Athena's Champion

Athena's Champion

David Hair and Cath Mayo

CANELO

First published in the United Kingdom in 2018 by Canelo

Canelo Digital Publishing Limited
57 Shepherds Lane
Beaconsfield, Bucks HP9 2DU
United Kingdom

Ebook ISBN 978 1 78863 279 9
Print ISBN 978 1 78863 421 2

Look for more great books at www.canelo.co

Dedications

Cath

To my husband Alan, for his unwavering support and his patience whenever that blank stare I give him means I have travelled 3,000 years or so back in time. Alan, please keep on repeating what you just said – it's a magic spell that will return me to the present.

David

New series, so the dedication has to go to my lovely wife Kerry, who is amazingly patient about having a husband whose head is full of imaginary people, places and events. Couldn't do this without you, love you to bits.

Prologue: A Dream of the Gods

'Tell me, Muse, of that resourceful man, twisting
and turning in the coiling arms of fate...'
—Homer, *The Odyssey*

I suffer from a recurring nightmare. In it I float above a great expanse, so vast my eyes can't encompass it. At one and the same time it's land and sea, mountains and woods and ocean; but it's also skin, a thin coating over blood and flesh. Creatures crawl over it, lifting their eyes occasionally from their scuttling, earthbound lives to bleed their souls into the sky.

Great, translucent creatures float above, like massive, gossamer mosquitoes, and they drink the soul-blood, subsisting upon it. There are hundreds, even thousands of them, filling the skies and hissing when another draws close.

I'm one of them.

The creatures below send us their hopes, their dreams, their desires, their needs... a cacophonous outpouring of desperation – to live and conquer and understand; to be understood and comforted and forgiven. A great spewing of their soul's blood. I barely listen as I guzzle it in, and nor do my kindred.

Those below are just ants – only *we* are truly alive.

But the feeding shapes us, ever-hungry as we are, and we become what we consume. Some of us morph into wind or water. Some attach to glowing stars and passing planets, orbiting in the void. Some cling like leeches to certain breeds of creature, feeding ever more intensely. Those prosper.

At times we flex our might and let the beetling creatures see us, and their awe grows. Those that feed deepest among us turn on their fellows. We war – we dominate or lose – and we herd the worshippers we've claimed like lion-shepherds.

They learn sounds and give us names, learn to use tools and how to sacrifice – to us.

Who am I?

I am fire. I am knowledge. I am among the great of my kind.

Time slows as it marches; the herds grow in complexity, and we grow with them. Our names change, so too our appearance and our behaviour. We learn how to negotiate, intimidate, compromise and betray.

I come to love my flock, and to loathe my kindred. I seek to elevate the former and emancipate them from the greed, the power-lust and cruelty of my own kind that holds them down... But my passion earns me the wrath of my kind, and they turn on me...

The dream ends in a dreadful place, a place of fire and smoke. I'm trapped in the body of one of my flock, screaming as the Great Ones – my kindred – close in, ripping at me like hawks devouring a vole. I can see them still, laughing in triumph as they claw me apart, gorging on my insides.

Zeus is there, his thunderous face drunk with gore. Proud Hera embraces him, relishing my fall.

Poseidon is there, bathing in the oceans of my blood.

Hades is there, his cold face gloating while his mad consort Persephone strokes his thigh, mocking me.

Ares hammers his nails through my wrists, to pin me, arms outstretched and feet dangling, to a rock for all eternity. Aphrodite sniggers, her luscious face alive with lust at the spectacle of my destruction. Hermes jeers as he pierces my side with his staff, and Dionysus toasts me with a chalice of my own heart blood.

Then Zeus becomes a massive eagle, tearing open my belly to feast once more, while his companions laugh...

... I burst screaming through smoke and fire, to wake with my heart hammering and my skin bathed in sweat. For long

2

moments all I can do is lie in my bed, rigid with terror lest the winds outside are the beating of giant wings.

Gradually, the distant kiss of the waves on the shore slows my pulse, and my heart ceases to pummel my ribs. My throat unclenches and I can breathe again. Ithaca, my island home, lends me her calm.

My name is Odysseus. I've dreamt that dream since I was a small child. I've told myself over and again that it can't be real. I'm a creature of reason, of rationality, a debunker of charlatan 'seers' that prey on fools in the port taverns. The gods are just primitive imaginings that we humans will someday outgrow.

But tomorrow, custom dictates that I set sail with my family to Pytho. At the age of twenty, I must stand before the great Pythia, there at the centre of the world, and she will judge my worthiness as heir to my father's kingdom.

And maybe, I will finally put my nightmare to rest.

Part One: The Prince of Ithaca

1 – The Centre of the World

'Cunning Cronos, that mighty being, was
deceived by Mother Earth... First he vomited up
the stone which he had swallowed last... Zeus
planted it in the broad-pathed earth of sacred
Pytho under the high valleys of Parnassos, to be a
sign thereafter and a marvel for mortal men.'
—Hesiod, *Theogony*

Pytho, Phocis

Fourth year of the reign of Agamemnon of Mycenae (1290 BC)

The rising sun has smeared a thin, rouged line along the eastern
horizon. The air is cool and apple-crisp, and the shadows are
lifting from the land below as another day begins here, high in
Pytho, the centre of the world. In the dawn of time, Zeus, the
Skyfather, commanded a stone – the omphalos – to be placed
here, to mark the heart of Creation: here, at the centre of the
world where the future is made known.

This morning, it's *my* destiny that the Seeress of Pytho will
pronounce upon.

And I'm frightened.

I shouldn't be: there's no rational reason for me to be afraid.
I have my beloved family with me, and even the Seeress – the
Pythia, the holy woman who walks the Serpent Path – is a
blood relative: my grandmother, no less. Generations of young
Achaean princes have undergone this rite before me when they
reached adulthood: to kneel before the Pythia in the Shrine of

Hera, Queen of Olympus, and receive the blessing of heaven. There's nothing that sets me apart from them.

Except that dreadful dream, which in the weeks leading up to this morning has plagued me every night, with greater intensity. Last night I was ordered to fast and forbidden sleep, a vigil to prepare me. I was delighted at the news, despite my hunger. Staying awake would be the best preparation I could have, to free me of the clutches of my nightmare. Or so I thought.

It's dawn now, and my judgement hour has come. The day is calm, but I'm uneasy; all night I felt a sense of foreboding, of some unnameable dread lying in wait for me. In the small shrine where I prayed before the sacred spherical boulder, the omphalos, I felt the painted images of the gods behind me were whispering and moving. The candles swayed to unfelt winds and a sensation plagued me, of a great serpent slithering by. Twice I was certain I glimpsed its coils in the gloom and once, I swear, I felt its touch – cold, smooth, sinuous – against my leg.

'Odysseus,' Eurybates calls. Eury is my father's half-Egyptian *keryx* – his herald, aide and indispensable master of the household. 'You'll be fine,' he says, as he joins me. 'It's just a ritual.'

I pray he's right.

Eury and I think alike – we share a healthy scepticism of the uncanny. But today, his reassurance doesn't ring true. This place is truly strange. I shiver as I take one last, longing look west across the hills towards my distant island home. I wish I was anywhere but here. But the sun's first rays are lighting up the cliffs behind Pytho, bathing them in orange and silver. The time has come. I square my shoulders and go to join my family waiting outside the shrine.

Pytho consists of a shrine complex surrounded by a cluster of outbuildings and a nearby village which contains houses for the senior priests and priestesses, the buildings large enough to accommodate distinguished visitors. Dormitories are provided for the acolytes and lesser guests. On our arrival yesterday evening, my family were housed by one of the senior priests; I assume their beds were comfortable and they were well fed.

Two sacred springs flow year-round: the first, just above the shrine, plunges into the deep chasm under the lowest and most holy shrine room, and the other issues from a great cleft beyond the village to tumble many hundreds of feet down into the river Pleistos.

Shrine and village are set on a small, sloping plateau high in the foothills of Mount Parnassus, studded with pines and ringed by breathtaking precipices. The nearest town is Krisa, far below us, perched on the inland edge of the wide plain that stretches out southwards to the coast and the Gulf of Corinth. The oldest place of worship at Pytho is the Omphalos House, but the holiest is the great shrine before which we have gathered this morning: the oracle of the Pythia.

My father, King Laertes of Ithaca, towers over the group; he's not an easy man to live up to, though the Gods must know I try. He's seen almost sixty summers, and sailed on the *Argo* when Jason of Argos captured the legendary tin and gold mines beyond the Axeinos Sea. As King of Ithaca, he built a fleet and burned out the pirate nests on the Ionian coast, and he hunted the Calydonian Boar. He's not a legendary hero, the subject of storytellers' tales, but he's a *name*. Clad in his breastplate with a helm under his arm, his chin jutting belligerently, he looks exactly like the man he is: someone who solves problems with force.

Me, I'm more than a full head shorter, though I have some of his heft at the shoulders. I take after my mother – I think and feel; Father has appetites and traditions. Sometimes I catch him staring at me, a puzzled look on his face, as if he's wondering how his son could be such a stranger.

But he tries. 'Well, boy,' he says, laying a heavy hand on my shoulder, 'there's nothing to worry about. It's just smoke and vapours. Hearken to whatever your grandmother tells you, say "yes, Lady" and "no, Lady", and we'll have a beer afterwards.'

To Father, there's nothing that can't be resolved with beers or spears.

My mother and sister exchange anxious glances. They feel it, the burgeoning power of this place, but Father is as sensitive as mudstone. I mumble something in reply, then pass on to Ctimene, my sister. 'Those bright colours suit you,' I murmur in her ear as we hug, and I'm rewarded by a blushing smile. She gives me a twirl in response, and the tassels dance. Her embroidered bodice is open at the front, though a linen slip hides her breasts. In Mycenae and the other major cities, bared breasts are the fashion, but we're from Ithaca, where old-fashioned values hold true, as they do here in Pytho.

Then I go to my mother Queen Anticleia, small and slight and worn-looking, yet with a durable air that suggests she can outlast all Father's blast and bluster. She fusses over me, trying to conceal her unease with trivia, adjusting my cloak and kilt, smoothing the tousled red mane that tumbles down my back in defiance of oil and grooming. Father and I are nothing alike but I'm clearly Anticleia's son: we share the same narrow facial features, the strongly defined nose and jaw, and that brilliant red-gold hue of our hair.

'Today, she's not your grandmother,' she reminds me: 'She's the Pythia. Make no reference to kinship. Be calm, listen hard, and…' She suddenly chokes and I stare at her in alarm.

'Mother?'

She shakes her head, but in the brief moment our eyes meet, I realize she's petrified.

'Mother, don't worry. Father tells me it's nothing to worry about. I'm excited, truly I am,' I lie. 'They say Grandmama can see the past, present and future as if she were there.'

If I was hoping to cheer Anticleia up, it has the opposite effect. 'Why would that ever be a good thing? Odysseus, keep your head down, do as you're told, and keep your secrets to yourself.'

'I don't have any secrets.'

Her gaze becomes sad. 'We all have secrets, darling.' She kisses my forehead. 'I love you, dear boy. Never forget that.' Then abruptly she pulls away, and takes Ctimene's hand.

What is *going on?*

But there's no time for more talk: at the door of the shrine, a tall, gaunt old woman appears, my grandmother Amphithea, robed in white linen embroidered with rich purple wool. She has a harsh, judgemental face and a nose that could function as an axe head. Eury throws me a sympathetic glance before announcing us.

'His Majesty, King Laertes Arcesiades of Ithaca; and his Queen Anticleia. They bring Odysseus Laertiades and Ctimene, their daughter. I, Eurybates, *keryx* to the King, do speak.'

'The King of Ithaca is very welcome,' Amphithea, Pythia of Pytho, replies. 'And my dear daughter and her children. Welcome, and welcome again. It brings me great happiness to see you.' She doesn't look happy though as she hobbles forward, kisses Laertes and holds her daughter briefly, neither woman at ease. Then she gestures to Ctimene, declaring that my sister should eat more 'to cover her bones' before embracing her.

Then it's my turn. Her eyes sharpen as she looks me over. 'Odysseus… "Born out of Grief". Your parents thought themselves barren until you were conceived. I trust you bring them joy.'

'I try,' I tell her. She doesn't appear to be someone to whom the word 'joy' is especially familiar, but caught in the beam of her chilling eyes I can see how people believe she has the power to see the future.

Can she see my dream?

'You remind me of…' she begins, then stops. 'No, no matter…' She beckons forward a bald, angular man with deep-set eyes. 'This is Doripanes, one of our most senior priests. He will take you through your preparations.' She looks me up and down again, clearly disturbed. 'I must also prepare… clear my mind…' She hesitates, her eyes boring into mine, as if there's something hidden within that she doesn't like, then stalks off, leaving me standing there.

Is such behaviour normal here?

'Come, Prince Odysseus,' Doripanes says. 'Follow me.'

–

The preparations are brief, and simple. Doripanes takes me to a small chamber where a copper bowl has been filled with water from the nearest, most sacred spring. I strip and wash to cleanse myself before being presented to the Goddess, then pull on a borrowed knee-length tunic. After that I'm made to kneel before an altar crowned with a rough statue of the Goddess that's old, darkened by ash and smooth from decades of hands. An open chalice of scented lamp oil burns slowly, filling the air with fragrant smoke.

Then a hissing voice whispers. '*Odysseus… Odysseus,*' it says. '*Man of fire…*'

I startle, and Doripanes looks at me. 'Prince?'

'Did you hear that?' I begin, but it's clear he's heard nothing.

He touches my shoulder. 'Come, the Pythia awaits.'

My rational mind has never quite believed this coming ceremony isn't mere formality, more elaboration than truth. False seers plague Achaea, the kingdoms of the Greeks, and I've heard Father and others often talk of this experience as being solemn, but not in any way uncanny. To believe in distant gods, whose lives barely touch a man's except in such huge incidents as storms, earthquakes and plagues, is quite different to believing they are watching *me*, and examining all the strands of *my* future. Despite the ominous pressure I've felt all day, it's solid and tangible things I usually fear – war, piracy, assassination – not the mystical.

I set my jaw and concentrate on bearing myself with dignity, rejoining my family but not looking at them as I follow Doripanes down curved stairs into a deep chamber, a circular subterranean vault around twenty feet in diameter. In the middle, oil lamps have been placed around the great central cleft in the rock, from which a vapour rises, drifting around the Pythia as she sits on a large bronze tripod. The rest of the vault lies in semi-darkness.

The old woman before me in her purple and white robe is no longer my grandmother Amphithea: she's entirely the

Pythia, voice of the Goddess, heir of a tradition of prophecy to whom even kings bow. Every few moments she lifts her veil to catch the steam, inhaling it deeply and moaning as she does. Behind her, in the shadows, a half-dozen shaven-haired priests are arrayed: thin, insubstantial figures, like ghosts haunting the chamber.

Doripanes takes me to stand before the Pythia. 'Remain standing,' he whispers. 'I'll do the talking.'

I nod, and glance back at my family: Mother and Ctimene are huddled together, with Laertes slightly apart, next to Eurybates, watching gravely. Eury gives me a reassuring nod, but my nerves only tighten.

That slithering voice whispers again: '*Odysseus... Fire...*'

The walls of the chamber change, mottling like snakeskin and moving, contracting around us. The air thins and I'm sure there's something poised behind me, its breath cold and stale and rotting. I flinch, wanting to spin round to confront it, but afraid to shift even my gaze. The Pythia coughs as she inhales more of the noxious vapours.

'Great Goddess! Hera Parthenos, Hera Basileia, Hera Khere!' Doripanes calls loudly, invoking the Virgin, the Queen and the Widowed Aspects of Hera. 'We come before you, seekers of truth and wisdom! We bow before you! We worship you and thank you!'

The Pythia takes yet another deep inhalation of the vapours that swirl around her before parting her veil to reveal her face, the wrinkles deep-etched in the lamplight, her eyes rolling back in her skull. 'Who comes?' she rasps, her voice a full octave lower than her speaking voice, a low rattle filled with menace.

'Odysseus, Prince of Ithaca, as a supplicant to your Holiness!' Doripanes announces. 'He comes before you humbly, purified and desirous of knowledge. His family await your judgement! Upon his line rests the peace and prosperity of his homeland! Will the kingdom of Ithaca pass into worthy hands? His parents have given consent, for he is their legacy, their heir! Will you walk the Viper's Path with him, and measure his worth?'

The Viper's Path? The phrase shocks me, alarmed already as I am by the slithering voice, and that monstrous serpentine presence I sense. The walls of the chamber seem to throb.

The Pythia's orbs turn a glowing white and pierce me through. My muscles clench, as if to prevent me from being blasted backwards by that empty, harrowing gaze, the air crushed from my lungs by the twin weights of tension and fear. Part of my brain, the emotive part, the boy inside the man, is struck dumb; but the rational part is even here trying to guess how this might be contrived… The vapours, strong and heavy, what are they?

Then the Pythia speaks, obliterating all thought. Her voice is at times shrill, at others a low growl, her face staring into a void, looking past me, looking *through* me.

'*Purified? Where is the purity? He came to be purged yet he has been touched by another! Another? Nay, by two! Spawned in fire, born of lust, the renegade, the trickster, eternal traitor, eagle's prey! Who dares! This is my place! Mine!*'

There is a collective gasp at each raving ejaculation. The Pythia is no longer seated but standing, her feet straddling the steaming fissure, her eyes still blind but her face enraged. And when she looks at me with those blind eyes, her whole face is overlaid with some kind of serpentine visage, with massive fangs and hooded eyes. The fingers she jabs at me are virulently accusing.

'*Wit before wisdom! Concealed hands and hearts! Faithful yet false! Loved and loathed! Touched, more than touched:* claimed, *by another! I see you, False Daughter, the owl that swoops! But this one is not for you! Tainted chalice! Envenomed blade! Honourless, perilous! Lost wanderer! Twin-finder! And dangerous: yes, most dangerous! Wall breaker! Lock picker! True-hearted deceiver!*'

I stare, petrified, as the Seeress sways towards me, holding her hands high as if admonishing the heavens, then twisting to hurl imprecations at the enclosing shadows. My mind is roiling: is this normal? Is it genuine, or some kind of performance?

Then she spins to leer into my face.

'*I see you, cuckoo's egg! Seed of the cursed! Rotted fruit of the tainted seed! I see you: son of Sisyphus!*'

The chamber is utterly quiet, the stillness broken by an awful sound – the startled sob of the woman I love most in the world: my mother, Anticleia. But I can't look away from the hooded, pupil-less eyes of the prophetess, her bared teeth a hand's breadth from my own, as the true horror of her words sinks in. Then I reel as the old woman gives an ear-splitting shriek and collapses to the ground.

The priests, led by an ashen-faced Doripanes, hurry to the Pythia's aid as I stare at her prone form, momentarily paralysed. Anticleia has fallen to her knees, staring open-mouthed at the crumpled figure of her mother, and Ctimene has dropped to hold her, her face upturned to see the reaction of Laertes, her mouth moving but no words coming out.

Cuckoo's egg... Seed of the cursed... Son of Sisyphus...

'Mother?' I croak.

The wretched look on her face tells me the rest. She'd resisted coming here because she'd feared this very moment. Her final words before we entered the shrine take on new resonance: '*We all have secrets...*'

My father... *No, not my father...* King Laertes is staring at me as if Hades himself has risen to claim him. His normally stolid face is torn open with anguish and rage.

Mother slept with another man... and the two of them, clasped in adultery, conceived me...

Anticleia crawls to her husband, tries to seize his knees. He bends and catches her arms, lifts her, and for a moment I hope for some kind of understanding.

Then Laertes's right hand cracks across Mother's face and she's sent flying, sprawling on her back, her head striking the stone floor. I rush to her side.

Her cheek is split, she's been struck senseless, but she still breathes. 'Mother, wake up,' I cry, 'Please, I beg you! Wake!' Then I look up. 'Father?' I plead.

'I'm not your father,' Laertes croaks. The King rocks on his heels, almost falling before he regains his balance. Then he turns and strides to the stairs, taking them at a run, and vanishes.

2 – Family Fissures

'My mother says I am indeed his son, but... no
man can be certain who his father is. If only I
was the son of a man lucky enough to grow old
while he was still in command of his own estate.
As things stand, the man whose son they say I am
is the most unfortunate man who ever lived.'
—Homer, *The Odyssey*

Krisa, Phocis

The short walk from the shrine to my family's accommodation
in the village is as terrible a journey as any legendary descent
into Hades's realm.

Doripanes initially leads us, but his arm is seized by another
priest who whispers urgently in his ear and drags him back
inside. Laertes has stalked on ahead and we follow, Eurybates
carrying my mother, conscious but dazed, bleeding and incon-
solable with grief. Ctimene is weeping, consumed by her own
misery. I stumble along behind, stricken by what I've seen and
heard, and with my future hanging in the balance.

I'm still hoping against hope that it's not true.

'Mother,' I try to ask. 'What happened? I *have* to know!' But
Anticleia only sobs the harder, leaving me feeling even more of
a monster, some vile creature that usurped her womb.

Finally we reach the house – Doripanes's own – and Eurybates carries Anticleia to the upstairs bedroom, which the priest
had vacated last night for her and Laertes to share. Ctimene
throws me a baleful look, as if this is all my fault, before scaling

the stairs after the *keryx*. I clamber up in their wake, already feeling like a dog that's been banished from the hearth.

Laertes is sitting on the balcony, his face as grey as his beard, staring away into the distance. He doesn't turn as we enter the room. Eurybates places Anticleia on the bed, where she lies like a dying woman, Ctimene perched beside her. For once, even Eurybates seems uncertain what to say.

Finally Laertes comes inside. 'Is it true?' he demands, in a flint-like voice.

'You should have asked that before you hit her!' Ctimene cries, wide-eyed at her own temerity.

Anticleia rolls onto her side and buries her face in the now blood-smeared pillow.

'Well?' Laertes demands.

'It's true,' she groans.

Oh gods, I think, as that thread of hope is cut.

'How?' Laertes asks, his face contorting with equal measures of misery and anger. 'Why?' he adds, as though determined to drink every drop of torment.

Anticleia sits up with difficulty, shivering, wrapping her arms about herself, hunched and woeful. Out of the corner of my eye I see a grim-faced Doripanes edge into the room to listen, as Anticleia confesses her secret.

'Husband, you went to Dodona to ask why you had no children, and they said you would never father a child unless you prayed to Eleuthia, Goddess of Childbirth. You told me Sisyphus was at Dodona also, for his own auguries. Afterwards you went off by yourself – you were angry, remember? You went into the wilds and railed at the gods. But Sisyphus came to Ithaca in secret. He said he had something to tell me, and I let him in…'

Laertes bunches his fists. 'That damned cockroach! A man in his fifties! You were nineteen!'

'I know,' she admits. 'But he was a king – how could I turn him away? And I…' Her voice trails off momentarily, then she rallies and goes on. 'He told me about the prophecy given you: that the fault of our childlessness was yours, but you were going to cast me aside anyway. I was so distressed, I don't remember the rest, the wine was so potent... I remember dismissing the servants and...'

I groan, because the moment Mother let Sisyphus see her alone, she lost recourse to say she was raped – even if she was. That's the law, harsh though it sometimes seems. Laertes knows it as well as I do, and it's the law – and the unwritten laws of appearance and honour, that will be uppermost in his mind now.

She's just condemned herself.

'I woke up in the bed...' she goes on. 'Everything was a blur... but he was dressing, leaving. He departed and a few days later you came home and my monthly courses ceased. Remember how happy we were that I was with child? I didn't know, couldn't know, whose it was. I've prayed every waking day that Odysseus is yours.'

Can this be true? I have a dozen questions, but daren't open my mouth.

Laertes looks as if he's swallowed poison. 'I would as soon be childless.'

'No, you wouldn't!' Anticleia flares. 'You're a king. You are compelled to produce heirs.'

'Some "heir".' Laertes stabs a finger at Ctimene. 'What of her? Another "cuckoo's egg"?'

'No! When I was slow to conceive again, you went to Eleuthia's shrine, as you had been bidden, and the priestesses gave you herbs to refresh your seed. Ctimene is yours, and yours alone. I swear.' Her eyes are huge with entreaty. 'Look at our son, husband. He is our pride, our joy!'

'But he's not *my* son!' Laertes shouts. He whirls on me; I see the punch coming but I'm too numb to react. His fist slams into my jaw and my head explodes with stars as I fall to the floor. I lie there, voided by a paralysing emptiness.

I am fatherless, I am nobody, I am less than nothing.

My father – *no, not my father* – looms over me, his face filled with inchoate grief and frustrated rage. He's never been an articulate man, and I can see all the anger and disappointment he can't express turning to violence.

'You're not mine!' he roars. 'You runtish bastard!' He draws back his foot, aiming the blow at my head. Mother and Ctimene are frozen, petrified with shock and fear.

'I'm sorry,' I manage to gasp.

Then both Eurybates and Doripanes step between us. 'It's not his fault, master,' the *keryx* says, firmly.

For a moment Laertes looks like he's going to take out his anger on the pair of them; instead he spits on the floor. 'I'm going out – I will arrange our immediate departure from this wretched place. We will sail for Ithaca this afternoon. It will take me half an hour at the most, and when I come back I want *him* gone! *Gone, you hear?* I don't want to look at him, I don't want a trace left of him, not a belt or a sandal or a bracelet. I refuse to hear his name! He is not mine, and he has no place in my house.'

Eurybates rashly speaks back. 'Master, he's—'

'Do it or I'll have you strangled!' Laertes roars. 'GET HIM OUT!' Then he whirls, stamps to the door and storms out. His footsteps on the stairs make the whole building shake and he almost breaks the front door when he slams it.

This is the end, I think. *Our family is finished.*

I get myself up, jaw throbbing and still seeing stars, but I go to Mother and Ctimene, pulling them both into a long, hard embrace. 'You're still my brother,' Ctimene whispers, which sets Anticleia weeping even harder.

I feel Doripanes's hand grip my shoulder and I ease Mother into Ctimene's arms so I can face him.

'I bring more bad news,' the priest murmurs, pulling me aside. 'Say your farewells quickly.'

'I know, Father says—'

'This has nothing to do with your father. There's a man coming to kill you.'

I stare at him, not comprehending. 'What do you mean?'

'Exactly what I said,' he whispers. 'Nigh on twenty years ago, King Sisyphus of Corinth – your true father – was dragged from his bed and murdered. They threw his body to the street dogs, and all of Olympus rejoiced. Why? Because he was the sole descendant of Prometheus, a line Zeus himself ordered to be expunged.'

Prometheus…?

He stabs a finger into my chest. 'That makes *you* the next one to die.'

'How do you know this?'

'I'm supposed to keep you here until Molebus comes.'

'Who's Molebus?'

'Molebus is the Pythia's hidden blade, her foremost hunter. Once the Pythia recovered from her prophetic trance, she sent for him. You're lucky he was down in Krisa, otherwise he'd be here already.'

I can barely comprehend: why would *my grandmother* order me dead?

I stare into his eyes, searching for the truth. Is he trying to panic me into a fatal act – or save my life? Instinct tells me it's the latter. 'Then I'll leave. But your Molebus isn't here yet, so I have time for goodbyes, don't I? And I have questions that need answers.'

'Very well,' Doripanes says, tight-lipped. 'But keep it brief. Eurybates, kindly guard the outside door.'

I turn to my mother and sister, standing white-faced behind me. I'm struck again by the loveliness of Anticleia's red hair, the hair I've inherited, and how young she still is – only forty – but so careworn. That I am hers can be seen at a glance. But I've never really seen Laertes in myself. Now I know why.

'Tell me about Sisyphus,' I say, in a choked voice.

Anticleia looks at Ctimene and me, her expression pleading for us to understand. 'Sisyphus was the most charming of men. Not in a smooth, sly way, but full of energy and dynamism. He and my father were friends, and as a child I longed for a husband just like him—'

'You loved him,' Ctimene accuses, her voice bitter.

'No! I *idolized* him—'

'You *loved* him!' Ctimene shouts, her compassion of a moment ago vanquished by rage. 'The most despicable man in Achaea? That's disgusting!' She thrusts Anticleia away, her face blazing. 'That's why you've never loved me! You only love Odysseus! It's always him, him, him! At least now I know why!' She bursts into tears and stumbles from the room, ignoring my distraught cry. The door slams, and we hear her shrieking at Eurybates before running from the house.

Anticleia collapses against me, crying uncontrollably. All I can do is hold her, unable to offer any kind of comfort other than my arms. It's the most horrible feeling, to be so helpless in the face of such grief. But after what seems forever, she gains some semblance of control. 'I suppose you want to know the rest?'

Doripanes moves towards me. 'Prince,' he pleads, 'you *must* leave. Now!' Out of Mother's sight, he mouths, 'Molebus…'

'Give me a minute,' I fume. 'I have to know this.'

Anticleia's lips tremble with resolve. 'You deserve the truth,' she says. 'But you have to understand, I had no intention of being unfaithful. I was never supposed to be alone: my serving women were always with me. But when Sisyphus started talking about Laertes's inability to give me a child, I *couldn't* let the servants hear. This was dangerous talk – a sterile king is an invitation to rebellion. So I dismissed them. It was already late into the night, and now that only Sisyphus and I were awake, I became nervous.'

I can feel Anticleia's distress as she reaches out to grip my hands, caught up in a vision of that night: the young, vulnerable queen and the worldly, cunning warrior.

'Then Sisyphus spoke of his own auguries from Dodona. "My enemies are closing in," he said. "People I trusted want me dead, as do the gods. I fear I soon will be murdered. But the prophecies say that one of my line may yet endure, and do a great deed that will bring salvation to all Achaea. None of my surviving sons are worthy, and Bellerophon, my magnificent grandson, is dead, destroyed by the gods. I need another son, a secret son…" Then he looked into my eyes. "And you, dear child, need any kind of son, to save your marriage and your life.'"

I see the same sick hopelessness on her face that I feel in my heart. *Trapped by fate. What choice did either Sisyphus or Mother have?*

Every choice, another part of me argues. *The choice to be faithful and loyal, and accept the ill-chances of life with honour and honesty.*

But she'd been frightened, on the verge of being utterly cast out.

'I wanted him, and I knew I was fertile that night,' Anticleia admits, quietly. Although I've already guessed it, my shock at her words is like a punch to my belly. 'Yes, he was much older than me, but he could have awakened passion in a woman made of ice. One night, and I knew it would haunt me forever. Laertes returned home a few days later, determined to defy the prophecies; I was already late with my cycles, but not so late that I couldn't pass the pregnancy off as his.'

'And Sisyphus?' *I cannot bring myself to call him 'My father'.*

'I never saw him again. A few months later, tidings came of his assassination.' She buries her head in her hands. 'If it becomes known whose son you are, his enemies will try and destroy you—'

'Madam, they already are,' Doripanes interrupts. 'You have said enough. Allow your son to escape.'

'Perhaps it would be better if I *were* dead.' I mutter, as despair hits me.

I'm the bastard of a murdered king. He seduced my mother, then he was poisoned and thrown to the dogs. Doripanes says Zeus himself wanted his death... and now mine... What kind of life can I ever have now?

But Dodona's prophecy said I will save all Achaea from some great peril...

Impossible. Sisyphus lied, to seduce her...

Or not...

I gaze into her eyes: she is my mother still, and I love her despite all her fallibility.

'Don't be a fool,' she says intently. 'Don't you dare give up. I jeopardized my entire life to create you, and I would do it again. Don't you throw that sacrifice away.'

'Of course I won't,' I tell her sincerely. 'But what will you do now?' I ask, aware Doripanes is exasperated.

'I want my family back,' she whispers. 'I do love your fath– …*Laertes*… He's my world: he, you and Ctimene. It's too late for me to start again.'

I want to say, *Mother, you're only forty, you've got years ahead*, but the fact is, she's right. A woman, even a queen, past child-bearing age and cast out for infidelity, has no future. 'Mother, you must hold on to your marriage—'

'I'm an adulteress! How can he forget that? You know him, he'll disown me too!'

I see Doripanes slip out of the room, for what reason I cannot tell. Is he going to betray me after all? But I still have more I need to say. 'No, Mother! Beg Laertes's forgiveness. He's a proud man – he won't want to admit to others that he's been cuckolded, and he can't afford to tell the Ithacans he has no heir! Do the things he loves: provide his favourite meals, comb your hair by the fire… It won't work straight away, but it'll work eventually.'

'My dear son, when did you become so calculating?' She stares at me, her eyes tremulous. 'You're so much like your real father, you know.'

I don't want to hear that.

'Mend bridges with Ctimene, Mother,' I tell her. 'She'll be either your greatest ally or your worst enemy.'

Her chin lifts. 'Yes. But you, what will you do?'

'I'll go to Menelaus in Mycenae. He'll take me in.'

Menelaus is the younger brother of the High King. He's also my best friend.

'Yes,' she says. 'Go to Menelaus. But don't admit you're Sisyphus's son to anyone. Even Menelaus.'

Footsteps come pounding up the stairs and we freeze. But it's only Eurybates and Doripanes, their faces set hard. 'It's time, Prince,' the priest announces.

Eurybates levers my travelling pack onto my back as I kiss Anticleia, both of us weeping once more. 'Look after her,' I tell the *keryx*, before Doripanes manhandles me through the door and down the stairs.

I collect my sword from the small room by the outside door where I would have slept tonight, had the Pythia not denounced me, sling the scabbard strap over my shoulder and take the staff Doripanes hands me. 'Which way should I go?' I ask. 'I can't make for Krisa, if that's where Molebus is coming from.' Krisa – the nearest port – is the only place here I know.

'Go inland,' he tells me. 'There's a zigzag path up to the cliffs behind the village. At the top, follow the goatherds' trail north to high mountain plateau. There's a distinctive outcrop near the base of a steep ridge, below it you'll find the Corycian Cave. Hide there – I'll come when I can.' He smiles a crooked smile. 'Now hit me – hit me like you mean it – and run.'

Hit him?

Then I realize: the blow will give him an alibi against betrayal. Though I still scarcely believe this is all real, I do it, striking his jaw crisply – despite my lack of height I've plenty of power. He staggers and slumps to the ground, while I cradle my now throbbing hand – his jaw is hard as rock.

Then I head out the door and run for my life.

3 – Corycia's Cave

'As a wild boar, high in the wooded mountain
glens, terrifying for a man to behold, determines
to fight... he gnashes and whets his pale tusks,
turning sideways, his eyes like flaming fire and his
mouth foaming, his mane and the hair around his
neck bristling...'
—Hesiod, *Shield of Heracles*

Pytho, Phocis

I'm still scrambling to make sense of it all: I'm suddenly a homeless outcast, a destitute bastard with no standing or honour. I'm
beyond distraught.

But right now, I have to run or die.

It's still early, the sun barely above the horizon. The narrow
path that twists up past the cliffs above the shrine is no great
obstacle for me. I'm a good runner with powerful thighs and
I've always trained hard; a warrior must be able to endure past
exhaustion, and rocky Ithaca is a testing training ground. Fitness
and fear propel me up the slope, breathing hard.

After the zigzag crests the cliff line, the track borders a swift
stream before plunging into pine forest. I pause to slake my
thirst, just enough to replace my perspiration – I'm sweating
hard despite a chill breeze that makes the pines ripple and
sigh. This is a land of rugged grandeur; the morning sky is
dappled with clouds, and to the east, the massive bulk of Mount
Parnassus is a patchwork of shadow and dazzling snow. To the
south, the way I've come, I can see right across the Corinthian
Gulf to the far shore, softened by haze. I feel utterly alone in

24

the world, a rugged, beautiful world of rocks and cliffs, rushing water, early summer flowers, old pines and gnarled scrub.

Achaea, my homeland.

My ears are straining for any strange sounds from the path below. Is Molebus coming – and who exactly is he? Why would the Pythia employ someone to kill on her behalf? And if he does find me, what chance do I have?

Best he never finds me.

I move on, jogging along a goat trail Doripanes told me of. It's heavy going, rocky and scoured deep by the spring melt, and I must watch my footing lest I twist an ankle or wrench a knee. At last I reach a rock outcrop, where I rest briefly before tackling the climb to my destination, the cave Doripanes described. Gradually the pines yield to *phrygana* – low, thorny scrub. The hillside is punctuated by tree stumps still bearing the charred marks of lightning strikes. I force a way up through the tangled branches, their prickly leaves tearing at my tunic and legs. Then abruptly the slope eases, harsh scrub yielding to soft grass, and there it is: Corycia's cave.

At first glance, there's nothing remarkable about it – just a hole in a cliff face punctuated by a single shard of rock like a tooth. Water trickles over a lip in the rock, into a clay jug with a cup beside it – the only signs of humanity. I fill the cup from the jug and drink.

'Corycia, I thank you for the gift of water,' I murmur, in appeasement, though I feel foolish doing so. Father is a great one for thanking every god and spirit, but I've never truly believed.

Not until I saw the Pythia change today: or did I? Is there something in the vapour from the cleft that breeds hallucinations?

I put such thoughts aside and explore: the cave proves surprisingly large inside. I set about making my stay a comfortable one, gathering fallen pine needles into a hollow in the cave floor in case I need to sleep here; after keeping vigil all last night – and Father's fist – I'm feeling heavy-headed, running on adrenalin and dread. Then I climb to the crest of the ridge above the cave and find a vantage point where I can watch the trail. The wind has swung west: if Laertes truly means to leave today, it will mean a lot of rowing.

I still can't believe he'll leave me behind. He's raised me as his heir; I'm Mother's only son. He'll see reason… He *has* to.

Wait! What's that?

Something moved on the plateau below: a dark shape in the clearing by the outcrop, where I'd stood only an hour ago… *there*! A man in a dark tunic, too far away to identify, but already my heart is pounding.

Is this the Pythia's killer – Molebus?

He's looking up at the ridge, right at me. I roll onto my belly to peer between two boulders. *Too late.* He lifts his hand as if in ironic salute, then vanishes into a tangle of pines. A few heartbeats pass, lengthened by fear…

Then a creature emerges from the trees: not a man, but a low-slung and bulky shape. A boar, perhaps. It thrusts through the bushes round the edge of the outcrop, then dashes across the clearing and plunges into the forest below me. I stare at the last point I'd seen it, guessing at its size and speed.

That it's coming for me, I have no doubt.

I spring to my feet and fight my way down through the scrub towards the cave, reaching it in moments, and seize my walking stave, shod with bronze at one end, bare wood at the other. I draw my short sword, with muttered apologies to Corycia for the naked blade, and begin to hack a point into the blunt end of the stave to make a spear – my sword will be little use against such a beast. All the while my ears are primed for the sound of an animal crashing up through the undergrowth.

Legendary boars are part of our lore: the Calydonian Boar that my father helped hunt, which Meleager slew; the Crommyonian Sow slain by Theseus; the Erymanthian Boar captured by Heracles – but even an ordinary boar is a dangerous beast. When roused to attack, they charge in with razor-sharp tusks, gouging at the upper thigh and groin, to sever arteries and rip open bellies. Men die on hunts, even experienced hunters armed with far longer, sharper spears than the one I've improvised.

I glance at the fire I've laid, wishing I'd already lit it. No time for fire sticks and tinder now. I need a place where a cloven-hooved creature can't reach me – like up a tree. I sling the sword and scabbard over my shoulder then scurry through the scrub to a tall pine, high on a rim above the cave. Pushing the stave into my shoulder strap, I haul myself up into the branches.

I'm barely ten yards from the ground when the creature bursts out of the trees. I go rigid, my heart hammering because it *surely* can't be natural. The boar is perhaps thrice the bulk of a man, bristling and tossing its head, snarling, its red-rimmed eyes livid. It ploughs through the scrub right to the base of my tree. I pull out my makeshift spear, blood drumming in my ears as I calculate angles and trajectories. No, better not to throw – the odds of piercing anything vital are negligible, and to be caught with no weapon afterwards would be to die.

For a few seconds it stares up at me, thwarted or so I think. What I see next confirms that I've stepped out of reality: it emits a heart-stopping bellow, its whole body rippling with shifting muscle and cracking joints. *Then it rises on its hind legs*, its forelegs becoming arms, hooves turning to claws. With a roar that's part agony, part bloodlust, the *creature* grips the lower branches, shoulders hunched, head low-set and jaws drooling as it hauls itself up the trunk.

With a terrified gasp, I climb higher, my makeshift spear tangling in the branches as I seek grip and leverage. Incredibly, the boar-man continues to follow, clambering after me as I struggle up to the thinner branches, seeking a place which might take my weight but not his.

Though I've gone as high as I dare, I'm not high enough. It climbs almost within reach and I jab at it with the sharpened stave. My hands are shaking, my breath rapid.

This CAN'T be real.

The boar-man looks up at me, a look of cunning in its piggy eyes. 'O… dee… zooz,' it snarls, and I almost drop the stave in shock.

It tried to say my name. It did *say my name.*

I jab again, jerking the spear back as the boar lunges at the haft to wrench it from me. It pulls back lips from a mouth full of yellowed teeth and tusks, and circles to the far side of the trunk, climbing again.

I force myself higher still, onto the flimsy branches above, panting for breath as I cast about for some means of escape. Then the monster's right claw shoots around the trunk and rakes at my ankle. I jerk away and ram the stave down, puncturing the creature's hairy arm enough to draw blood. It squeals and retreats, snorting.

This is impossible. I'll wake up any moment…

We're a good twenty yards up now; the tree is on the lip of a steep slope, which plunges away at least forty yards on the far side. If I jump that way, I'll break my neck. I discard one plan after another.

Then the boar-man moves – barrelling round the trunk, tusks and snout flashing into view. I jerk out of reach of a swinging claw, and thrust the stave at the creature's throat, but it's already gone – then it's lunging at me from the other side. I'm forced to let go of the trunk, balancing precariously out on a creaking, sagging branch. Somehow I get the stave interposed between us. The creature's laughing now, a sputtering sound that is horribly human.

Then it comes fully round the trunk. I give way, backing even further out onto the branch, which bends alarmingly under my weight. I glance down, picturing the movements needed…

The beast launches itself and I thrust with the spear, only to have it swatted away as if it were a willow wand. I bunch my limbs and, as I'm about to be engulfed, throw myself sideways into thin air. The beast hurtles past me, landing where I'd been standing and snapping the branch, even as I catch hold of another branch below, swinging and turning to plant my feet on an even lower one as the boar plummets past me.

It should have been perfect, *brilliant.* The boar-man should have crashed to the ground, winded and helpless…

But as the beast falls the air seems to bend around it. It lands on its hind legs on the ground below, the sharpened stave spinning into its clawed hands – then the branch under my feet breaks. My arms are almost wrenched from their sockets as I kick frantically, dangling until the top branch cracks too, swinging inwards towards the trunk. I twist to avoid being impaled on the jagged end of the lower branch, plummet through foliage and strike the sloped ground a dozen yards from the boar-creature, jarred and then rolling.

The beast-man hurls the makeshift spear, I jerk to one side frantically, and the weapon plunges into the turf beside my hip. I lunge for it, launch myself over the lip of the slope with the haft gripped in both hands, an instant before the boar's huge hind hoof slams down where my head had been.

I crash down the slope, bouncing off rocks and stumps, hearing the enraged roar of the beast as it tumbles after me. Then I'm rolling and sprawling in a small clearing, clambering to my feet, battered, bleeding and breathing hard, just as the beast lands nearby. It rises, snarling and pawing the earth with its clawed feet. Now we're on level ground and there's nowhere to climb, nothing to jump off or hide behind. If this boar-man stood, it'd be eight feet tall, and now its tusks seem to sprout in length as it crouches…

If I try to run, it'll mow me down. But running isn't my plan…

It comes at me in a massive, roaring blur, head thrashing from side to side and tusks raking, and I do as any good hunter would – dropping onto one knee, planting the butt end of the stave against a rock and aiming the point at the beast's torso. Let it impale itself upon the stave. Let it kill itself.

Had this been an ordinary boar, it might have worked.

But the creature flails a forearm and dashes the weapon aside, then its sweltering bulk slams into me, hurling me backwards with bone-shattering force. Suddenly my world is a scream of pain, as a razor-sharp tusk rips my inner right thigh from knee to groin. The impact shudders through me as the beast's weight and stench crash down, my vision goes bloody and the trees and the sky swirl above me, that ghastly, horribly human visage filling my sight…

The beast staggers as an arrow imbeds in his flank, a hand's breadth from another that must already have struck. The creature convulses, bloodied tusks splattering droplets of blood. Another shaft buries in its chest; it staggers, staring down at the shaft in a puzzled, disbelieving way… and crashes onto its side, twitching into stillness.

I've time to see a small, slender figure at the edge of the trees, like an icon to Artemis the huntress, poised to shoot again. Then I look down at my own body, with a sickening fear clutching at my bowels. The inner thigh of my right leg is laid open to the bone, and blood is fountaining out in frightening volumes, each terrified heartbeat causing my blood vessels to surge. A wave of numbing dizziness is drowning me.

I'm dying, I realize. *I'm actually dying…*

Suddenly that small figure is kneeling at my side, and I realize she's a young girl, barely into her second decade. She's clamping her hands over my bloody thigh and shrieking at me. '*Hold fast, Odysseus! Stay here with me!*'

I'm trying, but there's a dark tide pouring in, a roiling blackness that's engulfing me. I look up at her in panic, trying to cling to the sight of her, howling silently as fiery agony racks my body. Her face looms over me, blurs; an owl screeches and I see its huge eyes staring into mine, and then bizarrely the owl has become a woman, a woman with icy-grey eyes and a bronze helm, and she's shouting, '*ACCEPT ME AS YOUR QUEEN, ITHACAN!*'

Broken words bubble from my lips. 'Who? What? I…'

'*ACCEPT ME AS YOUR QUEEN, ODYSSEUS! PRAY TO ME! WORSHIP ME!*'

Her voice is a caress of thunder, reverberating through my being. I know who she is. I know what she is. And I realize that, in my nightmare of Prometheus, she's the only one of the Olympian gods who *isn't* there…

Somehow I get the words out. '*Athena,*' I gasp, '*You are my Queen…*'

The owl cries triumphantly and its claws grip my thigh, loosening a stream of glowing energy that for a few moments eclipses all my senses. My body is ablaze, the owl's face immense, hovering above me, its gaze piercing my flesh, my mind, my heart.

Then everything goes blank. I seem to be floating endlessly, back arched and limbs wide-spread, surrounded not by the darkness that earlier threatened me, but cocooned in a weightless embrace…

-

I drift through a delirium of dreams, in which a flitting, wispy creature stalks the edges of my consciousness. Then a cold, bitter liquid fills my throat. Some enters my windpipe and I jerk awake in a paroxysm of coughing. Someone *tsks* as I spit and retch.

I'm wrapped in a blanket, dimly aware of smoke, the only light a red glow beside me and a dim whiteness glimpsed far away in the darkness. I try to focus, make out a crescent moon, then something, *someone* bends over me and a high-pitched voice says, 'Try to drink some more.'

I manage another mouthful and then…

-

When I next wake, it's to pain, an awful throbbing as if I'm trying to give birth through my thigh. I scream silently, contorting and rigid in turns, unable to see through a red fog. Then a smoky rag is laid over my mouth; I breathe in a fragrance both heavy and sweet, and I'm in a floating haze again.

Dreams return as the pain recedes: I'm in a house, and something is outside the shutters, mewling to be let in. I go to unlatch the shutters…

'*Don't*,' a woman's voice advises, and I drop the latch and turn, fall out of the dream and wake.

It's dawn, I'm lying outside Corycia's cave, and I'm not alone.

At first I think my rescuer is a stranger, a boy, but then I see she's that girl – my Artemis. She's only about thirteen, but there's a mature composure to her. 'Don't try to move,' she says, as I groan. 'Here, drink this.' She hands me a mug of the same dark, bitter liquid I remember drinking before, and when it takes hold, I drift for a while in a state of warped euphoria.

After a while, my brain clears a little, though I'm left with a thunderous headache, and I'm able to observe her more closely. She's clad in a short brown tunic, man's garb, her bony legs deeply tanned and her hair hacked short. The smell of stale perspiration and smoke clings to her, the dust on her face is being sweated off in shiny streaks, and a copper bracelet of strange design has been pushed up her forearm until it's tight to her skin, the only unusual thing about her.

'Was that… beast… Was it Molebus?' I ask, curious to see how she responds, despite my pain and exhaustion.

She gives me an interested look. 'Mmm,' she says. 'The Pythia's going to be pissed off.'

'Is he…? Did he…?'

'He's in a hole,' she drawls, her manner more thirty than thirteen.

She killed a man… if that's what he was! From her manner, I doubt it's the first time.

'How did I get here?' I ask.

'I dragged you,' the girl says. 'Lucky you're a short-arse, otherwise I'd not have managed.'

I look down at my leg, wrapped tightly in a bloodied swathe of my own cloak, and shudder as I remember seeing my thigh bone amidst the torn meat and pumping blood. I grope at the bandages, my chest constricting in fear.

'Don't touch!' the girl snaps. 'Athena stopped the blood and closed the wound. That saved your life, but there's still much healing to be done. You interfere with it, you'll mess it up.'

Athena… Molebus… the Pythia… There has to be a rational explanation for all of this. But right now I can't find one – all I'm doing is making my head throb even worse than it was before. 'I suppose I'm in your hands,' I manage to murmur. 'Thank you.'

'You're welcome, O Prince of Ithaca.'

'You know who I am?'

She snickers. 'Yes – we had that conversation some hours ago, during one of your semi-lucid moments – though not lucid enough for you to remember, clearly.'

'If you say so.'

She turns her attention to the fire, and I realize she has a rabbit cooking on a makeshift spit made from green wood, while her bow and arrows lie propped against a rock. I'm lying on a bed of pine needles, perhaps the same ones I'd piled up inside the cave.

I peer at her hard, which isn't easy with my vision swimming. 'Who are you? Are you Corycia?' Not that I believe in nymphs.

Or gods and goddesses and shape-shifters... My worldview needs updating, it seems.

'Ha ha! No!' she cackles.

'Then who are you?'

'We've had that conversation too: I'm Bria.'

'Odd name.'

Bria shrugs. 'But Corycia's been creeping about, trying to get inside you.'

'*Inside me?*'

'Into your head, Ithaca,' Bria says, tapping her skull. 'Dirty little parasite. That's what these nymphs and *dryads* and the like do, you know – try to get inside for a ride. They target stupid people, wounded people, small children. You have to be careful in places like this. That's why we're outside the cave, not in it. You wouldn't have stood a chance in there. Lucky it didn't rain.'

She's just a peasant girl, she's talking nonsense.

I try to clear my head again with a brisk shake – bad move. Rattling my brain around only makes my headache worse. 'I'm expecting... um...'

'Doripanes,' she says brightly. 'He'll arrive later this morning.'

33

'You know Doripanes?'

'Mmm… we're kind of colleagues.'

I hesitate to ask the next question – surely I've been hallucinating – but I need her reaction. 'Yesterday, I was dying, wasn't I? Did Athena really come?' I stare at her pert, knowing little face and wait for her to scoff.

'Yes, Ithaca, that was real,' she replies. 'You were ten heartbeats from oblivion when she arrived.'

'Yes, but…' My words dry up as I try to reconcile what I've experienced since I arrived in Pytho with how I've always thought the world to be.

'Having a little trouble with all this, are you?' Bria says, with a trace of sympathy.

'You don't understand… or maybe you do, I don't know. To me, the gods have only ever been concepts,' I tell her. 'I've never seen anything remotely miraculous before, and the stories that explain weather and the moon and all the rest just sound childish to me. I've seen charlatans fleecing good people in the name of the gods, and priests living like kings while never doing a day's work.'

'But now it's all different, isn't it?' Bria says, in a smug purr.

I remember all the discussions I've had with Eurybates about this: 'It still makes no sense to me. How can every race of people have different gods for the same thing, if the gods are real? Why is the moon a goddess to us, but a male god to the Hittites? Does it suddenly grow a penis halfway across the Aegean Sea? The old tales are a mess of contradictory nonsense.' I throw up my hands in exasperation. 'So I've always believed they're just fantasies.'

Even as I'm saying that I'm thinking of my recurring dream, and wondering if I'm really just denying a dread that's been haunting me all my life.

Bria gazes at me with an oddly ambiguous expression. 'If only they were,' she sighs. 'But then you'd be dead. And so would I.' She strokes my face. 'Get some rest, Ithaca. You're going to need it.'

–

I sleep for what feels like a long time, and when I wake my headache is gone and the sun is high. Doripanes is sitting over me, wrapped in a traveller's cloak and watching me carefully.

'You're here!' I'm not prone to stating the obvious, but I'm not at my best.

'I am,' he agrees gravely. 'The Pythia is aware of Molebus's death and has sent out other servants to capture or kill you. But don't fear,' he says, laying a restraining hand on my shoulder, 'that's not my purpose.'

'That's comforting,' I say, summoning up a shred of sarcasm. 'Do my family know of this?'

'No. They left for Ithaca yesterday morning – Laertes would brook no delay.'

'Will the Pythia send more men like Molebus up here?'

'No: I've told the Pythia I've had reports that you've been sighted well east of here, heading for Boeotia.'

'Why are you helping me? You're one of Hera's senior priests.'

'Yes, but I have a higher allegiance.' He studies me, his expression inscrutable, then says, 'Let's have a look at that leg of yours.'

He removes the bandages to reveal a hideous tear in my thigh, running from just above the knee right up to within a hand span of my groin. It scares me. But it's also incredible: the wound looks weeks old, not something I suffered only yesterday.

I'm stunned – and chilled: despite its rapid healing, it's a massive injury, one that usually cripples any who survive it. And it's by no means completely repaired. *Will I ever walk properly again?*

For now though, I'm alive, something to be grateful for. While Doripanes rebinds my thigh, I swallow another dose of Bria's pain drugs, drain the water pitcher and eat my way through a breakfast of bread, olives and fruit she's placed beside me.

When that's done, they half carry me over to a latrine hole in the trees. Despite the drugs, I suffer agony trying to purge myself: bending my right leg is impossible and flexing my groin muscles nearly makes me scream. Doripanes offers to help me clean myself, but I wave him away with an angry hand. I can swab myself without his help, thank you.

Once I'm back on my pine-needle bed, Bria sits beside me. 'Are you ready for some truths, Ithaca?' she asks.

'I'm always ready for truth,' I tell her, while inside I'm wondering how much truth to reveal. Should I confess my nightmare to them? *No.* It's no business of theirs. 'Please, explain what I'm going through, because all my life I've sought to understand my world through reason and logic.'

'Then Athena did well to save you,' Doripanes says. 'For that's how she also thinks.'

'There didn't seem to be anything rational and logical about Athena yesterday – if that was really her.'

'It was.' Doripanes shares a look with Bria. 'I suspect the boy's beginning to realize that the world is a great deal more complex than he thought.' He turns his attention back to me. 'If the facts change, Odysseus, a wise man changes with them.'

It's a glib, but seductive aphorism – but if I embrace it I'll have to throw away everything I've ever believed in. And I've already lost my family and my identity. I feel I am standing on the brink of a crumbling precipice, with Doripanes urging me to fling myself over the edge.

'So,' Bria says, perhaps guessing at my rising panic. 'Let's start with who I am. The girl you see before you is a goatherd of Phocis. Her own name is Hebea; she and her father live alone in a wattle and daub hut seven miles west from here. Her mother's dead, and her father occasionally contemplates incestuous union with her, but he's tormented by guilt and grief, and flagellates himself instead.'

I stare at her, trying to work out if she's lying. But what young girl talks of incest and flagellation?

'Yet I, Bria, am not the girl you see. *I'm inside her.* The truth, Ithaca, is that I'm a centuries-old spirit – a "daemon", if you like – who can body-jump into a sympathetic host. This girl, Hebea, is one such host.'

I don't *want* to believe a word of it. But my brain is searching through all the superstitions I've dismissed since childhood. 'Daemons', the priests say, are a 'soul' or 'spirit' we all have, implying neither good nor evil. The daemon is the part of us that survives death, and goes to dwell in the Underworld. I've never believed in the Underworld either – priests are full of unknowable assertions of this sort.

'Prove it,' I retort.

Bria gives me a sniffy look. 'I could leave this body – that would show you – but it would be unkind. Hebea will most likely panic. I'll tell you this though: I knew your father – your real one – that dirty old man Sisyphus.'

That gets my attention. 'How? He's been dead nearly twenty years.'

'I was in Corinth, thirty years ago. People said he'd made deals with Hades himself, for eternal youth. But I think they were all jealous because he looked half his age, and could out-drink, out-eat, out-race, out-fight and out-fuck every man at court.'

I feel the colour drain from my face. 'So who were you, back then? Not a goatherd, surely?'

'A whore,' says Bria, preening her hair. 'He rode me several times, your father. Excellent technique, and perpetually horny.' She pats my unwounded thigh. 'Once you're healed fully, you're welcome to show me if you've got your old man's stamina.'

I push her hand away, scandalized. Because if she's telling the truth, it's not *her* body she's offering, but Hebea's, and that's repulsive.

But more than that, I don't *want* to believe in a world inhabited by age-old daemons. *Because if that's so, my nightmare about the gods could be real.* That doesn't bear thinking about.

I turn to Doripanes. 'And you?'

'I'm a priest, as you see,' he replies. 'But secretly of Athena, not Hera. I'm her eyes and ears in Pytho. I'm also a *theios*.' The term means little to me, and Doripanes doesn't explain it. 'Do you believe in the gods, Odysseus?'

'What do you mean by "gods"?' I riposte.

'Do you believe in gods who made the world,' says Doripanes, 'who dwell on Olympus and watch and judge us, who control the winds and the waves, the harvests and seasons, who preside over love and war and the Underworld, where our daemons will one day dwell for the rest of eternity?'

I groan: he's just giving me the same tired fairy tales that priests always tell. But my nightmare is pressing in on me, along with vivid images of the Pythia's ecstatic madness yesterday; the hissing serpent; the throbbing walls of Pytho's underground shrine; Molebus with his clawed hands transforming from a boar into a monster; Athena and her owl...

It could, I suppose, all be passed off as a hallucination, but then there's my wounded thigh, and that is incontrovertibly real: a miraculous healing that can't be explained by drugs and warped recollections. I spread my hands in appeal. 'After yesterday, I feel I don't know anything any more.'

If the facts change, a wise man changes with them...

'What about the Pythia?' Bria asks. 'Do you think she can really see the future?'

'Well, she's made a fucking mess of mine,' I retort.

'Ooo, sarcasm again... Don't roll your eyes at me, you look like a frog!' Bria leans forward, suddenly serious. 'Listen carefully, princeling. *The gods are real.* Not concepts. That is the most crucial truth you will ever hear.'

There's a long pause while I master my emotions – it feels as though I have indeed plunged off the lip of the precipice into a deep abyss, and I'm still falling. Then, as I have always done, I turn to questioning, as a path towards understanding. *As a lifeline.* 'Doripanes, you just called yourself a *theios.* It means "god-touched"? And Athena touched me, yesterday. Does that make me a *theios* too?'

They exchange another look, a more guarded one this time. Doripanes responds first: 'You are either born with that capacity or not; even gods cannot turn an ordinary mortal into a semi-divine one, touch or no touch.'

He hasn't answered my question, so I try again. 'But am *I* one?'

He shrugs. 'I don't know. *Theioi* are born of, or descend from, a coupling between a god or goddess and a human. Athena's healing should awaken your potential, if you have any, but it usually takes some time for that potential to emerge – or a crisis.'

'Spare me the crisis,' I remark drily, looking them both over. 'So, you're both *theioi*, then?'

They nod.

'So what's it like?'

Bria grins. 'It's a little like marriage, though without the fun aspects. You let them into you, and they leave something of themselves that you can use. More power, more speed... it depends what kind of *theios* you are, and what god bred you.'

This conversation is getting stranger and stranger, but it makes a certain sense: I'd always believed Theseus killed an ordinary bull on Crete, that Heracles killed a perfectly normal lion in Nemea, but perhaps these heroes were 'god-touched'? And maybe those mythical beasts were like Molebus?

Bria breaks in on my thoughts. 'So what are we going to do with him,' she asks, 'if even the Great Goddess isn't sure?'

Doripanes turns his head to mouth something at Bria, but I still make out the word: *Prometheus*. He's already mentioned Prometheus, back at Pytho, claiming him as a distant ancestor of mine – the original 'Man of Fire'. The trickster who fooled Zeus...

'Odysseus,' Doripanes says, addressing me again, 'only the Goddess knows who and what you truly are. But she must think you worth saving. What you experienced yesterday was a divine healing, an immense favour in itself. And she has a task for you. An urgent one.'

I blink in shock. 'Already?' I manage to stutter. 'With my wounded leg?'

'Yes, indeed,' Doripanes replies.

'Are you sure you can't find someone else?'

He shakes his head. 'Quite apart from the nature of the mission, which only you can perform, the chosen servants of Athena are few. As a virgin she cannot simply possess women during conception and breed *theioi* at will. That would damage her identity and weaken, even destroy, her religion. So we must always convert doubters like you, those who question, those who share her essential character. We're perpetually short-handed.'

I feel I can risk a joke: 'Perhaps I should've joined Aphrodite. She must have all sorts of helpers.'

'Our gods are chosen for us by our nature, Odysseus of Ithaca,' Doripanes says, seriously. 'And I didn't notice Aphrodite offering you the job. Now, let's see if you can walk unsupported.'

4 – The Trojan Prophecies

'...Cassandra, the fairest of the daughters of
Priam...'
—Homer, *Iliad* 13

Pytho, Phocis

Walking goes better than I expected. My first steps are excruciating, but the wound doesn't tear itself open and I don't
haemorrhage to death. Even so, I'm relieved I don't need to
travel until the next morning, by which time, they assure me,
I will be much improved again.

Doripanes departs soon after, to confirm to the Pythia that
I'm definitely not at the Corycian Cave and he hasn't seen any
trace of me anywhere nearby, leaving me with Bria's prickly,
sarcastic company. The priest has left us more flatbreads, olive
paste and goat's cheese, some dried figs and a flask of wine.
I gulp my share down ravenously – healing is hard work and
requires all the nourishment I can keep down.

By day's end I'm hobbling unaided, and the next morning I
can even jog. Incredible. Wonderful. *Miraculous.*

If this is the illogical world I have feared all my life, at least
there are tangible benefits.

I wash down the last mouthfuls of breakfast with water from
Corycia's spring, already dressed for the journey in clothes
Doripanes has left me – a servant's tunic – with my *xiphos* –
my short sword, which I've retrieved from the cave – along
with my pack. I have one last question before I go – no, I have
thousands, but I'm out of time.

'Did you know my father?' I ask Bria, then correct myself. 'I mean, Laertes. He was an Argonaut.'

Bria purses her lips. 'I wasn't on that little jaunt. I remember Laertes, though – he was a friend of Sisyphus's, after a fashion. Not someone you could laugh with, but he was good in a fight and he liked a drink.'

It's an apt enough description that I believe her – Laertes did used to visit Sisyphus too. It's not a big detail, but it does add to the credibility of her extraordinary claims. 'He hasn't changed,' I tell her, hefting my pack and stamping down the embers of the fire. 'I guess it's time to go.'

We set off, keeping a close watch for any of the Pythia's servants who might have ignored Doripanes's misinformation. When we reach the zigzag path, the only way down the upper cliff face above Pytho, we move even more carefully. The closer we come to the Pytho shrine, the more sick with dread I feel, so I'm vastly relieved when Bria deviates onto a more obscure and precipitous route which brings us to a point west of the shrine by a well-concealed path.

The terrain is hard on my injured leg. It seems divine healing is an imperfect process, for the pain has become almost unbearable and I'm limping badly by the time we halt. Bria has still not said where we're going and I've been in too much pain to ask. It's a relief when, in the late afternoon, we pause in a small copse of trees overlooking the main shrine and its outhouses.

This is too close to the shrine for my liking, especially as they haven't yet told me what this mission is that I'm expected to perform. It *can't* have anything to do with the shrine, not now they're all hunting me. That would be sheer madness, and certain death.

Bria and Doripanes rescued me, I remind myself. *They don't want me dead.*

I breathe slowly, to settle myself. Perhaps we're just waiting here to be given more instructions by Doripanes, before we move on?

Once the pain in my leg has eased a little, I join Bria in peering out from the thickly leaved oleanders. Pytho is bustling with people today, and I see a lot of visitors, including easterners in their distinctive clothes. A true Achaean man wears a knee-length kilt or tunic, but these men have tubes of cloth fitted to the legs, from hip to ankles – very strange. Their skin is darker, they sport oiled beards and braid them.

'Where are they from?' I ask Bria.

'Troy,' she says darkly.

I've never been there, but of course I know the name. Troy sits on the western edge of Anatolia, a client kingdom of the massive Hittite Empire. Racially they're Anatolian, with splashes of Achaean blood.

'What are they doing here?'

'Consulting the Pythia, of course,' Bria replies. 'Pytho accepts all comers, provided they pay.'

That seems wrong to me. 'Aren't they enemies?'

'Are we at war?' Bria shrugs. 'They have their own seers and oracular sites, of course. Their Queen Hekuba is said to be second only to the Pythia for oracular insights. But they like to come here sometimes to get a different perspective. It's to both our advantages: they verify their readings, and we learn what they're thinking.'

'We?'

'The Pythia and her mistress, Hera,' Bria replies, smirking, 'and Athena, through Doripanes.'

'Does my mission have anything to do with the Trojans?' I ask, with some trepidation.

Maybe they want me to spy on them once they leave the shrine? But I can't see the sense in that – surely Doripanes will be inside the shrine and hear it all. Besides, my leg will be a major handicap if I'm to do any slinking around.

'Your presence stirred up the spirits the other morning, Ithaca,' Bria says, suddenly serious. 'We'd like to see what comes out of the Pythia's mouth during the Trojans' session, with you present.'

'What?' I recoil in shock. 'You want me to go in there again? They're hunting for me right now!'

'They think you're many miles away, Ithaca,' Bria drawls. 'Just keep a fold of your cloak over your head and don't draw attention to yourself.'

Don't draw attention… Bria must be mad – stark, staring mad. I remember the Pythia's serpentine, piercing gaze. *Amphithea will see through any disguise I can muster.* 'I can't and I won't.'

'You worry like an old woman,' she scoffs.

'Says she who remembers the Argonauts.'

'Mmm, so I know what I'm talking about.'

I give her the full Laertiades glare. 'Going in there is suicide!'

'Hardly. Try breaking into the house of an Athenian merchant or a Spartan king if you want real danger. Those are priests down there, Ithaca – they had to send to Krisa for Molebus when they wanted some killing done. Or aren't you smart enough to outwit some dew-pated prayer-merchants?'

It's hard not to punch her, but I manage.

But her needling has done exactly what she intended: set my mind off on its own little journey of speculation. *You're clever, Odysseus*, it's whispering. *Cleverer than anyone else you know. Perhaps there's somewhere you can hide without being seen?… And think what you might learn about yourself…*

'What's so damn important that you need me to get killed over?'

'Not killed.' For the first time she looks a little apologetic. 'Listen, Ithaca. Doripanes says he's never seen such an arousal of the spirits as your session with the Pythia. What came of it didn't benefit you much—'

'Oh, you noticed?'

'…but we fear the Trojans and their ambitions,' she goes on, blithely. 'Both Hera and Athena will suffer if Troy gains ascendancy over Achaea. With you present in the shrine, the spirits of the oracle may reveal much, much more than otherwise about the Trojans' plans.'

I can't muster much excitement about helping Hera, who clearly wants me dead. But I owe Athena my life. And Ithaca is a part of the Achaean confederation and if it falls, we fall too.

Civilizations can vanish, their people exterminated. I would die rather than see this happen to my people.

We both tense as footsteps approach. I peer through the oleanders and see a cloaked and hatted figure clambering towards us through the trees. 'Doripanes,' I whisper, relieved.

The priest joins us – he's edgy, which does nothing for my nerves. 'Well?' he asks, looking at me.

'He's in,' Bria replies.

I shoot her a murderous glance, but my stupid brain is intrigued and I blurt, 'I'll do it.'

'Excellent,' Doripanes approves. 'Not that I expected otherwise.' His fleeting smile fades. 'I thought we'd have an extra day to plan how to smuggle you in,' he tells me, 'but the Trojans are insisting on a hearing at dawn tomorrow, to give them time to depart from Kirrha tomorrow afternoon. The wind is favourable for their voyage home and they are anxious not to miss it.'

Kirrha is the port south of Pytho where I landed with my family only a handful of days ago. It's built on a stretch of coast where large ships can safely approach the shore or even the beach. The Trojans will have sailed their own vessels across the Aegean, crossed the Isthmus of Corinth on foot, then hired Greek ships from Corinth for the last leg here.

'Who's in the Trojan party?' Bria asks.

'Prince Skaya-Mandu,' Doripanes replies, 'and his twin sister Kyshanda.'

Bria whistles. 'Skaya-Mandu is second in line to the throne, behind Prince Heka-Taru – and Kyshanda is King Piri-Yamu and Queen Hekuba's eldest daughter. Dear gods, are you sure we're not allowed to knife them?'

Doripanes shakes his head. 'Tempting, but Pytho must remain neutral and safe to all comers.'

'If you insist.' Bria scowls. I already know she can kill, but it seems she has a hunger for it too.

Doripanes perches in front of me, checks my wounded thigh and asks how I'm feeling.

'Fabulous,' I lie. Now I'm committed to this insanity, I might as well pretend I can pull it off.

He's clearly not fooled, but he says, 'Good to hear it. Listen, you'll sleep overnight in my house, then early tomorrow morning I'll get you into the shrine. There are alcoves overlooking the main chamber – one for each of the four winds. I'll disguise you and place you there, close enough stir up the spirits when the Pythia goes into her trance. Once the hearing is over, just slip away.'

He makes it sound suspiciously simple. 'How will you disguise me?' I stroke my mane of red hair. 'I'm somewhat distinctive.'

'Shave it off,' Bria suggests callously.

'No!' I'm rather proud of it, and anyway a warrior of Achaea would never do such a thing.

Doripanes sees my outrage. 'That won't be necessary, as well you know,' he tells Bria. He takes a handful of my hair and mutters something, and to my astonishment it turns brown.

'What have you done?' I gasp.

Bria laughs. 'Vain, isn't he? Don't worry, Ithaca, it's just an illusion: it'll last only as long as we want.'

I tell myself it's a good start, though my heart is still beating against my ribs as I don the grey acolyte robe Doripanes hands me and shroud my head with my cloak. Bria takes charge of my sword – no acolyte bears arms – and bids us farewell, for now. 'Put your fears aside, Ithaca,' she assures me. 'We'll be watching out for you, whatever happens.'

We don't exactly hug, but she killed Molebus, summoned Athena and has given me something like a reason to live. Though it's not a change I'm entirely grateful for, I owe her.

By now it's dusk and the air is chill. Doripanes and I walk over to the village, bold as you like. 'Just act as if you belong, and people will assume you do,' he tells me.

Reckless though that sounds, it actually works. There are dozens of acolytes here, all muffled in thick cloaks. No one gives me a second glance. Doripanes lays out a spare pallet for me in his own bedroom, the same room my parents used when visiting – and the very room where I was disowned. Is Doripanes reminding me how much I've lost, how much I now rely on Athena? Probably – and thinking about my family, right now returning to Ithaca without me, means it's a long time until I sleep.

–

Doripanes wakes me well before dawn and we breakfast on thick barley porridge that sticks in my throat. I force it down somehow and wrap a pair of honey cakes into cloth and tuck them into my pouch for later, while he briefs me on what I'm to do: just stay where he puts me and listen hard. He ensures my illusory hair colour persists, then swathed in our cloaks and with heads bowed, we go to the shrine. It's dark and we drift along the path through the pines like ghosts.

We're almost there when Doripanes pulls me aside, hissing in alarm. We duck behind one of the outhouses and peer out cautiously. At the main portal to the shrine, lit by a sputtering torch, there's a massive, bearded man with a dangerous, panther-like gait, wearing gaudy leggings, a blue cloak and a bronze corselet in the eastern style. He's positioning two sentries at the doors, obviously fellow Trojans. There were no guards during my family's visit.

'That's Aduwalli, a Trojan *theios*,' Doripanes mutters. 'One of the most dangerous men I've met. He must be here to protect Prince Skaya-Mandu and Princess Kyshanda. Best we wait until he leaves.'

The wait is anxious but brief, then Aduwalli sets off towards the village, presumably to fetch his charges. Once he's gone, Doripanes takes me inside the main portal, past the two Trojan guardsmen who question him brusquely but admit us when Doripanes shows them his priestly seal. He leads me around a circular passage around the upper level until we reach the northern alcove, which contains an altar to Boreas, the North Wind. It's here Doripanes leaves me.

'There's nothing you need do,' he tells me. 'Speak to no one, unless you must. If you're questioned, say you're new and

47

have been sent here by me to gain an understanding of the oracle.' He shows me a low opening in the wall behind the altar, which looks down into a brooding darkness: the dimly-lit inner sanctum where the Pythia makes her pronouncements. 'You're performing a crucial task,' he murmurs. 'If your presence stirs up the humours of this place, we may learn much. Once it's done, await me here.'

He leaves, and immediately I'm beset by memories of my confrontation with the Pythia, replete with that ghostly serpentine presence. Fighting for calm, I settle onto my knees, keeping my head bowed. At first I'm alone, but soon a group of priests and priestesses enter from the passage and begin lighting the shrine's lamps. One older priestess in grey robes asks me sharply who I am, but when I mention the magic word 'Doripanes' she loses all curiosity and I'm left alone again. I'm nervous – but oddly, I'm also vividly *alive* at all this intrigue and tension.

A few minutes pass, then I catch a woman's scent of roses and cinnamon, as someone kneels to my right, just out of reach. They're fidgeting rather than praying. I steal a glance and my throat goes dry.

The newcomer is a young woman and, once my eyes have been snared, I can't look away.

She's young, about my age I'm guessing. Her clothing, unlike our Achaean weaves, is of a diaphanous material finer than the most delicate Egyptian linen, and dyed in pale blues and sunset pinks like an evening sky. *Silk?* My mother has a few scraps, back on Ithaca, but nothing in this quantity. Gold earrings frame the most delicately beautiful face I've ever seen, narrow and equine and utterly enchanting.

She catches me staring, and something in her eyes flickers as she pulls a veil up and over her head, wrapping it around so that only her eyes show. *You don't get to look at me*, the gesture implies.

Flustered, I look away and there's an awkward silence, before she surprises me by speaking. 'What god does this altar honour?'

She speaks Achaean with a dusky, lilting accent – there's music in her, and a confident hauteur that's instantly appealing. She's obviously Trojan and, from her clothes and jewellery, I realize she must be one of the royal twins Doripanes and Bria spoke of: Kyshanda, the eldest daughter of King Piri-Yamu and Queen Hekuba. I can barely make my tongue work, I'm so stunned. Then my usual nature – garrulous, my sister calls it – takes over.

'This is the altar of Boreas,' I explain. 'He's God of the North Wind and a patron of Athens. He stole an Athenian princess and made her his wife, so the Athenians revere him.'

The Trojan princess arches an eyebrow. '"Stole"? So these Athenians admire kidnap and rape, then?'

Her directness shocks me, but I recover my wits before she thinks me a tongue-tied fool. 'No, no, it's not like that. In Achaea, a woman is expected to go unwillingly into marriage. It's customary that there is an element of "theft" in all wedding ceremonies. A good girl is expected to prefer to remain...' I blush. 'Er, virginal. Even when she loves the man who "steals" her.'

She looks at me fully, her veil slipping. Again I'm lost in her big, deep-set eyes, which are thoughtful as she takes this in. Then she startles me again by suppressing a giggle, which she only controls by putting her fingers to her cherry lips. 'Really?'

We share a smile that bathes me in the honey-warmth of empathy. 'It is indeed so,' I assure her.

'And do the men go all unwilling too?' she asks, and I sense a delightful and unexpected mischief in her, a worldly but playful curiosity akin to my own.

'No, we're expected to be experienced and full of ardour.'

'Then how,' she says, with faked coyness, 'do you acquire all this experience, Achaean?'

I glance about. This is a most improper conversation to be having before a sacred altar, but we're still alone. 'In truth, some young men go to their wedding virginal also, having only the knowledge given them by older mentors; but others have lain with widows or slaves, both of which are permitted.'

Her face hardens a fraction. 'Unprotected women, then. So you Achaeans *do* practise rape?'

I colour again. 'Lady, I can't pretend some are not exploited, but a good family looks after their servants and protects them. My mother forbids any woman servant in our house to be misused and we all respect that. And most widows have their dowries, and take younger lovers in consolation for their loss. My own...'

I've let my tongue run away with itself, and she latches unerringly on to my hesitation.

'Your own...?' she asks, her eyes teasing – and frankly curious. 'Do go on.'

'There is a widow I lay with at times,' I admit. This is true: her name's Issa, she dwells in a fine house outside Ithaca town, owns merchant ships and flocks and olive groves. She's one of the richest women in the islands, twice my age but still beautiful, and full of wisdom and grace. And a generous lover.'

Kyshanda hears something in my voice. 'Do you love her?' she asks.

'Lady, love would be awkward for both of us. I will marry someone my own age one day, someone my parents choose. And Issa is much courted. But were I free... who knows?'

The Trojan princess seems to accept that, her smile returning to charm me. 'Do you have a name, young priest?'

There's a game Eurybates and I play back on Ithaca. I like to befriend the traders and sailors that come to Ithaca, and learn of the world, but no one would speak truth to me if they knew my station. So we invented a false persona. 'Megon of Cephalonia is what they call me,' I say. 'It's a small island kingdom,' I add, in response to a questioning eyebrow, 'off the coast of western Achaea, with Ithaca as its capital. I've come as an acolyte, but also to seek guidance about the future, as have you, though my matters are of much less import.'

'Then you know who I am?'

'Of course – you are Princess Kyshanda of Troy, and I am at your service.' I don't pronounce her name well – the Luwian language has a weird 'sh' sound that comes out of my mouth as an 'ss', and I roll the final syllable – in Achaea we would render her name as something like 'Cas-san-d'rah', which is a pretty name.

We fall silent, smiling shyly. My face has character, not beauty, but I know I have a winning smile. And hers is like moonlight.

There's something about attraction that defies logic. I've heard many tales where two people meet and instantly want the other in their life. For me, Kyshanda is such a one. But her family is as far above mine as can be imagined, despite the fact that I am also a prince. King Piri-Yamu of Troy rules a rich kingdom, while my father rules a small cluster of islands. Laertes numbers his subjects in the thousands, and Piri-Yamu in the hundreds of thousands.

And, thanks to my subterfuge, to her I'm a mere commoner, Megon of Cephalonia, who doesn't even exist. I fear this brush with her will be over soon, and never repeated. And yet, I see an answering spark in her eyes.

'Megon,' she says, testing the sound of it on her tongue.

She glances over her shoulder. 'I'm supposed to be praying, Megon, but the truth is I'm nervous. Very soon my brother and I go to see the Pythia. Have you seen her? Do you know what happens here?'

'Yes, but I'm new – I've only witnessed an audience with the Pythia once before.' Then I remember that I still have Doripanes's honey cakes in my pouch, and pull out the parcel. 'Would you like to share these?'

Clearly, good manners, caution and decorum should all compel her to say 'no', especially before an altar, where the eating of non-sacrificial food isn't permitted. She glances left and right, as if suddenly aware she's alone with a male who isn't family. All men are animals, the old gossips say.

But honey is sweet. 'Why not?' she says, with just a hint of wickedness.

Thank you, Great Goddess!

I edge closer until we're almost touching, the fold of my cloak slipping from my head as I hand her a honey cake. With conspiratorial winks, we gobble them down like naughty children. Her delight at the honey cakes is clear, but she's watchful still. I sense a kindred spirit – another enquiring mind, eager to learn from this rare circumstance. I become aware that my fear has eased, and it's not just about her.

I'm quite enjoying all this intrigue and subterfuge…

'May I ask why you're here?' I risk asking.

She considers me for a moment, then shrugs. 'My parents sent us here. Troy is building a new harbour at Besikos Bay, to grow our sea trade, and my father the King is seeking fresh alliances. My mother is a great seeress in her own right, and wished to consult with the Pythia. But she's with child – *again* – so my brother and I were sent.'

As a prince, I've been raised to know something of the world, and as 'Megon' I've learnt much from the traders: Troy is at the southern end of the straits that lead through to the Axeinos Sea, and well placed to control the shipping from the tin mines. Their old harbour silted up some generations ago, however, so they've been unable to disrupt Achaean imports from the tin mines.

But this harbour she speaks of… that could change everything. My tutors drilled enough geography into me that I know Besikos Bay – it's south of Troy, sheltered from the strong currents of the Hellespont. Any ship entering or leaving Axeinos, the Inhospitable Sea, will want to use it – but the Trojans will exact heavy tolls, I don't doubt.

I'm careful to hide my concern though, just asking her more about Troy. She chats happily, and boasts a little of her father's might. His plans are certainly grand.

'Your harbour won't do much for Achaea,' I point out, curious to see her reaction.

'Achaea is tiny, and anyway, each nation must look to their own interests.'

At first I'm shocked at her dismissal of my people. Then I realize her misunderstanding. Historically, Achaea is a small kingdom on the north coast of the Peloponnese, an insignificant place, as she says – but the name has also come to mean the racial identity of all of our kingdoms, including the islands to the west, south and east, even those nudging the coast of Asia. 'I mean all the Achaean peoples,' I explain. 'We are many kingdoms, but we are also one, led by the High King in Mycenae.'

'I know,' she says, saving face. Or else she's provoking me, in order to tease my thoughts out of me. 'But why would our port affect the kingdoms of Achaea?'

Now I'm certain she's leading me on, testing my knowledge of the world. With any other person, I would have been irked, but I can't resist playing her game: she's charmed me.

'Almost all our tin – which we need for turning copper into bronze – comes from mines beyond the Axeinos Sea. If every ship stops at your new port, you can buy their tin and leave us none. Or charge tolls they must pass on to us, to make a profit. It will be like having a rope around our necks.'

'What are you saying – that we shouldn't build our new port and look after ourselves?' she challenges.

'No. But surely some kind of arrangement can be reached, so that we have our share?'

'A trade treaty, perhaps?' She strokes her hair, playing the wise queen. 'That would be better than conflict, surely. I will speak with my mother.'

'Please do,' I urge her. 'Life is hard enough without struggling for the basics.'

'I promise,' she says, eyes shining. 'And I hope we can still be friends, Megon of Cephalonia.'

By Aphrodite herself, so do I...

Our eyes are locked, and I experience that wonderful realization that the person you're so attracted to feels the same... I almost fancy that I could lean in and kiss her... 'You're very beautiful,' I murmur.

She preens unconsciously and says, 'And you have the most *wonderful* red hair.'

I stifle a gasp: a quick glance shows me my hair is still as brown as Doripanes made it this morning. But she's seen through Doripanes's illusions, perhaps without even knowing they were there.

My heart thumps against my ribs. Should I make my getaway while I can? No – she's shown no sign she's aware all Pytho is hunting a red-headed man. I master my shock smoothly – I think – and somehow we're leaning towards each other again, lips parting...

'*Kysha!*' A furious voice snarls as a slim young man, fully armed despite the prohibitions of the shrine, storms into the small recess, his face dark with anger. From his features I guess immediately that he's her twin brother Skaya-Mandu. 'Here you are! What are you doing? And who's this pig with you?'

I stand. 'We're only conversing.'

'You have no right to address my sister! She's a princess of Troy! No one speaks to her!'

I'd have been wise to shut up, but I'm not always wise: 'Sounds a dull existence. But no duller than putting up with you.'

His hand goes to his dagger, but Kyshanda grabs his arm. 'We were just talking, brother. He's been entirely honourable throughout.'

Skaya-Mandu glares at her. 'You sneaked out. I've been searching for you everywhere!'

'Dear Skaya, I didn't mean to alarm you – I just needed to think, that's all.' She strokes his bicep, gazing up at him with those amazing eyes. 'Nothing improper has occurred, I assure you. Megon has been the soul of honour.'

Apart from speaking openly of marital and sexual mores, and desecrating the altar by eating non-sacrificial honey cakes before it, she's absolutely right.

Skaya-Mandu scowls at me again, clearing seeing no more than a lowly novice. 'Piss off, dung beetle, before I slash your belly open.'

I'm not afraid. I've fought bigger men in the training yards all my life, most of them far more intimidating than this slender, arrogant pratfall of a prince. And I do have a temper, and his words have stung me.

Kyshanda senses impending violence and gives me a warning look. But then a massive figure fills the doorway: the big Trojan captain, Aduwalli. I remember what Doripanes has told me about him – he's a *theios* and dangerous.

'The Pythia has arrived, Great Ones,' Aduwalli growls. 'It's time.' He gives me a cold look – his face is scarred and pock-marked, and his eyes harbour menace. 'Is all well?'

Kyshanda speaks quickly: 'Of course. Skaya and I are ready.' She tugs on Skaya-Mandu's arm. 'Come, brother,' she says, with surprising authority, and he obeys. She glances over her shoulder at me as they walk out, her eyes twinkling. Aduwalli leaves last, staring down at me coldly before turning away.

Relief floods me, but so does adrenalin: I'm enjoying the danger. And I'd walk through fire to see Kyshanda again. But for now, I settle back onto my knees and peer through the low opening behind the altar to Boreas. I can see most of the inner chamber, which is now illuminated with smoking torches. The Pythia is positioning herself on her tall tripod stool, vapours are pouring up from the crack in the ground beneath her, wreathing her in smoke, and the priests and priestesses are beginning a hymn to Hera.

The Trojans' hearing is about to begin…

–

Three days ago, I came to Pytho as a supplicant, and the energies of this place almost overwhelmed my senses. To be here as an observer is quite a different experience: this time I'm prepared for the essential strangeness of the place. It's still an unearthly experience though, from the whisperings from unseen voices, the play of light on the walls, the stone floor – even the people seem to shift and flow as if they've been painted on the smoke.

I see the Trojans arrive, hear the ritual announcements of name, rank and purpose, Doripanes's voice reverberating through the chamber. The prince and princess are clearly visible through the opening I'm peering through, and I can bask in Kyshanda's angular beauty as I watch.

At first the Pythia – Amphithea, my grandmother – sits unmoving on her tripod, inhaling the vapours that rise from the fissure at her feet, her calm at odds with her surroundings. But then the cleft comes to life, issuing a thick black smoke rather than the translucent vapour I have seen before, and I hear the priests and priestesses giving little gasps of amazement. The Pythia looks around sharply, and I pull back from my little window.

Doripanes was right: my presence here really is stirring up the spirits.

I expected Prince Skaya-Mandu to lead the Trojan's supplication, but it's Kyshanda that steps forward. Of course – she's the eldest daughter of the famed Hekuba: *she must be a seer in her own right...*

Which only makes her more alluring, in my eyes.

'Greetings from my father, King Piri-Yamu of Troy,' Kyshanda begins. 'Know that Troy is completing a new harbour at Besikos Bay, six miles from our city fortress. Already the sea traders use it, and our markets thrive. My father wishes to know what this might mean for Troy and all the Aegean, for better or worse.'

The Pythia gathers her veils, drawing the smoke to her face and breathing it in, her torso swaying as she does. Once again the rock walls throb, as they did three days ago, but this time with greater intensity, accompanied by the same hissing sound I felt before.

Amphithea enters her trance-like state, venting an almost sexual moan, clutching at her left breast, then her eyes flash open, white and pupil-less. '*The hippocampus thrashes its tail,*' she cries, '*devouring the depths of the ocean. Pearls from oysters, coral and gold, glitter on the walls.*' She vents a croaking cough that trails on and on, but just as I think she's done, she continues. '*A shifting of stars in the firmament, a bloodletting, the end of a civilization... The lion rises and roars... the hippocampus has hooves and coils; from one can the lion flee but not the other. The comet plunges, the old king and the new, the rising and the setting of the sun, and the lion's roar is stifled...*'

As she falls silent, the earth rumbles and the whole shrine shakes. Dense smoke is pouring from the cleft to engulf the

Pythia, so thick she almost vanishes. The priests react with alarm, Skaya-Mandu looks terrified, but Kyshanda's eyes are shining and wide.

And as for the words: I've had no formal training in deciphering portents, but I'm a voracious student. The horse is a symbol of Troy and the hippocampus is a legendary beast of the seas, with a horse's foreparts and the tail of a fish – it could be a symbol of Troy's growing sea power. Pearls and coral must pertain to the wealth of the sea trade... and the lion is for Mycenae, seat of our High King, surely... The hoof and the coils: a sudden blow or slow strangulation... War, or economic dominance. '*From one can the lion flee but not the other.*'

When Kyshanda asks her next question, I can hear the excitement in her voice. 'In all things there is risk – what perils await Troy on the path we have taken?'

The Pythia answers instantly, her voice harsh. '*Brother to brother, family to kin, the horse gallops and the great eagle swoops. The Skyfather turns his eye: lightning for weakness; the quill for strength.*'

My mind races: the great eagle is the Hittite Emperor, overlord of all Anatolia. The Trojans dwell at the north-western edge of that Empire, and the traders say King Piri-Yamu has been courting the Emperor for over a decade. He's seeking alliance – the quill, not the lightning. But the Skyfather must be Zeus: how's he involved?

'By what means might the hippocampus defeat the lion?' Kyshanda asks.

The Pythia stalks forward from the edge of the fissure to confront Kyshanda. The smoke surges from the cleft to swirl around them both. '*Slow and certain are the coils that tighten, grip and asphyxiate!*' the Pythia cries. '*Swift the stamping hoof, that stuns and shatters! Against either, the lion is weak.*'

I'm horrified: I've just heard the fate of Achaea laid out, and it's doom for us, whichever way we take against mighty Troy. So much for my childish daydreams of working with Kyshanda for peace. But there's more.

'*But beware,*' the Pythia adds, '*for if the lion bites, the eagle turns.*'

A warning, surely, bearing some hope: Troy must be strong with Achaea, but be wary of showing too much strength, least the Hittites are aroused. But why? Surely they're allies of Troy?

'Who or what are the greatest risks to Troy, in any conflict with the Achaeans?' Kyshanda asks.

The Pythia tries to answer, but she's taken by a paroxysm of coughing, and almost falls. I sense that she can't bear much more of this. The gases and smoke must be racking her body for she starts lurching drunkenly. But still she rallies, and answers in a voice like an old serpent. '*The Lost One, abandoned, unworthy, awaits. Clouds gather, enticing promises blind the viper...*' Her voice falters, but she struggles on. '*Night hunter, pure watcher, skull-born – she sends the Bull-slayer, the dethroned, to contest thy will!*'

The first part of the prophecy eludes me but I understand this much: Theseus slew the Cretan Bull, and was dethroned as King of Athens some years ago. Is he also a servant of Athena? For 'skull-born' must mean Athena, referring as it does one of her origin legends.

The Pythia delivers what must surely be her final volley of words: '*The Consort stands firm, seeing and hearing all. She will not be betrayed again. Warn the Father, warn the Son: the Queen stands defiant.*'

So Hera will not countenance the conquest of Achaea.

And Troy and Kyshanda are to be my enemy...

That seems to be the end of it – but then the Pythia speaks again, her voice becoming the grinding of boulders in a landslide. '*Line of the Tormented, the Fire Giver,*' she groans. '*Man of Fire, Secret Son, revealed and shamed; taken up he rises, and altars crack! Let it not be! Take the quill and not the blade!*' She jabs a bony finger at Kyshanda. '*O Trojan priestess, the shadows gather about thee! While the flame burns, all thy schemes are threatened! Only his eyes see through thee! Bind or break him, or ruin take thee!*'

The Line of the Tormented? The Man of Fire... the Secret Son...

My heart hammers. *She means me...*

The hissing resumes and it seems to me that, somewhere, a giant serpent is searching for me. Then with a ragged cry the

Pythia pitches forward, her face striking the floor. The priests rush in, and I fear for her life. But she's twitching, and I realize she's only stunned, though her face is bloodied.

I hear Doripanes bid the Trojans leave: 'You have the answers you need,' he says.

'Thank you,' I hear Kyshanda reply. 'I am well satisfied.' But there's something in her voice, an unspoken question, that tells me she's hungry for more.

I know I'm now in even more danger than before, and not just from the Pythia's priests. The prophecy has just named Prometheus, the Fire Giver, and his Secret Son as a threat to the Trojans. They will want me dead too. My instinct is to pull the fold of my cloak over my head and try to slip away. But Doripanes ordered me to await him here.

I decide I have no choice but to obey.

For several moments no one comes as the Trojans depart and the priests and priestesses attend upon Amphithea. Once she regains her senses, I'm sure she'll realize that some alien presence – *my presence* – has agitated the spirits of this place. Every voice that carries up to me from below is full of amazement, and the phrase 'Man of Fire' is on every tongue.

Then I hear both booted and sandaled feet approach and there's nowhere to run. I drop to my knees again and pray, head down – to Athena, who I'm now rather more desperate to please than I could have imagined.

Kyshanda's fragrance washes over me as she reaches past me to place something on the floor beside the altar, then scoop it up again. 'There's my bracelet!' she exclaims, presumably to fool those with her. But as she rises, she murmurs, 'I wish to see you again. Come to Krisa, to the travellers' shrine near the inn, today at noon.'

Then she's gone.

My racing heart threatens to burst, but my soul is singing.

5 – The Choice

'…a race of bronze… fearsome and mighty, who embraced the woeful works of Ares and deeds of hubris… they were as hard-hearted as the mythic lodestone – terrifying men. Their strength was great… their armour was of bronze, their houses and tools were of bronze… but dreadful though they were, black Death took them and they fled the Sun's shining light.'
—Hesiod, *Works and Days*

Krisa, Phocis

Moments later, Doripanes finds me and marches me out of the shrine, past a cluster of acolytes jabbering about the prophecies, and up the slope beyond the shrine complex towards the cliffs. A low sun filters through the pines, and I realize it's still barely past dawn.

'Are you all right?' he mutters.

'I'm fine,' I tell him, quite honestly. Yes, there were some nerve-racking moments, and even being there, as an enemy of the shrine, was undoubtedly blasphemous. And the Pythia's words were frankly soul-crushing – but it was *exciting*. I feel like I was born to this life.

And Kyshanda… *Thank you, Aphrodite or whoever, for that encounter!*

Doripanes is clearly immensely pleased. 'Dear gods,' he murmurs, as we hurry towards his house. 'That was the fullest, most extraordinary prophecy I've witnessed! I was right to bring you here. If only you could stay, how much more we would learn!'

'What happens now?' I ask eagerly, my mind on Kyshanda's promised assignation. 'What do I do?'

'Go back to Corycia's Cave – take the secret path Bria led you down yesterday, and be sure not to be seen. Await my instructions there. It may take a day or so before the Pythia calls off the hunt, then I'll come.'

'And after that?'

'We'll take you to another place. We're still unsure how you may best serve our mistress.' He stares hard at me. 'You are truly of the line of Prometheus, the original "Man of Fire". How our Goddess views that I still don't know, but some say it was Prometheus who taught Athena about logic and reason.'

'Then we serve the same cause,' I reassure him. 'I'll see you at the cave.'

We clasp hands, he hurries off and I start climbing the trail…

But only until I'm out of sight. Because, despite my assurances to Doripanes, I've not told him of my conversation with Kyshanda; and I'm absolutely determined to see her again, whatever the risk.

I strip off the acolyte robes and poke them down a rabbit hole, bundle the cloak up and tuck it under my arm, then leave the trail to clamber down through rugged scrub, giving Pytho a wide berth. After a while, shins scratched and the wound in my thigh starting to ache, I find a goat track that takes me in the direction I need, invisible to any on the road.

Krisa, the nearest town to Pytho, is now only a few miles away at the base of the mountainside; it's still morning and I have plenty of time. So I pause to drink at a welcome spring, while I go over what I've learnt in my mind.

It's clear from my conversation with Kyshanda, and the Pythia's words, that this new port of Troy's at Besikos Bay could destabilize the whole region. As 'Megon of Cephalonia', I've spent many convivial hours in taverns learning how the world of commerce works. So I know that the rarest, most expensive trading commodity in our world is not gold or silver. It's not olive oil or finely woven wool or grain, wine, copper or timber. It's tin.

This is because without tin, copper can't be forged into bronze: the hardest known alloy, from which the most important tools and weapons are forged. Forty years ago, the great Jason led his Argonauts, a band of our finest warriors including Laertes, north-cast through the Bosporus and across the Axeinos Sea, where he defeated the local tribes and founded a mining settlement. It's since grown a hundredfold, drawing men from all over Achaea and employing countless slaves, all labouring to bring us tin. We don't keep it all – much we sell for immense profit around the Aegean. Thanks to the tin trade, Mycenae and the other kingdoms of Achaea thrive.

But Troy has also grown in this time. Once a smaller citadel that the great hero Heracles ransacked, the city has been rebuilt, the walls expanded and the kingdom it rules grown strong. This new harbour of theirs is like a knife at our throats, if I interpret the Pythia's prophecies and my own knowledge of commerce correctly. Sea travel is perilous, and a safe harbour is priceless. There are no good harbours in the narrow straits that lead to the Axeinos Sea, so by the time the ships reach its mouth, they need water and provisions. Troy will now give them that.

And she will also fleece us of the tin we must have. Traders are men of money, not patriots. They'll sell to the man offering the best price, on the easiest and safest routes. If that means selling all their tin to Troy and letting the Trojans distribute it – east and south into the Hittite lands, not west into Achaea – then they'll do it.

The Pythia has seen this: a future in which Troy ascends, safeguarding its relationship with its big, dangerous neighbour, the Hittite Empire, until it comes to dominate the entire Aegean. Achaea will die – strangled by commerce, or crushed by force of arms. My people and our way of life are doomed.

And somehow I – the Man of Fire – am a threat to this bleak future. I have no idea how. Nor do I wish to be the enemy of Kyshanda, whose lovely face floats constantly before my eyes.

This isn't mere infatuation, I tell myself. I feel clear-headed, and I remember the answering spark in her eyes.

I can even imagine a way that can fulfil Troy's ambitions yet save Achaea: *I marry her, and through our love we find a way to make both Troy and Achaea great.*

It seems ludicrous – but is it? I'm a prince of Achaea – albeit of one of the lowliest kingdoms. Perhaps I am a *theios, god-touched*, despite Bria's doubts. Surely I might be worthy of Trojan royalty?

Everything seems possible, when another soul touches yours.

–

I reach Krisa with the sun almost at its peak, but I put the cloak back on, pulling a fold of it over my once-more scarlet blaze of hair, and take the side streets through the town, seeking the travellers' shrine. My family stopped there to give thanks for our safe journey a few days ago, Father being a stickler for such rituals, so it's not hard for me to find it again. I slip into the rear of the building, which is empty at this hour, and settle myself into a shadowed spot near the door.

Soon after, Kyshanda arrives; I hear her tell her escorting guardsmen to wait outside. A moment later she enters, veiled and wrapped in a travelling cloak, going first to the altar and kneeling. After a surreptitious look over her shoulder, she rises and comes towards me, parting her veil and smiling. I rise and for a few breaths we just stare into each other's eyes.

We're both a little wary: afraid of being discovered, and also of rejection – there's been time for ardour to cool.

But it hasn't: she takes my hands in hers, her fingers twining in mine. She's a fraction shorter than me, and her upturned face studies mine, then with sudden decisiveness she's stepping close and breathing my breath, gazing into my eyes and then releasing my hands to lay her right hand on my chest, above my heart, while she strokes my hair with her left as if it's gold thread.

'The Man of Fire,' she whispers. 'That's you, isn't it? The Pythia spoke of a fugitive, a young flame-headed man whom we should capture if we could.'

My heartbeat skitters. I could deny it, but she won't believe me. 'There's not much of a reward,' I tell her. 'I wouldn't bother.'

I'm *longing* to kiss her mouth, and much more besides. I know from Issa, my widow-lover, how wonderful a stolen moment in a woman's arms can be. Even in a sacred place like this. But I also know better than to rush in, with so many pitfalls around us. So I just wait, gazing into her big eyes, luminous in this gloomy shrine.

'The Secret Son who could ruin us,' she whispers, tangling her fingers in strands of scarlet-gold hair. '"Taken up he rises, and altars crack." What does that mean?'

'I have no idea,' I tell her honestly.

'My mother Hekuba has also foreseen a Man of Fire… and we don't understand that prophecy either. "He who will redeem or damn us," Mother told me, on the very night before I set sail for Achaea.' Kyshanda's voice is filled with awe. 'She said we must "win his heart or cut it out".'

'Honestly,' I say with a twinkle, 'I'd prefer the former.'

'In Troy we think all Achaeans are barbarian giants, but you're not like that, are you?'

'Well, I'm not a giant, clearly.'

'Nor the other – barbarians don't have your wit or self-deprecation, or the audacity to speak to me as an equal. I feel like I've known you for years…'

Then we do kiss, a slow melting together of our mouths, tasting each other gently, caressing the other's lips and drawing each other in, full of warmth and softness and wanting.

Love's arrows can strike swiftly, they say.

So do the arrows of the War God.

Boots crunch on the gravel outside and there's barely a heartbeat in which to wrench apart as Prince Skaya-Mandu storms in, his face livid as he sees his sister too damned close to a stranger. 'Kysha! What are you doing?' he snarls. His eyes narrow as he peers into the shadows. '*You again!*'

I'm reeling in shock – my insistently logical mind is suggesting that Kyshanda lured me here to end whatever threat the prophecies spoke of. But when she tries to interpose herself between me and her brother, I discard that horrible suspicion. But it means I'm unprepared when he brushes her aside and smashes his fist into my face.

My world explodes in blood and white-hot pain and I stagger; the back of my head strikes the wall and constellations erupt. My knees wobble and I slide to the floor, my vision a wet smudge.

Kyshanda screams, her brother roars and they rail at each other in their own tongue. I know a little of it but not enough to follow their words when I'm stunned. Then he drags her, shrieking, out of the shrine…

…as Aduwalli and three other Trojans walk in, plant their feet and stare down at me just as my sight clears. I remember Doripanes's warning, only a few hours ago. *A dangerous man.* He looks it.

They draw their curved swords. 'Well?' says one of them, a thickset man with a paunch.

Aduwalli fixes me with a cold glare. 'We kill him.'

Paunchy grins savagely, testing the edge of the blade with his thumb. 'My pleasure.'

He draws back his arm, then slashes down hard at my neck. *I'm dead.*

Except that just as Paunchy's arm descends, the air thrums and a shaft whips through the open window above me and takes him in the chest, punching right through his brazen armour and piercing his heart. He convulses, then collapses backwards against his commander, dead.

His blade drops into my lap.

I snatch at the leather-wrapped hilt and lash out, sweeping the curved blade into the stomach of the nearest man. But the blow is foiled by his armour and only gashes him. By now, my trained combat reflexes are kicking in as I hammer my left boot into the side of the man's right knee. It buckles, and I rise as he falls.

As I come to my feet, an owl cries inside my skull, the sound piercing me through and through. All around me the air seems to glow and shimmer, and suddenly I'm clear-headed again. An incredible sense of well-being suffuses me, from the marrow in my bones to the tiny hairs on my skin. My wound scorches with a searing agony as flesh re-knits, and energy I've never felt before floods me.

You're mine, Odysseus, a woman's voice calls inside my skull. *Mine if you will it!*

The voice is accompanied by an incredible blend of puissance and well-being – *this is an awakening, surely* – and I shout in exultation, 'Yes, let it be!'

Then Aduwalli looms over me, a giant of a man, head and shoulders taller than me, and he's trying to cut my head off. A torrent of white energy streams through my veins as I batter his blade away. Suddenly, *magically*, I truly know what it means to be *god-touched*. I parry his blows with ease, counter-slash to buy a moment, and manage to get the altar between us as another arrow flashes across the space and buries itself in the throat of the man whose knee I've cracked. He collapses, gurgling...

Who is the archer?

The fourth guardsman has a dagger in his off hand. He's ducked away from the window as I elude Aduwalli, and before I've truly registered his presence, his arm flicks straight and the dagger flies, right at my throat.

I twist, faster than I've ever moved in my life, and the dagger flashes past...

...and I grasp the hilt with my trailing left arm, a miracle catch, made without thought. I turn and hurl it back wrong-handed while the Trojan is still frozen in amazement, and the blade buries in the man's breast, through his bronze corselet. With a choking cry he staggers back, his legs give way and he goes down, just as two more guards storm into the shrine.

I throw my curved sword at them. It loops through the air and takes one of them through the chest, as I feint one way then leap for the window, praying the archer outside won't shoot me by mistake. I feel Aduwalli's blade part the air behind me as I burst through the opening and out into the street. A moment later another arrow whizzes past my head and into the shrine. Someone cries out in pain, hopefully Aduwalli.

I strike the ground, feeling utterly *amazing*. Even my recently wounded thigh is like a coil of energy as I regain my feet. *Athena has decided to awaken me after all. And just as well...*

Bria is perched on an opposite rooftop, nocking another arrow. *Who else?*

'Run,' she shouts. I glance around. Beyond the shrine are Skaya-Mandu and more than a dozen armed men, some of them mounted. He's wrestled his sister to her knees, and he's calling her a whore, slapping her viciously.

I lose all self-control at the sight. 'Trojan cur!' I shout, stupidly.

He whirls. 'There he is!' he shouts at his footmen. 'Kill the bastard! I want his head!'

He clambers onto his horse, heaves his half-conscious sister up with him and gallops off towards the lower gates of Krisa and the coastal track, his horsemen closing in around him. Is he too much of a coward to face me? Or is he making sure his sister is secured? I haven't time to decide, for there's half a dozen footmen charging towards me, and one of them has a drawn bow.

There's a time for hopeless valour, but this isn't it. I may be awakened, but I don't know my capabilities and I never will unless I get out of this. So I run as if all of the Furies are behind me, pelting along the narrow street, weaving as I go. An arrow fizzes past my shoulder and buries itself in an earthen wall. Voices shout in Trojan; the locals have vanished and I can't blame them. I swerve into the first side alley I come to, my pursuers strung out behind me, their nailed boots pounding on the cobblestones...

Ahead of me, Bria's small frame drops from a rooftop, landing badly. She's clutching her bow but staggering like a drunk, making no effort to shoot. Then she drops her bow, her arrows spilling, and collapses onto her knees. I shout in alarm.

Then a known and trusted voice rings out unexpectedly: '*Odysseus, down!*'

I drop and roll as a dark shape steps from a doorway. *Eurybates, of all people...*

I've never been so pleased to see my father's *keryx* in all my life.

He swings what looks like a timber post, which bashes straight into the face of the nearest Trojan. The man's head and shoulders fly backwards while his legs keep running, and he's airborne before crashing down on his back. The *keryx* hurls the timber post like a spear, knocking the next Trojan back. The rest have to slow, and I seize the chance to race over to Bria.

There's no obvious wound, but she's unconscious. I swing her onto my back, the copper bracelet on her upper arm so hot it almost burns my fingers. Eury joins us, one – no, two sword scabbards slung over his shoulder. I catch him up effortlessly, despite the burden I'm carrying – I feel *immense*.

Eury looks like he's been caught up in a tavern brawl – he's got a black eye, a mottled bruise on his cheek and a gashed lip. 'What's happened to you?'

'No time!' he shouts. 'Run!'

Good idea.

We hurtle on through the backstreets, through the seaward gates and the dust cloud that Skaya-Mandu and his horsemen have left in their wake, onto the curving road that heads downhill to the plain, making for the shelter of an olive grove. Burdened by their bronze armour, shields, heavy boots and helms, the pursuing Trojans fall behind. We make the trees as they come into sight, and I lower Bria's limp form onto the grass behind a large, gnarled trunk. There's six of them, led by an unharmed Aduwalli.

Eury pulls my very own straight-bladed *xiphos* from one of his scabbards and thrusts it into my hands before drawing his own sword.

Six men on two: not good.

But I've got adrenalin pumping through me like never before, and I feel invincible.

The Trojans come charging at us across the field, but for some reason Aduwalli calls a halt when he's within shouting range. 'I see you have received the blessing,' he calls. 'The owl woman, yes? Attayana?'

'Athena,' I correct him, stepping into the open. 'I presume from all your scars you're not very good with a sword.'

'Rather, you should assume that the men I've killed were *very* good,' Aduwalli replies. He waves his guards back with a curt, 'He's mine.' His two curved blades snake out, a sword and dagger pairing that weaves complicated patterns. 'Much better than you, boy.'

Then, with a savage cry, he comes at me, sword first, trying to lock blades so he can ram the dagger into my face or throat. Behind him his men close in, three of them going for Eury, while their archer keeps watch over the approach from the town.

Out of the corner of my eye, I see Eury back up against an olive trunk, two of its lower branches flanking him so that his assailants can only attack one at a time. I return all my attention to Aduwalli, battering his scimitar aside and lunging. My short *xiphos* feels much more familiar than the curved blade I fought with back in the shrine, and it's answering to my every demand. It's cruel to feel so mighty, but I'm also aware that this man has as many gifts as I, and he's been fighting a lot longer.

I'm doomed, barring a miracle.

Aduwalli makes a sight-defying turn and almost takes my head off with a roundhouse swing. I duck beneath the blade, straining every muscle, and riposte even as I dart away. Every blow has been almost too swift to see, but I've been absolutely sure of foot and sword-stroke fighting out of my skin. I'm still in this.

Then with a shout, a grey-robed figure appears on the far side of the field, followed by three or four armed men. Doripanes, surely... but who are the men with him? Are they from Pytho? Whose side will they take?

The Trojan archer who's been hovering behind Aduwalli begins shooting, and one of Doripanes's men falls. Then, in between hacking at Aduwalli, I glimpse the Trojan archer collapse, clutching his face and screaming. I haven't time to wonder why or how because Aduwalli has redoubled his efforts to kill me. He swings at me powerfully with his sickle sword and our blades meet with a sickening crash that jars my whole arm. This time he manages to slide his sword down to lock onto my hilt, all his weight behind it as he punches the dagger at my eyes.

I twist aside and catch his wrist; we fall together and I hammer my forehead at his nose, but only batter his cheekbone. He kicks me viciously, in my newly healed thigh. The pain is excruciating and my grip on him fails, but I roll clear, almost losing my head to a sickle-sword swipe before slashing slantwise to catch Aduwalli's left hand. The *theios* staggers back, blood spurting from his wrist as his dagger spins away. Ha! But in the corner of my sight I see Eury take a lightning blow to the shoulder and stagger. The sight appals me, but with Aduwalli recovering – *somehow* – from his wound, there's nothing I can do to protect my friend.

But then Doripanes's men burst into the grove, and the Trojan who is poised to kill Eury has to turn to face them. Now they're all battering at each other, the fight still very much in the balance.

'Princess Kyshanda wants me to come to Troy,' I yell at Aduwalli, hoping to confuse him.

'And Prince Skaya wants you dead,' he sneers, driving at me with another flurry of blows I barely repel. 'Women don't matter, even princesses.' We circle again, dangerously close to Bria, who's still down.

She groans and lifts her head. Her eyes are blank and her face as pale as a ghost. Curiously the copper bracelet has disappeared. Perhaps it fell off during the chase.

'Who's your patron?' I ask Aduwalli, as a distraction. *Move,* I urge Bria silently. *Run.*

'Ishtar, Goddess of Love and War. It's quite the life for those dedicated to her – sex *and* blood. I'm going to enjoy giving your avatar girl there a taste of both.'

'You'll have to come through me for that.'

'That's very much my intention, Achaean.'

Then he roars in, slams a sword blow at my midriff and, once I'm committed to the block, turns his stroke into a feint and swings at my left shoulder. I manage to parry, but I'm knocked sideways, away from Bria.

He puts his sword to her throat. 'Yield, or the avatar dies.'

Around me, the fight goes quiet. I pause, caught by indecision. Bria has said she's a daemon, and the girl's body is possessed by her... So Bria might survive having her throat cut, but Hebea the goatherd is a living, breathing person, and she will die. Her eyes have widened in horror, and I realize Bria's knowing, calculating gaze is absent – it's the girl Hebea, terrified and bewildered, looking up at Aduwalli. *Bria's abandoned her.*

I'm furious: Bria has placed Hebea in danger, recklessly and without care. I'm not prepared to let her pay the price. 'She's an innocent girl,' I protest.

'Innocent?' Aduwalli sneers. 'That little slut's no innocent. She's a daemon, as we both know.'

His hard, scarred face is implacable, without an ounce of self-doubt as to his imminent triumph. Perhaps being god-touched makes men like him so arrogant. A weakness to be wary of, if I live through this.

'The daemon's gone,' I shout. 'All you'll murder is a girl. Have you no honour, Trojan?'

Aduwalli hesitates... and quick as light the girl pulls a dagger from her belt and buries it in his left calf. The Trojan gives a howl of pain and dismay. As he staggers, I leap and swing: a roundhouse slash that goes right over his flailing, blind parry, carving an arc that intercepts his neck and keeps going...

His torso crumples, blood pumping from the neck stump as his head bounds and rolls in the dirt. Hebea screams, her small face contorted. Then she staggers to her feet and dashes out of the olive grove as I stare at the still-twitching corpse.

This man was a theios, a champion of a god. But he still died young. Is that the fate I've signed up for?

As soon as they see their renowned captain fall, the Trojans flee, and Doripanes' men, who were doing no more than holding their own, are happy to let them go. Doripanes arrives, limping and strangely exhausted, just as I am kneeling down next to Eury. My friend is clutching his shoulder; there's blood splattered all over his face and seeping between his reddened fingers. He's in considerable pain.

Doripanes crouches down beside us and eases Eury's hands away. The wound is deep and welling fresh blood, the sight making my gorge rise. The priest swiftly hacks a length of grey cloth from the hem of his robe, binds the wound tight and presses down on it hard with the heels of both hands. 'A simple flesh wound,' he says, 'though a nasty one. Your friend will live.'

I grip Eury's wrist, my own hands shaking with relief, and am rewarded with a wan smile.

One of Doripanes's men goes over to the fallen Trojan archer, who is thrashing about on the ground nearby, and slits his throat with an ugly grunt of satisfaction. I catch a glimpse of the archer's face. His eyes look as though they have been boiled in their sockets. The rest of Doripanes's men are staring too – but at me.

Because, suddenly, all I can see is red. The stench of blood and voided bowels overwhelms my nostrils and I stagger from Eury's side, doubled over and vomiting. One of the soldiers comes over to pat my shoulder, but I push him away. Being comforted when I'm showing such weakness only makes it worse.

'First fight you've been in?' says the man. 'You'll get used to it.'

Part of me is reassured, the rest horrified, that I might become inured to violent death.

There's a noise in the distance, a cacophony of war horns wailing. It may well have been going on for some time but

I'm only becoming aware of it now. It seems Krisa has finally responded to the violence that has desecrated their sacred altar and littered the shrine and the nearby alley with bodies.

Moments later, a band of mounted men, helmet plumes waving and corselets gleaming, canter through the gates and head towards the coast, in pursuit of Skaya-Mandu's party. At the least, they should make short work of the fleeing Trojan foot soldiers, but the prince and his mounted men are already well ahead.

Doripanes asks one of his men to tend to Eury, then takes the dead Trojan archer's bow and arrow and thrusts them at me. 'You'll need these. If you hurry, you'll get to the coast before the Trojans take ship.'

'Isn't this enough?' I ask, wiping vomit from my lips. How can he be so bloodthirsty, and still serve a Goddess of Reason? *And War*, I remind myself.

'They're the *enemy*, Ithacan. They tried to kill you. And Eury's just told me that minx Kyshanda set a trap for you. Don't you want to make her pay too?'

It wasn't like that, I'm certain of it: otherwise why would Skaya have struck her?

But yes, I'd like a word with him about that blow...

My martial ardour returns. 'But Skaya and his men are on horseback.'

'Then you'd better hurry, especially now that the Trojans have heard the Krisan war horns. They'll be galloping hard now.'

'Won't they wait for Aduwalli?'

'Not for long. I fancy Skaya-Mandu cares more about his own safety than all else.'

'But I don't have a horse.'

Doripanes raises his eyes to the heavens. 'Use your legs.'

'You mean... *run*?'

'Yes. Run. One leg after the other, faster than a walk. A damn sight faster if you're going to get there in time.'

'You're mad.'

The priest smiles grimly. 'I'm as sane as I ever have been. Now listen carefully. The road to the coast makes a long dogleg, off to the west and then back again, as you already know from your journey in to Pytho. But you can take a direct route through the olive groves. There's more than a few drainage ditches, but they shouldn't slow you down, not now you've been awakened. Athena has given you more speed, strength and stamina than you've ever dreamt of.'

How does he know I've been awakened? By seeing me survive a fight with another theios, I suppose…

I probe my wounded thigh. It still feels good, despite Aduwalli's kick. Well enough to chance this crazy idea…

And, damn it, I want to see Skaya-Mandu pay!

Eurybates gives me an encouraging nod. And I remember the way Skaya-Mandu struck *my* Kyshanda.

I swing the quiver and the bow onto my back and shoulder my *xiphos* in its scabbard. Despite the exertion of the fight, I'm still burning – with energy and anger in equal measure.

I turn, and I *run*.

–

The land blurs beneath my feet as I bound and leap, ripping through tangled undergrowth, dodging between olive trees with their low branches and crazed trunks, and over countless ditches, vaulting over the slime and mud. The sun beats down but I barely feel it; undergrowth rakes my limbs, leaving welts and cuts, and a dozen or more times I almost lose my footing, risking broken bones or worse.

Instead I arrive, not long after, at the start of the very road my family and I had trod a few days ago on our way up to Pytho, when I was simply the son of a minor island king, seeking audience with the Pythia. Drenched in sweat, aching in every limb but unwavering, I run through the dirt streets of little Kirrha. Villagers stop to watch me, red-faced and panting like a bellows, and half-naked children recoil in alarm. I burst onto the beach, where leathery-faced fishermen look up from their nets of glittering fish which flop about as they asphyxiate, mouths and gills gaping. Women with baskets stare, and the gulls shriek and rise into the air.

But my eyes are on a Corinthian galley a little way offshore. Rowboats are clustered about it, loading stores as the last Trojans are clambering aboard, with only two mounted soldiers still on the beach. Those two turn as I appear.

I nock an arrow and fire in one motion, planting a shaft in the nearest rider's chest. At that, every one of the fisher-folk shrieks and scatters, and a hullaballoo erupts amongst the Trojans out on the ship. The second man, a mounted archer, tries to fire an arrow in reply, but I shoot him even as he takes aim. I heave him off his horse, a mare, and vault onto her back.

She fights me and I almost fall off. Ithaca is too mountainous and rocky for horses, but I learnt to ride when I was packed off to Mycenae during my adolescence – not so long ago. After a shaky few heartbeats, I've got her measure. I dig in my heels, urging her into the waves to get within firing range of the ship.

I see Skaya-Mandu in the stern. His sister joins him, her headscarf fallen around her shoulders and her black hair gleaming in the sunlight. She's breathtakingly lovely, but I'm consumed with fury at her brother as I urge the mount into the sea.

'*CUT THE ANCHOR ROPE*,' Skaya bawls at the ship's crew. '*ROW, YOU DOGS!*' He turns his head to mutter something accusing to his sister – because she's looking at me, not with hatred but with wide-eyed wonder. The sailors start hauling on their oars to drive the ship out into deeper water.

But now I'm in range: the mare is jittering about, jostled by the waves and trying to find her footing on the loose shingle of the seabed. With both my hands taken up with the bow, I have only my knees to keep the animal steady, to give me a steady platform for shooting. Somehow I calm her, draw the bowstring and take aim at Skaya…

And he grips his sister's shoulders and forces her in front of him.

For what feels like an eternity, we all stare at each other. I can see that Kyshanda is stiff with shame, rage and terror as she looks along the shaft I'm aiming straight at her.

'You piece of dung,' I hear her cry, and I know she doesn't mean me.

Swearing in disgust, I lower the bow. 'Coward!' I scream. 'Craven scum! Come back and settle this!'

Then a rogue wave slews into us, the horse staggers and it's all I can do to stay on her back. Skaya crows with laughter, clamping Kyshanda to him as the Trojan ship glides beyond range.

There's no point in giving vent to my fury, but I do anyway, before nudging the mare's nose shoreward and letting her pick a way back to dry land. 'You newt's pizzle, you gutter dog's vomit,' I roar, shaking my fist, but the Trojan just laughs more.

I now have to face the long inland journey back to Krisa. All my adrenalin is spent, I'm worn to the bone, my tunic is clotted and stiff with Aduwalli's blood, every bruise is beginning to throb and every welt and scratch stings from the saltwater.

I keep the horse. Yes, I know it isn't mine – the Kirrha man the Trojans rented it from comes running after me demanding payment, but I have no *obols* on me. I'll give her back later and pay him well, but frankly, I'm not going to make it back to Krisa without her.

6 – The Goatherd Girl

'Being the child of Invention and Need, Love is…
always poor, and far from gentle or fair as most
assume him to be him: instead he is bitter and
thirsty, barefoot and homeless…'
—Plato, *Symposium*

Krisa, Phocis

The evening shadows are lengthening as the mud-brick walls
of Krisa come into sight. I'm desperate to get to safety: my
right leg, which had borne up well in the long chase to the sea,
is now throbbing painfully, and every jolt makes me grit my
teeth. The wound isn't fully healed, despite Athena's touch. In
some bizarre and illogical way, it's reassuring that her powers
have limitations.

I trot the mare through the town gates as a grey-robed
man steps from the shadows – Doripanes. He has Eurybates
with him; the *keryx*'s left shoulder is heavily bandaged, and his
bruised face drawn. There's no sign of Hebea.

'Well?' the priest asks, as he leads me away from the gateway
and the listening guards.

I slip from the horse's back, grabbing the horse for support
as my wounded thigh struggles to take my weight again. 'They
got away,' I admit. 'I had Skaya-Mandu lined up, but he pushed
Kyshanda in front of him.'

'Then you should have shot her as well,' Doripanes says
irritably.

I've been anticipating this all the way back from the coast. If
I argue that Kyshanda didn't try to trap me, I'll have to confess

77

that she wants to convert me to the Trojan cause. Even if I try and couch it purely in political terms, Doripanes will probably guess I've fallen in love with her, and he'll never trust me again. So I can't.

Every act seems to lead me to a fresh lie these days.

'I have more honour than that,' I tell him, making him grunt a little derisively, but he accepts the explanation. We princes are infamous for our honour.

I ignore the priest's disapproval, turning to Eurybates. 'Dear friend,' I say, clasping his good hand. 'I'm glad you're on your feet – I feared for you.'

'Thank Doripanes,' Eury replies. 'He tended me well.'

My head is bursting with a myriad of questions, but they can wait till we have some privacy to talk.

It turns out Eury has been in Krisa for several days. He has a rather meagre room in a local tavern, and that's where we repair to. I bathe, shave and change into a clean tunic borrowed from the tavern owner, while my blood-caked clothes soak forlornly in a leather bucket. We continue our discussion over a platter of food, washed down with a half-decent wine, all purchased by Doripanes. Laertes left me no money at all.

Doripanes returns to my failure to shoot either Kyshanda or Skaya.

'I only had one arrow left,' I explain. Which is true. 'And I don't murder women.'

'She's a Trojan *theia*. Slaying either of them would have been an immense blow to Troy.'

'And probably would have launched the very war we're trying to prevent – remember? The one that Troy inevitably wins,' I reply.

To my surprise, Doripanes concedes the point with a frown.

'Eury,' I say, not only to change the subject, but because I'm burning to know: 'What are you doing here? I'd imagined you'd be back on Ithaca by now.'

The *keryx* gives me a rueful look. 'When we came to take ship, I tried to argue your case. Laertes wasn't best pleased, and he threw me out.' That explains Eury's blackened eye, bruised cheek and gashed lip – Laertes can be as quick with his fists as his judgements.

'I'm sorry. I can't thank you enough for standing up for me.' *Not for the first time – Eury's been doing it since I was a small child...* 'And then?'

'I was anxious for you, but I didn't think it wise to return to Pytho, when you're not so very popular there. Since there's only one road in and out – through Krisa – I decided to stay here and watch for you.' He gives me a quick grin. 'Just as well Laertes sacked me, don't you think?'

'My father can be a right bastard,' I say. Then I redden, as all the ironies of that statement hit me: Laertes isn't my father and *I'm* the bastard.

My name is not Odysseus Laertiades. My name is Odysseus Sisyphiades, and all the gods want me dead.

Except one: Athena.

I bow my head. 'I'm in Athena's hands,' I tell Doripanes.

'A timely thought, Ithacan. Though there is still much you need to learn about your craft.'

I wait for him to elaborate but he doesn't seem inclined to do so. 'And you?' I ask the priest.

'I'll return to the Pythia and tell her I pursued you but failed to kill you, and that you disappeared again after pursuing the Trojans. With luck, she'll believe me.'

I wonder at him, living every day with people who would cut his throat if his true allegiances were discovered. 'Who were the armed men with you?' I ask. 'They fought on our side. So they can't have been from Pytho, surely?'

'No.' Doripanes laughs. 'I have agents of my own here in Krisa. I gathered them up on my way through the town. They're back in their homes now, licking their wounds.'

'So the man who was shot survived?'

'Fortunately. A leg wound, no more.'

'But how did you know to come looking for me?'

'You mean, how did I know you disobeyed my orders – for which I'm awaiting an explanation?' Doripanes glares at me, but when I don't reply, he returns to my question. 'I spied you leaving the track up to the cave. Remember,' he adds, when I look surprised, 'keeping an eye on things is part of my job. But I couldn't follow you immediately, and risk drawing attention to you. And I had other concerns: I left for Krisa as soon as I was able.'

'What was Bria doing here in Krisa?'

'We realized that, if you stirred up too much trouble during the Trojan audience, you might not be able to head up the cliff track unnoticed. I'd stationed Bria up there to protect you; when you failed to show up she came back down – she's good at finding people, and happened upon Eurybates, just in time.'

Which is how Eury came to have my xiphos on him…

'But *why* did you disobey me?' Doripanes asks. 'Why did you come to Krisa? And *how* did you end up with that Trojan princess in the travellers' shrine?'

I need to keep this simple. 'I thought I saw someone higher up on the zigzag track, near the crest of the cliffs.' I pause, to give the lie weight. 'I figured then that I might be walking into danger, so I doubled back and went to Krisa as the logical place to lay low while I got a message to you. As for the shrine,' I continue, emboldened by their lack of contradictions or snorts of disbelief, 'I went in there to *pray*. It's what people do when life kicks them in the guts, and I had a lot to pray about. How was I to know Kyshanda *and* her blasted brother would turn up?'

I've made my voice sound aggrieved, and I'm well pleased when Doripanes not only seems to accept my story but looks a little shamefaced with it. 'That seems reasonable,' he admits.

I decide I've got a little leverage now, especially as I'm "awakened". 'So tell me then,' I say forcefully, 'how do I stand with you and Bria now? Because if I'm one of you now, I want to be treated as an equal, not some nonentity.'

'Nonentity? Never that.' The priest contemplates his hands for a moment, before looking at me again. 'It was more a matter of trust. And it seems, from your awakening, Athena has decided in your favour.'

'But why wouldn't she trust me?' Then it dawns on me. 'Because of Prometheus?'

'Aye,' he says, uncomfortably.

'What's so bad about Prometheus anyway? I've never understood why Zeus was angered by him? Surely the Skyfather didn't want humankind to remain ignorant of fire?'

'That is the tale we priests tell,' he concedes wryly. 'But the truth is more interesting – and dangerous. Prometheus was once a great god, rivalling Zeus himself.'

I'm staggered – I had no idea. Eury too is clearly amazed, leaning forward on his stool, his eyes shining as he glances from me to the priest and back. 'And the gift of fire?' he asks.

'The "fire" was knowledge,' Doripanes replied, 'secrets Zeus never wanted revealed. For those secrets Prometheus was cast down, nailed to a rock and condemned to constant torment for all eternity. Now we're told to forget him.'

My smugness of a moment before has vanished. My head is reeling, my nightmare beating in on me. I can see the crag and smell the blood as the eagle rips open Prometheus's gut and devours his liver. I can feel his agony.

In my dream, my hideous dream, *I am Prometheus…*

Somehow I pull myself together. 'What secrets?'

'Those secrets… are still secret,' Doripanes drawls.

I ponder what I know of Prometheus. 'But he left children. Sisyphus—'

'Sisyphus was Prometheus's great-great-grandson, and through him, a *theios*.'

'So you lied, two days ago. You and Bria knew I must be a *theios* too.'

'Not necessarily,' Doripanes replies. 'Divine bloodlines only last so many generations, and most of Sisyphus's children were born ordinary mortals. Nor do we yet know what your full potential might be. But from your behaviour today, we have good raw material.'

That's something, at least. Now for my two most burning questions. 'What happened to Bria during the fight?'

Doripanes sighs. 'She just burned out. Hebea's a young girl, and Bria tried to do too much. She overreached, trying to aid you, and was cast from Hebea's body.'

'When will she come back?'

'I know not.' Doripanes' face is emotionless, but I can hear the tension in his voice.

'And Hebea?' In some ways, I care more about her than the daemon.

'I found her and sent her back to her father.'

'That's not good enough,' I tell him. 'Bria says Hebea is at risk of abuse from her father. How can you just send her back?'

Doripanes shakes his head dismissively. Clearly, in his logical, reasoned world, the plight of such lowly ones is inconsequential. 'There are reasons.'

I set my jaw. 'I'll look after her if you won't.'

Eurybates gives me a look of quick approval – as usual, we're of one mind. 'Why don't we buy her?' he suggests. 'I should have enough *obols* for it.' I can only imagine where he got the long bronze skewers we use to purchase everyday items from. Laertes's travelling budget, perhaps?

Doripanes is not best pleased. 'Hebea is Bria's only host in this location,' he protests.

'She's at risk,' I tell him firmly. 'We're going to rescue her.'

'If you must,' he says reluctantly. 'She and her father live up in the hills to the west. I can describe the path to you. The father's name is Apis and he's a surly, unpleasant pig. I daresay you're right; she's better away from him. But see you do it properly or it'll reach the Pythia's ears.' He gives me a stern look, then relents and offers me his hand. 'Well done, Odysseus. You've survived your first test as a *theios*. Not everyone does.'

–

The next morning, Eurybates and I follow Doripanes's directions and emerge from a tangle of trees into a clearing. 'Apis?' I shout.

My call echoes about the small gully. I'm beneath a low cliff with a trickling waterfall that feeds a small stream, and there's a lean-to where the goatherd lives, shadowed by an overgrown wild fig. The tiny hut has a shoddy, ill-kept look; I can see a dozen improvements any diligent man would make.

'Apis!'

'Who're ye?' a rough voice calls from above. A man appears at the rim of the waterfall, idly spinning a loaded leather sling in his hand, the sort that can propel a small stone fast enough to burst a skull open. He's clad in an ill-fitting goatskin, as slovenly made as the hut, and peering uneasily from myself to Eury.

I show my empty hands, not wanting to intimidate him. Eury has charge of our *obols*, hidden in a bundle at his back. 'My name is Megon of Cephalonia. Are you Apis, father of the goatherd girl?'

The man's eyes narrow, the sling spinning faster. 'Wha' d'ye wan' with me daughter?'

'Nothing untoward. Some men attacked me. Her warning saved my life and I wish to thank her.'

'Saved yer life?' Apis rasps. 'How d'ye want to thank 'er?'

'With an *obol*,' I call. Eury slips the bundle from his back to emphasize the point.

The man becomes interested. 'Leave it below, an' I'll give it to 'er.'

'I wish to thank her in person.' This part is crucial to our plan – we've decided we won't talk about buying her until she appears, and we can grab her if needs be. Though I don't like the look of that sling. The best way is to play this *very* straight.

Apis pauses, head on one side. Then he puts his fingers to his mouth and emits a piercing whistle. 'Girl's simple,' he calls down. 'Dumber than a she-goat, like 'er mother was.'

I don't grace that with a reply. Most people work hard and keep their families well fed and clothed, but this Apis isn't of that sort. There are men who live like him on Ithaca too, putting their families through squalid, marginal existences. Some have excuses, genuine reasons why they can't provide, but others simply can't be bothered. I can guess which type Apis is.

And Bria claims he's a flagellant who fantasizes about raping his daughter…

Snapping twigs herald the arrival of the girl, pushing through the brush from some hiding place, wide-eyed and ragged, her spiky hair fouled with straw and leaves. The copper bracelet is absent from her arm.

When she sees me she freezes, recognition dawning. I can only guess at her emotions – hopefully she remembers me as her protector, back in the olive grove. How much she knows about the period Bria was inside her, I have no idea.

'What's her name?' I ask, pretending I don't know.

'Hebea. Called that by her mother, silly bitch.'

'Hebea,' I repeat.

The girl cocks her head, birdlike, making a mewing sound like a gull.

'Tol' you, she's an idiot,' Apis calls. 'I'm th'only one she understands.'

I struggle to hide my distaste for the man. 'Tell her I'm here to thank her.'

Apis gives me a sly look, and talks to her in a slow, sing-song voice. The girl looks back at me, her fear clear in her face, though which of us she's more frightened of, her father or me, I can't yet tell.

'Maybe ye jus' leave yer *obol* an' go, eh?' says Apis.

Eury extracts an *obol* from his bundle and places the long bronze skewer on a rock.

Apis grunts. 'She saved yer life, Megon. That all it's worth?'

'Another *obol*, and I take her away with me,' I reply.

Apis snorts. 'She's worth more'n that, Ithacan. Watches the herd. Cooks, when she 'members how. What ye wan' 'er for anyway?' Then he snickers. 'Nah, don' tell me, I already know.'

I shake my head. 'She saved my life. I can give her a better one than this.'

Apis spits. 'Four *obols*.'

'Two.' I have to be seen to bargain, otherwise Apis will be suspicious. The danger is, I might anger him instead.

'Three,' he says, finally. 'Or you can piss off.'

'Done,' I say, hugely relieved. On cue, Eury pulls out two more *obols* and places them beside the first.

Apis directs a stream of words at the girl in the same sing-song voice and, whimpering, she crabs across the open ground towards me. Apis scurries down and claims the *obols*, leering at us. But I concentrate on the girl. 'Bria?' I ask, but she shakes her head. 'It's all right,' I tell her. 'I'm taking you somewhere safe.'

Slowly she extends her hand to mine, giving Eurybates a doubtful look but letting me grip her fingers and lead her from the clearing.

'I doubt she's a virgin,' Apis calls after me. 'Been among the goats too long!' His jeers follow us as we walk away, the girl cringing at the sound of her father's voice. That in itself tells me I'm doing the right thing. As the distance from the hut increases, she stands straighter but she drops my hand too.

We are halfway back to Krisa when suddenly the girl tinkles with mocking laughter. Bria's sly, knowing presence completely transforms Hebea's anxious face. 'My, my! Odysseus of Ithaca! I didn't know you cared!'

'Bria!' I exclaim, trying to hide my relief. 'You're back!' I glance at her arm, just as she pushes a copper bracelet up under her sleeve and out of sight. I pretend I haven't noticed.

Bria makes a show of looking herself up and down. 'This one… the idiot girl! What joy! I prefer more mature bodies, you know. But she'll do for now. And here you are, *owning* me! That's exciting!'

'I bought her to protect her. You need a body – use this one if you must. But I'm telling you now: as soon as I can, I'm going to take her somewhere safe, so she can have a decent life. Perhaps among my mother's servants.'

If I ever see my mother again…

'Oh, that's so sweet!' Bria says, sarcastically.

'So I should have just left her to be abused and die?'

The daemon surprises me with a sombre look. 'What sort of life do you think *I* have, Odysseus? Do you think it's any better than hers?'

'Where have you been?' asks Eury, just as I'm about to ask the same question.

She rolls her eyes in her characteristic way. 'I overdid things,' she admits ruefully, confirming what Doripanes said. 'Things went blank. It's only when I heard you speaking my name just now that I found my way back.'

I have a *thousand* questions about that... but there are more urgent matters to deal with. 'I need to know as much as you can tell me about Athena, what I've agreed to do and what this means for Eury too.'

'Really,' she snorts. 'Get you, Ithaca.' She chuckles, then gives me a considering look. 'But as it happens, I've been sent back to her specifically to train you. Here's the thing, though: *I'm in charge*. If you're a prince, I'm your queen! I've been doing this for a long time – you're still wet behind the ears. And there's a damned lot you need to know if you're to be of any use to us.'

'Is that right?'

'It bloody well is: you'll follow my instructions to the full, without question.'

'It's not in my nature to do anything "without question". And I doubt your Goddess of Reason would think much of a mindless tool.'

'You'd be surprised. Stick around long enough and you'll see what I mean.'

I raise a finger. 'I'll agree on one condition: you will not do *anything* with that's girl's body that she wouldn't have consented to do herself.'

'*What?*' Bria's eyes go round. 'You have no idea what you're asking! I'm a disembodied spirit, Ithaca! It can take me months to find a body I'm compatible with, and when I do... *I have needs.*'

'I don't care. You're her body's caretaker. You'll look after it.'

Bria pouts. 'This is so unfair!'

'Enough. You have morals? You have honour? Then accept it.'

She throws me a very dirty look. 'I had no idea you'd be so difficult.' She looks at Eurybates, who is struggling unsuccessfully to suppress his amusement. 'You don't need to take his side,' she tells him. 'He doesn't own you.' When Eury laughs out loud, she stamps her foot. 'I've been alive for centuries!'

'Then act your age,' I retort, and Eury and I walk off, ignoring the steady stream of abuse Bria launches at our backs all the way to Krisa.

Part Two: The Judgement of Parassi

88

Part Two: The Judgement of Parassi

7 – The Hero and the Avatar

'...in keeping with his mother's character, [Love]
always lives in want. But he follows after his father
in striving after everything that is beautiful and
good; for he is courageous, eager and ardent;
a clever hunter, always plying some stratagem;
longing for wisdom and full of resolve to master
the truth until his dying day; a savant, skilled at
sorcery and magic potions.'
—Plato, *Symposium*

Near Kirrha, Phocis

'Keep your damned shield up, you flaccid little *phallos!*' Bria
screeches, like a flock of harpies. 'What do you think that spear
is, a cucumber? Stab with it, don't prod! *Stab!*'

I snarl wordlessly, heave the shield higher, despite my
shoulder muscles begging for mercy, and ram my spear at the
wooden target, sweating like a pig. Despite the rag wound
round the base of my boar's tusk helmet, perspiration is blinding
my eyes, and the bronze-plated corselet weighs as heavy as a
cattle yoke.

'Work, you slack-arse!' Bria yowls, cracking a whip. There
are welts on her own back as well as mine – she tends to get
carried away, and despite her centuries of experience, she's
pretty wayward with a lash. It's Hebea's body, of course, and
the girl's voice is hoarse from shrieking abuse.

Gods, save me: I've fallen in with one of the Erinyes, *those vengeful
black Furies who haunt children's nightmares.*

Lunge, thrust, retreat... over and over...

Then, finally: 'Now, up to the oak and back! Go!'

Instantly, I drop both sword and shield and take off, pumping my thighs hard and gasping for breath. By the time I'm at the top of the slope my legs are burning, but I force myself to leap from mound to mound on the way down, landing in an exhausted heap in the clearing below.

Bria throws me a water skin. 'Ten minutes, *princess*,' she chirrups, reclining on a fallen wooden column, the whip dandled in her lazy grip. I lie panting at her feet, feeling utter hatred.

We're in a hollow clearing, low on a hillside some fourteen miles inland of Kirrha, tucked under the westernmost arms of Mount Parnassus and well away from Pytho. Here, deep in the woodlands, is a shrine to some forgotten god or spirit. The altar's once-bright paint has faded and flaked, the horns of consecration that had once topped the now fallen pillar lie forlornly in the grass, and the shrine's attendant huts are long deserted by their original inhabitants. Bria has made a base out of this place for some time now, and planted a semi-wild garden filled with all manner of edibles, so we eat well.

Finally, after another hour of torture, I collapse onto a handy boulder, gasping in the late morning heat as I pull off the helmet and unstrap the corselet. The armour is a gift from Bria, from a hidden cache she's kept buried here, and fits passably well. I'd jestingly asked if it was forged by Hephaestus, the Smith God, but she just laughed.

'You've got a good physique for a short-arse,' she tells me. 'But a good big man will beat a good small one.'

I'm getting pretty tired of that jibe. 'I beat bigger men at Krisa.'

She sniffs. 'Aduwalli would have taken you apart if I'd not been there.' Presumably she's taking credit for Hebea's actions as well as her own. She pops a grape into her mouth.

Hebea is much changed: Bria is growing her hair longer, taming it with oil and ribbons, and the homespun man's tunic has been exchanged for an ankle-length linen dress with an embroidered neckline and fringed hem. Our diet is rather better than Hebea's had been, so her skinny body is filling out. Bria's even pulled jewellery out of the cache we'd dug up when we arrived, cooing over it in happy recognition. She moves like a woman, sometimes even like royalty... but she can still swear like a muleteer, giggle like a girl and deliver the insights of the ageless.

I look my own body over. My shoulders and chest are broad and well-muscled, but now there isn't a pinch of fat on me. My skin is sun-dark, and my long red hair bleaching to scarlet and gold. I've never been in better shape, but not all is perfect: my right thigh is still horribly scarred, and at times it can still cause pain. Something still isn't right in there.

But beyond that, I feel *great*. Already I can do things with a spear and sword I'd never dreamt of. I know, without question, I am now a far, far better warrior than any of Laertes's champions.

It's now almost five months since the fight outside Krisa, and Bria and I have been in the camp here through summer and much of autumn. Eurybates has mostly been here too, training by my side. But he has also made several journeys to Ithaca, to find out how my mother and sister fare and get news. I've spent many sleepless nights worrying about them, and I was vastly relieved that he found them both well, and desperate for news of me.

There's been no public announcement about my true ancestry, and Laertes is telling people I'm travelling with a sea trader. It's an easy fiction, and hopefully will deflect anyone seeking out the 'Man of Fire' for unsavoury purposes.

The news from Ithaca is somewhat comforting: Mother's relationship with Laertes is still precarious, but Laertes has discovered that the smooth running of his kingdom is very dependent on both his *keryx* and his wife. So when Anticleia told Laertes she was re-hiring Eury as her own servant, he put up little resistance. Whenever Eury returns to Ithaca to help Anticleia, he keeps out of Laertes's way, but does much of his old work. He's there now, but we're expecting his return any day.

It's autumn now, the air is bracing and the nights are turning chilly. Winter will bring rain and bleak grey days, storms in the Aegean, the beaching of ships and the temporary halt of most trade and travel. The wildlife we see and hunt – goats, hares, and the occasional wolves, boars and bears – have started growing shaggy coats in preparation for the coldest season.

In the tales, winter occurs because Persephone, the daughter of Demeter, was kidnapped and forced to marry Hades, Lord of the Underworld. Demeter in her rage and grief turned the world cold and grey, but Zeus intervened and enforced a compromise, whereby Persephone spends part of the year in Erebus and the rest in the world above, creating winter and summer. I'd always regarded the tale as a fable, but now, as an awakened *theios*, I wonder. If gods are real, what can or can't they do? This is no mere idle speculation: I'm wondering, if Zeus really can hurl thunderbolts, whether I need to be watching the skies.

Bria, of course, tells me nothing.

'So,' I ask, once my chest has stopped heaving. 'What's next?'

'Archery,' Bria replies. 'From now until sunset.'

So be it. I examine the calluses on my hand. For the first few weeks they'd blistered and bled, but now they're hardening like old leather. And my shooting is improving all the time, both in speed and accuracy. 'Let's get going.'

A strong composite bow can drive an arrow through a thick oxhide shield with enough force to pierce the bronze corselet beyond. After months of practice, I can fire an arrow every three heartbeats, for hours at a time and with a precision I would have thought impossible five months ago.

This afternoon is almost windless, and I slam arrow after arrow into the row of targets set up across the clearing until even Bria declares herself impressed. 'You've an eye for it, Ithaca,' she praises, swaying up and offering me a small wineskin. 'We're done for the day.'

'Where in Tartarus did you get this?' She's told me we have no wine.

'Never you mind.'

Too thirsty to puzzle it out, I take a solid swallow and return the skin, giving her a reproving look as she downs a mouthful herself. She snorts. 'You think the girl didn't drink? Her father made beer and she used to steal it.'

'She's still a child. You promised to look after her.' I try to snatch the wineskin but she darts away, then gives me a flirtatious wink.

'Hey, Ithaca, if I let you have some more, will you share my blanket tonight?'

'No!' I reply. We have some variant of this conversation every night, and the answer's not going to change. It's all part of the routine by now – she's tried it on both Eurybates and me, but we're presenting a united front.

'It's not fair,' Bria pouts. 'You parading around in your near-naked glory, and expecting me not to get ideas. Hebea is of age, you know – and she likes you, more fool her.'

'Why don't I believe you?'

Bria decides she's found a chink in my resolve. 'But it's true – and it makes a difference, doesn't it, Ithaca? She's willing, you know – more than willing.'

'No! Drop it. And take your wine somewhere else.'

She rolls her eyes, then shrugs, and we get on with our chores more amiably. If she could just get over all her posturing and flirting I'd like Bria a lot more.

But once she's asleep, her spirit will often come adrift of the girl Hebea's body – she's incapable of controlling the girl for too long at a stretch – so many mornings it's Hebea, not Bria, that Eury and I have for company. I like Hebea – she's far from the idiot Apis portrayed her as: he'd just been too lazy to teach her anything, including proper speech. And Bria's comment just now about awakening Hebea explains a few things that have been puzzling Eury and me recently. We've both caught Bria in the midst of two-way conversations, a dialogue where seemingly she's been more aware of our daily goings-on than I expected.

But this evening, Bria is firmly in charge. We're taking the air outside the hut where we do our cooking when Eurybates's return is heralded by a shrill whistle. I hurry to greet him, we embrace warmly and I shoulder some of his load back to our campsite. One of the bundles I take from him makes my breath catch in my throat, but I wait until we're back at the huts before I comment on it.

It's a long leather bow case, the outside surface tooled with pictures of mythical tales of both hunting and war. I love and loathe what's inside, a composite bow of immense strength, its incurving arms made of laminated goat's horn and wood.

It's both a great treasure and my personal nemesis. I was given it by an old man after I'd won a court case two years ago, on my return home from four years in Lacedaemon, where I'd been learning courtly manners. It was my first time leading a case – an important one involving the return of hundreds of stolen sheep. Winning it avoided war with Messenia, and the old man who owned the bow – Hagias – gave it to me afterwards out of admiration for my eloquence.

Since the gift was made, I've tried many times to string the bow but failed at every attempt, a fact Laertes didn't hesitate to mention whenever he could. The only consolation is that he failed to string it too. Since then it has lain in the palace storeroom, amongst other precious things, gathering dust. After I was cast out of the family at Pytho, I'd expected never to see the bow again.

But here it is – I open the bow case and take it out. 'Did my mother give this to you?' I ask Eury.

'Yes – remember how Hagias said you'd be able to string it when you matured? Your mother has decided that if you're not "matured" by now, you never will be.'

I don't bother asking if Laertes was asked for his agreement. Instead I raise the bow and examine it.

Bria's impressed, putting aside her wineskin and coming over. 'You know that's one of the Great Bows?' she remarks, as she strokes the smooth goat's horn. 'What's a nobody like you doing with it?'

I'm too amazed to protest her withering dismissal. As far as I know, there are only two weapons worthy of the name 'Great

Bow'. One, the most famous, belonged to Heracles. Everyone knows the fabled hero gifted it to his friend Poeas when he died, and Poeas passed it on to his son. As for the other... Eury and I look from her to the bow and back. 'You think this is Eurytus's bow?' I say, in a hushed voice.

In the legends, Eurytus taught Heracles archery, only to be murdered by his pupil.

'I don't *think*,' Bria says irritably. 'I *know*.'

'But this was just a gift, from old Hagias.'

'Except there's no such person.'

'I *met* him.'

She snickers at my confusion. 'Don't get your toenails in a tangle, Ithaca. I know the name "Hagias": it's a false name used by Iphitus, when he was being hunted by the sons of Heracles. You must have heard of Iphitus, even in your backwater island.'

'Iphitus, son of Eurytus? But Heracles killed Eurytus and all his family.'

Bria shakes her head. 'It suited Iphitus to have everyone think so. He feigned death, stole back his father's bow under cover of darkness and fled to Corinth – to Sisyphus, his father's old friend. I rather imagine Sisyphus made Iphitus swear to look out for you – and behold, here's his Great Bow.'

Now my head is swimming. *I've been given one of the two Great Bows... a weapon that rivals Heracles's own...*

'Well, are you going to string the damn thing?' asks Bria.

I groan inwardly. It was bad enough not being able to string it in front of Laertes, but to give Bria more excuses to tease me doesn't bear thinking about.

But I'm a *theios* now. Just maybe, I'm ready.

Stringing a bow looks easy, but it's far from it. It's not just a test of strength, but coordination as well, and it requires your whole body, especially a really powerful bow like this one. I hook one of the bow string's loops over the tip of the lower arm and brace myself, one leg over, one leg behind, in the complex stance required. I breathe slowly to get my focus under control. Bria is fidgeting beside me, but I can't let her impatience rush me.

Now! I bring all my weight onto the top arm, bending it down, down... My hands are sweating, my muscles shaking with the strain. Just when I feel I am certain to fail, I find reserves. With one last effort, I ease the top loop over the tip of the upper arm and pluck the string, before flinging my arms wide in triumph. The bow string sings – a deep, powerful note unlike anything I've ever heard before.

Eury is thumping me on the back, while Bria pushes the wineskin into my hands – she does at least appreciate the difficulty of what I've just done.

'Wine?' Eurybates exclaims, as she bustles back. 'We have *wine?*'

'Pure water is far better for you than alcoholic poisons,' says Bria, wagging a hypocritical finger at us. We ignore her, taking turns to swig from the skin.

So we are more than a little tipsy when Bria says, 'Boys, we have visitors!'

She doesn't seem unduly worried, even though we have had no other people come here since we arrived in early summer. 'What kind of visitors?' I ask, as I notch an arrow. *Will I be able to draw the bow? Stringing it is only the first step...* To my relief, the bow yields to my arms as I draw the bow string back.

'They're friends,' Bria says, scooping more raw vegetables into the stew and blowing on the embers under the cooking tripod. 'You won't need your new toy. Go and greet them, Ithaca. Where are your manners?'

I lay the bow down on the nearest bench, feeling vastly deflated.

'*And* you've drunk all the wine,' she adds, quite unjustly. 'Eurybates, go behind the next hut, to the old sundial. There's a hole beneath full of wine amphorae and goblets. Bring one amphora and five goblets.'

Eury and I share a look. 'You've been hiding these from us for months!' I protest.

Bria pulls a face. 'It's a fine vintage – too good to waste on you lot. Hurry along, they're nearly here.'

Eury goes off to find Bria's cache, while I scan the forest fringe for our visitors. Two figures soon appear amidst the pines, one a tall man, armed and leading a pack mule. The other is a woman, riding another mule, her legs astride it in manly fashion. Despite Bria's reassurances, I'm wary: what constitutes a friend, in a daemon's world?

The man isn't merely tall, he's immense, well over six foot, with limbs like tree trunks and huge shoulders and chest. Yet, even at this distance, I can see he isn't in the best shape: he has a paunch, and his face, thick-lipped and overripe, is sweating freely. It's obvious he hasn't shaved for days for his chin is covered in silvery stubble, and his golden-brown mane of hair, shot through with grey, is thinning at the temples.

Nonetheless, he'd have been handsome in his prime, with his square jaw, bronzed skin and deep-set green eyes. He moves with a heavy grace, alert to my presence but not unduly troubled. When Eury appears he pauses momentarily, then, spotting the amphora, he urges the mule forward.

The woman mounted on the other mule has pulled a veil over her hair, but I've already noticed that it's long, grey and tightly tied. She has a judgemental face, with narrow eyes and a thin-lipped mouth – the face of one who's reached a point in her life where she wonders whether anything has been worthwhile.

'Greetings,' I call formally, as they halt before me.

The giant warrior gives a tired grunt. 'You're the Ithacan, eh?'

'Odysseus.' I neglect to include a patronymic, against all polite custom. 'Laertiades' would be a lie, and 'Sisyphiades' is none of his business.

The warrior towers over me as he offers a big hand. 'Theseus, of Attica.'

Theseus of Attica! I am instantly awestruck. Theseus is the greatest living warrior in Achaea, if not the known world. Once King of Athens, and said to be a son of Poseidon, his feats are almost as prodigious as Heracles's, a slayer of monsters and evil men.

I offer my hand in return, and his huge paw engulfs mine in a firm grip.

An instant later I am slammed face first into the ground, my arm contorted behind my back, blood and dust clogging my mouth and nose. Theseus's huge foot presses down on my back, grinding me flat. I try to rise but the giant Attican almost wrenches my arm from its socket.

'Lesson one, Ithacan: trust nobody,' Theseus chuckles. He saunters past while I spit dust, burning with shame and anger. The woman gives me a cool, unimpressed look as she rides by. I feel another surge of temper, but Bria sends me a warning look. She's placed an arm across Eurybates's chest to keep him from coming to my aid. I clamber to my feet ruefully, dusting myself off.

'Are you still pulling that stupid stunt, you great oaf?' Bria asks Theseus, sniffing with suppressed laughter.

'Bria, you little strumpet, is that you?' Theseus embraces her in a bear hug that lifts her off the ground, roaring in mock rage as she slaps his chops. He drops her, but she lands spryly and strikes a pose, hands on hips.

'Don't think you're getting any more than a hug, after that scene you made in Thessaly last year,' she scolds. 'Anyway, I'm keeping this host-body chaste until I can find an older one.' She throws me a 'see how noble I'm being' look. 'So, keep your hands in seemly places, Attica!'

'What made you choose a child?' Theseus grumbles. 'I'd been looking forward to a good tumble.'

'It was chosen for me, and anyway, you're a long way from being in my good graces, you great lump.' She waves airily at the older woman, who is dismounting from her mule. 'Welcome, Lady Iodama. This is Odysseus of Ithaca, the latest of our Queen's champions,' she announces, then indicates Eurybates. 'And this is his friend, Eurybates. Odysseus, Eurybates, this lady is Iodama.'

Close up, Iodama looks to be in her sixties, perhaps older, with deep-set wrinkles on her forehead and under her eyes, and loose skin around her neck. But her gaze is sharp and penetrating.

'The sister of Athena?' I blurt. In some tales, Iodama is Athena's sibling; in a few, the Attican goddess kills her, though this woman is very much alive.

'Athena has no sisters – she gave me this name as a joke,' Iodama says, coolly. She looks me up and down. 'Couldn't you find anyone taller?' she asks Bria.

'Size isn't everything,' Bria replies.

'That's not what you usually say,' Theseus snickers. 'I hope you have wine or beer – I'm parched.'

'Water, until dinner,' Bria replies.

He stumps over to the bench where I've laid Eurytos's bow and brushes it onto the ground in a fit either of pique or dismissal, before sitting himself down.

Outraged, I try to appeal to Bria but she is busy embracing Iodama. When they've finished their greeting, Iodama looks me over more thoroughly. 'So this is the young man whose very existence has Pytho in turmoil? The line of Prometheus was thought extinct when Sisyphus died – and most of Olympus rejoiced at that news. What have you told him of the *theioi*, and the gods?'

'As little as possible,' Bria replies.

I shoot Bria a look: *Really?*

'Good,' says Iodama. 'We'll speak after the meal, young man.'

It's obvious I've been dismissed. I thank her as courteously as I can, given my suppressed fury, before hurrying over to pick up the bow. I put it well out of reach before daring to confront Theseus. 'That is Eurytos's bow,' I tell him. 'One of the two Great Bows of legend.'

'I eat archers for breakfast, boy. Cowardly runts who're too scared to go toe to toe with a real man.'

'Cowardly runts like Heracles?' I reply, my blood up.

Theseus stands; my eyes are level with his nipples. 'I'll Heracles you, runt.'

Iodama forces her way between us. Interestingly, it's at me she directs her scorn. 'Learn to take better care of your possessions, Ithacan,' she snaps. 'Leave them lying around at your peril.'

Fuming, I carry the bow and its case into Eury's and my sleeping hut, checking the bow for any damage before placing it inside its case and safely under my bed covers. When I emerge, Theseus is as jovial as Dionysus again, mollified by a goblet of wine.

Bria now produces all manner of foods she's concealed from Eury and me: olives, pickles, cheeses, cured and spiced meats, sesame oil and dried figs, which she places on wooden platters with freshly harvested vegetables from her garden. And I know she's right about the wine: Eury, who was in charge of Laertes's wine cellar for some years and has an excellent palate, is finding it delicious. But I'm in no mood to appreciate it.

Eury and I are silent for most of the meal, which isn't our way. But I don't trust myself to speak and he's being both sympathetic towards me and overawed by such illustrious guests. So it's Theseus who talks most. His manner is boisterous and boasting, filled with references to his past deeds. I find, despite my love of the Theseus legends, that I am increasingly irritated by the hero's refusal to talk about anything but himself.

'Remember that bandit fellow who used to kick his victims off the cliffs?' he's crowing to Bria. 'Gave him a damn good kicking myself. That's my way, you know: give a man a bit of what he's been handing out, and see how he likes it! By the Owl, Achaea was a brutal place back then, eh! The gods were shitting out monsters every time they took a dump! Heh heh! Break open another amphora, will you?'

He's like a giant child, I think. But I still listen closely. His world is my world now, and Theseus can't be a legend for nothing.

Finally, they all look at me. 'So, Odysseus, you survived your awakening,' Iodama observes. 'We weren't sure you would, when our Queen came to empower you.'

'I've been in easier places,' I reply.

'A tricky situation,' Iodama concedes. 'Badly outnumbered, with your leg barely healed. What happened?'

I describe the fight with Aduwalli and his Trojans, making much of the courage and steadfastness of Eurybates and Bria in helping me survive. I expect praise once I finish, but when I recount the final confrontation with Kyshanda and Skaya-Mandu, Iodama gives me an angry look.

'You should have shot the Trojan princess – she's worse than her brother.'

I'm shocked – I can understand Doripanes being so brutal, but Iodama must surely feel some compassion for her own sex. 'Shoot a *woman*?'

'She's the daughter of Hekuba of Troy! You could have crippled our enemies. But then, I suppose we had no time to explain the kind of world you've been thrown into. By the Owl, though, if you ever aim another arrow at an enemy of our mistress, loose it!'

I bow my head to hide my true feelings. I don't regret my decision not to shoot. Kyshanda's lovely face still fills my dreams.

'I know you'll have questions about what kind of life you've entered, and what service to the mistress entails,' Iodama goes on, 'but first let me give you the basics.' She holds out her goblet to Bria. 'Be a darling and fetch more wine. I'm not going to spend the evening listening to Theseus complaining of thirst.'

Bria brings another amphora, omitting to water the wine she pours into their goblets, then she and Theseus leave together. I eye them doubtfully as they wander off, not trusting either of them.

She'd better behave, for Hebea's sake.

Iodama then looks at Eurybates pointedly until he gets the hint and makes himself busy elsewhere, leaving me alone with the stern old woman. 'So, let me tell you of gods and men,' she begins, gathering her cloak around her against the evening chill. 'The first, most simple fact, you know already: the gods are real. Most people insist they believe, but are shocked nonetheless: their belief is usually in distant beings.' She cocks her head at me. 'I'm sure that used to include you, if you ever believed at all.'

Damn, she's perceptive…

She silences my explanations with a gesture. 'The gods made this world, and they raised us from the beasts. They deserve our reverence, for they chose us as their flock, and they protect us.'

'So why—'

'Hush. You were going to ask why there are other gods than ours? As you did with Bria? Non-Achaean gods – Egyptian, Trojan, Hittite, Thracian and so on?'

What can Iodama possibly know of a conversation I had with Bria five months ago? Athena's servants must have some way of sharing information, for I've been with Bria ever since. I shift uncomfortably on my stool.

'Our priests tell the common folk that these are false gods – imaginary beings,' Iodama continues. 'But those other gods are as real as ours. They are myriad, and they are at war. A god with no worshippers dies. A forgotten god dies. So too do their people, for they are two sides of one coin. Think of the Earth Mother, proud Hera. Once, there were many such divinities in Achaea, from Demeter to Themis to Gaia and beyond. But the worship of Hera has lived on, spreading near and far, while her predecessors are gradually forgotten, and perish.'

Questions fill my mouth. 'But why—'

'Don't interrupt! Bria warned me of your impatience!' Iodama snaps. 'I tell you this so you understand the war we fight. We who serve Athena struggle to ensure that she continues. If she thrives, so too do her flock.' She taps the emptied amphora. 'Imagine our world is an amphora like this one, too small for the gods to enter lest they destroy it, but with many holes through which they can reach inside. They do so to protect those they love – their people – from the people of other gods. But they can only act through those with the right blood. You already know about *theioi* – the god-touched. You are such a one, and you have pledged yourself to Athena. The man who tried to kill you – the Trojan, Aduwalli – is another, but pledged to one of his own gods: Ishtar. The Trojans desire ascendancy over Achaea, and so they attacked you, our "Man of Fire".'

'But why would Athena approach me?' I ask. 'My family have mostly given reverence to Zeus and Hera. And Poseidon of course.'

'Because you are by nature suited to Athena,' Iodama replies. 'Just as I am, and Bria and Theseus too. We are rational people, who prize skill and logic and order. I know this of you because my mistress was able to awaken you – if you'd been a crude barbarian, she'd have failed to bring you to her service.'

It's true – I've always had a questioning mind, never taken anything on faith, always sought for reasons. But Iodama's statements open up many more questions. 'We're raised to revere all the gods of Olympus,' I say. 'Why would we pledge service to just one?'

'It's no coincidence that the tales of the gods often have them in conflict,' Iodama replies. 'The Olympian gods displaced the Titans, who displaced their forebears. Gods compete; gods die. In this world, we *theioi* are their weapons, and can be turned on each other.' She looks at me intently. 'Prometheus was the fire bringer, but now we revere Hephaestus. Poseidon supplanted Oceanus as God of the Sea... Need I go on?'

'If there were no gods, would there be no war?'

Iodama snorts. 'We are mankind, doomed to struggle and strive and fight and kill. As above, so below.' She jabs my chest with a bony finger. 'Life is struggle, Ithacan. Would you not prefer a world shaped by Athena – a place of wisdom and reason – than one made in the image of Skaya-Mandu's Ishtar, or even Ares, the War God of Olympus?'

That makes sense to me: if this struggle she describes leads to a better, more rational world, then it's a cause I can believe in. *And how like a rational person to need a rationale for my service.*

'I can see how serving Athena suits me,' I acknowledge. 'What else must I know?'

Iodama considers, as if measuring how much she need reveal, or how much she thinks I can handle. 'There are four known paths for a *theios*,' she tells me. 'The champion, the seer, the avatar and the magus. The path is determined by your nature, when you are awakened. You are a champion, blessed now with superior strength, speed and endurance. Because you are Athena's, your skill in battle is enhanced; Theseus is another like you. A seer is one like your grandmother, the Pythia, who can walk the Viper's Path and see the future.'

It occurs to me that Kyshanda, ever-constant in my thoughts, is probably a seer. *How much can she see?* The thought makes me shiver. 'What are you?' I ask.

'I'm an avatar, one who can call their chosen god or goddess into themselves, and become their vessel. Finally there is the magus, the sorcerer, drawing upon the powers of their patron – they're the most complex of the *theioi*.'

'Like Molebus?' I shiver as I remember the half-human monster that fought me below the cave. 'Doripanes called him a shape-shifter.'

'Yes, indeed. Molebus was a son of Pan, God of Wild Places. So his affinities were with mountain and forest creatures, and with hunting.'

'And Doripanes himself? He blinded one of the Trojans from the other side of a field.'

'He too is a magus. But he has other powers. Some can walk more than one path, but they are seldom as strong in a given field as those that specialize. No two *theioi* are alike – you will learn that soon enough.'

'So how is a *theios* made?'

'In the first instance, they are created by a god possessing – taking over control – of the body of an avatar, and *conceiving* a child. And later, by the child of such a union producing children of their own. Take Heracles, the son of Zeus, or Theseus, a son of Poseidon: they are first-generation *theioi*. Name any Achaean hero and I'll tell you their divine lineage and patronage. It's what gives them their edge. But you're a great-great-grandson. Your bloodline is diffused, so you have potential, but less than many. You'll need to make up for your lack of raw power with skill and wits.'

Though I'm disappointed, I'm only facing the same obstacles I've dealt with since I was a child, except on a larger scale. But I have a more pressing question. 'I take it, from my own situation, that the original god might not end up as their *theios* child's patron?'

'Indeed not. It would be difficult for our mistress Athena, a virginal goddess, to breed her own *theioi*. Her virginity is an essential part of her identity.'

'What is Bria? She usually calls herself a daemon, rather than a *theia*.'

'She is what she says she is – she can possess humans, like this slip of a girl, Hebea. Her origin... is her own business.'

'And monsters? The Typhon? The Chimera? The creatures Heracles slew? Satyrs? Nymphs?'

'All real too,' Iodama replies. 'A few of the gods – the mightiest, most primal ones – can possess random beasts as easily as human avatars; the offspring are always monstrous in some way.'

I recoil, remembering some of the more grotesque tales of the past. 'Then the Minotaur... Poseidon possessed a *bull*? And seduced – or raped – the Queen of Crete in that form? Why?'

'Because he could,' Iodama replies. 'Perhaps he desired a monstrous offspring. Or to demonstrate his power. Or from lust. Or to *punish* her.' Her voice is scornful and bitter. 'Athena represents a different ethos to those old, lustful male gods. Most of the gods are in contention because they are fundamentally opposed, in many ways. The other Olympians are no less a threat to my mistress than any Hittite god.'

I glance across the clearing, where Theseus and Bria still joke and drink. Eurybates is cleaning up, but has his eye on us all. I drop my voice: 'So Theseus, son of Poseidon, slew the Minotaur, bred by Poseidon? The son of a god against his own half-brother?'

'Think rather that a modern hero – a champion of Athena, regardless of who sired him – slew a monstrous being bred in an earlier age,' Iodama replies. 'Think on this – the Minotaur was an embodiment of a primitive and barbarous religion, used to give credence to a bloody religion of sacrifice. Athena's hero came to end it, championing reason, and ending the dominance of Crete over Achaea. Real people, real events.'

So Heracles is truly Zeus's son, I think, *and he really slew monsters begat by Titans.* The sons of Heracles are still alive; less than twenty years ago they rampaged through the Peloponnese. Heracles is accounted a god now, raised to Olympus by Zeus. As I ponder this, my gaze drifts upwards, where the stars are coming out. Many have a tale of divine origin. Orion strides across the winter sky, forever aiming his mighty bow at Taurus the bull, both of them immortalized in the stars.

My mind is spinning. Doripanes has already shown me a world very different from the rational one I believed in. But for months now, I have pushed this realization aside as I focused on hardening my body and honing my reflexes under Bria's lash. Iodama's words make the very earth beneath my feet feel untrustworthy, as if at any moment I could fall through an abyss into Erebus, the underworld realm of Hades.

Iodama touches my knee. 'It's much to take in, Ithacan. Sleep now. It will be clearer in the morning. And our mistress has a task for us. You'll need to be well-rested.'

Easily said, but it's a long time before I can sleep.

–

The next morning, Theseus, reeking of wine, offers to show me a few wrestling moves. His real intention quickly becomes apparent.

We strip off in the clearing. Naked but for a loincloth, Theseus is an even more imposing figure – his giant stature layered with slabs of muscle, the oil he slathers over himself gleaming in the sunlight. I pride myself that, though smaller than most, I am well-built, but Theseus is ridiculously massive.

We begin by crouching, grappling for a hold on each other's arms or shoulders, shoving and twisting, trying to make the other man buckle and fall. Eury's gone to hunt more meat to feed our unexpected guests, but the two women are watching. Within moments, I've forgotten they're there, because it's clear Theseus isn't going to hold back. I'm soon driven backwards and into the dirt by the bigger man's crushing weight.

Theseus snorts like a bull, holding me down for just a bit longer than he needs. 'You aren't big enough for this, boy,' he jeers.

Bastard, I think, my face mashed into the dirt. I stagger to my feet, angrily wiping away the dust.

This time Theseus drives in hard, ramming me backwards until my left leg slips and down I go once more. 'Too fucking easy,' the big Athenian grunts, getting up and flexing his muscles. 'If he's the best you could find,' he calls to Bria, 'you're not looking hard enough.'

I feel my face burning. 'Again!' I shout as I get back to my feet.

This time, as the Athenian rushes in, I go lower, twisting my body at the hip to let the giant's momentum push him past me so I can flip him hard, using the hero's own weight. It might have worked, but Theseus is so heavily oiled I lose my grip. But I adjust as my hold fails, drive in from the side and force him to one knee, straining and roaring, body to body... Theseus's feet begin to slide...

Then the Attican batters his forehead into my temple. My vision explodes in pain as Theseus tumbles me over and crushes me with a full body slam. I lie in the dust, winded and dazed, while the other man presses me down, his breath hot on my neck, chuckling darkly.

I clutch my bloodied temple. 'You filthy cheat—'

'You think the Minotaur played by the rules, boy?' Theseus snorts. 'You think any of the men you'll come up against are going to care how they win?'

'You used to be a hero of mine,' I snarl, 'but you're just a prehistoric *phallos*.' Something snaps inside me, and I punch Theseus right in the groin, an uppercut that crushes the man's scrotum into his pubis. Theseus convulses and doubles over, roaring in pain, but almost immediately launches himself at me. We both throw punches, but my blows strike a belly with a layer hard as bronze beneath the surface fat, while Theseus's fist almost breaks my ribs.

'Stop!' Iodama snaps, leaping to her feet. When neither of us pays any attention, a spear appears in her right arm, and she hurls it between us to land quivering in the dirt.

For a moment I think Theseus is going to grab the spear and come at me. I contemplate doing it myself. Then, reluctantly, we both back away, panting.

'That's enough,' Iodama tells us. 'Grow up, the pair of you. Our mistress doesn't want her champions killing each other in some absurd pissing competition.'

'The boy needs to know what's what,' Theseus growls back.

'I'm not a boy.'

'In this world you are, Sisyphus-spawn,' the Athenian retorts.

So he knows... Oh gods, does the whole world know?

'Enough,' Iodama repeats. 'I've had a bellyful of you both. Theseus, watch your tongue – I warned you to say nothing of his father.' With that, she flounces away.

To my annoyance, Bria's sympathy is for Theseus, going to him and murmuring something placating.

Fickle bitch! Feeling thoroughly ill-treated, I grab my tunic and stamp off to a pool in a nearby stream to rinse off. Once clean and dressed, I find a spot in the sun and sulk. After a while, I begin picturing moves I could and *should* have pulled to use some leverage and grind that *suagros* – that *pig fucker* – Theseus's face into the dirt.

I wish Eurybates was here, but he's not. So I'm left to stew until Bria comes over, to either sympathize or gloat. 'You all right?' she asks.

'I'm fine,' I lie.

'There's no shame in being beaten by Theseus, Odysseus. He's a great warrior.'

'No he's not, he's an egotistical, bullying brute. No wonder the Athenians threw him out.'

'Threw? An underhand political manoeuvre by Menestheus and his conniving comrades.'

'Harpy's balls! Everyone knows that, after Crete, Theseus used his fame to engineer his way onto the throne, then spent most of his days drunk or bedding other men's wives.' I have this from Laertes. As a wide-eyed teenager, I'd chosen to believe better of the Minotaur-slaying hero but, having met him, I now believe Laertes's version. 'He might still be ruling Attica if he hadn't been such a disaster. Good luck to Menestheus – he has a right mess to sort out.'

'And a colder-hearted *phallos* than Menestheus it would be hard to find,' Bria replies. She ruffles my hair in a gesture that deliberately belittles me. 'Theseus is right about you, Ithaca: in our world, you're still a boy. You fight like it's a sport. It's not, it's a battle for survival. Real warriors don't care about rules – only about winning. The best punch you threw was the one at his *peos*. That's what our mistress needs.'

I spit, which does nothing to wipe the bitter taste from my mouth. 'I thought Athena stood for honour.'

'Honour? No, she stands for logic, and logic has little place for irrational concepts like honour. Pay lip service to it, then cheat and stab and win just the same – that's my advice.' She pats my shoulder amiably. 'Believe me, the champions of Ares and Zeus and the rest will fight just as dirty. So will Trojans like Skaya-Mandu and his brothers. They know what's at stake.'

'Fine. I understand.' *I do and I hate it. But there's no going back.*

'That's as well. This afternoon, there's a gathering of the court of Olympus – and you're invited.'

I stare. 'Are you serious?'

'I am indeed. Sometimes a matter arises that must be dealt with through a meeting of the gods. Iodama came here because one such has arisen.'

'Where are we going?'

'You'll see.' Bria smiles secretively.

'Shouldn't we be preparing for the journey?'

'No! We'll cross the world without leaving this clearing.' Bria giggles at my confusion. 'Don't worry, you'll see. Anyway, what did you make of Iodama's spiel about the gods?'

Spiel? 'It explained a lot,' I reply, hesitantly. 'But it opened up another thousand questions.'

'Iodama is Athena's mouthpiece, Ithaca. She'll tell you only what she wants you to know.'

Those words surprise me: I've assumed Bria and Iodama would be telling me much the same things, but there's a very real sense of contrariness in Bria's voice. 'What do you mean?' I ask.

'That story she fed you – of gods creating the world, and of gods and men intertwined in a battle for survival – might not be the only explanation.' She pulls a duck egg from her pouch and displays it. 'Here's a thought for you – which came first: the egg, or the bird that laid it?'

She places the egg into my hand, gives me a winning smile and walks away.

8 – Soul Journey

'Many tales are told in many ways: new forms are
found
to rub upon the touchstone,
Herein hazard lies'
—Pindar, *Nemean Ode 8*

Phocis

Eurybates returns before midday with a hare for us to stew. I clap him over the shoulder. 'Well done, those little beasts are tough to catch.'

He grins, deservedly pleased with himself to have snared such a swift and elusive creature. It was he who taught me how to do it: not only how to tie the fine mesh nets needed, but where to place them without betraying either human scent or presence, before surprising the hare, driving it into its final, fatal run.

Iodama calls us together for an unusually early dinner: a stew made from Eury's hare, with herbs and vegetables from Bria's wild garden – and a few wild duck eggs. I eat the latter while giving Bria a thoughtful look, but she doesn't meet my eye.

While we finish the meal, I take a moment to gather my thoughts. It's difficult to articulate what I'm going through, even to Eury. Athena's appearance in Krisa had been like a lightning bolt to my brain. The healing of my wounded thigh was an indisputable miracle, and since then I've felt as if my physical potential has been extended past the limit of what I'd thought possible. It's magical, supernatural – terrifyingly, gloriously irrational.

And yet… set beside the personal vision I'd tried to explain to Eurybates on our first arrival in Pytho – of the gods as vast, invisible powers that drive and suffuse the entire world – to find that no, the gods are bickering rivals setting tribe against tribe for their own gain is curiously disappointing.

And now there's this new bird-and-egg puzzle Bria has planted in my head, which has me wondering if I'm still being lied to, by people who have claimed my allegiance and who owe me more.

But that's a future worry – I have enough on my platter right now.

Theseus spends the meal moaning to Iodama about how much he misses Athens. 'I've been waiting a long time to return to my kingdom. When are you going to deliver on your promises of support?'

'When I believe there's strong desire for your return,' Iodama replies. 'Right now, I'm not seeing it.' She makes a chopping gesture with her right hand. 'That's enough – we have a more pressing need.' She looks directly at me. 'Theseus and I have done this several times, but for you it'll be a new experience, Ithacan. There are potions that draw a person's daemon – their spirit – from their body. Once freed, the daemon can travel vast distances in moments. By such means, the gods can hold physical meetings on earth, and that's what we're summoned to. I brewed the potions this morning, and very soon we will partake.' She shows us three small flasks, before adding, 'Knowing you, Ithacan, you'll have questions.'

'Of course… How long does it take? What are the dangers? Where are we going? How will we get back? What happens if we're separated? Can we take any weapons with us? Do we—'

'All right, all right,' Iodama harrumphs. 'The short answer is – stay with me. If we're separated, just visualize this place. Theseus and you will accompany me. Bria and Eurybates will remain here, to keep our bodies safe. They will continue breathing, the hearts will keep beating, albeit only for a few days unless well-tended. But I'm only expecting we'll be away a few hours.'

'Where are we going?' I ask.

'Luwia,' Iodama replies.

Luwia is on the Trojan side of the Aegean Sea. The announcement makes even Theseus frown. 'Why there?'

'Do I look like Zeus?' Iodama snaps. 'The Skyfather gave us the date, time and place – he didn't give reasons. I suggest you purge your bowels and bladder, to save Bria and Eurybates some unpleasantness, then join me back here in twenty minutes.' She rises and stalks away.

'She's always bitchy, just like Herself,' Theseus remarks. 'Virgins!' He winks at me and swaggers towards the latrine trench, whistling.

I give Bria a doubtful look. 'What?' she asks, truculently.

'Given we know Athena is real, and we do her will, shouldn't Theseus be more... er...?'

'Reverential? Blindly devoted? Fanatically obedient? But we're the ones who've seen behind the curtains, Ithaca. "True believers" are priggish, righteous, ugly souls, full of rigid certainties and brutal prejudices. Steer clear of them. Scepticism will serve you far better than faith in this life.'

It's a disturbing thought, but I can relate to it: to know more, to see more, to question more – isn't that exactly what I want?

I join Theseus in pissing into the trench, the Athenian unable to resist demonstrating just how far he can direct his thick stream. 'Better than wetting yourself while you're floating in the clouds,' he chuckles, smacking me on the shoulder and almost sending me into the pit. Then, suddenly serious, he says: 'Wherever we go today, Ithacan, follow my orders and keep your mouth shut. There are going to be men there who can break you in half, and the only thing between them and you is *me*. And I've not yet worked out if you're worth protecting.'

He laughs and strolls off.

I respected you more when you were a campfire tale.

I finish my ablutions and head back, joining Eurybates in our hut. 'What do you think of the *theioi* now, after meeting one of the greatest of them?' I fume.

'Much as you do,' he murmurs, keeping an eye on the door.

'That's hardly an answer. What do *you* think is their true nature?'

'What is the true nature of any man? We all have faults and virtues. Perhaps these are more exaggerated in a *theios*?'

'Very much so,' I agree. 'How many of them do you think there are?'

'Well, they say the old gods were lusty buggers! Laertes thought there were half a dozen at most of the larger royal courts, and dozens more scattered through the roving war bands, like that of Heracles's son Hyllus.'

'Father knew?' I'm stunned… again.

'He could hardly have been an Argonaut and not notice the prowess of men like Jason.'

'Good point. What about Ithaca? Are any of Father's warriors a *theios*?'

Eury shakes his head. 'With respect, my prince, Ithaca is the backwater of a backwater.'

I can't argue with that. 'Theseus worries me,' I whisper, returning to my main concern. 'He treats Iodama with very little respect, and me with none, but I'm expected to trust him. What should I do?'

'Whatever Iodama demands,' he replies, suddenly very serious. 'This is her world, and she at least means you no harm. I'll watch over your body, have no fear.'

Bria has lit a fire and assembled a pile of blankets, explaining that our bodies will be prone to chills without souls to animate them. 'I'll cover you, once you've lain down.'

Theseus hoists up his tunic and waggles his cock at Bria. 'If this gets hard while I'm asleep, feel free to climb aboard, sweetie.'

'I'm more likely to chop it off and sell it,' Bria replies tartly. 'Should fetch a decent price in Athens, provided I could convince anyone that tiny thing is actually yours.'

Theseus guffaws. 'It'd get a good price anywhere, but only when I'm attached.'

Iodama joins me. 'Lie near the fire, but not too close,' she counsels. 'Find a comfortable position on your side, to help keep your air passages clear.'

It's a clear autumn afternoon, the heat oppressive even though the sun is well past its zenith. Despite this, Bria is adding more fuel to the fire, which already has us sweating.

Iodama offers me one of the small flasks. 'Odysseus, this potion will make you feel numb, as if you're losing control of your body. Feeling, taste and scent will go, but you'll retain sight and sound. It's not a pleasant sensation, but stay calm. Keep your thoughts disciplined. Don't wander off into a reverie about home, or that could be where you end up. Listen to my voice, and follow my instructions.'

It's with as much fear as anticipation that I swallow the bitter-tasting fluid in the flask. I'm going to see the gods! I feel a version of that hyper-alert mix of nerves and exhilaration I experienced at Pytho. Yes, I'm a little scared, but I wouldn't miss this for the world.

Theseus swigs his flask and belches, while Iodama drinks with a kind of reverence, giving me a reassuring nod and lying down. I drink – it's tasteless – and lie down too, as Bria kneels by my head.

'Just breathe,' she murmurs. 'Soon you'll start to feel hollowed out – that's normal. When you hear Iodama speak, cling to that. Think only of her, and what she's saying. She's done this many times, and so has Theseus. We've never lost anyone. Remember, you can always come back to me here.'

She goes on, but as the dislocating sensation takes over, I find myself less able to follow what she's saying, while a creeping numbness in my limbs heralds the onset of the drug. Soon I can no longer feel my fingers or my feet.

'…and you'll gradually become aware of…' Bria drones on. A floating sensation washes through me, like childhood dreams I'd occasionally had of drifting around my room. My body is almost completely numb now, an inert slab of meat. Then Bria's voice fades, and I hear another.

'...*awaken and pray with me*,' Iodama is saying, her words more felt than heard. '*I sing of Pallas Athena, illustrious grey-eyed goddess. Oh, Crafty One, with a heart relentless, modest Virgin, Protectress of the city...*'

I know the prayer but only vaguely: Athena is an Attican goddess, peripheral in Ithaca.

'*...The valiant Tritogeneia was roused by Zeus the Wise from his own awesome brow, the tools of battle on her arm, glittering gold: all the immortals were amazed. Without delay she leapt from the ever-living skull to come before Zeus, master of the aegis, and the sharp javelin rattled in her hand. Mighty Olympus was sent madly spinning by the potency of her, the grey-eyed one.*'

Iodama ends her chant. '*Rise,*' she cries, in a voice that commands instant obedience. I sit up, enduring the weird sensation of peeling myself from my flesh. As if in a dream I see Iodama and Theseus do the same, their daemons filmy and opaque, their abandoned bodies pale and empty looking. I can't help but look down at my own face, and I'm chilled by the slackness of my features. My mouth hangs open, the rise and fall of my chest imperceptible, and for a moment I panic that my body has died, and I'll never return to it.

By contrast, Bria and Eury seem to shine, the combination of body and spirit brimming with energy, and I feel a visceral sense of envy for their warmth and vitality. Eury looks puzzled, even alarmed, but Bria can see us, watching my spirit-face and giving me a wink of approval.

Then Iodama grips my 'arm' – my spirit's arm – and the sensation is exactly as if her real hand had gripped my real arm. She pulls me completely free of my body as she rises into the air, seizing Theseus with her other hand. As we drift upwards I try tapping my own chest – my spirit's chest. It feels like an eggshell: unyielding, but bloodless and empty inside.

My clothes are the same as the ones my body still wears but they've taken on a filmy essence, like mist draped over the hills on a chill morning. The dagger at my side feels sharp to the touch, but what can it now cut, I wonder?

Our surroundings are altered also. A kind of twilight prevails, the colours muted even though the sun is high in the sky. The stream nearby sounds louder, the birdsong jarring in my ears.

I have many questions, but Iodama doesn't permit them. 'Hold fast to me,' she commands, and I grip her forearm tight. Then she shouts aloud and soars into the air with astonishing speed, pulling Theseus and me with her as though we're weightless, the ground spinning and swirling away. For a moment everything around us blurs; then, looking down, I see with giddy exhilaration that the land is already far below, the shape of the hills and coasts suddenly clear as we flash like comets across the sky, until we're travelling so fast the world below becomes an indistinct smear of grey.

I chance a glance to my right, see that Theseus is caught up in the experience, while Iodama is focused and purposeful. Already we're shooting over white-topped waves, over a surf-edged coastline and then rolling brown hills with valleys and plains. A great mountain looms ahead and we bear down on it at a terrifying speed. I cry in alarm, causing Theseus to laugh at my fright, and then without transition, we're standing on solid ground. Only Iodama's grip prevents me from slamming face first into the turf. I cling to her, even after Theseus has disentangled himself from her grasp and stepped away with a characteristic swagger.

'Look at me,' Iodama rasps. 'Get your feet planted, and now watch the horizon. We all find this disorienting at first.'

When the world has stopped spinning, Iodama nods approvingly. 'Well done, Odysseus. You did well. Walk around now, get used to being in this state. Test the limits.'

She indicates Theseus. The giant Attican is flexing as if in his own body, then suddenly he turns and whips out his blade, lashing at the branch of a tree.

The blade passes through as if it doesn't exist, and the branch doesn't even move. I stare, as Theseus chuckles wryly. 'One day I'll learn how to do some damage in this state,' he says, with purposeful menace. 'Then there'll be no stopping me.'

I reach out and tentatively touch the branch. Despite its slender breadth, I can't budge it at all. The grass beneath my sandals doesn't even bend when I walk on it – a most strange sensation.

'Your daemon is insubstantial,' Iodama explains. 'All of ours are. We can't affect the physical world.'

'But we can damned well affect each other,' Theseus growls. 'See this sword – it's as deadly to you in this state as a real blade is to the body you left behind in Phocis. So watch yourself, Ithaca.' He pats my cheek condescendingly, then turns to Iodama. 'Come on, let's go, I'm thirsty.'

I hesitate, looking at Iodama. 'If a normal human was here, what would they see?'

'Nothing more than an empty mountain meadow,' she replies. 'Not sight nor scent nor sound. Not even the disembodied daemon of a god could shift even a hair on their head, much less communicate.'

'What could a *theios* see?'

She gives that curt, approving nod. 'Our awakening as *theioi* opens our eyes. We can see, feel and hear other daemons, and even the gods themselves if they're present.'

'Just when we're in our daemon state?'

'No. In our physical form as well.' She gives me a taut smile. 'No gods or daemons will be able to spy on you, and I can teach you how to banish those that try.'

'You must give me the potion's recipe.' I'm already envisaging flashing about the Aegean, seeing sights I've barely dreamt of.

Iodama dispels such pleasant fantasies. 'That potion is made from very rare and secret ingredients. We don't use it lightly.' She fixes me with a meaningful look. 'Odysseus, tonight you'll see beings that spend their entire existence in this form – the gods, and many lesser beings, nymphs, *naiads* and the like. Very few of the latter can possess a human, but all of them would love to. That's why Bria is protecting our bodies – to ensure they stay empty.'

It's a chilling thought. 'Why are we here?'

'Because Zeus has called the gods of Olympus together, here on Mount Ida, in Luwia. These "courts" seldom happen, and never before outside Achaea. Athena must attend; you and Theseus are here to guard her.'

Even in such strangeness, there *must* be rules. 'What's your role here?'

'I am the avatar that Athena will enter to interact with her fellow deities this evening. That way, if she's attacked, it's I who might perish, not her.'

I'm stunned. 'But why would you risk that?'

She looks me in the eye. 'She's my *goddess*, Odysseus. When she possesses me, the world is perfect, a state of timeless bliss. I love her, and I'd die for her a thousand times.'

Her fervour is *unreasoning*, a terrifying fanaticism I can't approach. But I now know what drives her. 'We'll keep you safe,' I tell her.

'That's why you're here.' She looks hard at Theseus. 'Don't start any fights.'

'You know me.' The giant champion scratches his groin. 'I don't start fights – I finish them.'

'If only,' Iodama retorts.

'Can we die in this form?' I ask.

Theseus snorts. 'You bet, kid. Stay close to me.'

I bite back a retort, not least because I'm relieved he's with us. 'Why was this gathering called?' I ask, as we take a path that climbs the hillside.

'To discuss Dodona,' Iodama tells me as we walk. 'The priests of Zeus have seized Dodona, the second-most important oracular site in Achaea, and the priestesses of the Triple Goddess – Hera in all her forms – are outraged. This is a threat to Hera's status as equal partner with Zeus, an arrangement that has stood as long as Olympus. Hera is *murderous* about this little apple.'

'Apple?' I ask.

'The Olympians like to call an argument an "apple of discord".'

'I'd quite like an apple right now,' Theseus remarks.

'Shut up and listen. The real issue is that Hera's role as Queen of Olympus is under threat.'

'What, they're going to unmarry?' I quip. Surely gods don't casually uncouple.

'Don't think of Zeus and Hera as wedded,' Iodama tells me. 'They're an alliance of two religious cults that have dominated Achaea for many generations. But the *instant* Zeus feels that Hera is more impediment than asset, she will be passed over – and Hera would do the same, if the boot was on the other foot. Zeus claims the Dodona oracle was losing its potency, hence the seizure. Now, so Hera maintains, he's casting avaricious eyes on Pytho.'

'So why are we here?' I ask. 'And why Luwia? These are Trojan lands.'

'Why indeed?' Iodama says grimly. 'We know the priests of Zeus and Tarhum – the Luwian Skyfather – have begun to speak of them as one being. Recently, the *Trojan* Apaliunas has assumed the name of Apollo, calling himself a twin of Artemis and a son of Zeus: not by Hera but a minor Earth Mother, Leto, whose cult Hera absorbed decades ago. Decoded, that's a clear threat to Hera, and any other purely Achaean god. And who's next? Ishtar, perhaps? She embodies both love and war: I've heard rumours that Aphrodite and Ares are seeking alignment with her.'

'Then what will happen today?'

'Hopefully, no more than rhetoric – but Zeus likes to spring surprises.'

The cold resentment in her tone has me even more puzzled. 'But isn't he Athena's father?'

Theseus does one of his sniggers and Iodama throws him a dirty look. 'No more than Hera is his "wife". Athena is synonymous with Athens, and Zeus wanted full acceptance in Attica. Hence that foolish tale of our patron being born of his head – not his loins, note. No true daughter of *his* would be a virgin. The worshippers of Ares *hate* our inclusion. What pantheon needs two war gods, they argue, and especially a woman?'

My head reels. And yet, it makes sense. 'The tales we tell of the gods reflect their history and status, then?'

'Yes. And now a new tale is forming.'

She stops, looking ahead. The path has reached an intersection with another, and three immense warriors are awaiting us.

'Ares,' Theseus growls.

I squint. *Which is the War God?* Then I catch my breath as the middle one of the trio seems to grow three hand-spans taller, his bronzed face a visage of power and arrogance, framed by a ferocious mane of hair. Golden armour and a giant sword now hang from his body, and his eyes flash with the hint of lightning.

Glancing across at Iodama, I catch my breath as she also changes. Instead of a slight, ageing woman, I behold the majestic being I'd glimpsed after my thigh was ripped open. She's a head taller than Theseus, grey-eyed, helmed and this time armoured in radiant gold, holding a glittering shield and a spear. *Athena.*

As if in response, Theseus seems to increase in size. Athena turns on him, her face livid. 'I remind, you, Attican, to keep your place.'

Theseus duly returns to his normal size. 'Just practicing, my Queen,' he says, with an unrepentant grin.

Athena strides on up the path. Clearly having a taller stature is of major importance here. One day I'm going to find a land where short people are valued. They'll make me king.

'You wanted to know who our chief enemy is?' mutters Theseus. 'That *lastauros*, Ares.'

Theseus might feel free to call Ares a hairy arse, but there's nothing whimsical about the War God. I lay a hand on my sword hilt, feeling like a toddler who's mistakenly wandered into a pitched battle.

'Hail, mighty-thewed Ares, excelling in strength, doughty of heart,' Athena intones, managing to sound both polite and ironic.

'Greetings, grey-eyed Athena, craftiest of virgins,' the War God replies in similar tones, before barking with laughter. 'I'd rather die than endure eternal virginity. But that's Athenians for you – they'd rather pray than fuck.'

His companions guffaw, while eyeing up Theseus and me with cold eyes. Ares turns to introduce them. The immense man with straggling hair halfway down his chest and a lion's hide cloak is Hyllus. 'Yes, the son of Heracles, ravager of the Peloponnese,' Ares snickers. 'Where he'll soon return.'

I only come up to the man's armpit.

'And this is Aias, son of Telamon,' Ares continues, indicating a man just as huge, with a big, stupid face and broken teeth. 'The strongest warrior in all of Achaea, bar Hyllus himself. All the greatest fighting men pledge to me, unless they're Attican...' He looks sourly at Theseus, then trails his eyes over me. 'Or runts from the Isles.'

Hyllus and Aias laugh. 'An Ithacan, Athena? Scraping the bottom of the apple barrel, eh?' Hyllus jeers. 'A great-grandson of Hermes, yes? Barely a *theios*, and only suited to the Messenger's service.' He fixes me with a derisive eye. 'Anything to say, Errand Boy?'

'Why don't you ask—' I begin, but Athena cuts me off.

'He can fight – pray you don't find out how well,' she says, crisply. 'And he can *think*, which puts him well ahead of apes like you.'

Hyllus steps forward, but Theseus meets him, chest to chest. The giant son of Heracles is taller by half a head, but the Attican doesn't give ground. Aias takes a while longer to understand the insult, before taking a step in my direction, fists bunched.

'What a shame you have to poach all your followers, Athena,' Ares says smugly. 'Without this aversion to cocks, you could breed your own – they'd prove more reliable than the *ex*-King of Athens.'

Theseus looks over Hyllus's shoulder. 'Take my advice – keep hiding behind your men, O Mighty-thewed One.'

'You said he was intelligent?' Ares scoffs at Athena. 'If he wants to challenge me, let him.'

This is going to end in blood, I think. *Assuming we bleed in this form*. My brain feeds me six plans in three wild heartbeats, all of them suicidal. Then a clear male voice rings out.

'The Skyfather gave explicit instructions. No violence!'

I peer past – or rather *around* – Aias, where a thin youth in a skullcap has appeared. *A* keryx *of Hermes?*

'Behold,' says Ares. 'Another errand boy.'

'The Skyfather bids his daughter join him,' the herald calls. 'Ares, please wait here until summoned.'

Ares colours as Athena stalks past him, saying, 'Wait here, Ares – the grown-ups need to talk.'

That leaves Theseus and me with Ares's giant escorts. Theseus pushes his chest against Hyllus's, then makes a mischievous moue with his lips, stepping round him composedly as Hyllus flinches away.

I make the mistake of letting that distract me. A moment later Aias's giant hand slams open-palmed into my chest and sends me sprawling. Ares and his men roar with laughter as I scramble to my feet, blade half-drawn. Theseus catches my shoulder. 'Don't,' he snaps.

I go scarlet as I allow Theseus to lead me away, both irritated at my companion and profoundly angry with myself for the lapse. 'I'm sorry,' I stammer to Athena as we catch up.

'It's your first time,' she replies coolly. 'Learn from it.'

A crumbling stone arch stands before us, the broken portal through a tumbledown wall guarding a ruined fortress. The air beyond it is glowing. I'm still smarting from my encounter with Aias, but as we step through the stone arch, that emotion is erased by wonder as the world changes. The arch is seemingly a portal not into another world, but an enhanced vision of this one.

A large lawn spreads before us, dotted with men and women, before a raised dais of gold. The ruined fortress is – at least to our eyes – restored to an improbable glory. Above us, enormous stars hang in a shimmering purple sky.

Many of those on the lawn are fighting men, the escorts of their patrons. Here and there are glowing figures that tower over their surrounding attendants – gods and goddesses, surely. My stomach tightens in awe, dread and the rising excitement of curiosity.

'What is this place?' I whisper, awestruck, to Athena.

She gestures offhandedly at the restored palace. 'We gods have made it from the same energies as these daemon forms. It has no substance except to those in the same state. So be as impressed as you choose – it's all just show.'

Illusory or not, it's breathtaking, a vision of kingly – no, *divine* – splendour, unrepeatable in our world. Every detail is a small sculpted piece of perfection, as real as any brick made by men.

Theseus and I surrender our weapons at a table just beyond the entrance arch, then a lissom girl sways towards us, dressed in a vivid white knee-length dress, vines tangled in her hair and one breast displayed, offering us a tray of gold goblets.

Her lower legs are furry and cloven-hoofed.

'Now that's more like it,' Theseus crows, sweeping up a goblet and just happening to brush the girl's nipple as he reaches over, ignoring Athena's scowl. 'The wine at these gatherings is as delicious as those who serve it,' he says, earning a flirtatious smile from the serving girl.

She offers the tray to me. 'Wine, my hero?' she purrs.

I give the goblet a longing look, but catch Athena's frown. 'I'd prefer water.'

The girl waves a hand over the goblet and passes it to me, and lo, it is merely water, though cool and pure as a mountain spring. Athena nods in approval, then she takes wine herself and surveys the gathering. I study the servants as I sip from my goblet. Most are hoofed, and many horned as well.

'What are they?' I ask when our serving girl has moved on.

'Nymphs, satyrs,' Theseus says. 'Are you *that* ignorant?' He downs his wine and saunters off.

'Think of them as the daemon offspring of the gods,' Athena tells me, as Theseus leaves. 'You'll stay with me,' she says. 'He's going to seek out his peers and gather the latest tidings.'

She scans the gathering, pointing out a supremely regal female figure who is already enthroned on the dais, attractive in a handsome, mature way and clad in the customary ceremonial garb of Achaea – a tiered, heavily tasselled skirt and an elaborately decorated bodice open at the front to frame a pair of substantial, naked breasts, their nipples painted a brilliant red: Hera, the Great Goddess and patron of Mycenae and Pytho.

'I suppose we must pay our respects to my not-mother,' Athena sighs. 'Come.'

I follow her, gazing open-mouthed at the cloud of extravagantly dressed priestesses and warriors behind Hera. Evidently status dictates the number of attendants; we're obviously not rated very highly. I realize in alarm that the Earth Mother's people include my own grandmother, the Pythia, but have no choice but to follow Athena to the foot of the dais, where I kneel at Athena's gesture, though the Attican goddess merely inclines her head. 'My thanks for the invitation, my Queen,' she murmurs.

'The King insisted,' Hera answers in a rich, melodic voice, full of experience and brooding bitterness. The tales speak of Hera as one who resents her 'husband' for his infidelities; now the old stories make more sense.

The cult of Zeus is constantly seeking a stronger partner, flirting with all the female cults, seeking another who will enhance his power without challenging it. Which means Hera has lived an eternity under siege.

Then the Pythia whispers in her patron's ear, and I find myself transfixed by the goddess's stare, as though my blood has clotted in my veins. *Son of Sisyphus*, her piercing gaze seems to whisper.

I swallow, wondering suddenly what role she might have played in my father's death.

'So this is the "secret son",' Hera comments. 'The interdict against the worship of his ancestor still stands. Why does this young man still breathe?'

'He's been claimed by me, and I give warrant for him,' Athena declares. 'No one may strike at him without my leave.'

Brave words, for which I am profoundly grateful. But she still leads me quickly away.

'She knows your true sire,' she notes, 'but Ares was ignorant of it. I wonder who else knows?'

She doesn't wait for a reply, taking me back across the lawn, brushing past a clever-looking, youthful god with flyaway golden hair that streams out behind him, though there's no wind: *Hermes*?

We steer well clear of a dark-haired, brooding god, the air around him stained with darkness like a seeping poison. A tall, female figure in a death shroud stands beside him. My skin clenches into a rash of goose bumps as I stare. 'That's Hades and his consort,' Athena comments. 'They don't normally come.'

The Death God looks every bit the gloomy ruler of the Underworld. I can almost see the bones beneath his pale flesh. His consort is young: Persephone, if the tales are true. The right side of her face is lovely – sun-kissed and full of ripe life – but when she senses my gaze, she turns to face me fully. The left side is white-skinned and skeletal; a black eye shines from a deep-set socket with chilling allure.

'Did he really kidnap her and take her down to Erebus?' I murmur, averting my eyes.

Athena snorts. 'Demeter and the King of the Underworld have been allies for millennia. The girl loves both her lives, the sun-filled months above and the winters below.'

'I'd always thought of Persephone merely as an explanation for the seasons,' I confess.

'Now you know better,' Athena says, tartly. 'Don't voice such thoughts again, Ithacan. They have no place in my service. Now, follow!'

Abashed – and, remembering Bria's riddle of the egg, some-what intrigued by Athena's annoyance – I obey, noticing an unusual figure, a big barbarian in rough clothes with a shaved and tattooed skull, who has approached Hades before kissing Persephone's hands. Theseus joins them; he and the barbarian are clearly old friends, judging by their greetings.

Then Ares arrives, flanked by his two giant escorts, Hyllus and Aias. The War God is glaring around the lawn belligerently. I'm a little concerned they will replicate our earlier encounter, but Athena leads me to the far end of the lawn, where a pair of young divinities stand in splendour, a head taller than the loftiest of their attendants, who are all Trojan, with their braided hair, colourful leggings, and narrow, hook-nosed faces. None of them looks older than twenty.

'Appally-nah-nah!' Athena calls, deliberately mangling the Trojan name. 'No, wait: don't you prefer "Apollo" these days?'

The tall, beautiful young god at the heart of the group silences the hisses of annoyance from his attendants with a languid wave. 'Lady Athena! How good to see Attica represented! I'd been worried such a *regional* divinity as yourself would not be considered *important* enough to attend these gatherings any more. Not when the courts of Achaea and Troy are becoming so aligned!'

Athena tinkles with ironic laughter. 'My father Zeus, my only parent and protector, would never hear of such a thing. Attica is the heart of Achaea, and I am the heart of Attica.' She peers at the willowy slip of a goddess, dressed in male hunting gear, standing in Apollo's shadow. 'Oh, there you are, Artemis! Congratulations on having a brother now – it must have been *such* a shock.'

Artemis looks at Athena sourly. 'Only one attendant, Athena? And such a *small* one.' She puts a fond hand on the arm of the large figure hovering protectively beside her, and I realize that her escort is female, though taller than most men, with a strong figure but an ageing face framed in greying blond hair. 'Atalanta is nigh twice his size, and she's a mere woman.'

Atalanta. So she's the champion of the Huntress...

My heart quickens. When will I get used to meeting legendary figures? Atalanta, heroine of the Calydonian boar hunt, gives me an intimidating stare, accentuated by her languid, cat-like quality. 'Who is he?' she asks, in a husky, deep voice.

'Odysseus of Ithaca,' Athena replies. 'Remember the name.' She turns. And freezes.

While we'd been talking, another party has approached, and without warning I find myself confronting the most bewitchingly beautiful creature I've ever seen. She has a perfectly formed face, immaculately sculpted blond tresses, honeyed skin and a voluptuous yet slender form that is exaggeratedly attractive, yet wholly lovely. She radiates sensual charm, from her pouting lips and come-hither eyes to the thrust-out bosom protruding from her tight bodice, the wasp-like waist, and her full, moist, parted lips. Gorgeous beyond compare, and she towers over her escorts, marking her out as another deity.

Aphrodite... I'm enchanted and intimidated in equal measure.

But she isn't all that steals my breath away.

Flanking her are Prince Skaya-Mandu of Troy and his dark-haired sister, Kyshanda.

9 – The Beauty Contest

> 'They clad her in godly garments and placed
> a beautiful, finely wrought crown of gold on
> her immortal head, and hung jewellery made of
> mountain copper and precious gold in her pierced
> ears, and decked her with necklaces around her
> soft throat and shining breasts...'
> —Homeric, *Hymn to Aphrodite*

Luwia

I stare in shock. These two, *here* – and so soon after our last encounter! My fists flex at the mere sight of Skaya-Mandu's lean, smug face, while Kyshanda stirs up conflicting, yearning emotions.

'Ooo,' Aphrodite purrs. 'Have you all met already?'

Athena lays a cold hand on my forearm. '"Sister"... charming to see you. But couldn't you find any Achaean escorts?'

'None as much to my liking.'

I glare at Skaya-Mandu, remembering the last time I'd seen him: sighting along an arrow shaft, until he pulled his sister between us. 'Do you always hide behind women, Trojan?' I challenge.

Skaya-Mandu sniffs. 'So says a dirty Achaean who sneaks around women like a fecund rat.'

Aphrodite claps her hands in a girlish display of delight, but her eyes are diamond-hard. 'I do enjoy a little creative tension! Shall we have them duel, "Sister"? We could wager, oh, I don't know... Athens? Your hymen?'

'But Aphrodite, to make the wager equal, you'd need a patron city or some semblance of virtue,' Athena retorts. 'Alas, you have neither! And our host has forbidden violence. So let's just talk, yes?'

Aphrodite's eyes bore straight through me, and it's as if she's pulling memories from my head, of the last time I held my widowed Ithacan lover, her tongue caressing my lips and her body undulating against mine... and suddenly it's as though it's Kyshanda I'm holding, kissing, and then this divine creature... dragging my heart out of my chest. I know I've reddened to the roots of my hair, but I can't look away.

The Goddess of Love smirks, then turns back to Athena. 'Yes, sister, we have much to discuss.' She addresses her escorts. 'Skaya-Mandu, darling, fetch me my cloak.' And to Kyshanda, with a knowing smile, 'Why don't you entertain this young man, my dear?' Her sidelong look at me seems to command gratitude, and grateful I am indeed, though in other ways I feel violated.

Under Aphrodite's firm gaze, Skaya-Mandu retreats, mutinous over his dismissal. Kyshanda takes my arm. 'Is this your first time, Megon? It's mine, and I'm overwhelmed—'

'Er, well, actually, Cass... er, Kyshanda,' I stammer. 'My real name is Odysseus. Of Ithaca. I... ah... I—'

'You're sorry you misled me?' She gazes at me with those amazing eyes. Then, to my immense relief, she gives me a knowing smile. 'Now, why would a servant of Athena have given a false name while spying on a shrine sacred to Hera?' She puts a slender finger over my lips. 'No, you don't need to say.'

Her touch has all my senses racing, and it takes me a moment to collect myself. 'Why are you here – with *Aphrodite*?'

'Our Ishtar is Goddess of both Love and War, our equivalent to your Ares and Aphrodite. Recently, under the aegis of Zeus-Tarhum, the two cults have been cooperating. My mother arranged for us to be sent, instead of Aphrodite's usual Achaean champions.'

'Then are you a worshipper of this Ishtar?' I remember what Aduwalli told me of Ishtar.

She shakes her head. 'I am an initiate of Kamrusepa, our Goddess of Wisdom and Magic. Not so different from your Athena, perhaps?' She lays a hesitant hand on my arm. 'I'm so glad you escaped. I wish… I wish I could have warned you. Skaya was wrong, and I tried to tell him so.'

Just to be so close to her makes me sweat. She is one of the few here who doesn't tower over me, and as I meet her steady gaze, I become sure that her remorse is genuine, and that at least some of my feelings for her are reciprocated. That brings me more relief than I'd have thought possible. 'I believe you.'

Even though you're a princess of a hostile kingdom.

Her smile widens. 'Friends, Odysseus of Ithaca?'

'Friends.' I look away, absolutely smitten. 'What's this meeting really about?' I ask, to cover my reaction.

'Ah,' Kyshanda says, giving me a conspiratorial smile. 'Are you going to ply me with wine to loosen my tongue?' She proffers her empty goblet. 'I prefer red,' she adds, helpfully.

I grin, and wave over another nymph with a tray, glancing over my shoulder – Athena is still deep in conversation with Aphrodite – so I take two goblets. We sip – I have no clear idea what we're drinking, except that it's delicious – then Kyshanda says, 'My mother – Queen Hekuba – suspects something out of the ordinary has been planned for today. If I knew, of course, I couldn't tell. But,' she says, dropping her voice to a whisper, 'everything – *everything* – hinges on our new harbour, and the prophecies of war.'

'Between Achaea and Troy?'

'Exactly.' She meets my eyes. 'I like you, Odysseus of Ithaca. But where do you stand on the question of war?'

I know, without needing to be told, that my reply will determine our relationship.

War is waste, Laertes has always said, one thing he and I agree on. And I've never believed in pretending to be other than who I am, even to impress a beautiful woman. 'There must be a better way,' I reply.

'Most men see war as glory,' she comments, in a probing manner. 'Especially the *theioi* – stronger, faster, more resilient than the rest. All the *theios* men I know see war as a chance to shine. Why should you be different? Are you afraid, as my brother suggests?'

I bristle at that. 'I'm no more afraid than any other sensible man. But the Peloponnesian kingdoms are still recovering from Hyllus's war band and its trail of destruction, fifteen years ago. No one sings of the innocents slaughtered, raped or enslaved... or the plague that followed. Craftsmen slain, farmers ruined – if they were lucky enough to survive. Families sundered or destroyed. Fields burned and crops lost. No rational person wants war.'

It's a gamble, to speak my mind like this when most of the noble caste see war as a pinnacle of glory, but to my relief, she gives me an approving smile. 'Then we are of like mind, Odysseus.'

I hesitate, then murmur, 'That kiss?'

She looks at me slyly, from under lowered eyebrows. 'Yes?'

'If I overstepped, I'm sorry.'

'Overstepped?' She flutters her eyelashes. 'I thought you'd never take the hint.'

My heart does a series of somersaults. Maybe, if there's somewhere private we can go...

But then she looks over my shoulder. 'Lady Aphrodite summons me.'

Indeed, the two goddesses are parting, Skaya-Mandu brooding behind them, clutching a dark blue cloak.

'It's good to see you, friend,' Kyshanda murmurs, touching my hand. 'I hope it won't be the last time.'

I struggle to contain the longing to taste her mouth again – an impulse I'm now sure she also feels – before I return to Athena's side, passing my now empty goblet to a servant and taking water again.

'So that's the minx you spared at Kirrha,' Athena remarks. 'Beautiful certainly, but I have little use for a champion who's too soft-hearted to slay my enemies.'

'She's not an enemy,' I breathe. 'She doesn't believe in war.'

Athena's grey eyes flicker dismissively. 'But I do – provided I win. Our problem is that no oracle will back Achaea against Troy.' She peers about her. 'Note the patterns, Odysseus. Hera sits alone – no god will stand close beside her, despite her rank. Hades and Persephone also, but no one ever speaks to them anyway. Apollo and Artemis – the youth divinities – are surrounded by Trojans, even though this is an Achaean assembly. Aphrodite also flaunts her Trojan connections. Ares shows off his command of the Achaean giants of warfare. Hermes flits and flirts and flees.' She scowls. 'And I too stand alone.'

A new thought strikes me. 'My Lady, if I may ask? Where is everyone else?'

'Everyone else?'

'Poseidon, and Dionysus; Hephaestus; the Gods of the Four Winds, and all the others.'

'Poseidon is a sea god. Here he'd be a fish out of water,' Athena sneers. 'Dionysus… Gods of wine don't make for sober counsel. And Hephaestus, who *cares* what that cripple thinks? Certainly not his *loving* wife Aphrodite. As for the Wind Gods…' She pauses, giving me an assessing look. 'The truth is that they don't exist. We've grown beyond that sort of *kopros*. Even a Scythian savage doesn't worship wind, beyond their own farting.'

'What about "Strife" and "Harmony"? The Furies, or the Muses?'

'They're just emotions. No one worships an emotion – except "Love" of course.' She glowers across the lawn at Aphrodite. 'Your tales pretend they have status, but there are no sacrifices to them. No one *worships* them.'

'And that's what's important?' I prompt.

'Aye – that's what's important.' She gives me a pointed look. 'That amphora Iodama told you of, with the gods reaching in… sometimes arms get lopped off. We're at war, and there are casualties.' She looks around the gathering. 'The Titans were primal beings – sky, water, earth, darkness… and fire, of course.

See any of them here? The gods of this age are rational beings – like me.'

'Concepts,' I say, thinking about Bria's egg. 'Like war, love, thought, healing...'

'Aye. Concepts. But still rooted in primal truths, Ithacan.'

Athena seems to be inviting a further question, so I ask. 'Zeus – was he *always* God of Judgement, as well as the heavens, or did he *become* that?'

She flashes me an approving look. 'That's a very dangerous question. Let this suffice: Zeus was always what he is now, as was I, but humans had to learn to recognize our essence. We are unchanging, but our worship evolves.'

Bird or egg...? I ponder. *Bria warned that I'll only be told what she wants me to believe...*

Athena pats my arm. 'That's enough theorising for tonight. I'm impressed – in one day you've made a mental leap that Theseus has never made. Perhaps Bria is right about you.' Then a trumpet blares. 'Eyes and mind open, Odysseus: the show's about to begin.'

Theseus slaps his friend with the tattooed head on the shoulder and rejoins us as a crowd of nymphs and satyrs burst through the entrance arch, tossing flower petals in the air, playing flutes and dancing, followed by a group of fully armed warriors, richly caparisoned in bronze chaised with gold. Their leader is larger even than Hyllus and Aias, with a lion's pelt about his shoulders. As he approaches, he gives Theseus a belligerent stare, returned in full.

My jaw drops: it's *Heracles*!

Heracles: the greatest hero of them all, the son of Zeus and conqueror of anything worth conquering. And now worshipped as a god – there's an altar to him at every shrine to Zeus, even on Ithaca.

I've come to regard Theseus as the ultimate primitive strongman, but I realize I'm wrong: Heracles is nothing *but* raw, brutal power. His gaze is so blank he might as well be a bull in mating season. Strength, fecundity... all that is there, in the blockish musculature, scarred limbs and bulging crotch...

but with a hint of something akin to cunning as well. A devious, instinctive understanding of when to leave the trappings of civilization behind and become a beast in the name of victory. It's almost as if the lion's pelt were his own hide.

As a small man, I am beneath Heracles's notice. But Theseus isn't. The giant demigod steps sideways to measure his height and bulk against the Athenian's, chest to chest, growling obscenities that must have made even the stupendous ego of the Athenian hero shrink, before swaggering on.

And now Zeus… My instinct is to raise my arms in the traditional Achaean gesture of supplication, but when the whole gathering, bar the gods and goddesses, drops to one knee, I quickly follow suit. Is Zeus already so absorbed by eastern ritual? Or is this only because we have assembled in Luwia?

At least it keeps my face well hidden. I'm suddenly, painfully aware of my lineage: *I am the son of Sisyphus, of the line of Prometheus, a god Zeus crushed without mercy…* I keep my head down as the Skyfather pauses before Athena.

'Daughter,' a resonant voice pronounces. I hear a cursory kiss, a cold whisper. Then the immense, gold-clad feet move on, shaking the ground at every step. His bodily form is another head taller again than any male here. From Athena's stony expression, the whispered message has not been to her liking; nor does she appear to appreciate Zeus's warmth towards Aphrodite as he greets her, or his bare acknowledgement of his 'wife' Hera.

Zeus is as every story portrays him: a mighty creature, loosely robed, broad of chest and effortlessly majestic. In Achaea the custom is for men to go clean shaven unless they are very old, but the Skyfather's form combines both power and experience in his massive frame and his silver-frosted mane of hair, projecting eternal strength and age-old wisdom. Energy crackles from his hands, as if a thunderbolt might form at any moment. His eyes seem to sweep the gathering in a heartbeat, yet I feel that everyone here has been noted and examined – myself included.

Zeus takes his throne, and Hermes leaps to the dais, the divine *keryx* raising a hand for silence. 'The court of Olympus is now in session. Welcome all, from far and wide. Mighty Zeus, Father of the Skies, Victor over Cronos, Ruler of Olympus, greets his kindred.'

The herald has barely paused when Apollo – Apaliunas – strides forward, calling, 'Welcome to the lands of Luwia, Great Zeus-Tarhum! Welcome and thrice-welcome! It is a joy to see you enthroned here, at the heart of your eastern demesne. The lands themselves have thirsted for you, and now they are salved!'

'The children of East and West bow to you, Great Father,' Artemis calls, her reedy voice soaring as Apollo pauses. 'Man, woman and child hunger for your words!'

Straight to the flattery. Apollo and his sister, cementing their status, highlighting their eastern ties – of which Zeus clearly approves...

'Achaea bows before its king,' Ares bellows in response, as if he were Achaea's spokesman.

'To our Lord and King!' Apollo shouts, brandishing a goblet and pouring a libation. *He knows we'll all have to drink the toast – another status point scored.*

The toast duly consumed, Zeus raises a hand for silence. Beside him, on her lesser throne, Hera sits immobile, thin-lipped and tense. There have been no welcoming speeches for her. 'I thank you for your due greetings,' the Skyfather says, his deep voice resounding effortlessly across the crowd. 'As you all know, these gatherings are too rare – we have so many pressing concerns. The prosperity of our people must come first. But sometimes a matter arises that demands our attention.'

The Skyfather leaves the statement hanging, his eyes roving over us once more. I feel my pulse race, fearing some dreadful pronouncement, but instead Zeus laughs merrily. 'But first, I hope you will indulge me. Today is the thirteenth birthday of two of my precious children.' He makes a grand gesture as two figures are led forth, muffled head to toe in dark cloaks, amidst a stir of surprise.

I steal a glance at Hera, who looks angry now, to have these children flaunted before her. *Iodama said their 'marriage' is more an alliance, but this must still matter on some level. At some point in the past, they must have been truly aligned, and truly a couple…*

'We must not let mortals forget that our capacity for miracles remains,' Zeus goes on. 'And a well-built woman is an invitation, is it not? Behold, my latest offspring.'

Women, so the gossip runs, often claim a god has impregnated them. Often it's an excuse to cover a much more mortal liaison. But I now know that such liaisons are possible, and that my own origins lie in two such acts. I wonder if Hermes knows who I am, and that my mother is his descendant?

The two cloaked figures reach the dais, make their obeisance and turn to face the crowd. Their attendants rearrange the folds that have draped their heads, and there's a buzz of comment: the boy, if he is truly only pubescent, is prodigious – the size of most grown men. Both have golden hair and a statuesque bearing – but their faces are concealed behind beaten gold masks, the boy a lion and the girl a falcon.

Despite the masks and the daemon forms, I know who they are. I know the shape of their bodies, the way their hair whorls at the crown as if they were family. We know our own, and these twins are people I've watched grow for half my teenage years.

I look about carefully. No one else appears to know them, so I conceal my recognition. I shrink behind Athena – I have no desire for the twins to identify me either, especially here.

'Come!' Zeus calls. 'Will my family bless my offspring? Let me start proceedings! This will be an "awakening" as we used to perform it in earlier days, each of us blessing our new *theioi* in turn!' He places a hand on each of their masked heads. 'I awaken thee, as my progeny, and extend my protection. What gifts are mine, I grant to thee!'

I frown. This is like but yet unlike my own awakening. I glance questioningly at Athena, but she's watching the dais, engrossed but alert. Then Apollo – ever swift on the uptake – steps forward. 'I will gladly bestow my blessing on your son, sire!' he cries, laying his hand on the boy's forehead. 'Let this young man have the seer's eye.'

I didn't know your gift could be chosen when awakened. It's something to ask Athena about, later.

Artemis hurries forward and rests her hand on the girl's forehead. The girl flinches, but stands her ground. 'Let her be a huntress,' Artemis announces. 'Let her be ever-youthful!'

Zeus makes an approving gesture.

Hermes steps to the boy's side. 'May he be fleet of foot and perceptive of eye,' he says, in a high, carrying voice. I fancy that, behind the lion mask, the boy swells with excitement.

Ares is hot on Hermes's heels, his massive hand almost engulfing the boy's skull. 'Let him become a supreme warrior, leading armies to victory!' he roars, buffeting the boy's shoulder good-naturedly. 'Let glory accrue to his name!'

Aphrodite follows close behind. 'May this girl be the loveliest of mortals,' she cries, cupping the girl's chin, staring through the mask into her eyes. 'Be confident of bearing, my dear. Shine, and all men will want you. Your place will be assured and you will never want.'

'Compare the gifts of Artemis and Aphrodite,' Athena whispers in my ear, then she straightens, pursing her lips sourly. 'It seems I must contribute to this farce.'

She coolly approaches the dais, pausing before the girl, then moving to the boy. He flinches at her touch and she laughs drily. 'Just testing you, lad.' She turns to place her hand on the girl's head. 'Be sound of judgement. Think before you act, and act with reason.' She sniffs at the boy. 'There, you'd have liked that, wouldn't you? Might've done you good.' She inclines her head to Zeus and backs away.

The gathering falls silent.

'What says my good brother Hades?' Zeus announces.

'They don't *want* my blessing,' Hades replies archly, and indeed the twins' bodies have stiffened – they look terrified.

Zeus makes a gesture of acknowledgement then twists on his throne to look at Hera. 'Then it remains only for my consort to give her blessing, on this auspicious day.'

Hera looks as though she'd rather slap someone.

I'm trying to fathom the interplay here: Zeus and Hera might not be married as a human understands marriage, so she isn't a jilted wife, but this is symbolic – Zeus seduced another woman, and Hera must either bless the results or deepen their rift. I've seen love end like this – where one person holds the upper hand and slowly grinds the other down, exploiting their vulnerability. And the matter of Dodona is yet to be raised: Zeus wanted it, and Hera was powerless to stop him. This is another demonstration of his mastery over her.

But what else *is it?*

While Hera broods, I question Athena in a low voice. 'What's just been done to those children?'

'They've been awakened as *theioi*, only their gifts will be manifold; they will be everything – magus, seer, champion and avatar – with the personal gifts each god brings also.'

'I thought there was only one awakening, and you received the gifts suited to your nature?'

'That's the ideal. Forcing gifts upon *theioi* children like this rarely ends well. Unless they have the mental and emotional strength not to be crushed by those gifts, they'll crack. Think of Icarus, or Bellerophon.'

I give her a startled look. Bellerophon, dead twenty years, was also descended from Sisyphus. He flew to Olympus to challenge the gods, the tale goes, and was cast down. *My own blood...* Is she warning me?

Hera rises stiffly from her throne and walks over to the young girl with a slow, measured tread. 'Let my gift be of a fruitful womb, and let that and all her other gifts accrue upon her *marriage*,' she says, with sullen solemnity. 'She is now sealed,' she adds, and for a moment the girl is touched with radiance.

The Queen of the Gods sits again, amidst a fresh stir, and now it's Zeus shifting uncomfortably in his seat. 'What did Hera do?' I whisper.

Athena gives me an impatient look. 'Hera is Goddess of Womanhood – she's just bound up all these changes to the girl's *theia*-nature to her marriage. And by *sealing* her, Hera is preventing any others from revoking what's already been given.'

Athena looks like she's cursing inwardly that she hadn't thought to do something similar.

I am still taking that in when Zeus's voice booms out again.

'Thank you all,' he says in a put-out voice, as if Hera has surprised and undermined him. 'It has been long since we united in such a blessing.' He gestures and the two masked children are taken aside, surrounded by men of Zeus's retinue.

Am I the only one who's identified them, apart from Zeus's people?

The servants circulate with more wine and honey cakes, which Theseus wolfs down. Athena is still gazing after the children. 'Those of us who bless *theioi* invest something of ourselves in them, Odysseus. When you die, it will kill part of me. Was that the real purpose of this "birthday blessing"? To ensure that if one of these children falls, we're all damaged? It's how we used to do things.'

'Then the fate of those children matters, doesn't it?'

'Only if they fulfil their promise. You *theioi* have your advantages, but not all kings are god-touched, nor are all the best warriors. Even the greatest spear must still be wielded well.'

After an initial burst of chatter, the gathering settles again, everyone's attention returning to the throne. Zeus waits until the last voice subsides before rising.

'And now for the real matter at hand,' he announces. 'There is an apple of discord, which we must bite. The name of the apple is *Dodona*.'

The tension of the gathering resurfaces. Glancing towards Hera, I see the Pythia whispering urgently in her ear.

'The oracle at Dodona had fallen silent!' Zeus says, his voice cracking out across the gathering like a thunderclap. 'You all know the place: a shrine that was once of Gaia, then Themis, but taken under the aegis of my consort Hera. But for years now the oracles have grown increasingly fallible, and my consort's sisterhood of crones did nothing.'

'There was nothing to be done,' Hera retorts, her voice strained and angry.

'There is always something to be done!' Zeus replies. 'Worship! *Sacrifice!* When my priests entered Dodona in the spring, the answer was apparent: the spinsters that served the shrine had lost their fervour! They needed to give more! They needed to *sacrifice* more! And so they have!'

Hera's face becomes ashen. 'What have you done with *my* priestesses?'

The Skyfather smiles smoothly. 'We reminded them that at the inception of the shrine, a dozen women had been trapped by an earthquake in a subterranean ritual chamber. In their final suffering, those poor tortured creatures broke through to the Viper's Path. It is to their spirits we hearken to gain prophecies at Dodona.'

'What's happened?' Athena breathes, in a faintly appalled voice.

'We put it to your women that a fresh sacrifice was required,' Zeus says. 'A noble sacrifice, for which they needed little persuasion.'

'*No!*' Hera cries.

I feel like a poisonous snake is writhing in my gut.

Zeus conjures parchment from the air. 'And from Dodona we have our first prophecy in more than a year, received in vivid clarity by *my* priests! "*Fast comes the season of wrath, and the avenging sons.*" Intriguing, yes? And thanks to *my* action, not my consort's idleness!'

Hera rises, her wrath like a huge, vengeful shadow. 'What did you do to them?'

'We walled them into the old ritual chamber,' Zeus says. 'They entered willingly.'

'My seers... My avatars...' Hera snarls. 'Murderer.'

'*They entered willingly*,' the Skyfather repeats.

For a few moments Hera can't even speak, then she grates out, 'I have other such sites, Pytho supreme among them. I see the future clearer than thou, *my husband*, and I counsel you to step away from this brink!'

But Zeus has no such intention of backing down – that seems clear to me.

'I see we're no longer of one mind... *Consort*,' the Skyfather replies. He turns to face the gathered court. 'And that is the true nature of this apple of discord. I am King of the Gods; my mastery is undisputed. But armour is only as strong as its weakest point, and mine is my consort. The Goddess rules a cult of *women*, who guard their secrets and rituals from outsiders. In doing so, they limit their worship! Yet Attican men as well as women give reverence to Athena. Look how her worship is increasing. And reverence to Aphrodite grows apace.'

'I am the prime goddess of Mycenae, and of all Achaea,' Hera replies, grim-faced. 'The mightiest rulers of Achaea offer prayer and sacrifice to me! Me!'

'But would they offer it, if you weren't my stated consort?' Zeus asks, in a diffident voice.

'The worship of the Earth Mother is as ancient as that of the Sky,' Hera answers, with an arrogant tilt of the head. 'It is inextricable from the land itself. Perhaps you forget that half of all mankind is female?'

'But the world is changing, Lady Hera, in ways that you *aren't*. Women are half the world, but are they the half that *matters*? "The weaker sex" are mostly confined to home and hearth: that is the role allotted by *nature*. It has become a man's world, my Lady. Such a world requires a different kind of queen.'

'A world where women grovel before men? Where did that deluded fantasy come from? Your eastern friends?'

'It is the new world! Achaea is failing! The Hittite Empire is the mightiest power in our hemisphere, and they have a different vision to yours. That is why I called this gathering here, in Luwia! Because this is where the beating heart of the Aegean now lies! There are more people in a single kingdom of Luwia – Seha or Arzawa or Troy – than all of Achaea! More fighting men, more worshippers! That is the reality!'

I glance over at Athena, and see her biting her lip in vexation. Yet her eyes are intent, as if she sees opportunity here, not just threat.

Zeus spreads his arms wide. 'But why listen to my word? Let us hear the voice of the common man!'

'What?' Hera sneers. 'What would such an untutored *beast* have to contribute?'

'That is my point!' Zeus cries out, jabbing a finger at Hera. 'You dismiss men as beasts, but they father the next generations of *worshippers*. The dominant gender, the decision makers, the protectors, the earners! Their voice must be heard first, and shall be!' He strides to the front of the dais. 'Find me a man, any local man, and bring him here! Let him be the judge – yes, the judge! Who is best suited to be Queen of the Gods?'

I feel my eyes bulge in surprise, even though Athena has warned me that the King of the Gods likes to surprise his court. And almost immediately, someone from within Zeus's retinue shouts, 'Here's a skulker!', and shoves a ragged young man into our midst, a shepherd by his garb. A male satyr rubs the shepherd's eyes, and then he seems to see us. He visibly shrinks into himself, falling to his knees.

The newcomer is half-naked, dressed only in sheepskins, with a narrow, angular skull and jet-black hair. *He's a Trojan*, is my first thought. He's not unlike Skaya-Mandu, in fact: the same deep-set eyes and jaw, but burlier, taller, harder – a man bred to the wilds. He's staring about in awe. I wonder if he has any idea what he's stumbled into? Or has this whole scene been stage-managed?

And then I'm wondering how he can see us, and why the satyr was able to manhandle him. But no one else seems to be asking these questions, so I infer that there are ways and means to do what Theseus earlier couldn't.

Hera has retreated to her throne, clearly enraged, as is her retinue. I can see that Athena is torn, and I realize there must be some very deep-rooted enmity between Hera and my patron. *In the myths Athena is purely Zeus's child*, I remember. I come up with an explanation for that, based on my new understanding of the gods: *Athena's cult has been a reaction against, and a rival to, Hera's. They give scant regard to Hera in Attica, as I recall. But Athena is no happier with Zeus's pronouncements about women than Hera. That's why she's torn.*

'What is your name, shepherd?' Zeus says, silencing the court with a gesture.

'My name is Parassi,' the shepherd replies, in broken Achaean.

'You speak our tongue?'

The shepherd bows his head. 'My father taught me,' he stammers, 'so I may speak to traders.'

'Are you married, Parassi?'

'No... er, Honoured Sir...?'

'Majesty,' Zeus corrects.

The shepherd falls to his knees and buries his face in his hands. 'I meant no offence,' he pleads.

'And none was taken,' Zeus says, in a magnanimous voice. 'Rise, good shepherd. You are welcome amongst us. Someone bring him wine.'

There is a pause while the shepherd drinks, with everyone too confused to do more than mutter to their neighbours. I look for Kyshanda, and find her beside Aphrodite. Skaya-Mandu is in urgent conversation with the Goddess of Love, but Kyshanda is staring at the shepherd with searing intensity. Perhaps she feels my gaze, for she glances at me, a warning on her face that I can't interpret.

'Now!' Zeus says from the dais, bringing our attention back to the shepherd. 'Let me simplify matters for our new friend. We're debating what sort of woman a man desires as wife.' He holds up a hand to forestall a tirade from Hera. 'No! This is the crux! A queen is still a wife! A wife rules the home, never mind whether it is a hut or a palace. She bears peasants or princes – they are implanted the same way, and come out the same way! But what manner of woman should she be?'

'Why not ask women what they need in a man,' Hera heckles.

'If we ever need to know, perhaps I shall,' Zeus answers. 'Come here, friend Parassi. Don't be afraid.' He pulls the trembling young man onto the dais. 'We merely want your *opinion* – there's no right or wrong answer.' With a cruel smile, Zeus turns to the gathered court. 'Let the women of my family state their cases: why should they be considered the perfect mate?'

'Oh, you arsehole,' Athena mutters.

I am filled with foreboding. 'Say nothing,' I urge her. 'Don't play his game.'

Athena shoots me a forbidding look. It's been too easy to forget I'm not standing next to an ordinary woman. 'Don't presume to tell me what to do.'

Zeus looks around the court. 'Artemis, daughter, have you nothing to say?'

'Virgin girls are my concern, Father. Marriage is nothing to me.' Her answer sounds rehearsed.

Zeus turns towards Athena. 'And you, daughter?'

'Say nothing,' I urge her again, risking her anger.

She ignores me. 'Father, it's *obvious* I cannot be your consort.'

'This is a hypothetical discussion, dear daughter.' Zeus gestures floridly. 'I only wish this young man to have as wide a choice as possible.'

Despite my advice, Athena replies once more – perhaps she feels this is a chance to make a point that will otherwise be lost?

'Very well,' she says. 'Despite my sacred virginity, I do have something to say about womanhood and marriage.' She steps through the press, removing her helm and standing before the shepherd. 'Parassi, do you see this helm? What does it mean? I'll tell you – it signifies that all women are warriors. You are confused? Let me elucidate: life is a struggle – for survival, for food, water, shelter, and the means to support a family. Do you agree?'

The shepherd seems too overcome by her magnificence to respond, but belatedly his brain catches up with his eyes. 'Ye-yes, I understand,' he stammers.

'A woman fights that battle every bit as much as her man. He goes to war, she to the birthing bed. From both, many do not return. She tills the pitiless fields. She puts food in his mouth as surely as he puts it in hers. Men and women must be partners: two wills and two wits, as together they are twice as strong, twice as wise as one person alone. Think of your own parents: the long suffering they have shared to provide for you. If your mother was an idler or a coward, would you even be alive today?' Athena puts her hand on her heart and then his. 'Choose a warrior-wife, Parassi, and no matter the challenge, together you will conquer.'

The Trojan shepherd raises a shaking hand and covers hers, pressed to his heart.

'A warrior-wife,' he echoes.

Well done, I think, impressed beyond my expectations. And unable not to steal a glance at Kyshanda: our eyes meet for a heartbeat before she looks swiftly away.

I would fight for you. Believe it.

As Athena descends from the dais, Zeus strides to the fore again. 'A warrior-wife,' he echoes. He gestures towards Aphrodite, now staring at Athena with a fierce look on her lovely face. 'Does the Goddess of Love have anything?' the Skyfather asks. 'Or indeed, does the patron of marriage, my good consort Hera, wish to speak up for her gender? Or do you no longer offer counsel for those eager to learn of wedlock?'

Hera rises, giving Zeus a foul look, and stalks towards the young shepherd. 'What a man needs from his wife is a *provider*. Ignore Athena, Parassi: what can she, a cold-hearted virgin, know of these things? You need a young woman, lissom in youth, who will become the mother of your children and your comfort in old age. Someone who understands the turning seasons of the land, and of her body and yours. Who can unlock the bounty of life and present it to you. Your ease, your comfort, your wealth and your joy. With such a one, you will have all the fruits of the world.'

The shepherd looks overwhelmed. 'Everything I want will be mine?'

'All,' Hera repeats. 'A true woman can give you whatever you wish.'

For a few moments, silence reigns, and even Zeus looks uncertain, as if he is reappraising this charade. For 'charade' is what it is – I know it, deep in my bones. *What has Zeus already planned?*

Then Aphrodite claps her hands twice, slowly and sarcastically, and sways forward. 'The virgin and the crone think they know about what lies between a man and a woman,' she mocks, as she circles to Parassi's left, drawing his eyes away from Hera and Athena. 'Parassi,' she croons, gliding into his reach. 'Poor lonely shepherd, with just your pipes and your sheep, sleeping rough in the wilds for months on end. What do you dream of? Mmm? A virgin with a spear to drive off the wolves? Of course not: *you* drive off the wolves. You are the warrior, the only warrior you need. So not *her* then,' she concludes, flicking a disdainful hand towards Athena, then leaning closer – clearly giving the stunned shepherd a very good look at her bosom. 'Maybe a "provider", but for heaven's sakes, man, you *have* a mother! Who needs another?'

A raucous laugh from Aphrodite's and Apollo's attendants punctuates this salvo.

'What you want,' Aphrodite murmurs, in a lush, sensuous voice, 'is a woman who wants to give you *herself*. Every *inch* of herself.' She unpins her hair and tosses it free, then pulls her embroidered bodice wide, fully exposing her voluptuous breasts. 'From her heart,' she purrs hoarsely, as if overcome with need herself, 'to her belly, where she'll carry the child your love engenders…' The bodice is gone, the sashes binding her flounced skirts loosened, exposing her belly, her pubis…

The shepherd's eyes are going to explode, I think. My own heart is thudding, my throat like a desert. Aphrodite is, after all, *Goddess of Love*.

She lets the remaining cloth slide off her hips. 'All she wants is you inside her *wet, empty cleft*, which she *longs* for you to fill, as often and in as many ways as you desire… *Because. All. She. Desires. Is. You.*'

It's not just her words or her extraordinary, naked body. The very air about her is throbbing now with heat and ripe sexuality, so much so that everyone is flushed of face and staring, or staring away, with equal intensity.

Parassi falls to his knees, clutching his now no doubt fully aroused loins in embarrassed desire. 'You,' he sobs. 'You. I need you.'

Athena rolls her eyes in utter disgust. On the dais, Hera is doing the same.

'Please, Lady, marry me,' Parassi begs Aphrodite.

'She's taken, boy,' Ares growls, striding to the Love Goddess's side to scoop up her garments and thrust them at her. 'She's mine.'

Ironic, considering she's supposedly Hephaestus's wife, not Ares's... Not that you'd know to see them.

'But... I...' the shepherd wails.

'Hush,' Aphrodite says, though I can hear cold cruelty coiled inside her overt kindness. 'I know, I know... But I swear to you, I'll see you wed to the most beautiful woman in the world.'

It sounds like a consolatory platitude, but I have a sudden thought. I look around, wondering...

Aphrodite gestures, and a swarm of her female attendants close in around the shepherd and lead him away. I cast a glance at Kyshanda, a suspicion forming.

Who, I wonder, actually is the most beautiful woman in the world?

10 – A Goddess Scorned

'...yet Hera saw what passed... and straight away she taunted Zeus son of Cronos: "O devious one, which of the gods has been plotting with you now? You always love to wait until I am absent before scheming secret things and hatching plans. Never are you willing to tell me openly what you are purposing to do."'
—Homer, *Iliad*

Luwia

Athena has her back to the dais, grinding her heel savagely into the turf. Peering around her, I can see mocking looks from the retinues of Apollo and Artemis, and triumphal crowing among those of Ares and Aphrodite. Those about Hermes seem indifferent, their attention on Zeus, while Hades and his consort are detached and alert. There seems no imminent threat, but I have no doubt that my mistress's standing has been weakened.

I was right, she shouldn't have spoken. She should have poured scorn on this farce.

But done is done. The real loser has been Hera.

Amidst the swirl of attendants about her throne, the goddess rises to speak, her face pale but dignified, her voice as inflexible as bronze. 'So the harlot wins the beauty contest by flashing her crotch. What next, husband – will Hermes prove he can run faster than crippled Hephaestus?' She snaps her fingers. 'All this proved was that Trojan shepherds can't think past the end of their cocks. And, perhaps, nor can the King of the Gods?'

'We all know what it showed,' Zeus replies. 'Your cult has lost touch with half of humanity. But Aphrodite's hasn't.'

'So?' Hera demands, drawing herself to her full height. 'Am I still your consort?'

That impresses me – confronting the question head-on. It requires courage, and I see immediately that Zeus is taken aback. He'd expected some kind of meek collapse or conciliatory words, not blunt defiance.

'I have never been hasty,' the Skyfather replies carefully, backing away from a potential precipice. 'These are momentous matters. One shepherd's opinion, however heartfelt, does not decide the will of Olympus. We must take counsel and consider deeply, as we did when our alliance was forged so long ago.'

'And?' Hera demands.

Zeus frowns. 'You are still my Queen.' He makes a move to embrace her, a public show of unity.

'Excellent. Are we done here?' In a swirl of robes Hera and her attendants sweep from the dais, leaving Zeus marooned mid-gesture. He lowers his arms, glowering at her retreating back. Then Aphrodite, clothed once more, appears at his side, whispering urgently in his ear. The other deities are already drifting apart, as though they can no longer bear to be near each other.

Athena touches my arm. 'Go – tell Hera I need to speak to her directly.'

I obey instantly, hurrying towards the Queen's retinue, to be intercepted by my grandmother, the Pythia. 'Yes?' Amphithea says, her voice as cold as her eyes.

'Greetings, Grandmother,' I reply, suppressing my emotions. *This is the woman who ordered my death.* 'My Lady wishes to speak to yours.'

'The Queen has nothing to say to one who would usurp her.'

'My mistress has disavowed the contest – she made that clear,' I reply, improvising. 'She thought it demeaning and insulting, and offers her counsel.'

The Pythia considers, before leaving me and speaking with Hera. 'Very well,' she says on her return. 'Take the third path on the right; it will bring you to a clearing.'

I catch her arm. 'Grandmother, at Pytho – how much could you have left unsaid in the presence of my parents?'

The old seeress scowls. 'None of it. When I walk the Viper's Path, what comes, comes.' She shakes her arm free. 'My daughter was always a disappointment to me, and when the Viper spoke, I was appalled. To betray her husband and bear another man's child is despicable. Especially to that man! Anticleia is dead to me, and I would that you were never born. Many people have sought to extinguish the line of Prometheus, boy. Some of them are here tonight.'

Then she turns and stalks away.

I stand, stock-still. It's not just the viciousness of her words that appals me. All my fears are returning. Across the lawn, Kyshanda and Skaya-Mandu are staring at me. *They know me as the 'Man of Fire'; they must have guessed 'the Tormented' is Prometheus. Does that mean they know about Sisyphus and my mother? If so, who have they told?* Sickened, I hurry back to Athena and Theseus.

'By Tartarus, she's got a magnificent pair,' Theseus is enthusing, gawping towards Aphrodite. 'I know it's her daemon, but that's what you get when you bed her true aspect, isn't it? By the Balls of Cronos, I could—'

'Theseus, shut up!' Athena snaps in exasperation, before turning to me. 'Well?'

'She'll speak with you, Lady.'

Athena sighs in relief. Around us the crowd has dissolved into knots of people gossiping. The shepherd Parassi has been hurried away, as have the two children, which is doubtless prudent. I'd have loved a few minutes with either party – there seems much more to learn.

'Come – we're short of time,' Athena says. When I give her a quizzical look, she adds, 'I can't stay in an avatar body for more than an hour or two.'

Once again, I feel strangely confused. How can Athena be so vulnerable when her whole presence, her thrilling, mesmerising aura, projects such power and strength? But I thrust those questions among the others stacked like spears in the back of my mind.

We regain our weapons and leave, passing bushes that are alive with amorous grunts and squeals from nymphs and their companions. The sky remains a limpid blue, but the twilight is darkening towards night. We stride down the path, taking the third right to enter a small dell.

Hera, the Pythia and her other attendants are already present, including two warriors who step in front of us. Both are mature men, big-boned veterans. Theseus goes to greet them, but I hang back, listening in on Athena's conversation with Hera.

The two goddesses exchange perfunctory kisses, then face each other, expressions grim.

'You took part in that stupid contest,' Hera says.

'So did you,' Athena snaps back.

'I had no choice, once you had,' Hera retorts. 'You gave credence to the Skyfather's game. Who ever heard of such nonsense – a shepherd judging goddesses! You should have laughed at him!'

'Aphrodite would have spoken regardless. It was set up for her. Did you want that vixen's voice to be the only one heard? Exploiting the fantasy that women are mere vessels for men's lust? As if she really believes that! At least you and I defended what a woman should be.'

'In so far as a dry virgin can ever speak for all women. Only *I* represent all the seasons of our gender. Only *I* recognize that men and women must be equals for both to thrive in harmony. My worship is as old as time; Zeus-Tarhum cannot discard me! I've swallowed pretenders before and I'll do it again. The highest goddess in Troy is Arriniti, and she is *subservient* to Tarhum. I'll never become what she is.'

Athena seizes on this: 'That's the real issue: Zeus thinks to spread his worship across the Aegean, knowing ours is tied to Achaea. Why? Because the oracles speak of war between Troy and Achaea, a war we can't win!' She extends a hand halfway between them. 'Hera, we face the same threat.'

'Then serve me!' Hera exclaims, ignoring the offered hand. 'I'll protect you.'

'Protect yourself,' Athena retorts. 'I'm not beholden to you. Every fighting man in Attica offers prayer to me, and the women too. My worship thrives.'

'In Attica alone,' Hera sneers. 'Little fool. I could crush you – any one of us could.'

'Try it.'

'Don't you think Zeus would be laughing to hear you both?' I exclaim. It's probably wiser to keep my mouth shut. But I can hear this discussion descending into mayhem fast.

The mountainous weight of Hera's sudden gaze bears down on me. 'Who gave this creature leave to speak?' she cries, striding towards me, eyes blazing. 'Yes, I see the lineage, the flame-hair burning. What game are you playing, Athena, protecting the last of Prometheus's blood?' She stops in front of me as my bowels turn to water, glaring down at me from an immense height – and in one startling instant, she's maid, mother and crone all at once. 'Speak unbidden again, and I'll rip your tongue out and feed it to the crows.'

Athena lays a hand on my shoulder, her fingers biting deep. 'He's mine to punish, not yours.'

'Beware the dog you feed, Virgin. He'll bite you – treachery is bred into him.' Hera throws me one last look of pure contempt. 'If you won't serve me in this struggle, Athena, I have nothing further to say.'

'An alliance of equals, or nothing,' Athena says, flatly.

'Equals?' Hera shakes with derisory laughter. 'Go *fuck* yourself… Oh, wait, you're even denied that pleasure!' She waves a dismissive hand. 'Don't you ever try and put yourself ahead of me again or I'll shunt you off to Tartarus and find you a white-hot pile of coals to squat on, so you can warm your sterile little twat on it for all eternity.'

Athena stiffens, then spins on her heels to storm from the dell. Theseus throws her two champions an apologetic 'it's her, not me' look, feigns drinking a pint of ale and follows. I send one final glance towards my grandmother, hoping for some scrap of empathy, but Amphithea's face is stony and pitiless.

For a moment, I feel like a man who's wagered his fortune on a horse, only for it to pull up lame before the race begins. But bets once placed can't be redeemed. I look at Theseus, hoping for some scrap of comfort. 'What did you make of that?' I ask.

Of course, he just laughs. 'Have to say, I'd have picked Aphrodite, given my druthers. Rather share my bed with a willing bit of snatch than some woman who thinks she rules you.'

'I heard that,' Athena calls back, 'and guess what? I *do* rule you! Keep up!'

–

As we reach our original meadow, Athena vanishes without a word, leaving Iodama slumped over with her shoulders drooping; she looks as dog-tired as I'm feeling. It's quickly apparent that she's aware of all that has happened, and is in a foul mood. 'You can't say it wasn't coming,' she mutters. 'That damned new Trojan harbour has changed everything.'

'Do *all* the prophecies say Achaea is doomed?' I ask.

'Aye,' Iodama admits sourly. 'They'll cut off our tin trade, and Achaea will run out of bronze for tools and weaponry. We'll be strangled, as the Pythia foretold.'

I think hard for a moment, then ask, 'Do prophecies always come true?'

Theseus gives me an odd look, but Iodama gestures dismissively. 'It's time to return.'

It's now late in the evening, and twilight is almost spent. Far across the foothills, I can make out the shining expanse of the Aegean Sea, shimmering in the last light of evening. It's a beautiful sight, but my mind is on Kyshanda. Why was she so intense, so *worried* at the sight of that shepherd, Parassi?

Then Iodama says something in a tongue I don't recognize, and a silvery thread appears at each of our navels that runs straight and true to the south-west. 'Your cord of life will always lead you home,' she tells me.

I feel it thrum as I touch it. Then Iodama grasps our hands and draws us spiralling through the twilight. Time is hard to measure here, but it seems our journey lasts only a few minutes before I fall back into my own body in a dizzying rush. *Perhaps the silver cord helps to pull you home?* Whatever the reason, feeling my own skin enclose me is a profound relief. I have a blurred vision of Eurybates hovering above me, and then I'm sinking into darkness…

–

Phocis

'Get up – we all need to talk,' a voice says from the doorway of the hut.

From its timbre, it seems Iodama has been inhabited by Athena again. I rise from my bed, clumsy with sleep, and stop, confused as it's Iodama's body that I see: thin, serious, clad in a plain blue-grey cloak, with straggling grey-brown hair. Only her eyes are different – grey orbs flecked with gold, penetrating, vibrant and remote.

Presumably she doesn't feel the need to impress anyone here with her appearance, I guess, knowing now as I do that any form of magic is exhausting, even for a goddess.

It's evening, the day after the Olympian Court. I slept far into the morning, as did Iodama and Theseus. At midday we'd all besieged Bria and Eurybates, seeking food and water and bringing them up to date with the events of the previous day, before heading back to bed. Now twilight is claiming the last of the day as I emerge and join the others around the campfire.

Theseus is holding forth once more with Bria. 'Honestly, she had the best tits I've ever—' Then, catching sight of Athena's angry glare, he breaks off to say, 'Uh, good morning, evening, whatever. If you'd flashed yours, you might've come second. Although that Hera… A fine figure of a woman! Mother's milk, heh!'

'It's hard to imagine why you were once considered the smartest of the *theioi*,' Athena comments acidly. 'Simpler times, I suppose.'

'Better times,' Theseus says heartily, missing the jibe. 'Go in, kill the monster, nail the girl. Hey, Ithacan, have I told you about Ariadne? Silly chit really thought it was true love, but it was her sister I really fancied—'

'Stop wasting my time!' Athena snaps. 'Iodama can't sustain my presence all night. So, what really happened at that damned Olympian Court last night? Your opinions, please.'

Everyone looks down at their feet, then I say, 'I've got some questions.'

'All you've ever got is bloody questions,' Theseus jeers. Bria presses her finger to the big man's lips, shaking her head. Eurybates meets my eyes, and we share a look of resignation.

I launch my case: 'First, what kind of shepherd speaks a foreign tongue? Two: why did his face resemble Skaya-Mandu's? Three: who were Zeus's twin children, and what can they now *not* do? Four: who's the most beautiful woman in the world?'

Eury winks approvingly, Bria gives me an appreciative look, while Athena's glittering eyes narrow. 'You think the shepherd is a Trojan prince?' the goddess asks.

'I think "Parassi" is a shepherd in the same way Laertes is a farmer: he owns flocks of sheep. And he just *happens* to wander by? I think he was preselected. Then Aphrodite promised him "the most beautiful woman in the world". Who might that be?'

'According to "Parassi", it's the Clamshell herself.'

Clamshell? Ah, yes, that Cypriot myth about Aphrodite's birth. I suppress a smile.

'Can't be – Aphrodite said "woman", so goddesses are off the list,' Bria says. 'I've heard the seer Tiresias's daughter is stunning: Manto, her name is.'

'Must look her up,' Theseus grunts. He nudges me. 'That Trojan piece of tail you were working on was a looker too – Cassandra or whatever? The Trojan King's eldest too – quite a catch, Ithacan!' He manages to make it sound as though I have absolutely no chance with Kyshanda at all – but that *he* does, given the chance.

As for 'piece of tail'… I want to smash his nose out the other side of his head.

'My point,' I say, restraining my temper with difficulty, 'is that whoever it *was*, they're about to be usurped by that girl every Olympian goddess has just blessed. You heard all those gifts she was given. Beauty, power, intelligence, prowess.'

'Wasted on a woman, apart from the beauty bit,' Theseus sighs, earning filthy looks from Athena and Bria.

'But who is she?' Athena asks, tersely.

The thing is, I already know. But I'm not sure I should tell my new associates – especially Theseus. But then the Pythia's vapour-maddened words come back to me in a rush. '*Twin-finder*', she called me. The oracle had known I'd meet them and that it would be significant. Perhaps I have no choice but to share what I know; perhaps the future depends upon it – but is it a good future?

Feeling like a king passing judgement on some monstrous crime, I say, 'I recognized both those children: the girl is Princess Helen of Lacedaemon, and the boy is her twin brother, Polydeuces.'

'By Cronos's balls, how do you know?' Athena demands. 'They were masked!'

'When I turned fourteen, I was sent to Sparta in Lacedaemon, to learn of courtly life. Laertes is beholden to King Tyndareus of Sparta, and he was grateful for the chance given to me. At that time, the sons of Atreus – Agamemnon and Menelaus – were refugees in Sparta, because they were still too young to challenge his murderer, the usurper Thyestes, for the throne of Mycenae. I'm much the same age as Agamemnon's brother Menelaus, and we became good friends. So I was permitted into the Spartan royal family's inner circles. I last saw the twins two years ago, but I'd recognize them anywhere.'

Theseus speaks up, his voice testy. 'For those of us who don't give a liquid *kopros* about other men's children, who's who in Sparta these days?'

'You must know Tyndareus is still king,' I answer, trying not to sound condescending, but likely failing. 'He's in his fifties now. Leda, his wife, is much younger – thirty-something. They were married when she was barely of age.'

'I know *that*,' Theseus interrupts. 'Gorgeous little peach, she was.'

Evidently Zeus thought so too...

'Leda had twins,' I continue. 'A boy, Castor, and a girl, Clytemnestra. But a year later, while Tyndareus was on campaign, Leda became pregnant again. Tyndareus has raised the second pair of twins as his own, but those of us close to the family know he's not the father. The whisper was that Queen Leda claimed some wild tale of sleepwalking and waking up beside a *swan*.'

'The queen fucked a swan in her sleep! Now I've heard everything!' Theseus roars with laughter. 'I tell you, if your woman ever says she's been with a god, she means your best friend or your brother.'

'After you, anyone would seem godlike,' Bria says, snidely.

'Are you children done?' Athena snaps. 'Go on, Odysseus.'

'Leda insisted it was *Zeus* making love to her. But Menelaus suspects she was drunk – when I was in Sparta, she often was.'

'Indeed?' Athena says. 'That might give her story veracity: people who've lain with a divinity pine after that moment for the rest of their lives.'

'I have that effect too,' Theseus puts in.

'Except in reverse,' Bria answers, ducking as Theseus swats at her ear.

'But now Zeus claims them,' Athena muses. 'And he's awakened them as *theioi* in the old fashioned way. *Fascinating*.'

'Tell me again why their awakening was different, and what it means?' I ask.

'It's simple enough,' Athena replies. 'In the past, when we gods were more unified, it was common for *theioi* to be blessed by several gods. It gave each of us a stake in that hero, so theoretically we'd work together. But it led to many problems, and in these jealous times, the practice has been neglected. We now keep our chosen *theioi* very much to ourselves. If those two young people can cope with these multiple gifts, they'll be extraordinarily talented and powerful. But it's just as likely they'll go mad, and be a danger to themselves and those they love. So these days, most heroes – like yourselves – are awoken singly, then sealed.'

'Sealed, meaning no one else can claim us?' I ask, watching hard for her reaction.

'Exactly,' Athena replies. *Did she flinch? For just a fraction of a moment? Have I been sealed?*

'Except to the *theios*'s divine sire, if they're different to their patron,' Bria puts in.

Athena shoots her an annoyed look. 'Oh yes, and that.'

She wasn't going to tell me, I note. *But Bria thinks I should know...*

'So this Helen really could become the most beautiful woman in the world?' Bria asks, perhaps anxious to change the subject before Athena decides exactly how annoyed she is.

'Beauty is in the eye of the beholder,' Athena mutters. 'Some *barbarians* even think the Clamshell is attractive.'

'You lost. Get over it,' Theseus responds.

'That contest was a *farce.*'

'Zeus said "What gifts are mine, I grant to thee",' I put in hastily, to keep the peace. 'What gifts has Zeus actually given to them?'

It's Bria who responds. 'With Zeus, they usually relate to the sky: wind, lightning, flight, wisdom – meaning divine guidance, not logic, I might add – and majesty. They have to have the potential anyway,' she adds: 'You can't make a leaden oaf into a genius.'

'Apollo gifted the boy – Polydeuces, yes? – with a seer's insight,' Athena notes. 'Ares granted him warrior skills, and Hermes gave him speed and keen eyes. He will be an athlete, warrior and war leader, seer and king. One to watch, provided his little brain hasn't been fried inside his skull by all that divine energy.'

'And the girl, Helen?' I ask, as Eury tops up Athena's goblet and fills the other four.

'She received the same blessings from Zeus, plus hunting skills from Artemis, beauty from Aphrodite – which is as much about confidence and glamour as appearance. And I, of course, augmented her native intelligence.' Athena sighs. 'All of which ought to make her quite formidable.'

'Does divine intelligence wear off eventually?' I ask, glancing at Theseus, who is staring vacantly into space.

Athena follows my gaze, and her eyes narrow – but she smiles faintly. Sharing a joke with a goddess is a strange sensation, especially as Athena doesn't really have a sense of humour. 'Perhaps.'

'But then there's Hera's blessing,' Bria says. 'She's postponed Helen's gifts until marriage. Presumably so Helen's more mature by the time she's awakened. But marriage is merely a ceremony.'

'A ceremonial *screwing*,' Theseus throws in, just when I'm sure he's nodded off. 'Awakening is usually tied to a physical event. That bitch Hera tied it to the girl's maidenhead.'

'That's how I interpret it also,' Athena agrees. 'In the early days, we often tied awakening to a physical change in the body that signified maturity. When multi-gifted *theioi* were awakened too soon, they were even more prone to madness. Think about Heracles and all his fits of murderous insanity! Nowadays, we seldom awaken anyone younger than fifteen.'

'So when Helen loses her virginity, she'll suddenly receive all her gifts?' I muse. 'That's going to be quite a first night of marriage.'

'It's cruel,' Eurybates puts in, a sentiment I wholly agree with. He's been mostly silent, perhaps intimidated by the presence of Athena and Theseus, but his comment reminds us all of the reason and human decency Athena is supposed to personify.

'The daughter of Tyndareus, eh…' Theseus says, reflectively. 'He's a shrewd man, Tyndareus, with a nose for gold. He didn't put Agamemnon back on the throne of Mycenae for nothing.

If he knows what his daughter is worth, she'll be sold for a high price.'

'He'll know,' I reply. 'Think about it: she and her brother weren't yet awakened, so they couldn't travel to Luwia as we did. So Tyndareus must have been in on the plan – he must have handed them over to Zeus's people, for them to be taken to Mount Ida. And another thing: within minutes of Helen being transformed into a future prize-bride, Aphrodite is offering that Trojan "shepherd" the most beautiful girl in the world. Coincidence?'

Athena slaps her thigh. 'Zeus was creating an offering for Troy! A wife for their prince, in Helen! And a husband for one of their princesses, in Polydeuces, who will undoubtedly be Zeus's new champion in the near future! He was showing the Trojan royalty what he would bring them. He was displaying the might of Zeus-Tarhum!'

There's a stunned silence, though there shouldn't be – Athena's conclusion had been obvious to me since the start of our discussion. 'Then he really is shifting his power base to Troy,' Bria says. 'It's just a matter of when.'

Our little group falls silent as we sip our wine – which tastes a little bitter now, due to our worries. Athena's worship is tied irrevocably to Attica, so if Zeus is beginning to sever ties to Achaea in favour of Troy, then it could spell the beginning of Athena's end – and by proxy, our own.

Who'll protect me if she disappears? I wonder. It's an ugly scenario, but I have to confront it: I no longer have a homeland or a family – I'm an exile.

But I've never been one to shy away from a puzzle... 'If I were Zeus,' I begin...

Theseus chokes on his wine. '"If I were the King of the Gods", says the Ithacan runt,' he chortles.

'...I'd be looking to marry Helen off to Troy as quickly as possible,' I go on, ignoring the Attican ape. 'We can't be the only ones who've worked out who she is.' Then I pause, reconsidering. 'No, no, wait: Tyndareus allowed those two children to be taken away, but surely with some assurances about their safety. He must *value* them, even if he doesn't love them as his own... Tyndareus knows the price of everything. He would never give anything to the Trojans that might be used against Achaea.'

'He's a trader-king,' Athena says, sourly. 'All things have a price to such men – especially two children who aren't his. And maybe even his loyalty to Achaea?'

'Not Tyndareus,' Eurybates puts in. 'He put Agamemnon on the throne in Mycenae. He is Achaean through and through. I can't believe he would marry those children off to enemies of his people.'

'Unless he's been told that such a marriage would *prevent* war?' I suggest.

'I'm sure Zeus's people would tell him exactly what they thought he wanted to hear,' Athena says bitterly. 'But all we know for sure is that Zeus has plans for those children, and not plans I would approve of. We need to find them...' She purses her lips. 'And kill them.'

'They're *children*!' I exclaim, my natural outrage backed by a flood of guilt. I've been the one to identify them. Beside me, Eurybates looks just as appalled.

'All tyrants, traitors and killers were once children,' Athena replies. 'And with the gifts we were tricked into laying upon them, those two won't be children much longer. If Zeus-Tarhum wishes to hand them to the King of Troy, I'd rather slaughter the pair of them.'

I'm horrified. This is all my fault... *But wait, what if...*

'They're *valuable*, as you've pointed out,' I say. 'But who to? Whoever controls them, that's who! They've been blessed by all the senior gods and goddesses of Olympus, so they're not beholden to any particular one. Polydeuces is free to fight for whoever he chooses, and Helen, once she is... er... *married*, will give her gifts to whoever wins her heart.'

'Sparta is the heart of the Peloponnese,' Eurybates adds. 'Sparta would never betray Achaea.'

Athena studies us with her penetrating grey eyes. Bria is pondering, chin in hand, and even Theseus has a calculating look on his face.

'If those children are left in the hands of Zeus's people,' the Goddess muses, 'they'll grow up thinking whatever Zeus wants them to think. Whether they're in Troy or Sparta, they'll be surrounded by the Skyfather's toadies.' She fixes a hard look on Theseus. 'Could you worm your way into Sparta, and steal them?'

I'm only slightly less unhappy at this turn, but abduction is more acceptable than murder. 'Kidnapping them could be just as damaging,' I put in, before Theseus can respond. 'Tyndareus won't take it lying down. It could even provoke the war you're trying to prevent.'

But Athena isn't listening to me – she's waiting for her trusted champion, the man who's been fighting on her behalf all his life, to speak.

'It's been a while since I was last in Sparta,' Theseus replies, ruminating over his wine cup. 'There's no one there I can't best, but I'd want someone with me I can trust… Pirithous would be perfect.'

I know the name – a northerner, a barbarian chieftain who'd married an Achaean woman named Hippodamia. Their wedding feast was a colossal disaster – the guests were attacked by, well, I've always assumed it was Scythian horsemen, not "centaurs". But maybe men with horses' hindquarters are more plausible than I'd imagined?

'Was that Pirithous I saw you with at the Olympian Court yesterday?' I ask. 'With Hades.'

Theseus grins. 'Yes – he's pledged to Hades. But we've worked together before. I nabbed the old beggar stealing cattle when I was ruling Attica. After I caught him, I found I rather liked him. And the Hades connection has helped us both out,' he adds, speaking directly to Athena.

'At times,' Athena agrees, in a reserved voice. 'I'd rather Hades wasn't involved with this.'

'But Erebus could be the perfect hiding place for these twins, once we've got them out,' Theseus suggests. 'Even Zeus would hesitate to try and extract them from the Underworld.'

'No, not Erebus. We'd never get them back – Hades and Zeus have arrangements I'm not privy to. The Lord of the Underworld has been the Skyfather's gaoler for centuries, and he's close to Hera too. No, I don't want Pirithous involved. Take Hippasus. He's level-headed and capable.'

'But Pirithous is worth three of Hippasus! And he could mediate between us and Hades if we need help.'

Athena falls silent, contemplating.

'Is Erebus an actual place?' I ask. *If gods and monsters are real, I suppose the Underworld might be also...*

'Obviously it's real,' Theseus says scornfully, annoyed at the distracting question.

'No, Theseus!' Athena decides. 'No Erebus, no Pirithous! You'll take them to Attica; I'll deal with them after that. I've plans to raise the boy myself. And I'll choose the girl's husband from among those I favour.'

Theseus scowls. 'You mean that backstabbing mule's arse *Menestheus*, don't you?'

Athena looks him in the eye. 'She'll marry whomsoever I choose, Theseus. If that means the man who deposed you, so be it. You hated being King of Athens anyway – you moaned about it the entire time.'

'That's not the point! He threw me out of *my own city*!'

'And did you a favour,' Athena ripostes. 'Bria will go with you as my eyes and ears. And you'll take Odysseus; he's been in Sparta far more recently than you. You'll heed him. I want this done properly.'

Theseus doesn't look happy. 'It'd be his first mission, and—'

'We all start somewhere. Odysseus, you'll do this?' When I nod, despite my profound misgivings, she turns to Bria. 'I need you to find someone to look after the girl Helen once we've got her: someone calm and maternal.'

'Anticleia would help—' Eurybates begins, and I silence him with a look – there's no way I want my family dragged into this.

'What about my mother, Aethra?' Theseus asks.

Athena looks doubtful, but she acquiesces. 'Very well.' She's clearly tired now, as if she's been in Iodama's body longer than she can easily manage. I'm intrigued by her weaknesses and fallibilities, but clearly I can't ask about them. So my new self, a *theios* insider who knows more than ordinary men about the gods, and conversely reveres them less, simply notes with interest the way Athena's posture – straight-backed, square-shouldered – is sagging, the wrinkles deepening around her eyes and dragging down from the corners of her mouth. I hear an owl shriek in the trees outside, and then I'm looking at an ashen-faced and weary Iodama again.

'I heard it all,' she yawns, in her own voice. 'Theseus, send word to Hippasus and to Aethra, your mother. Odysseus, I want you to draw maps of Sparta and the palace wing where the children dwell, so we can make our plans accordingly.' Then she yawns again and totters out, heading for the hut where she and Bria sleep.

Theseus is toying with his wine goblet; behind his ageing and florid features he's clearly thinking hard. Bria is bright-eyed and eager – she seems to thrive on activity. I draw Eurybates aside. 'This is insanity!' I mutter.

'I know, but I don't think we have a choice,' he replies. Then he heads off to do some chores, while I sit back down, replaying all the events of the last two days in my mind and reviewing the decision that Athena has reached. I decide Eury's right – we have no option but to go along with this scheme.

'I have a question,' I say.

Theseus barks with scornful laughter. 'Another fucking question! Now *there's* a surprise.' He downs his wine and staggers off towards the pissing trench.

'What is it?' asks Bria, leaning towards me, and I'm grateful that one person here will listen.

'Eurybates schooled me in the old tales. He said Aphrodite was once considered Zeus's daughter, though not by Hera. But now I understand the priests say a Titan fathered her?'

'In the old teachings, Aphrodite's mother was Dione,' Bria replies. 'But "Dione" is a feminine form of "Dios", an old word meaning "of Zeus". It implies that Zeus conjured her from his own body. An even earlier tale tells how the titan Uranus had his genitals chopped off. When his semen fell into the sea, Aphrodite appeared, floating on a clamshell. Hence the nickname Theseus loves to use.' Bria strokes her chin, the gesture incongruous in a barely pubescent girl. 'And it's that old tale that's being revived. Perhaps Zeus's priests are trying to deny his fatherhood of her, to prepare Aphrodite as his new consort. Father–daughter marriages are a stretch, even for gods,' she adds, with a sly grin.

'So Zeus has been planning this a long time?' I reply.

'A luxury available to immortals. We can wait generations for the right moment to put the knife in. You've only got a few years.'

'You're such a comfort. Oh, and I trust you'll take a new body to Sparta.'

Bria rolls her eyes. 'Of course. My next one will be built like a *hamazan*.'

The cult of the *hamazan*, as I understand it, is a far-distant one, from east of the Hittite lands – women pledged to live as warriors. They are few, by all accounts, and seldom leave the east, but some travel as mercenaries. It must be a hard life, for they are constantly tested by every man they meet.

'Where will you find her?' I ask, wondering if she has dozens of bodies stashed somewhere, awaiting her needs.

'That, prince of Ithaca, you'll never know. But I'm tired of being trapped in Hebea's body, I can tell you that for free. When you next see me, I'll be *all* woman.' Bria rises, drains her cup and leaves me with the empty amphora. 'Better get busy with those maps – Iodama will want results by the time she wakes tomorrow.'

11 – The Abduction of Helen

'HESIOD: Under what circumstances might one truly trust in men?
HOMER: Where danger itself follows on the heels of action.'
—*Contest of Homer and Hesiod*

Lacedaemon, the Peloponnese

A fortnight after the Olympian Court, I find myself pressed flat on a rocky outcrop in Lacedaemon, overlooking the junction of two dusty roads, with the Bow of Eurytus strung and ready beside me and a quiver on my back. One road comes west from the bustling port of Helos, where we'd disembarked four days ago; the other winds north through forest-clad hills from the islet of Kranae, its stony beaches favoured by smugglers and others who have no wish to be noticed. Naturally I am watching the latter closely.

It's from that direction that the expected traveller appears, a giant of a man on a shambling nag. Clad only in a leather kilt, despite the autumn chill, he's perched his helm in front of him and rides with comfortable assurance, reins loose in one hand and a long spear cradled in the other. He's scanned my hiding place several times, but he doesn't seem to have spotted me, and that's just as I like it.

So this is Hippasus… I know the name from Laertes's stories about the Calydonian Boar: Hippasus, an Arcadian, had joined Laertes and others to hunt down a monstrous beast laying waste to Aetolia. Privately, Laertes has admitted it had been a very ordinary boar, slaughtered in honour of Artemis during a gathering of local rulers. It's odd how some legends grow from ordinary roots, but others – as I'm learning – do have a truly supernatural origin.

I am about to rise and greet Hippasus when I hear a faint sound behind me. I twist round, gripping the bow, mouth dry and heart beating, to discover a woman in a warrior's tunic perched on a boulder twenty feet above me, with an arrow aimed at my head. She has a blockish face, broad, masculine shoulders, a deep tan, pugnacious eyes and black hair tied tightly back.

'Got you, Ithaca,' she says, smugly.

How did I let that happen? 'Good to see you too, Bria,' I grunt. 'Whose body have you stolen this time?'

She strikes a side-on pose, thrusting out her bosom and behind. 'You like? This one's Lanabrea. She was a slave until I found her. Now she lives with Iodama, when I'm not inside her. She and I get on fine, and just so we're clear, she and I will do exactly as we please. Keep your moralising to yourself, Ithaca.'

I study her carefully, looking for a copper bracelet, but "Lanabrea" wears long sleeves. 'Just as long as you keep your mind on the job. Theseus has barely had a sober moment since we parted.'

Bria shrugs. 'He'll be fine. And Hippasus is very solid. They've done this sort of thing for years. When Theseus goes into action, he'll be completely focused.' She slings her bow over her shoulder and sashays down to plant a muscular yet sloppy kiss on my cheek. 'Relax, Ithaca, I'm here.' Then she steps to the edge of the outcrop. 'Hey, Hippasus! I found him right where you said he'd be!'

The big Arcadian snorts with laughter as he swings from his mount. 'Kids think they know it all.'

'It's a good spot,' I say, ruefully, wiping Bria's saliva from my face.

'It is: *too* good. Don't be so obvious in future,' Bria advises.

I look about, taking that advice in. *There's one, two... no, three other vantages that would've done as well, less dominating. Not where*

I'd expect to find someone. I follow Bria down the slope, feeling slightly foolish.

The Arcadian Hippasus has a wild look – he's clearly mountain stock, from the heartland of the Peloponnese. But he has a stolid, businesslike air to him that I warm to. He claps Bria on the back, and gives me a firm grip and an appraising look. 'So you're Athena's new champion. I know your father.'

'Know' in the present tense... So he doesn't know about Sisyphus. Or is he being ironic? Or merely polite? 'Laertes has spoken often of you,' I reply, giving him the benefit of the doubt. 'Theseus and my *keryx* are camped nearby with our horses – I'll take you there.'

Our plans are coming together. The morning after Athena resolved on kidnap, we left Phocis and journeyed to the coast, taking ship at the small port of Haleion. There our ways parted, with Bria abandoning Hebea's body. Iodama has taken the Phocian girl, who is a lot more mature and articulate now, and seems grateful for her new life away from her father. They've gone to our rendezvous point – the town of Aphidna, in Attica, where Aethra, Theseus's mother, has a house.

Theseus, Eurybates and I, equipped by Iodama with a stock of tooled oxhide handcrafts and copper trinkets, have been posing as traders. We headed south for Lacedaemon, landing at Helos, where we bought a mule to carry our merchandise. I'm acting as the supposed merchant, with Eurybates in the role of servant and Theseus as our guard. The Athenian had wanted our roles reversed so he could claim the better rooms at the taverns, but Iodama overruled him – he knows nothing of commerce and cares less. Not that he's much good at fake subservience either.

The main problem has been stopping him going into every tavern and boasting of his exploits. I was at a loss, but Eurybates quickly hit on a solution: a few *obols*, three amphorae of wine and the best whore at whichever hostelry we happened to be staying at. With Theseus occupied, Eury and I have worked the wharves, market corners and bars of Helos, with me resurrecting the persona of Megon of Cephalonia, this time as a purveyor of fine Thessalian wares. 'Megon' has been generous with *obols*, curious about everyone, especially the wealthy whom he might sell to, and the roads and places he might encounter on his new routes. He's been a fun person to be for a while.

In the market town of Krokeia, a short day's walk north-west from Helos, 'Megon' has sold the remainder of his goods at a decent profit, enough to buy woollen yarn stained with the local purple dye, a compact but valuable consignment – no point abandoning our false identities yet. Ostensibly heading north to Sparta, we've been camping near the junction with the road from Kranae, waiting for Hippasus. Which is to say, Eury and I do the camp chores, while Theseus drinks. Travelling with the 'hero' is wearing thin.

The advent of Hippasus sobers Theseus up with remarkable speed: the Arcadian announces his arrival in camp by dumping the contents of a water ewer over Theseus's sleeping head, then hurling him face down into the dirt when he tries to rise, the Attican too drunk to break his hold. Then they hug, backslap and laugh about it – though I find Theseus's jollity a little forced. But he doesn't touch wine at dinner, instead making a public show of swearing off it until we're safely in Attica.

And it turns out Hippasus even knows Eurybates – he's visited Ithaca a few times, while I was away in Lacedaemon, and remembers the *keryx* fondly. 'I don't know how Laertes is coping without you,' he comments, when he hears how we both came to be here. 'But I doubt he's managing well. I'll look in on Ithaca when we're done with this mission.'

It feels good to have someone so sensible and experienced with us, and I'm reassured that Hippasus seems to share many of the misgivings about this mission that Eury and I have. But there's no suggestion we won't follow through with it. The following dawn, we leave the main road to take an unmarked route through forested hills, Hippasus proving his bushcraft many times over. Arcadia is a hunter's land, with the nature gods Hermes and Artemis pre-eminent. In the Arcadian mythos, it's Hermes, not Apollo, who is Artemis's brother.

The landscape is rugged, but it's clearly richer than Phocis: the lowlands are all tamed, the wide river flats chequered with crops, and the more rolling country planted out in olives and fruit trees. It's late autumn though, and the harvest is over.

I keep as close to Hippasus as I can, sensing an opportunity to learn. At every stop, I ask him about this or that: I already know to approach deer from downwind, but what masking scents can fool your prey? And what are the best ways to obliterate your own trail quickly? He's happy enough to oblige me, and we get on well.

Theseus and Bria follow none too closely behind. I suspect, from the occasional flushed face, that they are taking the opportunity to couple whenever they can.

'You've absolutely no taste in men,' I remark to her one afternoon a few days later, as we slither up to a vantage point atop an ancient beehive tomb overlooking Sparta's palace and northern gates.

'In this body, I'm Lanabrea. She *likes* getting dirty with one of the great heroes of the age,' she sniffs.

'Never mind that he's a drunk and a boor.'

'And funny and daft and larger than life. He's seen and done everything. No wonder you hate him.'

'I don't hate him. But he's an unreliable drunk!'

'Actually his drunkenness is pretty reliable. Get over it, Ithaca – I like men who make me laugh. You're all business. You had your chance with me in Phocis and you thought you were too good for it.'

'You know why! Hebea is a child!'

'She's a young woman, and totally willing, as was I. You rescued her, so you're her hero, for all that's worth. And now you're jealous of me and Theseus? Well, too bad!'

I grab her arm. 'I'm not jealous. I'm just sick of you two not concentrating on doing your job!'

'Sure you are, Ithaca!' She slaps my grip away. 'I don't give men second chances.'

Without a backward look she snakes forward, joining Hippasus at the tomb mound's crest. A moment later, a grinning Theseus arrives – he's probably overheard every word.

A harsh late-afternoon sun is beating down on us. Hollow Lacedaemon, the singers call this land, the cultivated plain cupped between the great mountain wall of Taygetos to the west and the Parnon Mountains to the east. The sea is far to the south now, hidden by the tangle of hills we travelled through. How prosperous it all looks, I think, richer even than I recall it only two years ago when I last guested here, with its silted valley soil and many snow-fed streams irrigating the fields.

Ithaca's a barren rock in comparison. The sudden thought drives a now familiar knife into my guts. *Oh gods, what's happening at home? Is Mother all right? What if she's not?*

But it's impossible to do anything about it and pointless dwelling on it. I drag my attention back once more to Tyndareus's palace, white-walled and splendid on its crescent of rock above the northern end of the town.

'Formidable,' Hippasus concedes, grudgingly. Lacedaemon and Arcadia aren't the best of neighbours.

'I can think of at least three ways to get into the royal family's living quarters unseen,' I tell him, pulling out the parchment maps I drew back in Phocis. My three companions cluster around me – Eurybates is tending our camp, and ensuring our livestock are tended. He's not going to be going into the Spartan palace, on Bria's insistence, and though he's frustrated, I'm glad – I would rather he wasn't involved at all in this treacherous mission.

Breaking into the home of friends still doesn't sit well with me, but we have a job to do. I show the others how my line drawing matches up to what we see yonder, pointing out the buildings, the public and private courtyards and gardens. 'There are two megarons – Tyndareus has done himself proud for assembly rooms – while the eastern wall encircles administration offices, a big kitchen, storerooms and baths—'

'Must seem immense to an Ithacan,' Bria says, snidely. I ignore her – though she's right, damn her.

'Here,' I say, pointing to the map, 'is Tyndareus's suite, along with Queen Leda's rooms and a bedroom for honoured guests – these are the rooms at the furthest end of the western wing. His sons, Castor and Polydeuces, are at the end of the opposite wing, off the same corridor as the older daughters' room and the nursery.'

Hippasus is giving me a curious look, then he clicks his fingers. 'I do remember you! I visited Sparta with an Arcadian delegation five years hence. You and Atreus's younger boy Menelaus used to run amok, as I recall.'

'Those were good times,' I smile. 'I was here when they built this palace. Menelaus and I climbed scaffolding like monkeys. We stole anything that wasn't nailed down for our own hideaway.'

'The old palace in Pharis burned down, didn't it?' Bria comments. She looks at me teasingly: 'Was it you that set fire to it, Ithaca?'

'Very funny,' I reply. 'They think it was a handmaid with an oil lamp, tripping over something. Menelaus and I were asleep upstairs.'

A flash of memory hits me, of waking to choking fumes, hauling Menelaus out of bed, then crawling, throats raw and eyes blinded by smoke, along the corridors, down the stairs, hearing screams, the crashing of timber and tiles, feeling the glorious rush of clean midnight air outside, shedding tears amid the overwhelming relief of being alive.

'I heard it was assassins, sent by Thyestes to murder his nephews,' Hippasus murmurs.

'Perhaps. But nothing could be proved.'

'Well, at least we know Zeus's offspring are still here,' Bria notes eagerly.

We've confirmed that in an unexpected way. At the first glimmer of dawn this morning, the whole royal family and their entourage paraded out of the city gates, through the olive groves and up this very hill to an altar erected at the mouth of the long, earth-filled passage that leads to the tomb entrance. Some ancient ritual, we guessed, which Tyndareus must have resurrected to honour the long-dead kings interred beneath the mound. We'd been roused from sleep by the wail of *auloses* and the rattling of *sistrums*, with enough time to hide in the thickets overlooking the tomb, but no time to lay a plan to take advantage of the moment.

First had come the King and his plump wife, Leda, accompanied by a tall man with long golden hair, the early morning light still too dim for me to identify him. Then the children, led by the eldest son, Castor. Castor's twin sister, Clytemnestra, wasn't present, of course; she'd been claimed, in the months before Thyestes was deposed, as a hostage bride by Thyestes's son Tantalus, a man with a sinister reputation. Tantalus refused to return the girl after the death of Thyestes, his assurances of her happiness ringing as false as everything else about him, but no one has been in any position to do anything other than accept the situation, in the wake of the conflict that brought Agamemnon to the throne of Mycenae.

The two figures I was hoping to see came next: Polydeuces and Helen, walking hand in hand. However life had been for them before – isolated and a virtual secret – their awakening at the Olympian Court must have changed everything. Polydeuces's new gifts would make him the envy – and possibly the enemy – of every young man in Achaea. But the girl had only a promise she would be awakened when she weds – or more precisely, when she loses her virginity.

She'll be like honey to the bees...

At least we seem to be getting in first.

After the twins came Tyndareus's and Leda's youngest daughters, Timandra and Philonoe, cheerful little girls jostling and laughing, followed by a procession of women and heavily-armed guards. I saw no chance of a lightning swoop to seize the twins. It seemed better to stick to our original plan anyway.

Having confirmed that our quarry is in Sparta, we've passed the day in planning, and now here we are, perched across from the palace and almost ready to move. I take the map from Hippasus and show them all a mark I've made. 'I've drawn a circle *here*... It's a drainage hole, at the base of the circuit walls, just big enough to crawl through. If you look closely at the actual walls, it's to the left of that tower by the main gates. You can see a couple of bushes that have grown up in front of it.'

'Thriving on shit, no doubt,' grunts Theseus.

'They'll give us some cover. Menelaus and I had to be pretty stealthy when the drain was new. There's a grill at the top end to catch flotsam and prevent the drain blocking up; hopefully it's still loose. Lift it out of the way, and six yards further up the culvert you can take cover behind some small buildings where the slope steepens. Then stick to the shadows, stay off the main paths, climb over a courtyard wall and you're inside the palace.'

'But how do we get as far as the bushes?' Hippasus asks. 'There's a good ten yards of open ground from the last olive tree.'

'Each sentry has a set beat, back and forth,' I explain. 'There's a moment when they meet and face each other's torches, so they lose night-sight for a dozen heartbeats. Tyndareus is a stickler for routine, so once we know the rhythm, it won't change. Time it right, and they'll not see us. Trust me – I've done this often.'

I return to the map and the floor plan of the palace. 'As I said before, the little girls are in a nursery – here – but the older children have rooms on either side. Polydeuces will be sharing with Castor, at the far end of the corridor, but Helen will be alone since Clytemnestra's forced marriage to Tantalus.' I point carefully at the respective rooms.

'These kings, eh?' Theseus chuckles. 'They treat their children like puppets.' He pats Bria's behind. 'Personally, I prefer independent, low-born girls with dirty minds.'

'You just prefer available,' Bria retorts. 'Who says I was low-born anyway? I was a princess, stolen by my nurse and sold to pirates.'

'That's what they all say.'

'Hush, you two! How many guards are stationed inside the palace at night?' Hippasus asks. 'How quickly can they deploy? Are the children's rooms guarded?'

I answer his questions as best I can, and eventually we decide we are ready. By now, the sun is kissing the western crest of Mount Taygetus. 'We should avoid bloodshed if we can,' I remind them. 'Spartans make bad enemies – they can hold a grudge for generations.'

'You could say that of anyone in Achaea,' Bria comments. 'But you know what Athena wants: no blood unless it's unavoidable.'

'I can't see that the twins will be willing to come with us,' Hippasus comments. 'How do we handle them?'

'Iodama gave me two vials of pure spirits of wine to soak into cloth,' Bria says. 'As soon as we find the twins, we hold those soaked cloths over their faces until they fall unconscious. I've brought a cloth for Castor as well. Easy!' She sounds excited by the mission, especially the morally questionable aspects of it. 'It's an early moon tonight – we'll go in once it's fully dark.'

As we turn to go back to camp, Theseus lays a hand on my arm. 'Sometimes bloodshed isn't avoidable, boy. Don't hesitate if someone tries to raise the alarm, even if you know them.'

'Yes, of course,' I reply, though I've been trying not to think about that. I have too many friends in Sparta for this to go wrong. I study Theseus – these last few days are the first time I've seen him fully sober since he arrived at the camp in Phocis. 'But don't you go killing anyone unnecessarily.'

To my surprise, he doesn't brush me off. 'I know you think I'm a drunken, barbarous relic,' he says. 'But I've been doing this for more than thirty years. Let's see if you can sleep without having to drown the memories, when you're my age.' He claps my shoulder and adds, 'If you ever live so long.'

'What keeps you going?' I ask. 'The kingship – the hope you'll get it back?'

He pauses, his big florid face contorting. Then our eyes meet, and I catch a glimpse of the boy inside the man. 'Crowns and gold are just trophies, boy. It's the glory of the moment that drives you on. The instant when your blade goes in and the other bastard falls, and you realize that you're going to survive. Or when you emerge from the struggle and every man still standing raises their bloodied *xiphos* and screams your name. Or when you drive your cock into the most beautiful creature in creation, and she looks up at you in utter adoration. *Glory.* You can't touch it, or hold it, or store it. It satisfies every need you have and yet leaves you hungry for more. You'll crave glory more than food and water, in time. It's the lust you'll never satisfy, the dream you'll never stop dreaming.'

For a moment his soul is naked, and I can feel that hunger.

You really are a relic, I think. *Killing, adulation and someone to sate your body's lust.*

But I know him now.

You have to know your enemies, Father always said. And the more I know Theseus, the more I'm certain he'll never be a friend of mine. And he, I'm sure, feels exactly the same way.

–

As soon as it's dark, we *theioi* leave Eurybates with the Great Bow in his keeping and set off on our mission. Much as I would like to take the bow with me, it will only get in the way inside the drain.

We reach the edge of the olive grove without incident. It goes against all my instincts to run across open ground lit by flickering torchlight, but my many excursions with Menelaus have proved it can work – you just have to get the timing right. Tyndareus's military routines prove as rigid as ever; I bend double and dart from the shelter of an olive trunk just as the sentries' helmeted heads turn away, and I reach shelter without uproar.

The drain angles steeply up, as smelly as ever, my fingers and toes finding the old familiar holds to help me climb. Thankfully, the grill at the top end of the drain is still loose. In the old days, I needed Menelaus to help me shift it, but now, with my new *theios* strength, I can manage it alone.

Inside the wall, the large, fan-shaped culvert feeding the drain is lit briefly by the passing sentry. Pressing myself into the narrow band of dark shadow hard against the base of the wall, I wait silently until the guard passes on. One by one my fellow conspirators emerge through the tunnel, their breath hardly audible despite their exertions.

Since I've been awakened as a *theios*, my night-sight has improved immensely. As we traversed our clandestine path across from the tomb, none of us needed more than starlight to see every contour of the land, every blade of grass, in sharp detail. All that's missing is colour.

'Avert your eyes from any torches,' Bria had warned when she first showed me this ability. 'Light will dazzle you, twice as badly as previously, if your night-sight is fully opened.'

At the moment all is going to plan, but we've yet to penetrate the palace. Once again we wait for the sentries to face and turn, to traverse the culvert to the steep hillside leading up to the main buildings, which is scattered with small dwellings and criss-crossed with narrow alleys. All depends on the occupants not stirring, or a dog barking, or a sentry glancing our way. But sleep seems to be holding the Spartan citizenry and their dogs in its grasp as we creep along, silent as ghosts.

Now the palace is rising sheer above us, its plastered walls a ghostly white. Hidden from the sentries by a row of sheds, I lead the others along to a lower wall that borders a garden courtyard. Thankfully no one has cut down the cypress tree on the other side. As the sentries meet and turn once again, Hippasus gives me a leg up and I slither over into a colonnaded courtyard.

I'm about to signal the all-clear when I hear a familiar voice.

'They expect us to bow down,' a man says, sounding stressed and tired. 'To feel blessed. But I *don't* feel blessed.'

It's Tyndareus, the King of Sparta himself – I know his voice from my years here, and I like him greatly. He has no huge fame as a warrior, yet he's the acknowledged kingmaker of Achaea, his ability to amass wealth and influence making him key to Agamemnon's return to the High King's throne of Mycenae. But rumour has it that Tyndareus is in poor health now, and this morning he looked and moved like an old man.

'I came back from campaign to find my wife pregnant to another,' he's saying – to whom? 'I almost cast Leda aside, but she claimed *Zeus* took her, and the priests backed her tale. Rejoice, they told me!' Tyndareus sighs painfully. 'Rejoice? I've worked hard to hide the truth, but Leda has lost interest in the world, despite two further pregnancies, two new, beautiful daughters. She drinks heavily all the time – to forget, she says – and grows hysterical when I try to forbid her. She has no interest in her children, except those two by Zeus.'

I wince in empathy. *Tyndareus, I never realized it was so hard for you.*

Then another voice replies, this one so well-known to me it sends a shock through my body. 'You've done so much for us. You know how grateful we are.'

Menelaus! What are you doing here?

I realize it must have been Menelaus I glimpsed with Tyndareus and Leda this morning. He's grown taller than ever, lost his adolescent stoop – born mostly of embarrassment at his gangly height – and filled out. I'd not even guessed it was him. But his presence complicates matters even further.

I always knew this was a bad idea.

I force my mind back to the matter at hand. My fellow conspirators are waiting, undoubtedly growing impatient, but I'm too close to the two men to risk making a sound. I can only hope that my companions can hear voices and realize there's a problem.

I think back to my conversation with Theseus this afternoon – these are the last two men I would ever wish to harm, let alone kill. And would Athena really want me to murder one of the most powerful kings in Achaea?

'What you can do?' Tyndareus's laugh is a mix of affection and bitterness. 'Nothing, my young friend, unless you know how to stop my wife drowning in wine and melancholy.' He drops his voice, so I have to strain my newly-enhanced senses to hear what the King says next.

'A group of priests took Polydeuces and Helen away; they told me it was required – that Zeus himself demanded it. I was sceptical, as any rational man would be. Then one of them *changed*. He *became* the Skyfather.' There is awe in the Spartan king's voice, but resentment too. 'I *met* the King of the Gods, man to man. I should have felt reverence, awe, adoration. But all I could think was, "You took my wife, my proud, beautiful wife, and turned her into a drunken sot."'

I hear Menelaus suck in a sharp breath. 'You didn't *say* that…'

'Oh no! I'm not a fool, Menelaus! But he knew… Inside, he was laughing at me. Then he took them away.'

'Where?' Menelaus asks. 'Why?'

'I know not, nor are the two of them saying. You remember what they're like, those twins? And what power they have over their older siblings? Castor won't breathe without Polydeuces's permission. And Helen and Clytemnestra… The intensity of those two, I've never known whether it's hate or love.'

'How have Poly and Helen been since they returned?'

'Helen's been like a ghost – miserable and angry. She assaulted a slave, nearly killed the poor girl. And then…' His voice trails off. 'But you don't need to know all the details. Let it suffice that we've had to keep her confined with Leda.'

I catch my breath. *What luck I've heard this, or we'd have wasted time looking for Helen in the wrong room.*

'What about Polydeuces?' says Menelaus.

'Polydeuces is…' Tyndareus groans. 'On his return, he threw his wrestling tutor – a man far greater in size – and almost broke his neck. He can hurl a javelin further than grown warriors, and outrun anyone in Sparta.'

'He's been awakened?' Menelaus asks.

Awakened? When did you learn of such things, my friend? I feel a flare of hope. Perhaps Menelaus has enough divinity in his blood to be a *theios* too? *But surely it's many generations since the gods touched the line of Atreus.*

'Aye, he's been awakened,' Tyndareus mutters. 'I knew it would come, one day. I've seen many such men in my life. Few live long, despite their advantages. The world won't let them. And they're seldom unchanged after awakening – they turn arrogant. By Hades, if I were superhuman and divinely touched, maybe I'd be that way too. It's hard enough staying humble when you're raised to rule.'

'You're among the most humble men I know,' Menelaus says.

Bless you, my friend. My thoughts too.

'I try,' Tyndareus replies, tiredly. 'There are moments I can be just Tyndareus. But most other times I have to be King of Lacedaemon, wielding the power of life and death, untangling the criminal from the victim. I have to choose which allies will keep us safe, even when I know some allies are worse men than my enemies. Which brings us back to the reason for your visit, Menelaus.'

'We don't have to speak of it now. Wait until you're rested.'

'Ha! You're no negotiator! The best time to nail down a negotiation is when your adversary is tired, in pain and half-gone in his cups! As I am now.'

'You're not my adversary, Tyndareus.'

'In negotiation, all men are opponents,' Tyndareus counters. 'When I agreed to help Agamemnon reclaim his throne four years ago he was in no position to reward me; since then, he's had to fight hard to restore the wealth of Mycenae. Any demands I might have made, before now, could well have destabilized his reign – a reign I took considerable risks to set up.'

'My brother knows,' Menelaus replies earnestly. 'He is grateful. As I said, anything we can do—'

'*Anything?*' Tyndareus laughs drily. 'I repeat – you're no negotiator, lad! You know what I need: my eldest daughter back from the hands of that dark-hearted scum, Tantalus. I send my *keryx* there every few months and Tantalus displays my Clytemnestra – my darling girl! First, big in the belly with that snake's spawn! Then cradling their offspring. And she smiles, and tells my *keryx* she's *happy*. But I know the man – there's none crueller. I want her freed.'

So that's why Menelaus is here: summoned by Tyndareus to start a war... and what a war. Tantalus's kingdom is west of here, at Pisastis, and he's a powerful man.

'I hear you,' Menelaus responds. 'Agamemnon hears you. But the citadel of Tantalus is strong and he's allied to all of Arcadia and the western Peloponnese. Many there see him as the true High King – as they saw Thyestes himself! It would be suicidal to attack him, now that all the oracles say our true enemy is Troy.'

'Agamemnon promised his aid in return for mine,' Tyndareus reminds Menelaus. 'He promised to unite our families. He was betrothed to Clytemnestra, an arrangement Tantalus knowingly broke when he took her.'

'My brother will keep his promise,' Menelaus insists. 'But Clytemnestra is unobtainable, and… well, not all men want another's man's widow, should it come to that. You have other daughters. Helen is of age. Timandra will be, in a few years. You're our father, Tyndareus, in all but name. We love you, and we will never forget what we owe you. Offer Agamemnon Helen. Or give him more time to unite his subjects against Tantalus.'

The two men fall silent. I lean back against the courtyard wall, my mind whirling. *Agamemnon might become betrothed to Helen. Is that an outcome Athena would want?* The urge to see my dearest friend, and pay my respects to Tyndareus, is almost overwhelming, and I'm ashamed of why I'm here.

Thankfully they decide they've had enough night air. I hear their footsteps retreat, a door opens and closes again, and they're gone.

I wait a few more breaths, in case any guards came with them and still remain. But all is quiet – they must have come here for privacy: Tyndareus would never have spoken of Leda as he did with any other person present.

I give the all-clear, the hoot of an owl, and the other three slither over the wall to join me.

'What in Tartarus caused the delay?' Theseus demands.

'There were people here talking,' I reply.

'Why didn't you just kill them—?'

'No unnecessary deaths,' Hippasus interjects, reassuring me that he at least isn't a bloodthirsty murderer. 'Where from here, Odysseus?'

I point out the two wings where the royal family sleep. 'It was lucky I overheard what I did. Princess Helen is confined to her mother's suite, instead of her room in the east wing near her brothers. We need to split up.'

'If we must...' Hippasus mutters. 'How shall we do it?'

'I'll take the girl, with Odysseus,' Bria says. 'Theseus, you and Hippasus capture Polydeuces. We meet back at the culvert.'

That agreed, the next phase depends on timing. The palace guards change at midnight, coming into the palace complex through several entrances, all of it creating a momentary confusion that Menelaus and I had often capitalized on. *Night-time swims in the river, stealing fruit, hunting in the woods*— despite the tension I'm feeling, I grin at the memories, then shake my head at the irony that Menelaus is also here.

We wait, and then the bell chimes for the change of the guard. It isn't loud, just a faint tinkling so as not to wake the sleeping household, followed by the muffled tread of many boots. We're ready though, detaching ourselves from the shadows to enter the palace behind the men coming on-duty. It is somewhat brazen, but thanks to the shadows, the flickering torch-light, and our casual manner, we enter the building unchallenged.

As the door swings shut behind us, I steer Bria into a pantry beside the main storerooms and the other two follow close on our heels. I've chosen this room because it has shuttered windows opening into the courtyard, and a back stairs to the living quarters above, used for discreetly servicing the rooms of Tyndareus's family and any of their guests honoured enough to stay in the royal wings.

Finally, everything falls silent outside and we take the back stairs, parting at the top. I lead Bria left along a dark corridor, leaving the two champions to locate the boys' bedroom in the other direction. My eyes meet Theseus's as the Attican turns away, the hero giving me a doubtful look, as if he fears I'm not up to this.

The King's rooms lie at the furthest end of this corridor, with two other suites on either side of the preceding corridor, one belonging to the Queen, the other for favoured guests. This back way is unguarded, provided one is quiet – the only guards are at the top of the main stairs. Tyndareus likes his privacy.

Inside a minute, Bria and I are in the corridor, which takes us past a sitting room. A glow of light comes from under the door, and the sound of male voices: Tyndareus and Menelaus, still talking.

Good – they're less likely to hear any noise we make…

Bria silently works the lock on Leda's main door. Peering round her shoulder I notice a shimmer in the air, and a faint itching at my senses – she's not using lock picks but some magical art. I resolve to ask about it later… if we survive the night.

As the door opens, we pull out the cloths soaked in alcohol from our pouches and slip inside the anteroom. Three maids lie sleeping on pallets in a small room to the left – we tiptoe past the doorway, aided by a tiny wall lamp. The inner bedroom is unlocked and contains two beds: Leda lolling in the larger one, snoring, in a fug of wine. Bria heads for the other bed, while I stand by Leda's head in case she wakes. My pulse sounds deafening in my ears, loud enough to wake the whole palace.

Bria bends over Helen and holds the dripping cloth over her face. The girl rouses, trying to fight back, but Bria presses her whole weight down on her.

The sound of the struggle is enough to wake Leda. Her eyes fly open as I lunge in. '*Zeus, Lord! Yes!*' the Queen gasps, baring her breasts as she half rises from the sheets to greet me. Her eyes bulge as my alcohol-soaked cloth covers her mouth and nose, her struggles soon subsiding as years of indolence weaken her resistance. Fuelled by fear, guilt and an almost hysterical mirth, I hold her until she sags back, unconscious.

She thought I was Zeus! It's tragically comic, and makes me hate the Skyfather more than a little. Do these gods we revere do us anything other than damage?

Bria is already pulling the unconscious Helen from the sheets. 'Cloak,' she murmurs, and I fumble with a pile of discarded clothes to find what she wants. Together we wrap the girl – Helen's body is shapely, her breasts budding already, and her face has a natural beauty, graceful and oddly birdlike, even in repose.

Bria is thrusting the girl's jewellery into her own pouch, before grabbing a day dress laid out ready for the morning. A wordless nod and we are creeping back through the anteroom with the wrapped-up girl over my shoulder and Bria leading the way. Then we hear the sitting-room door open suddenly, and one – no, two – sets of footsteps approach along the corridor.

'It's been good to relax after our talk outside, Menelaus,' Tyndareus says, his voice alarmingly close, as he and Menelaus exchange the slurred and emotive goodnights of the drunk. Then the door across the corridor opens, Menelaus murmurs 'Goodnight,' and it closes again.

Bria draws her knife as Tyndareus's footsteps come right to Leda's door.

No, I silently will. *No, please, no...*

A key clatters in the lock. Bria's face turns bleak as she raises her blade. I tense – unsure, if that door opens, whose side I will take...

Then Tyndareus gives a sad, soft sigh and withdraws his key. I'm sick with relief as the King shuffles away towards his own room. Bria gives me a soft smile, which tells me that she hadn't wanted to kill him either. It's a pleasant surprise.

I look yearningly at Menelaus's door as we pass it, aching to be this close to my best friend, but keenly aware that I'm doing something Menelaus would find utterly reprehensible. Then we're away, stealing along the corridor to the back stairs and down. The girl is an awkward bundle to carry, but with Bria's help I ease her through the pantry's outer window and we slip across the courtyard again, without disaster.

The gate in the courtyard wall has been relocked, as we'd expected, but Bria swiftly works her magic once again, leaving it open for Theseus and Hippasus to follow. Then we time our exit to the now familiar patterns of the sentries, regaining the safety of the alleyways leading down to the culvert.

Still in good time, we reach the welcome shadow behind the last hut, an equipment shed and unlikely to be inhabited. This close to the citadel ramparts, the sentinels' torches are casting what seems an almost blinding light on the intervening ground. Moment upon moment passes, with Bria more and more fretful. 'Where are they?' she whispers at last.

But after another agonizing wait, Theseus and Hippasus arrive, panting hard. Neither is carrying anyone at all. 'Where's the boy?' Bria demands, in a low, clipped whisper.

'He wasn't there,' Theseus mutters. 'Neither of them were. There were a couple of bolsters in the beds, and the window was open, with a rope dangling down the wall outside.'

I have to stifle a laugh: *They've slipped out on some midnight escapade.* I can almost picture 'Uncle' Menelaus giving them tips on how to do it.

'Where will they be?' Hippasus asks me.

'No idea,' I reply. 'This isn't the only way in or out of the citadel—'

'You mean you brought us up that stinking sewer when we had other options?' Theseus demands.

'This is the only route that's practical for carrying out prizes...' I point to Helen, still limp on my shoulder. 'As for the boys, Castor might be old enough to head to a tavern, down in the town, but Polydeuces may be a bit young for that kind of fun. There are at least a dozen swimming spots in the river, and there are woods and copses to hunt in, or orchards to raid. They could be anywhere.'

Bria swears under her breath. 'Either we find them, we wait for them, or we take what we've got and go.' She looks at Theseus. 'What do you think?'

'We can't hang around here on the off-chance we'll stumble into those lads. We have to get our princess as far away as possible before dawn. After sunrise, we're sure to be seen exiting the drain. And if it turns into a chase, they'll have riders and hounds. Let's cut our losses.' The giant Attican leers at the sleeping Helen. 'Pretty, up close. She's going to ripen into something special. Here, Ithacan, I'll take her.'

'She's for Athena, not you,' I remind him.

'Don't go telling me my job,' Theseus sneers. 'How's a short-arse like you going to carry her when the going gets rough?'

'He's got a point,' Bria whispers. 'Give her to Hippasus.'

Ah. So she doesn't like the way Theseus is looking at Helen either...

Hippasus takes Helen from me with a reassuring nod, which settles some of my misgivings. I peer round the side of the hut. 'The sentries will be turning in a moment,' I murmur. 'Who's going first?'

'Odysseus and Hippasus,' Bria whispers back, putting a restraining hand on Theseus's shoulders.

Now... I drop into the culvert, help Hippasus clamber down with his burden, then we hurry to the shadows under the wall. Booted feet pass over our heads and stop. Heartbeat follows heartbeat in an endless suspension of time.

Then the footsteps resume again.

I let out a long, slow breath. Maybe the sentry has merely stopped to scratch his balls.

Another cycle, and Bria and Theseus are dropping into the culvert, skidding on muck as they scurry to join us in the shadows, just before more boots sound overhead and we all go still. Then they move on. The Attican gives us a wolfish grin. 'Last stage, friends.' He gestures at me. 'You first.'

'No, I'll stay back, to keep watch.' It's the most dangerous role, but I back myself to remain concealed in this familiar place. So Hippasus takes the lead, edging across the culvert to the drain with Helen in his arms, his eyes on the position of his feet. Then a movement catches my eye.

Someone else is at the entrance to the culvert, peering up at us...

I squint, but the darkness defeats even my night-sight.

Then a dark, helmed figure appears beside Hippasus, and a bronze dagger flashes, slamming into the Arcadian's back. Hippasus staggers as the dagger is withdrawn, stupidly trying to keep Helen in his grasp when he should be protecting himself. The blade rams into him again. Bria's knife is already drawn as she turns to Theseus, her mouth open to warn him…

And Theseus drives his own dagger into her left breast.

A look of utter shock and betrayal flashes across her face, but even as the Attican wrenches out the dagger her stricken features are going slack. She staggers, takes one step as she tries to right herself, then pitches face first against the culvert wall. Behind her, the hidden assassin wrenches Hippasus's head back and slashes his throat open, and the Arcadian slumps, all askew, spilling Helen to the muddy floor of the culvert.

I'm already in motion, pulling the *xiphos* from my shoulder scabbard, but Theseus is coming at me and I've only time to block his thrust, barely turning it aside. I lash out with my left foot, catching the Athenian an ineffectual kick to the chest. Theseus's bloodied dagger plunges into my calf and I cry out in agony as I lurch sideways, all but sprawling on the ground.

My cry is answered by shouts from above.

With a frustrated roar, Theseus comes at me again, but I slice wildly and somehow pierce his guard. All I manage is to slash open his tunic and gouge the tip of my blade along his ribs, but it's enough to save me. As he convulses, I pivot on the injured leg and kick him in the midriff. Theseus staggers backwards, but my wounded leg buckles and we stagger apart.

'Come on!' the assassin calls from the end of the drain in a Thessalian accent. Theseus hurls his knife at me, and it slams into my chest as I try to twist away. A wave of weakness strikes me and I sag to my knees, not quite believing the sight of the hilt that juts crookedly from my right breast. Men are shouting, footsteps pounding. Then a face looms over me, bellowing furiously, and a fist batters into my jaw. The night erupts into vivid white, then goes black…

12 – Silver-Tongued Prince

'HESIOD: What is the sure sign of wisdom among men?
HOMER: To judge the present rightly, and to march with the times.'
—*Contest of Homer and Hesiod*

Sparta, Lacedaemon

Cold water splashes onto my face and I come awake with a jolt, my heart pounding. Light and dark blur around me: human shapes, bronze weapons, red cloaks and shouting voices, all male.

Then someone shakes me, and a voice says, '*Odysseus! What in Tartarus are you doing here?*'

My calf is throbbing and there's a sharp, liquid pain in my chest, the taste of blood is in my mouth and my sight is a smear. But then the man shaking me resolves himself into Menelaus and I clutch him, half sobbing in sheer relief at being alive, reassured a fraction to see my friend… and then I try to *think*, asking and answering questions internally, balancing risks and consequences. Some men can think under stress, others freeze. I am learning that I'm of the former kind, thankfully.

But I still almost panic: *Oh gods, Bria's dead… and Hippasus! And if I don't come up with a plan – NOW – I'm going to die too!* Then my thoughts go to Eurybates. *Has Theseus killed him too?* I picture Eury lying dead in our camp – and Theseus with the Bow of Eurytus. The mental image puts me in a mix of wild panic and cold fury, both of which I'm careful to hide.

'Menelaus,' I make myself splutter. 'The thieves... did they...?'

Before he can answer, one of those rough-faced giants that infest royal courts thrusts Menelaus aside. 'This piece of shit has woken up!' he roars, spittle spraying, his fists bunched as though he wants to punch and punch me until I'm pulp, and I can't blame him. 'Send for the King!' he shouts.

'The guards said he was fighting the intruders!' Menelaus says, angrily. 'Let him be, Alycus!'

Alycus, that's right... one of Tyndareus's younger champions back when Menelaus and I dwelt here. He looks senior now; if he recognizes me, he's giving no sign of it.

'Did they get away?' I groan.

'Yes, they—' Menelaus begins.

'Tell him nothing!' Alycus snarls. 'What in Erebus was he doing here?'

I stifle another groan. 'I was tracking them... It's a long story... Menelaus, I'm so glad you're here.'

Menelaus pats my arm. 'I vouch for this man, Alycus. He'll tell you all he knows – just let him recover!' Then he bends close to whisper: 'Agamemnon gets regular news from Pytho. The last messenger had some wild tale about you quarrelling with your father?' From his expression, he clearly knows more – which makes sense. Pytho, Hera's main shrine, will be keeping the King of Mycenae, Hera's sacred city, well informed. And Agamemnon will tend to pass anything about me on to Menelaus.

Thank the gods Menelaus knows when to keep his mouth shut. 'It'll be resolved,' I whisper back. 'My loyalties are as they always have been.' *If only that were true.*

I've just lied to my dearest friend, and I utterly despise myself. But I already know what I have to do: survive, find Theseus, and bring Helen back. Anything else, and all my life will amount to is a cautionary tale, like that of Sisyphus. And right now, I hate Theseus so passionately, I'll do anything for the chance to bring him down.

I glance around. I find I'm lying on a table in some functionary's office, surrounded by more than a dozen stony-eyed Spartan warriors, who all look as ready as Alycus to turn me to mash. My hands aren't bound, nor my legs, but with my calf slashed and my chest welling blood, I'm unlikely to be able to flee. I realize that if I hadn't twisted as I did, Theseus's dagger would have punctured my right lung.

Then Tyndareus appears. The Spartan king is haggard, his face pale as clotted ash, and his eyes like open wounds. 'Odysseus,' he manages. 'What is your part in this?'

Inwardly I groan at the necessity to tell more lies, but I owe it to the world to split Theseus's black heart… 'Did they escape?' I croak, wincing as I struggle to sit up.

'Two of them, and they took Princess Helen,' Alycus snarls. 'Who were they?'

'The princess? Oh no!' I collapse back, and it's only half an act. 'I saw a bundle, a large one… and I assumed… Oh gods!' I look Tyndareus in the eye. 'I'm sorry: I failed you. I… I didn't understand what they were after. I thought it was gold.' I close my eyes to focus on the pain in my chest, letting that speak for me.

'Odysseus, you were my house guest for years. Upon your honour, tell me what happened tonight,' Tyndareus demands. 'Why are you here?'

'Menelaus may have told you – my father and I have fallen out,' I reply. 'The reasons are private, but I swear there is no dishonour on my part, nor his. Families quarrel – you know that.' Tyndareus gives me a tired nod. 'I'd been wounded by a boar…' I pull at the bloodied fringe of my tunic to bare the scar, to a hiss of indrawn breath. 'I recuperated for a few months, with Eurybates's help, and now we're seeking a haven until I can resolve things with my father.'

'Why didn't you come to Mycenae,' says Menelaus, clearly horrified.

I give my friend an apologetic smile. 'I couldn't travel. All I could do was hole up in Phocis until it healed—'

'Or send word—'

'I was too proud.' Everyone in this room can interpret that: honour is everything in our world, and disgrace, its converse is worse than death. Most if not all would do as I'm saying I did: hide and wait out their shame.

'*Too proud?*' exclaims Menelaus, predictably. 'You idiot. I'd have come to you!'

'I know, I know. But I had my father's *keryx*, Eurybates, with me. We managed. When I finally left Phocis, I headed here, remembering Tyndareus's welcome when I was a youth. But in a tavern in Helos, I overheard two men plotting theft, talking about some great prize – as I said, I assumed it was gold – and a secret way in, using a drain. *Sparta*, I thought. They must be heading for Sparta. And like a fool, I decided to play the hero.'

'Or the ass,' says Tyndareus, frowning. 'I'd have thought Eurybates at least had more sense.'

'I overruled him. To be honest, I hoped to prove something to my father. I've never felt good enough for him – Menelaus knows that. And I ran into Hippasus of Arcadia, and he agreed to help us.' This is a gamble, but Hippasus is a well-known fighting man and his body is sure to have been recognized. 'But there were three of them, not two. I killed one...' *Oh blessed Athena! Bria! You are dead and I'm lying here on this table saying I killed you!* With an effort, I pull myself together. 'But the leader of the thieves turned out to be Theseus—'

'Theseus!' Tyndareus exchanges an angry look with Menelaus.

'By Cronos, I knew it!' Alycus snarls. 'I glimpsed the Athenian's face in that rat hole of a drain!'

I can see most of the Spartan guards starting to relax, caught up in my story. But Tyndareus's frown has deepened, and when he speaks, his tones are doubtful. 'If you thought these men were planning to raid my palace, why did you not come straight here and warn me?'

'I needed to be sure where they were going, sire – there are other drains in Lacedaemon, and other treasures to rob. But at dawn the next day, I woke to find they had already left the tavern. That's when Eurybates and I enlisted Hippasus – he was staying at the same place. We tracked them as best we could, with my wounded leg, but they were travelling fast. To cut a long story short, we lost them. The general direction seemed right for Sparta though, so we headed straight here, arriving around midnight. There was no sign of them, and I was beginning to think they'd made for Pharis or Amyklai after all, but then we saw movement around the culvert and realized that, quite possibly, their plans were already being carried out.'

I pause, wincing in unfeigned pain: this much talking hurts.

'Where's Eurybates now?' Menelaus asks.

'At our camp, a mile into the woods,' I reply. 'If Theseus hasn't killed him.'

'I'll send men later, if you give directions,' Tyndareus promises. 'What happened next?'

This is the weakest part of my tale, the part where my improvised logic is shakiest. I take another breath, and focus on the King. 'Instead of hammering on the gate, as I should have done, I decided to enter via the drain and catch the intruders in the act. I'm afraid, sire, that culvert is an old haunt of Menelaus's and mine.'

'It's true,' Menelaus admits, blushing.

Tyndareus snorts, but in amusement, not condemnation. 'You two,' he says ruefully. 'Go on.'

'This is all my fault,' I claim. 'When I saw the grill over the top end of the drain had been removed, I realized the thieves were already inside. Hippasus and I should have raised the alarm then and there. But I wanted to do something that would make my name, and I thought... damn it, I thought Father might respect me anew. Hippasus and I went in, hoping to stop them as they left.'

I close my eyes, deliberately calling to mind the look of betrayal on Bria's face, because it gives me such genuine pain and fury.

'But how did these men know about the drain in the first place, if not from you?' the King asks.

Menelaus and I exchange a look. 'We weren't the only ones to use it,' my friend explains, blushing even deeper. 'We were told about it by… er, one of the guards, who used it to visit his mistress in one of the villages nearby. And there were others, I suspect.'

'So a *secret entrance* to my citadel is the subject of tavern gossip?' Tyndareus swears under his breath.

'I'm sure not *everyone* knows it,' I mumble. 'Anyway, once we were inside I realized that, if I raised the alarm, I might be speared as an intruder myself. And then…' I cover my face in my hands. 'I had no idea there were three of them. As Theseus emerged with his bundle – Helen, I now realize – his companions came up behind us. They must have been watching from the woods. They struck us down… they were so *damned* fast.'

'They must be *theioi*,' Menelaus says, then he stops, clearly wanting to bite the words back. Tyndareus shoots him a warning look, then gestures for me to go on. I pretend not to know what Menelaus meant.

'Once Hippasus fell, I was fighting for my life. Only arrows from the ramparts kept Theseus from killing me. I swear, I owe your archers my life. I misjudged so many things,' I add, wiping my eyes angrily. 'I only pray you will allow me to make it right.'

All through this story, I've been following a trick Eurybates taught me as a child, the first time I'd been caught trying to filch honey cakes from the kitchens at home. *Lie with utter conviction*, he'd told me. Keep it simple, easy to remember, and don't ever hint you're worried that you mightn't be believed.

Menelaus squeezes my hand. 'No one would have done differently,' he murmurs.

Alycus looks like he might beg to differ, while Tyndareus is contemplating me with an air of… what? Hesitation? Scepticism? He's probably remembering all the times he'd had to call Menelaus and me to account after some escapade or other. He knows I have a silver tongue. 'You can talk your way through the eye of a darning needle, young man', he used to say. But boys are expected to get into scrapes, and some adults take secret pleasure in that fact – or at least Tyndareus seemed to. *Get caught? Take your punishment.* Those were his rules, when we were younger.

After what seems like an eternity, Tyndareus appears to make up his mind. 'I've never known this young man to perform a malicious act,' he says. 'To do idiotic things, yes. To explain the almost implausible in a delightfully plausible way, yes. But not to act in malice.' He turns to Alycus. 'For those of you still in doubt, we have a witness. My good wife insists she saw one of the intruders who stole Helen. Please, have her brought in.'

By Cerberus! I've forgotten Leda woke before the drug took her... Suddenly I'm squirming inside, wondering if I'm to be unmasked after all.

Tyndareus's *keryx* – a rather dull, scholarly man called Gedus – brings Queen Leda waddling in, wrapped in a cloak, her puffy cheeks tear-streaked and a bright scarlet colour... probably burnt by the spirits I'd smothered her with – pure spirits can be brutal.

When she sees Tyndareus, she huddles against the *keryx* rather than allowing her husband to comfort her. 'They stole my beautiful Helen!' she wails. 'Tell me you've found her!'

'My love,' Tyndareus says, in a pained voice. 'You said you saw someone by your bed.' He points dramatically to me. 'Was it this man?'

Leda looks at me, and gasps. Her big eyes, the only beautiful thing left to her after a decade of pining for one lost moment of divine ecstasy, are swimming with tears, her lips working as she struggles to reply. My heart feels as though it's going to leap up my throat, but I manage, only just, to keep my face blank.

'It was... it was...' she pants, fighting for breath. I see the Spartan soldiers reach for their weapons. Then something snaps behind her eyes. 'It was the Skyfather!' she moans. 'He came back to me! I stayed beautiful for him, and he returned!'

My relief is intense, but laced with fury. *Curse you, Zeus. This is the destruction you and your kind leave behind you, with your 'miracles'.*

Tyndareus gestures for Gedus to take Leda away, still rhapsodizing of her joy, before sinking into a chair and staring into space. Menelaus puts a hand on the King's shoulder in a mute attempt to comfort him, while the warriors gaze awkwardly away, clearly trying to pretend they've never seen the Queen in such a state.

Then one of the younger men, Melipas, a soldier I've always liked, presses a goblet of wine into my hand. 'I'm sorry we mistrusted you,' he murmurs, with an earnest look.

'Thank you,' I reply, my gratitude quickly swamped by self-disgust. I've just passed my greatest test as a liar – and I hate myself for doing so.

–

Five hours later, after a deep but all too brief sleep, I am roused. Before I was able to wash and rest, Tyndareus had a surgeon stitch my wounds. I'm vastly relieved to find that my injuries are healing fast: being a *theios* has many advantages. I'm able to enter Tyndareus's private rooms with little discomfort, though I conceal that fact.

A serving woman, grey-haired and stooped, is hobbling about in the dawn light, laying out food and ladling well-watered wine into goblets from a *krater*, a tall mixing bowl. The King is reclining on a cushioned ebony sofa, wrapped in a crumpled cloak. He looks like he's slept here. Or not slept at all, more likely.

Menelaus is here already, with Alycus and Laas, a kinsman of Tyndareus who has lands in the south-west. Gedus, the *keryx*, is standing in the corner. The two young princes, sixteen year-old Castor, and Polydeuces, three years younger, are also here, returned from whatever adventure they had last night. *Thank all the gods they're safe!* Both are bursting with anger, and eager to take it out on any target.

Menelaus is closest to me, and I lean towards him. 'Did Tyndareus's people find Eurybates?'

My friend shakes his head faintly. 'The campsite was empty – it had been abandoned hastily, but there was no sign of violence,' he whispers.

I thank him with a small inclination of the head. *Eurybates, where are you?* I wonder, trying to decide if this is good news or bad. I've not mentioned the Great Bow to the Spartans, but I'm sure someone would have mentioned it if it had been found, so I have to presume that either Eurybates has it... or Theseus.

Tyndareus motions for the serving woman to leave – she gives me a close and curious look as she goes – and the moment the door is shut, the younger of the twins leaps to his feet. 'It's the Athenians!' Polydeuces shouts. 'Give us an army, Father! We'll burn every village in Attica until we find her!'

Because Theseus is involved, he thinks all of Attica is – impulsive and illogical. I wait for Tyndareus, indeed for anyone, to point this out. But they all seem to be taking the boy seriously.

Because he's a theios? But do Alycus and Laas and Gedus know about theioi? Then I look closer at Alycus and Laas, and decide there's every chance they might also be *theios* champions – Bria and Eurybates both said that god-touched warriors are drawn into royal courts, and what king doesn't want superior fighting men?

Regardless, someone has to contradict the young prince, and no one else seems willing. 'Theseus was thrown out of Athens,' I reply, pitching my voice as that of reason. 'And the new ruler, Menestheus, hates and despises him. Why would Menestheus commission Theseus to steal Helen?'

Polydeuces glares at me. 'They're Attican! Swindlers and cheats, every one of them!'

But the older men are nodding at my words.

'What if Theseus plans to use Helen to overthrow Menestheus?' Laas suggests. He's a tough-looking warrior in his prime, and known for his temper. 'To those in the know, Helen is more valuable than gold. Perhaps he thinks marrying her will bring his old followers flocking back to him.'

I've been wondering exactly that. 'Theseus is universally hated,' I remind them, raising my voice above the two boys' highly vocal disgust at the idea of such a marriage. 'He was once a hero of Athens, but through his drunken lechery, he squandered their affection. The only reason he was deposed, rather than murdered, was gratitude for his past deeds. But *nobody* in Athens wants him back.'

'What if Tantalus is involved?' Menelaus suggests, turning to Tyndareus. 'If Tantalus and Theseus are allied, then having the two eldest princesses of Sparta in their hands might help them bring you down, and through you, strike at Agamemnon?'

Tyndareus's face becomes even more drawn as he considers that.

I hide a smile. It's so characteristic of Menelaus to be both perceptive and wrong. But the more Menelaus obfuscates the truth, the more of a smokescreen I have to hide my real part in last night's disaster. Because, while Menelaus can't conceive of my being guilty in this, the others won't be blind to any holes in my story. And I have to keep probing, to try and work out what Theseus is up to…

He's murdered Bria, and his companion – Pirithous, surely – has killed Hippasus. That means he's betrayed Athena. *Unless Athena is behind the change in plan…* I reject that as unthinkable. Theseus must be doing this on his own – but in that case, what's he planning to do with Helen? Somehow I have to make sense of all this, while keeping my own role secret, and find a way to escape, or even turn this situation to Athena's advantage.

'We should march on Tantalus and burn his palace to the ground!' Polydeuces exclaims, seizing on this next potential target for his anger. Castor growls in furious agreement.

'It may have nothing to do with Tantalus,' Alycus says, shaking his head. 'I think Theseus's partner in this must have been that bastard Pirithous. Anything like this, they team up – they always have.'

'Who's Pirithous?' I ask, grateful Alycus has not only confirmed my suspicions but steered the conversation in a more promising direction.

'He's a Lapith, from northern Thessaly. An animal.'

'Let's march on Thessaly!' Castor shouts.

'Peace, my son.' Tyndareus says, with a touch of exasperation. 'We can't accuse half of Achaea of this crime – we need proof.' He looks at Alycus. 'Any reports from your trackers?'

'None. Our men lost them in the dark. And there was no sign of Odysseus's man Eurybates either.'

'Eurybates is very resourceful,' I tell them, quite honestly. 'He may have realized what was afoot, and be tracking them.'

'Good luck to him,' Laas grunted. '*Theioi* move fast, day or night.'

Menelaus glances at me. 'Do you know of the *theioi*?'

I decide this is something I can safely confess. 'The "god-touched"? I know of them. My mother is granddaughter to Hermes, some say – and her mother is the Pythia.'

From Menelaus's expression, I can tell that he's been told what the Pythia has said about me, and is longing to ask me about it, but he holds his tongue.

None of the Spartans seem to know about Sisyphus, and Menelaus is saying nothing. Only a true friend would keep such a secret.

'The fact is,' Menelaus says, 'Theseus and Pirithous, as *theioi*, can run all day and night, even carrying Helen, and think nothing of it. They could be miles away by now.'

'Yet we waste our time here, talking!' Polydeuces shouts.

'Peace!' Tyndareus snaps, before Castor can chorus his brother's outburst. No wonder he looks permanently exhausted, with those two storming about. 'To use an analogy, bringing them down will take an arrow,' he says: 'This discussion is designed to aim the shaft. Be silent, my young arrows: you will be loosed when I am ready!'

I am impressed with Tyndareus's show of mettle. 'Have you *theioi* of your own?' I ask.

Alycus grunts assent. 'I am descended from Hephaestus, and Laas is grandson of Ares. We'll lead the pursuit.' He gestures to Polydeuces. 'And the prince here is the son of Zeus himself.'

I look suitably impressed.

'Who are Theseus and Pirithous pledged to?' Castor asks, showing that he isn't too bright, or attentive when others speak.

'Athena, and Hades,' Tyndareus replies, patiently. 'But Athena is an Attican goddess only; our warriors hold to Ares. As for Hades... well, death is eternal. He doesn't usually bother with earthly politics. That's Athena's game.'

This is getting dangerously close to the truth. 'But if Princess Helen is the twin of Polydeuces, she must be a *theia*, a prize even Hades might covet,' I suggest. 'Hades may be acting untypically, in a bid for greater power.'

That should get them thinking.

'Maybe so,' Laas replies. 'But Theseus was always ambitious. He wanted to be king to feed his own legend, not because he had any desire to serve his people.'

'Then we must get her back!' Castor cries. 'And we'll have the Athenian's head into the bargain!'

Does he always state the obvious as if it were a fresh insight of blinding penetration? Though he isn't a *theios*, Castor is speaking with exactly the same angry intensity and self-confidence as Polydeuces, as if he and his brother are the same.

Tyndareus sighs as Castor's bold words echo about the room. 'If they're working together, we must assume that Athena and Hades are too,' the King says. 'But where might they go?'

That question leaves us all silent.

Then, without a knock, the door opens. Hands fly to knife hilts, but it's only the old serving woman, bearing a bowl full of fruit – ripe figs, golden apricots and dark purple plums – to add to our breakfast, which we haven't touched as yet. Tyndareus gestures for her to enter, and she shuffles to the table and stoops over it to lay the bowl down. Then, after directing another searching look at me, she stands up, her back straight as a spear haft as her grey hair tumbles free. Her rheumy eyes dart around the room, questing and questioning in a very un-servile way.

We are still staring open-mouthed at the change in her demeanour when she undergoes a complete transformation. Her hair darkens, flowing in glistening curls over her shoulders and down her back, framing an unlined, square-jawed face. She is now towering over Polydeuces, who, alone among us, is on his feet. A shining helm appears on her head as her intense grey eyes lock onto the Lacedaemon king.

I knew there was something strange about her...

'Greetings, King Tyndareus,' she says, in ice-clear tones that slice through the shocked silence. 'I hear you need to find your daughter's kidnappers.'

'Athena!' Polydeuces roars in fury. 'Give me back my sister!'

Incredibly, he launches himself at the Goddess, but a spear flashes into her hand, dealing him a slanting blow across his chest to knock him off balance. She puts her weight behind it, thrusting him backwards and down so that he crashes onto the table, sending dishes flying, and lies pinned there, the haft over his throat.

Castor starts forward, but freezes as Athena turns to him, grey eyes flashing. 'Move and I crush his windpipe,' she says calmly.

Laas pulls Castor backwards before the prince does anything rash. And then the woman changes again, reverting to the shape of the old serving woman, though without her bent timidity. The spear across Polydeuces's throat remains firmly in place.

'Are you indeed Athena?' Tyndareus asks, as we all gape.

'No, though you have indeed just witnessed her dread presence,' the woman replies, avoiding my startled look. 'I am here to speak for her. My name is Bria.' My eyes flash to a copper bracelet on her arm. 'I apologize for borrowing your servant's body – please be assured that, once I have left her, she can be trusted as before.'

So Theseus only killed Bria's host body... That in itself is somewhat chilling and alarming, but I must say my immediate reaction is relief, despite our differences. I'm not alone any more – my goddess hasn't abandoned me.

Alycus voices something I am wondering myself. 'How have you possessed her?' he demands. '*Theioi* can't possess people who aren't avatars themselves...'

'Because I'm special,' Bria replies, offhandedly, which doesn't answer the question at all.

I recall what I'd been told of the four types of *theioi*: seer, champion, avatar and magus. As Iodama had said, Bria seems to be a little of all of them, much as Zeus has contrived Polydeuces and Helen to be. I wonder again who she truly is – but this is no place to ask, or to hint that I've ever met her. Alycus doesn't look happy with her reply either, but he lapses into silence for now.

She looks down at the trapped Polydeuces. 'You have huge potential, Prince, but you're not the finished product. Be careful who you take on, until you've learnt how to *really* fight.'

The young *theios* glares up at her. 'I'm going to—'

'No, you're not,' she says. 'You're going to get up slowly, when I let you, and then you're going to return to your seat and listen to your elders. Understood?'

Polydeuces has absolute hatred on his face, but when no one moves to help him, he nods sullenly. As he takes his seat again, he exchanges a vengeful look with Castor.

Bria spins the spear, causing it to vanish, and perches on the table amidst the broken dishes. She's just smashed Tyndareus's finest Cretan tableware but she's either completely relaxed about it, or oblivious. I stare down at a broken shard on the floor; half an octopus head with severed tentacles stares back at me.

Alycus and Laas are *theioi*, not men to be overawed by this sort of encounter; as for the others, Menelaus is clearly aware of the deeper world behind the shrines and rituals, and everyone seems to assume that my own ancestry and training give me similar knowledge. So the miracle of having a goddess appear is taken in their stride by all present, even Castor and Polydeuces.

'Don't worry about introductions or explanations,' Bria says. 'I know who you all are, and I've been listening at the door. I'm here to help, with my mistress's blessing.'

'Then clearly your mistress knows what's happened here?' Tyndareus demands. 'Why should she offer aid, when one of her champions kidnapped my daughter?'

'Athena is the Goddess of Reason, and there is no *reason* she would wish your daughter harm,' Bria replies in a chilly voice. 'Theseus of Athens has betrayed her, and she wants his *blood*.'

The room takes Bria's statement in with cautious, sideways glances. Personally, I believe her: I can see no reason Athena would betray Bria and me, and back Theseus in this matter.

'Theseus was working on his own,' Bria states. 'Athena didn't know of or sanction this outrage. Helen of Sparta is a child of Zeus, Athena's sire, and she desires her return most fervently. I am to place myself at your service in recovering her.'

I'm impressed – Bria's lies are simple and plausible, demonstrating the adaptability and cunning I would expect. My only concern now is that she forgets herself and somehow betrays that she knows me, but I have faith in her cunning – lying minx that she is.

'Where are they likely to have fled, Lady?' I ask her, to initiate what has to be seen as the first exchange between strangers.

'There are several places, Prince Odysseus,' she replies, with just the right note of diffidence. 'It won't become apparent until we've picked up their trail. But the most likely candidates are in Attica – the land Theseus knows best. May I make a suggestion, King Tyndareus?'

'By all means,' Tyndareus replies.

'Allow me to find a more suitable host body and rejoin you as swiftly as I may. In the meantime, assemble a war band small enough to move unseen in hostile lands, but large enough to deal with two of the most dangerous *theioi* in Achaea.'

'Where do I send it?'

'To a place I know in Attica. Every man has a weakness, and Theseus, invincible warrior that he is, is not immune. Her name is Aethra, his mother: she's the one serious relationship in a life crowded with wives, children and lovers. She dwells in a mansion he built for her in the countryside near Aphidna. We'll find him there.'

'We won't need you, then,' Polydeuces sneers.

'Without my intercession,' Bria replies, 'King Menestheus of Athens will view your incursion as war.'

'Then we accept your aid,' Tyndareus says gravely.

Bria smiles sweetly. 'Thank you, wise King! Send your party to embark at Epidaurus Limera, on the coast. A swift ship will reach Attica faster than by land. Do you know the tavern beneath the three oaks, near the landward gates? Good. Meet me there this evening, and tell no one outside this room what you're doing.' She looks at the King determinedly. 'Are we agreed?'

Tyndareus rubs his chin. 'Yes, yes, we are agreed. But surely Zeus's priests will aid us as well?'

'Not them,' Bria replies. 'They were entrusted with her safety at a certain recent court event, yes? She was supposedly anonymous, correct? So how did Theseus learn who she is? You need to keep the number of people who know of this crime to the minimum. Trust to your warriors, and to my mistress.'

'I will sacrifice to Athena myself,' Tyndareus pledges.

I have to school myself not to roll my eyes at the irony.

'Then farewell, for now,' Bria says. 'This evening, at Epidaurus Limera!'

Her face flickers, then the body sags back into the posture of the old servant, who would have collapsed had I not caught her. After giving me a grateful look, she notices the broken dishes.

'Oh no! Did I faint…?'

'Don't fret, Solea,' Tyndareus reassures her. 'You've had a little dizzy spell, that's all. Go and lie down – I'll call someone else to clean up.'

The woman leaves, looking dazed and distressed. It feels cruel to let her imagine she's disgraced herself, but I doubt the truth would be any more palatable.

Once she's gone, Polydeuces leaps to his feet. 'Castor and I must lead the war band, Father! I have been blessed by the gods! I can defeat Theseus, I swear!'

'You were rendered helpless by an old woman,' Tyndareus reminds his son.

'Athena surprised me with a dirty trick,' Polydeuces snarls.

'And you think Theseus will fight fair?' the King retorts. 'No, I want experienced warriors on this chase, not my two sons.'

'Father, let us go!' Castor begs.

'To be honest, I don't think I have any men who can defeat Polydeuces, barring myself,' Alycus says, unexpectedly. 'And Castor is already a fine warrior in his own right. This would be good experience for them.'

'You're not taking my sons into battle against Theseus!'

'It won't come to that. We'll be pursuing two men on their own, and we'll have the numbers to handle them,' Alycus asserts. 'I won't allow the princes to endanger themselves.'

Polydeuces looks set to make an outraged reply, but restrains himself when Castor touches his arm in warning. I watch Tyndareus waver, clearly torn between wanting to protect his sons, but also knowing that young men must be permitted to learn and grow. And the two brothers are clearly burning to rescue their sister – if they're left behind, there's every chance they'll run away to follow us anyway.

'Very well,' Tyndareus says, at last. 'Both my sons shall join the war band.'

'May I join them?' asks Menelaus.

'No,' Tyndareus says, throwing up his hands. 'Your brother Agamemnon would have my head. I didn't risk my entire kingdom backing the House of Atreus to put the heir to the throne of Mycenae in danger.'

'Then allow me to aid you,' I put in, as I've been burning to do from the moment Bria announced her plan. 'My father has already disowned me. And it was my misjudgement that saw Helen kidnapped in the first place! Please, let me atone!'

'By your own admission, Odysseus, it wasn't your fault,' Tyndareus replies. Is there an edge of sarcasm in his voice? 'Still…' He gives my bandages a considering look. 'Very well, provided your wounds allow it. They seem to be more superficial than I thought. And your tracking skills, as evidenced over these past few days, may prove useful.' He turns back to Alycus.

'Assemble a dozen men, plus my sons and Odysseus. Laas, will you go?'

'I would relish the chance,' Laas growls. 'The fame of defeating Theseus would be everlasting.'

Menelaus gets to his feet. 'If I may not come with you, I'll return to Mycenae immediately, to inform my brother. If they pass through our lands, we'll net them.' He clasps hands with Tyndareus, then embraces me. 'I want the full story of this one day, my friend,' he murmurs.

He knows there's far more to this than I've told. But he's still prepared to give me his trust. And I don't deserve a scrap of it. I'm moved by that, but I can't risk showing it, instead masking my guilt behind the very real sadness at being parted from my friend so soon. 'I'll come to Mycenae when I can,' I promise.

'And I will write to Laertes immediately, begging him to relent.'

'Bless you, my friend,' I whisper, though my heart tells me that even a plea from the heir to the High Kingship may have little success in the face of Laertes's obstinacy.

Once Menelaus has left, the serious planning begins. Alycus rattles off names, with Tyndareus nodding approval. The *keryx* Gedus compiles lists of provisions, equipment and mounts we will need, and maps the route to Epidaurus Limera, the main port on Lacedaemon's eastern coast, and the ship and crew we will take north. It's clear they don't need me for that, so I take my leave of the meeting, along with the two young princes, and go off to ready myself for a hard ride to the coast. I need armour, a *xiphos* and a dagger, and a new and I hope temporary bow – I feel the absence of Eurytus's bow deeply.

Polydeuces turns on me as we leave. 'What gods do you worship, Ithacan?'

'The gods of Olympus,' I reply.

'But especially?'

'Ithaca is an island, my prince. Poseidon is ever in our thoughts, and Zeus and Hera are paramount.'

Polydeuces's eyes narrow. 'What about Athena?'

Did he see me on Mount Ida? Surely not… 'My mother is a grandchild of Hermes,' I point out, which seems to satisfy them.

'A shame for you the ties aren't closer,' Castor remarks. 'If *you* were Hermes's grandchild, you'd be like my brother: god-touched.'

'We must make do with what we are,' I reply. 'What choice is there?'

'Someday, my brother will be immortal, as I am,' Polydeuces says, confidently. 'I'll find a way, even if I have to go down to Erebus to bring him back from the dead.'

13 – The Gates of Hades

'Spartans pay honour to Fear, not as something harmful – something akin to the unseen powers they try to avert – but because it is their belief that Fear is the primary foundation of the state… The men of old appeared to regard bravery not as a lack of fear, but as a fear of condemnation and a horror of disgrace.'

—Plutarch, *'On Sparta', Cleomenes 9*

Port Epidaurus to Attica

Bria is good as her word, lounging outside the rendezvous in Port Epidaurus this evening, as our small troop of Spartan warriors ride in. Her new body seems barely female at first glance – in fact she seems to be trying to pass as male. It looks like a labourer's body, with very dark skin, black frizzy hair and North African features – the body of a Nubian farm slave, perhaps. But she's outfitted for war, with bow and *xiphos*, and a boiled leather breastplate contoured to her shape – no chance-acquired body this.

Since the terrible events of last night, I've spent a lot of time thinking about Lanabrea. For all Bria's claims of willingness and compatibility, she'd taken another person's body into danger, and *that* person had died, not Bria. She'd come close to doing the same thing with Hebea. The immorality of it offends me deeply.

One day there'll be a reckoning, I've promised the dead woman's shade.

So I feel little warmth for her, holding back as Alycus and the princes greet Bria, instead acknowledging her distantly. *After all, I'm only supposed to have met her once, in Tyndareus's suite. And that suits me fine.* I nudge my mount up beside that of Melipas, who'd been first to show me kindness after Tyndareus's interrogation, and who of all the Spartans has been most willing to speak with me on the journey.

'Do you trust her?' I ask the soldier.

Melipas – in his early twenties, only a few years older than me – runs his fingers through his long, sweaty hair, and shrugs. 'I'll follow Alycus's lead. He's a good judge of people.' He looks crossways at me. 'He's still trying to work *you* out, my friend.'

'I thought I was fairly straightforward,' I say, with a grin.

'You? No, you're complicated – you always were. You and Menelaus were forever up to something. Always elaborately planned too – passwords and secret gestures, even if it was just to steal some apples or make an idiot of your tutors. And now, no sooner does one show up, the other's right behind him. Just like old times.'

'A total coincidence. And we were boys back then.'

'All men are still boys deep down, my mother says.' Melipas smiles. 'If you can guide us to Theseus, I suspect you'll be as keen to take the Attican down as any of us. An inch further left with that dagger and you'd have drowned in your own blood.'

'That's the truth.'

Laas joins us, giving Melipas a pointed look that prompts the younger man to edge his mount away. The older man glances at me, then back at Bria, who is giving directions as if she were in charge. 'Is she a *hamazan*?' Laas wonders. 'Like the woman Theseus killed in the culvert?'

'I doubt it,' I answer. 'A runaway slave, more like, but one this "Bria" creature has used before, judging by her gear. Bria makes my gut turn, but I suspect we need her guidance.'

'For now,' Laas agrees, spitting in distaste. 'It's a damned cold thing, to steal someone's body.'

'Yes,' I reply, truthfully.

Laas turns to me. 'I don't like riding with outsiders, but you lived among us as a lad, so I'm giving you the benefit of the doubt, Ithacan – for now. That story you spun about why you were in that culvert? There are other explanations – thieves falling out, perhaps. So I'll be watching you.'

I meet the man's eyes – hard, ruthless – and bow my head respectfully. 'I would expect nothing less.'

'For a young man, you're good at masking your thoughts,' he comments. 'But that's not a trait that makes me inclined to trust you.' He touches his mount's flank and walks it away, leaving me to digest his comments. It might well be that Tyndareus allowed me to join this expedition to keep an eye on me, rather than for my tracking skills.

Our group are soon in motion again, trotting our mounts through the narrow night-time streets to the shoreline. Although it's well past sunset, the long sandy beach is crowded with ships dragged up on wooden rollers and fishing boats pulled high on the sand, fishermen still unloading the catches, the smell of rotten fish guts rank, and the air filled with buzzing flies and the clamour of men and women shouting over each other, buying and selling and gossiping.

The advent of fifteen riders causes quite a stir, but Alycus's documents from Gedus, stamped with the King's own seal and accompanied by silver from his treasury, soon set things in motion. We leave our horses, sweat-soaked and tired after a long day's travel, at the royal stables. Then Alycus leads us to the local barracks, before heading off to find the ship's captain and crew who have been assigned to us.

It's too late to think of embarking. Hopefully, if the southerly wind holds, we can make a good passage up the coast tomorrow morning. Alycus and Laas are invited, with the two young princes, to stay at the house of the port governor, while the rest of us are offered pallets and food in the sparse barracks – crude accommodation that has us all grumbling.

Melipas touches my arm. 'I've a fistful of *obols* in my pack,' he says. 'Why don't we find something a little more comfortable?'

It sounds good to me, but as we leave, Bria blithely saunters up with a mannish walk. 'I travelled to Ithaca when I was younger,' she declares. 'How is the old lump of seaweed and rock?'

Knowing I'm going to have to make the best of this, I manage to reply with a semblance of politeness. 'Unchanged, I imagine,' I tell her.

'Mind if I join you?' she asks Melipas, making close eye contact, with the hint of flirtation.

Melipas seems intrigued, and I'm badly in need of news, despite my anger, so the three of us end up wandering off together and find a tavern on the landward side of the town, a quiet place where the locals look at us suspiciously but leave us alone as we eat and drink at a corner table. Bria keeps the conversation light. It's strange to watch and hear her, noting the similarities and differences in her mannerisms while inhabiting first Hebea, then poor Lanabrea, and now this burly, armoured North African woman. She flirts with Melipas – mostly to irritate me, I suspect. But when the young warrior indicates a willingness to take her on, she puts him off – for the time being.

'I'll see you soon, handsome. But I just want to ask Odysseus here about a mutual friend in Cephalonia.' She strokes the back of Melipas's hand. 'I won't be long.'

Melipas grins, gives me a triumphant glance and heads to the rooms upstairs – we've booked two, one for Bria and one for Melipas and me. Evidently that's about to change.

'No lecture,' Bria warns me, as soon as Melipas is gone.

'You got Lanabrea killed,' I fire back. 'By the man you were screwing.'

Bria bares her teeth. 'You think I don't care? I *adored* Lanabrea! We were kindred spirits! You don't understand what it's like to find a simpatico soul like her. I didn't see it coming, and I'll never forgive Theseus for it. But he's been Athena's most trusted warrior for decades! How could I have realized?'

'I thought you were part-seer?'

She bares her teeth. 'Seers get insights into the big picture, not the chance blows of battle, or treachery. Don't try and make me blame myself more than I am, Ithaca.'

The vehemence in her eyes and voice go some way towards persuading me to forgive her, or at the least, suspend judgement. But the notion that she can just ride someone else's body until it fails her still leaves me queasy.

However, she's currently my only link to Athena. I need her. Wordlessly, I pull up her sleeve and find the copper bracelet – it's identical to the one I'd seen on Hebea's arm and, most recently, worn by the old serving woman while Bria possessed her, with that distinctive pattern of the deerhound biting its own tail. 'What's this?'

'None of your business.'

'Very well. How did you get into the old serving woman, Solea, back in Sparta?'

'She's been mine for years. I planted her in Tyndareus's household,' she replies.

'Very well. But what's Athena doing to find Theseus and Helen?'

Bria lowers her voice. 'Athena was completely blindsided – we all were. She's lost two of her best men – one dead and the other now an enemy. Enraged doesn't begin to describe it. She wants Theseus more than dead: she wants him crushed, humiliated. She wants his legend destroyed.'

'Where is he? Where's he going?'

'We don't know yet, but he can only be a day ahead of us.'

'We have to find him fast, Bria. The Spartans might half believe my story for now, but if we fail, suspicion will fall back on me again. And if Theseus is trying to use Helen as a bargaining tool with the gods, to become immortal like Heracles, he'll be in a position to destroy us all. Perhaps even Athena herself.'

'Our mistress knows that only too well,' Bria replies. 'It was easy to hate Theseus as king, but people *worship* a hero. He'll be envisaging a new cult in his name, a chance to forget the bad years and concentrate on his glories. He's always measured himself against Heracles, who is now a god.'

'Theseus as a new God of Reason and War?' I suggest. The notion *hurts*.

'Precisely,' Bria intones.

We share a grim look. 'So where do we head to?' I ask.

'Aphidna is still our best hope. Even if Theseus is making a bid for immortality, I can't imagine him leaving his mother behind. He worships her. We're watching her house as discreetly as possible – we don't want to scare him off. Iodama is with her, and another of Athena's champions, Diakates. If Theseus arrives, they'll let his party in, trap him and await us.'

'Will Athena return Helen to Sparta, if we recover her?'

'Of course not. She still intends to gift Helen to Menestheus. But Athena's resources are spread thin. How many Achaean *theioi* do you think there are, Odysseus? Less than a hundred – even Zeus has barely two dozen *theioi* to call on. Our mistress plans to use the Spartans as much as she can, but when the time comes, we take the girl and vanish.'

That isn't what I've promised Tyndareus, and the dishonour of breaking my word, when a man I respect has extended his trust to me, tastes foul in my mouth. But arguing the point with Bria isn't going to get me anywhere at the moment. 'Very well,' I say. 'But it may get complicated.'

'Then we'll think on our feet, Ithaca. You're good at that.' She stands. 'You take the single room, laddie boy. Sleep well – we'll try not to be too noisy next door.'

'Do you make any lasting friends?' I ask, sarcastically. 'Or have you lost that art?'

She gives me a sour smile over her shoulder as she leaves, but unexpectedly turns back. 'Odysseus, Athena is pleased that you escaped, and used your wits to stay involved. You have her favour. That's no small thing.' Then she's gone, bounding up the stairs to the guest rooms without another backward glance.

Ignoring the come-hither glances of the tavern girls and the narrowed eyes of the local men, I finish my wine. Being in a port town reminds me cruelly of home, and that sets me to wondering, as I have so often done over the last months, about Ithaca and the people there that I love. Is Mother keeping well since Eury's last visit? Has Laertes managed to forgive her yet? Have they rescued their marriage or are they still living at arm's length? Is Ctimene missing me, as I am missing her?

Then a muffled figure detaches himself from the shadows and slides into the chair opposite me. My hand goes to my dagger, but the newcomer isn't some local thug – he slips the folds of his cloak from his head and it's all I can do not to cry out in relief and joy. 'Eurybates!'

We maintain distance, not to make a scene, but we're beaming at each other as I hastily order more wine, then ply him with questions. Where was he? Did he see Theseus? Does he know what's happened?

'You left me watching your approach to the palace,' he reminds me. 'I heard the fight at the head of the drain and the uproar on the walls. Then I saw two men exit the mouth of the drain with a bundle I presumed to be one of the twins. At that stage I didn't know who'd escaped, but I'd seen another man approach the drain while you were inside, so I was already suspecting treachery. I couldn't do a thing, so I raced back to camp and grabbed the mule and our gear – including Eurytus's bow.'

I don't bother to hide my delight at that last piece of news.

'I only had time to hide in the bushes,' Eury continues, 'before Theseus arrived with another man – a Thessalian, from the way he talked. Pirithous, I assume. They had Helen, and they were in a mad hurry. Theseus cursed at not finding me, but they took the horse and left.'

'Was Helen harmed?' I ask anxiously.

'Not that I could see. She was unconscious, and apart from being lashed onto a horse, she wasn't ill-used – though of course I only got a glimpse. Then they were gone. I could have followed, but I was more concerned about you. I hung about, watching the citadel from cover. Then this morning I saw you leave the citadel with a bunch of Spartans and trailed you here, riding the mule – not a bad little animal when she's given her head. I have a room at a tavern down the next alley.'

My friend's reappearance is about the best thing I could have wished for. And as I'd already made it known that he was with me, I have high hopes I can get him officially into the war party.

But tomorrow will be a long, hard day. We finish our drinks. 'Join us as we go on board tomorrow morning, and I'll talk to Alycus on your behalf,' I tell him.

We part company with some of my optimism restored. And despite the night noises, even from my immediate neighbours, I sleep like a log.

–

Aphidna, Attica

I have little problem convincing Alycus and Laas to allow Eurybates to join us. We embark at dawn, with Notos, the south wind, urging us northward in fine style, my heart high now I have my friend and my own glorious bow back. By early afternoon, we've left the Peloponnesian coast well behind, hopeful of reaching the coast of Marathon by nightfall.

But then the Etesiai, the notorious north-easterlies of the Aegean, set in. That means hard work at the oars all afternoon, and I'm not spared, despite my rank or wounds. We force the ship into the welcome lee of Cape Sounion, just as the last evening light ebbs from the sky. After a quiet night spent sleeping on the decks, next morning a light south wind returns and we make landfall on a quiet stretch of beach north of Marathon around midday, and set off inland for Aphidna.

The forced march across the coastal plain of Marathon and into the hills taxes our strength, but haste is needed. We're clad in lighter leather armour rather than bronze, to aid our speed and endurance, and we avoid the main roads, following goat tracks that Bria knows, so that we don't run into trouble with Attican soldiers. Low cloud and late autumnal rain have turned the dust to mud but provide a welcome coolness.

I hide my fatigue and the residual pain of my not-quite-healed wounds as best I can. As the afternoon wears into evening, Eury and I find ourselves alongside Melipas. The young soldier is watching Bria's behind with irritating smugness. 'She kept me up all that night,' he enthuses. 'The way she used her hips, I've never had anyone like her. And her appetite was insatiable! I wish we could stop somewhere so—'

'I can hear you,' Bria sing-songs as she crests the next rise. 'Keep your voices down, we're almost there...'

I am so busy trying to blot the inevitable images out of my mind that I run smack into her as she stops dead, staring down into the valley below.

A country house, square, double-storeyed, and gardened with pillared walkways, lies half a mile ahead. Even from here, it's clear that some disaster has ravaged it. A trail of grey smoke smears across the sky to merge with the still-falling rain. Sections of blackened roof have collapsed, and a pack of wild dogs are gathered around more than a few prone forms.

'Oh no!' Bria groans. 'That's Aethra's house!'

We all stare, as I envisage everything that could have happened here – a vivid imagination can be a curse. Worst is the thought of finding Helen's ravished corpse – in the ruins, or torn apart by the wild dogs. But we can't afford to hurry when we are deep in potentially hostile lands. Alycus's men are edgy as we approach.

There's no sign of any living person. After a volley of arrows has driven off the wild dogs, we move in and examine the corpses that lie scattered around the building. They're all cold and rigid, with no signs of decay, suggesting that the carnage occurred last night. At first glance, the dead are house slaves, all of them male. They've all died of wounds, as best as can be ascertained, given they've been chewed by the dogs.

Sickened through and through, Eury and I keep to ourselves, leaving the Spartans and Bria to search through the wreckage of the house. Some, to my disgust, emerge with plunder – jewellery and other valuables. With Eury's help I re-examine each of the bodies outside in turn, before checking the gardens and outhouses around the house. Slowly a picture of what has happened begins to form in my mind. We are poking at newly turned-over soil in the vegetable plot when Alycus and Laas emerge from the rear of the building, the two Spartan *theioi* looking troubled and frustrated.

'What've you found?' Alycus calls.

'That they were in a hurry but, despite that, they've taken some trouble to cover their tracks,' I reply. 'And one of the corpses out here is built like a warrior, stripped of his weapons and armour, and dumped with the slaves.'

Laas peers at the body, then shrugs; he doesn't know the dead man, and nor do we. But Eury and I can guess his name: it has to be Diakates, the *theios* champion Bria said would be here with Iodama.

'What have you found inside?' Eury asks.

'More dead bodies, mostly women.'

'Raped?' I ask.

To my relief, Laas shakes his head. 'No.'

'Either the killers were merciful, or acting under urgency,' I surmise.

'Most of the bodies have arrow wounds,' Eury notes, 'but the shafts have been forcibly removed. They had time enough for that.'

'But there's precious little looting,' says Alycus.

'Your lot are making up for that,' I say with some heat, to be met with carefully blank faces. *Uncaring* phalloi, *both of them.* 'At least we know the motive wasn't robbery. And now this.' I point at the disturbed soil. 'They've buried something large here, and smoothed it over.'

Eury and I exchange a look. *Helen's corpse?* I wonder, my stomach churning. *Or...?*

'Then we'd better dig it up,' Laas growls. He marches off to a nearby gardener's hut to return with a shovel, setting to work with savage efficiency, as if digging were a proxy for slaughtering whoever has done this.

A moment later, Bria joins us, her face drawn and her skin waxy. She draws me aside. 'It's a bloody disaster,' she murmurs in my ear. 'I've found Iodama's body. Murdering bastards!'

Iodama? I didn't think I could be shocked any more than I already am. 'Eury and I think we've found Diakates among the dead outside,' I tell her. I sound like I'm helping compile a shopping list, so flat and banal do my words sound in comparison with my grief and anger. 'He was felled with one blow.'

'Iodama as well. That's *two theioi* dead, with single killing wounds. They weren't overwhelmed, they were *ambushed*. Theseus must have arrived, pretending all was well, then killed them before they could react.' All Bria's habitual flippancy has vanished. 'Theseus will pay for this.'

'And Hebea?' I ask, dreading the answer.

'I've not found her among the dead,' Bria replies, hesitantly. 'I can usually sense where my host bodies are, and she's not here. There's a chance she's alive.'

That's something of a relief, but I'm still furious. 'I'm not so sure Theseus did all of this,' I say, once I've mastered my emotions enough to mask them. 'He may have slain Iodama and Diakates, but I doubt he killed all these servants – they've mostly been shot. I think there were others involved.' I indicate the hole Laas is digging. 'I have a theory – but let's see what Laas finds.'

We don't have long to wait. In a short time the Spartan has excavated a shallow trench containing four corpses. They've been laid out on their backs, with arms crossed over their chests, and what is immediately clear from their hooked noses, braided beards and long trousers, is that they are men of eastern origin: Trojans.

'A respectful burial, though in haste,' Alycus comments.

'But out of character,' I observe, glancing at Eury, who knows as much of foreign customs as I do, if not more.

'Unlike us,' the *keryx* explains, 'the Trojans burn their dead before interring the remains, but something has prevented them performing their standard rites. My guess is, they arrived here, fought, were victorious but had to press on swiftly.'

'Too swiftly to despoil the women or to loot,' I point out, 'but they still took the time to hide their dead.' I point towards the stables at the rear. 'There's stabling for three horses, but the stalls are empty. The wet ground shows three sets of hoof prints heading north-west, followed by many men on foot.'

Laas rubs a hand over his chin, leaving a muddy smear. 'But this is absurd. How can the Trojans be involved?'

'Perhaps Theseus offered Helen to Troy,' Bria suggests. 'However you see it, his theft of Helen must have been carefully planned. He and Pirithous organized the kidnapping, while perhaps offering her to King Piri-Yamu in exchange for gold and a safe haven.'

'But then, who did the Trojans fight here?' Alycus asks.

'Perhaps the Trojans decided stealing her was cheaper than buying her,' Eury suggests.

'Yes,' Bria exclaims. 'But Theseus resisted – he's not blind or stupid. Just colossally arrogant and convinced of his own immortality.'

'That sounds plausible to me,' I put in. 'I think the Trojans tried to use force to avoid whatever price Theseus was demanding. But they clearly failed: neither Theseus or Pirithous are among the dead, nor is Aethra, Theseus's mother. Or Helen. I think the three horses were taken by Theseus's party, with one of the men carrying Helen. And the footprints are the Trojans in pursuit. Either side might have killed the slaves and the two *theioi*.'

'The Trojans must have a ship somewhere,' Laas comments. 'What of Theseus?'

'I expect he's now fleeing towards Thessaly – Pirithous's homelands,' Bria says, pointing north-west. 'He's going to escape: he's on horseback, and the Trojans don't know the lay of the land – and if they run into any local soldiers, they'll be attacked.'

I agree with that also. 'For the Trojans to have any chance of keeping up with him, they'll have to return to their ship and follow Theseus by sea. The vessel must be in the straits of Euboea, but north of Chalcis, to avoid being trapped at the

Narrows. Judging by the number of footprints, I'm estimating they brought thirty men ashore.'

'If they've brought a big war galley, they'll have fifty-to-sixty men in all – half in the raiding party, and half still manning the ship,' Alycus calculates. 'They'll easily outnumber us, if we do have to face them.'

At this point, Castor and Polydeuces join us, the older prince looking sickened, though struggling hard to hide it. These are probably the first dead bodies he's seen. Polydeuces seems unaffected.

'Have you found any clues?' Castor asks Alycus.

The Spartan *theios* points out the opened trench, and explains what we've deduced.

'I would pursue my sister to the walls of Troy,' Polydeuces declares, striking an overtly heroic pose. 'Or to the gates of Erebus itself! Enough! We have enemies to pursue!'

It's almost evening, but there's still an hour or two of daylight remaining. So off we set, jogging north-west behind Bria, who seems tireless. Before we leave, Eury and I take one last, quick look around. In a far corner of the garden, close to a wall, we discover a few small footprints, widely spaced as if the person has been running. They could belong to any child of the household. Or they could be Hebea's...

Knowing what I now know of the gods, praying for her safety seems both futile and hypocritical, but I do anyway – to Athena, who might at least care.

–

That evening and the next three days pass in a debilitating slog through hostile lands, evading settlements, resting for minimal periods and sleeping rough. We jog when able, weighed down as we are by war gear, food and water, and pretty soon all of us are struggling. The *theioi* fare best – though the ordinary soldiers are unlikely to know of their captains' god-touched abilities, they are well aware Alycus and Laas have endurance beyond theirs. Bria manages as well as the two captains, but although I am aided by my own gifts, I still struggle, for those wounds to my chest and leg aren't being given the chance to heal properly. Eurybates aids me, but he's exhausted too and it's all we can do to keep up.

Polydeuces, as a *theios*, could have left his elder brother behind, but he refuses to do so, cajoling, praising, carrying extra gear; Castor for his part is uncomplaining, striving to match his brother despite the gulf between their physical abilities.

Having a brother of my own would have been wonderful… but then, I have Eury. And Menelaus.

The first full day takes us through the rugged terrain of northern Attica, the hills broken and the tracks punishing, before emerging onto a broad inland plain. Alycus increases the pace accordingly, and we sweat and curse as we keep up the gruelling pace. Now we're using more frequented paths, I use my hunting experience to spot their telltale hoof prints amid the jumble of other signs.

The afternoon of the second day takes us back into the hills, this time near the coast, rather than the expected inland route through the plains. Just before dusk, we glimpse a galley in the straits of Euboea, overtaking us on its way north up the straits. The craft looks eastern, though it's hard to tell at this distance.

'If it *is* Trojan, they must have some way of working out where Theseus and his party are heading,' Eury comments to Bria as we set up camp that night. We've been making a show of getting to know Bria, so that any slips in our roles as strangers only lately met can be explained away. That, and the business of pursuit, have meant she's kept Melipas at arm's length, despite his clear desire to renew their liaison. The young warrior is now watching the three of us sullenly.

He thinks I'm to blame for Bria ignoring him. It's another potential problem, but hopefully one that can wait.

'They must have seen which direction Theseus headed off in,' Bria replies. 'And this coast is the only way north, unless you want to go mountain climbing.'

'But if Theseus's party is on horseback,' Eury wonders, 'why are they taking this trail through the hills? The terrain's too rough for them to do more than walk their mounts. Why didn't they take the main roads, and outstrip us all?'

Bria gives Eury an approving look. 'You've a brain in that skull of yours, *keryx*,' she comments. 'Theseus may think we've alerted all of Achaea to his crime, and fears travelling openly. By now, he can presume Zeus's people are aware of the abduction too. Once the Skyfather is involved, no road in Achaea is safe for him.'

That gets me thinking: 'Zeus has been working closely with the Trojans all along, and Helen and Polydeuces are clearly a prize he's dangling in front of Troy. The Skyfather sent Helen and Polydeuces back to Sparta after the Olympian Court – to hide them, or so we thought. But what if they were returned as bait, knowing someone would try to seize them once they deduced their identity? Is he hoping to provoke a war? Remember: Zeus's priests backed Thyestes against the House of Atreus. And the Atreiades line reveres Hera first, not Zeus.'

Even Bria looks impressed at the connections I've made. 'But Theseus could still have been taking Helen to Troy,' she replies.

'Perhaps that was his first choice? But if the Trojans tried to double-cross him, and he's trying to escape them, perhaps he's just running blind?'

'He's a *theios*,' Bria replies. 'He's not stupid, despite what you think. He'll have a plan.'

'He needs a place to hide, not just from the Trojans, but from every king, every *god*, in Achaea,' Eury exclaims. 'But where?'

Suddenly Bria looks startled. 'North of here, there's a place called Thermopylae.'

'The "Hot Gates",' says Eury. 'I've heard the name.'

So have I. It's due north of Pytho by around thirty miles, on the far side of Mount Parnassus. 'What about it?'

'It's a place where the coast road becomes a narrow track,' explains Bria. 'The locals call it a "pass" but it's at sea level, squashed between the mountain cliffs and the shore. Hot springs come gushing out from the base of the cliffs, next to a cave. But not just any cave. This one is a gate to Erebus.'

'And Pirithous's patron god is Hades,' I say, putting aside the impossibility of a "gate to Erebus" for now.

'Can such a place be?' Eury wonders.

'Oh yes,' Bria says. 'If men can imagine it, gods can make it.'

I drop my voice, so the Spartans can't overhear. 'Back in Phocis, Theseus said we should hide the twins in Erebus. I confess, at the time I didn't take him seriously.'

'I keep telling you, Ithaca – he's a fool, but he's not stupid.'

'We've been wondering all along if Theseus is seeking immortality. For that, he'd need a patron, a god other than Zeus, but of similar status – Hades himself.'

'That must be his current plan,' Eury says. 'But what exactly is a "gate to Erebus"? Can a living person just wander into the cave at Thermopylae and enter the Underworld?'

'It's not so simple,' Bria replies. 'You need to know how to leave this world behind.'

I stare at her. 'Leave *this* world behind?'

'Places that are deeply tied to legends develop their own secret landscape. They take on an alternative reality, one that conforms to the tales, not the natural world. If you climb Mount Olympus, all you'll find is rock and snow, but if you have the ability to unlock the mythic side, you'll find the home of the gods. That's what we did on Mount Ida – remember that archway at the Olympian Court? If you enter the right cave and do the right things, you pass through a "gate" from the earthly cave, and enter the mythic Underworld.'

I've seen so much these past months, there's no point being amazed any more...

'Does that mean that Erebus would contain everything the tales suggest? Cerberus, Tartarus, Charon the boatman – they're all real?'

'You're catching on.'

'Wonderful,' I groan. 'I presume Theseus knows all this.'

'Of course – and he's with Pirithous, a champion of Hades. But it's possible the Trojans don't know.'

'Well, that's something to hope for.' I give Eury a troubled look – another problem has entered my mind, one I can't yet see the solution to...

'The Trojans are probably led by *theioi* too,' says Bria, breaking in on my thoughts. 'So don't get too confident. I suspect that before the end of this, we'll be facing Trojan swords in earnest.'

I meet her gaze. 'Then I hope Skaya-Mandu is among them.'

We share a grim look, then Bria smiles. 'Prince Poly said he'd pursue his sister *to* the Gates of Erebus. I wonder how he'll feel about going *through* them.'

–

Next evening we all stand on a desolate gravel beach outside a cave, as the sun sets and the colour leaches from the world, as if Hades himself were reaching out from Erebus to paint his threshold in hues of gloom and loss. It's a desolate place, the coastal path going right beneath those formidable cliffs, with no alternative route for many mountain-bound miles. The only sounds are the swish of the waves and the bleating of a goat Bria captured earlier, and now has on a tether.

'A few hundred men could block an army here,' I muse aloud, staring up at the heights above.

'Provided they're Spartans,' Laas grunts, before turning to confer with Alycus.

Other than ourselves, the only signs of life are the horses Theseus's party have abandoned some distance down the beach, a few gulls circling mournfully above, and a single war galley standing about three hundred yards offshore – definitely a Trojan vessel, fully manned and very much alert to our presence. Among the Trojan warriors on board, I can see a feminine figure whose long black hair flutters like a banner in the gentle breeze. She has her arms raised, as if imploring the heavens. Her voice carries across the waves, raised in a song with a strange, lilting cadence.

My heart jolts at the sight, and the timbre of her voice. *Kyshanda*…

The Trojan ship is hoisting sail, and anyone who isn't rowing is lining the sides with bows at the ready, though we're well out of range. There's a sea mist just beyond them, which thickens into a dense bank of fog, creeping closer as Kyshanda sings, threatening to engulf the ship.

'What are the oily bastards up to?' Alycus growls.

We all stare as the sluggish winds turn onshore, filling the sails of the Trojan vessel as it sets its prow towards us and begins to surge forward, oars flashing as they churn the sea white.

'Are those *gunandroi*, those women-men, coming to take us on?' Laas growls. 'By Hades, I think they are!'

'Skirmish lines,' Alycus shouts to his Spartans. 'Form up, and ready your bows!'

We line up and nock our arrows as the Trojan craft approaches, Eurybates beside me using the Spartan bow I'd been given, now I have the Great Bow again. Kyshanda's voice floats eerily across the water as the fog rolls in behind it, dank and cold. Despite growing larger and larger in our vision, the Trojan ship is now harder to see, its outlines blurred, the coloured sails muting to grey. The shouts of the shipmaster and the drums marking the strokes roll over the waves, counterpointed by Kyshanda's spectral wail, and the almost human shrieking of a gull that I can see, its legs held in Kyshanda's left hand, upside down and flapping frantically.

In her left hand is a dagger. But as her blade flashes and the blood spurts, the fog swallows the Trojan ship, and they become just a dark blur in the swirling mist. The bird shrieks and goes silent, and the fog congeals, concealing the oncoming ship completely.

'Take aim!' Alycus shouts, though there's no longer anything to aim at. We brace ourselves for a volley of enemy shafts whipping out of the fog. The two fingers on my bowstring are sweating…

…and then something happens I've never seen or felt before. A flash of lightning jags overhead amidst a peal of thunder that shocks the very air. A circle blazes in the mist, where the Trojan vessel should be, and the wind whips at my skin without so much as swirling the enveloping fog.

The world falls utterly silent. Kyshanda's voice is gone, so too the drums and the chants of the rowers, and the shouted commands of the Trojan shipmaster. All of it gone, but for the waves.

We stare, waiting for the dark shape of the galley to break from the fog, but instead the mist rolls over us as well. We huddle together, nervous, exchanging glances, and even Bria looks bemused. Then in the space of a few moments the fog around us lifts, though it still lingers far out beyond the inshore surf.

The Trojan ship has vanished.

There's no dark shape out to sea, no hull heeled over on the shore or wreckage in the waves. It's *gone*, and so too is the wind that had propelled it towards us.

The Spartan soldiers gasp, making gestures to ward off evil and muttering among themselves as they look to their captains for reassurance. Alycus makes a determined effort to convey calm, telling them the ship has simply veered off in the mist and is now somewhere in the fog bank offshore. 'They turned around, that's all,' he tells them. No one looks convinced.

'What happened?' I mutter to Bria.

She purses her thick, dark lips, beads of sweat on her black forehead despite the chill in the sea air, and runs her fingers through her short, tightly curled hair. 'I think – and I'm guessing – that they just beat us to the punch.'

'What do you mean?'

She meets my eyes, then waves Alycus and Laas in close, so she can speak to the three of us without being overheard. 'I could be wrong, but I think they just *sailed* into Hades's realm.'

Alycus starts. 'Is that possible? They're Trojans – they don't even worship Hades!'

'But the Luwians and Hittites do have gods of death, and a goddess of sorcery too, akin to our Hecate: they call their sorcery goddess Kamrusepa. Perhaps there are already links between those deities and Hades?'

Kyshanda told me she is an initiate of Kamrusepa…

'But can a ship sail the Styx?' I ask, feeling foolish to be discussing the topography of a place I've barely believed in until now. Alycus and Laas look just as uncomfortable, for all their years as *theioi*. Clearly this is beyond their experience too.

'Erebus is girt by several rivers – it's a dangerous journey but it has advantages also,' Bria replies, as if discussing the route to a market in Athens. 'They can avoid Charon and Cerberus, for a start. We must hurry if we're to catch Theseus before they do.'

The two princes join us. 'What is this place?' Polydeuces demands. 'Where did that ship go?'

The two princes are determined to a degree that's almost fanatical – they've been raised on tales of heroism and are desperate to prove themselves equal to the best, especially with their sister's safety at stake.

Alycus looks wretched, trapped between two imperatives. 'My prince, I promised your father you would not be placed in undue danger.'

'Why, what's dangerous about this cave?' Polydeuces asks.

'It's a gateway to Erebus,' Alycus answers, avoiding his eyes.

'Is that so?' Castor replies, without batting an eyelid – in his world, gates to the Underworld are clearly as real as water and stone. 'We're not frightened. We'd break the pillars of the world to get Helen back!'

'Forbid us entry and you'll never serve the House of Tyndareus again,' Polydeuces adds.

Alycus looks about him for support, but Laas has stepped away and Bria has found something fascinating to look at on the cliffs above.

I take pity on him. 'To hold them back would be to shame them forever,' I advise Alycus.

Castor and Polydeuces cast me a grudgingly grateful look before turning back to Alycus. The Spartan *theios* gives a fatalistic sigh. 'Very well. Let's take a look.'

The cave isn't large – a dark cleft next to a sulphurous hot spring pouring out of a hole in the adjacent rock face that emits a rotten, noxious smell. Eury and I lead the way, finding footprints that mark the sandy soil beyond the spring. Some of them are small, and several others match the distinctive imprint of Theseus's boots. I also find what seems to be a strand of Helen's long golden hair. 'It's them, I'm sure of it,' I murmur to Bria. 'Their prints go in, and don't come out.'

Bria waves Alycus in, and shows him the tracks. 'This is the place,' she tells him. 'You shouldn't take anyone through who doesn't want to go. Erebus has a way of swallowing people for eternity.'

Alycus wipes his brow, then leads us back outside. I don't envy him the somewhat incredible tale he has to spin. 'Men,' he says, raising his voice and waving the soldiers in close. Melipas makes a point of standing beside Bria, glaring at me from under heavy eyebrows. He still thinks I'm trying to steal her from him.

'You're wondering why we're here, and where our quarry have gone,' Alycus tells his men. He points to the cave mouth. 'The answer is in there.'

One of the warriors, Aendros, gives a puzzled snort. 'They ain't here, sir – it's just a little hole.'

'You've only seen what's easy to see, Aendros. There is a way onwards, into the earth.' Alycus swallows, then goes on. 'It leads into Hades's realm.'

Some of the men go pale and start muttering prayers. Others, more inclined to scepticism, react to his pronouncement with suspicious glances and raised eyebrows.

'The actual Underworld? Erebus?' Aendros asks. 'Are you serious?'

Alycus gives him a frosty look. 'Yes, I'm serious. If you've been believing that the old tales are just old women's stories, think again, because we're about to walk into one. If any of you don't have the guts for this, you can wait outside, if that's more your way.'

This is a cold-hearted way of asking for volunteers, but I sense Alycus is worried that if he doesn't make it a point of honour and shame, no one at all will volunteer. They still waver.

Then Bria speaks up. 'This is *real*, and it will be dangerous and frightening. You may see things you've spent your whole lives not wanting to believe in. You may meet your own dead – kin and friends. And enemies too. *They* won't be pleased to see you – the dead envy the living, for possessing what they've lost. But if we move swiftly and have fortune on our side, we'll reclaim the princess and kill those who took her.' She tosses her head. 'I'm doing this, even though I'm not a Spartan and I've never met your princess. Why? For glory. For the immortality of being remembered. I expect no less of you men.'

After that, no one has the courage or cowardice to back out. Quite coldly and deliberately, Alycus and Bria have ensured that every man here will be volunteering, to avoid shame. They all raise their hands and step forward.

I need to remember what moments like this tell me about my companions.

'Good lads,' Alycus approves. 'True Spartans! Prepare your gear and get something in your stomachs.'

'No!' Bria interjects. 'Don't eat until we're inside. The transition can affect some people badly, and they vomit uncontrollably. Wait until we're inside, and you've adjusted.'

This earns her hard stares from everyone. 'You've done this before,' Melipas accuses, backing away from her.

'Clearly. Does that make me in charge?' She looks at Alycus and winks. 'Just joking.' Then she edges closer to the Spartan *theios*. 'You'll need to pay the ferryman,' she murmurs.

Alycus looks a little startled. 'How much?'

'The usual fee.'

'Ah.' He points to the pack at his feet. 'Tyndareus has given me more than enough silver for that.'

We prepare in an air of unreality, as the thick mist gathers around us again. I draw Eurybates aside, for there's something I've been brooding on since last night that I must say.

'My friend,' I say in a low voice, 'I can't ask you to come on this journey.'

'You don't have to,' he replies. 'I am with you wherever you go.'

'You misunderstand – I don't want you to come.'

Eury's stricken expression replies more eloquently than words could. 'I'm not afraid,' he insists.

'I know, Eury. But that's irrelevant.' I bite my lower lip, then press on. 'The thing is, if I don't return I want someone to go to my parents – the only parents that matter to me, Laertes and Anticleia – and my sister, and tell them where I went and why. If you don't do this, they'll never know what became of me, and that would hurt me more than any torment devised in Tartarus.'

Eury goes to refuse, but then he sees something in my face and bows his head. 'As you command, my prince,' he says, in his most formal voice, to hide either his disappointment or his concern and fear for me.

'If I return, I'll be forever in your debt,' I tell him fervently.

He grips my hands, wordless, a moment as powerful as any we have shared. I don't think we'll ever see each other again, and I suspect he feels the same.

But then a resounding crack breaks our silent reverie. Everyone turns their heads.

Melipas has been pressing Bria, trying to pull her aside, whether to argue with her or steal a kiss I can't say, and it's her open-handed slap which echoes about us, sending the Spartan warrior sprawling, Then she's striding away. I'm wanting to speak with her anyway, so I grip Eury's arm one last time and hurry after her. The furious Melipas regains his feet and catches my shoulder, her hand print livid on his cheek.

'You've poisoned her against me, Ithacan,' he snarls, bunching a fist.

I duck instinctively even as Melipas strikes out. His fist flies past my ear, then I grab his forearm and jackknife, using the Spartan's momentum to send him crashing over on his back. 'Stay down,' I hiss, planting my knee in Melipas's chest. 'I've no interest in her, bar what she knows. And I'd advise you to stay well away from her too – people she gets close to end up dead.'

That said, I rise and storm off, to find Bria on the other side of a barnacle-encrusted boulder, squatting over a scooped hole in the sand. I pull back to the far side of the stone, calling in a low voice. 'See where your greedy little escapades get you to?' I call.

'I'm pissing, Ithaca. Get lost.'

'You've made an enemy out of a good man. Congratulations.'

'Go to Hades,' she rasps, amidst wet splashing sounds.

'I'm about to.'

Bria grunts, finishes her business and joins me. 'Listen, I know you don't approve of what I am – I'm not exactly enraptured by it either. I used to be... No, never mind. But I am *compelled* to serve our mistress, and I'll use whatever tools I have to hand. You'll learn in time that morals get blurred, Odysseus. Right becomes wrong and wrong right. You can either climb aboard, or jump ship and see how long it is before Sisyphus's enemies find you.'

It's the word *compelled* that gets my attention. She's not used that before to describe her situation, and it strongly hints that she has even less choice than I do in all this. And she's used my name, not the derisive 'Ithaca'. It's enough to calm me. I give her a cold glare, but my temper has dissipated.

'What's the name of this body you're using?' I ask, by way of a peace offering.

She rubs her dark cheeks, then abruptly makes a very coy feminine gesture. 'You like? This one's called Ikumbi, from the upper Nile Valley. She's got lash scars on her back from her time as a slave, but I freed her.'

'How do these non-*theioi* women become your, um... "partners"?'

She puts a finger to her thick dark lips. 'That's a secret, Ithaca. Shall we go?'

I grab her arm. 'Not until you tell me where we will emerge, if we ever return from this?'

'What makes you think I know?'

'You've been there before,' I reminded her.

She rolls her eyes. 'All right. There's a cave on the Spartan coast south of Messe. It's said to be another gate to Erebus, but in fact it's an exit. I take it you've forbidden Eurybates from coming with us – that's a good decision. He's not a *theios* or much of a warrior, for all his recent training – he'd never make it. Have him go to the cave near Messe and await us there. But tell him this: if we haven't emerged by the time three days have elapsed, we're not coming back.'

It's a frightening thought, but I let Eurybates know. If he catches one of Theseus's horses and rides hard, along the main roads south into Attica, a ship from Athens will take him south in time to meet us, winds and fate allowing.

When we've finished discussing his route, we embrace again. He drifts to the rear, his eyes downcast, as Bria steps in front of the thirteen Spartans. 'Right,' she says. 'Let's be clear about a few things – the first being that I'm the only one who's done this before, so I expect to be listened to! I'm going to open a secret way, and we'll enter another place. We will find ourselves on the banks of the legendary river Styx. These are the rules: don't drink or eat anything except what you've brought with you. Don't kill anything that isn't trying to kill you. Stick together, protect one another. Listen to the creatures you encounter, but don't believe all they say! They want to harm you. They will mix truth and lies to entrap you, especially if they tell you that one of your fellows is your enemy.'

She waits until they've all nodded in agreement, then seizes the tethered goat in her arms. 'What opens the gate is a death. The Underworld opens up to claim the soul.' I remember the flailing seagull in Kyshanda's hand, the flash of the knife and the red blood spraying. 'We can fool it with this poor beast,' Bria continues. 'Come.'

She carries the bleating goat into the cave and we follow, eyeing each other uneasily. Most of the Spartans look doubtful, perhaps still unwilling to believe this is real, but Alycus and Laas and the two princes are bearing themselves with utter conviction, and their certainty sets the tone among their men.

I'm last to enter, turning to raise a hand to Eurybates. He does the same, then places his palm against his heart. I mirror the gesture of respect, then turn and enter the cave, wondering if this is the last time I'll ever see my friend.

The cave is dark and redolent with sulphur, the air sultry from the steam of the hot spring. The waves on the shore outside fade into the distance as the stealthy onset of night takes hold, turning the pale fog to deep grey gloom. Twilight – the liminal time, the threshold period – has begun.

'Great Hades, hear me!' Bria shouts. 'You spirits that convey the dying, hearken! Here is a soul, seeking the ways! Here is one to walk the shadow path into eternity!'

Her cries echo in the confined space as she plunges her dagger into the animal's neck. Blood spatters, the goat gives a choked bleating, thrashes briefly then subsides, quivering, into death. It reminds me of one of the men I killed in Krisa, big-eyed and shocked that life could end in so banal a fashion. Then the goat's eyes become glassy and its body stills.

And the shadows subtly shift.

It could be no more than the flames of a torch, except we have none. I'm struck by a sense of perspective changing, a shifting of light that reveals a crack in a hitherto solid wall.

'Come,' says Bria. We all gasp as she walks right into that jagged line of darkness on the back wall of the cave, and vanishes. A few men step backwards, but with the Bow of Eurytus gripped in my sweating left hand and my fears held in a stranglehold, I follow her. The closer I get to the rock face, the less solid it seems, until I am pressing through it as though wading through water. Inside the stone, there are stars, bright pinpricks of light swirling about me, and coppery clouds of shifting dust. Momentarily I'm weightless, floating upwards then plunging, then just as abruptly I am on stony ground, staggering until I catch my balance. If I'd eaten I would certainly have vomited as I spun. Then I hear a slow trickle of water, and let the sound guide me onwards.

I step out of *nowhere* onto the grey banks of a dismal river, winding through a slime-encrusted swamp beneath a sky of burnished bronze. The skeletal silhouettes of trees droop thin branches into the water that flows by, left to right, the far shore lost in fog.

Bria is standing on the banks, looking around with a sour face. 'Ithaca,' she hails. 'You've followed me all the way to Erebus. It must be love.'

'What did you mean by being "compelled" to serve Athena?' I ask.

She puts a finger to her lips, a now familiar gesture. 'I'd need to know you a whole lot better before I say another word on that subject, Odysseus.' She glances around the chilling surroundings. 'Let's see if we both make it back from here, eh?'

What has she not told me? 'Can *you* die here?'

'Just assume I can. Watch my back, Odysseus, and I'll watch yours.'

Then other shapes loom out of the mist: Alycus, watchful and unemotional; Castor and Polydeuces, holding hands and tense, but making a show of boldness; then Aendros, wide-eyed and fearful, making superstitious signs with his hands. Gradually the rest appear, with Laas bringing up the rear, presumably to make sure no one changes his mind and flees. All look queasy from the vertiginous passage here, and a couple who'd disregarded Bria's exhortation not to eat are vomiting. They all huddle nervously around Bria.

'Right,' she says, in a voice of forced cheer. 'Alycus, you're the pay master. The boatman will want an *obol* per man.'

Alycus unslings his pack and pulls out a bundle of bronze *obol* spits – probably about ten or a dozen, at a quick glance – which he puts to one side, followed by several silver nuggets. 'Each of these nuggets is worth four drachmas by weight,' he says.

He doesn't need to explain the arithmetic – even a child knows that four drachmas make twenty-four *obols*. More than enough for our needs.

'Very good,' says Bria. 'Keep a nugget handy. But don't expect any change.'

'They say Heracles wrestled him to gain passage,' Melipas comments.

'What about swimming the river?' suggests Aendros.

'Go ahead,' Laas invites. 'But I'm for paying.'

I walk to the river and peer down at the grey, murky water. Any fish that swim by are either bloated or half-skeletal, already dead but still moving. Some are longer than my body, dimly glimpsed in the depths. Nothing at all could induce me to swim.

'How long do we wait?' Aendros asks.

'Never long,' Bria replies. She waves away Melipas, who's approached her to either renew their argument or apologize, and joins me at the riverbank. 'Ithaca,' she mutters, 'the boatman takes his passengers to the other side to face Cerberus. The hound is there to keep the dead in, and the living out.'

'I've heard many conflicting tales about Cerberus.'

'That's the problem. The Underworld is made of belief, and what people believe keeps shifting. Dog heads, snake heads, furred skin or brazen, man-size or giant. The unifying theme is this: it's just possible for the living to get past Cerberus but almost impossible for them to escape.'

'I've heard death's like that – for *most* people.'

'I am what I am,' she replies, a little truculent, a little sad.

I decide I've made my point. 'Do we have a plan?'

'Cerberus can be distracted, but only for a moment. For all I know, Theseus's group are dog feed already. But if they've got past, we'll have to follow.' She eyes the Great Bow. 'Your weapon may come in handy, Ithaca – if you must use it, aim well.'

We're interrupted by the rippling of water as a dark shape glides out of the river mist, a long, low barge being poled from the rear by a huge, shrouded shape who guides the craft in smoothly, resting it alongside the riverbank – a giant of a man with long, ragged white hair and beard, and hollow eyes. Charon, the boatman – said to be a child of Nyx, Goddess of Night, if she is or was ever real. His lips move as he counts us. 'Fifteen *obols*,' he grunts.

'Here you are.' Alycus proffers his silver nugget.

The boat man spits into the river. 'Fifteen *obols*.'

Bria's eyes widen. 'He wants an *actual obol* per person?'

'What?' Alycus snarls, grabbing her collar. 'I thought you said you'd been here before?'

She shoves him away, forcefully. 'I have – but I didn't have to handle the bloody money that time.' She grabs the nuggets and shouts, 'These are worth more than your fifteen *obols*, you fucking moron.'

The giant's eyes narrow. 'Fifteen *obols*,' he grates.

She stamps her feet, swearing under her breath, then whirls away. 'I'm going talk to your master, you piece of stale *kopros*,' she shouts. 'I'll get you banished to the Tartarus for this.'

'Fifteen *obols*,' the boatmen says again, his voice flinty.

Alycus dumps his pack down and pulls out the bundle of bronze spits again. 'Two fistfuls,' he says, grimly. 'Twelve.'

'Who else has *obols*?'

'Do we look like merchants?' Castor replies, sullenly. 'Princes don't carry money.'

'We're on a hunt, not a market expedition,' Laas drawls.

The rest of the soldiers shake their heads – they dwell in the palace at Sparta, eat from the King's table and deal mostly in favours and obligations. They seldom need actual money. And Melipas has spent all of his *obols* on our accommodation in Lacedaemon.

And of course, noble me sent Eurybates away with whatever we had…

'What does he actually do with the *obols*?' I mutter to Bria.

'Nothing. It's merely a habit humans have developed.'

'Stupid damned custom,' I growl.

Bria turns away, cursing under her breath – probably the closest she's going to get to apologizing for this mess.

Alycus waves his silver nugget under the boatman's nose again. 'Look here, Charon, twenty four *obols* for the lot of us – it shouldn't damned well matter anyway.'

The boatman watches him stonily, not in the least intimidated. 'One man, one *obol*,' he repeats.

'Fuck this for a joke!' Aendros says, stepping onto the ferry. 'Take us across!'

The bargepole sweeps around in one brutal movement, spraying drops of dirty water as it arches, to slam into Aendros's midriff and hurl him into the river with an immense splash. The water goes still for a few heartbeats. Then he comes to the surface, thrashing about and gasping for breath.

'Help me!' he cries, 'I can't swim!'

As everyone else gapes, I rip my cloak off and throw one end towards Aendros. 'Grab hold!'

Aendros reaches, stretches, grasps the floating cloth and holds on, spluttering as he goes under again. Castor springs to my aid and together we heave…

…until the water around Aendros boils and he's jerked backwards and wrenched under by some large creature with black-scaled flanks, his final cry dying in the air.

The war band stare – frozen in horror – at the ripples that are all that mark their lost comrade. My cloak floats away. Castor retreats to his brother's side, pale with terror.

'You killed him!' Polydeuces shouts at the boatman. 'You'll answer for this! Don't you know who we are?'

Charon turns his head slowly to survey the young prince. 'One man, one *obol*,' he says, planting his pole in the water again, to push away.

'Wait!' Bria shouts. 'Wait! We'll pay!'

Charon pauses, looking from her to Alycus then Polydeuces. 'One man, one *obol*.'

Alycus stares at Bria. 'Do you mean two men will be left behind?'

'All they have to do is walk back the way they came, and they'll find the cave,' Bria replies, smoothly. *Too smoothly*. But Alycus doesn't resist as she grabs the twelve spits from his hands.

'Twelve *obols*, twelve men,' she says, passing them to the boatman.

Charon counts the spits painstakingly. 'Aye. Twelve.'

Alycus gestures to the two princes to clamber aboard, before running his eyes around the circle. *Twelve men left; ten places.* 'Right, you know the situation: two of you can return to the cave. To safety. Any volunteers?'

To be branded as cowards? I am unsurprised when no one speaks.

'Then Castor and I will decide,' Polydeuces says, with surprising maturity. 'You'll come, Alycus, of course. Bria, as our guide. Laas, you're of a noble Spartan house – you too will come.' He surveys the rest of us.

Seven places left; nine men. 'Pandos, Myrcos, Philoton, Eunomos, Thaumas, Samo...' Polydeuces eyes up the three remaining men: two Spartans, a veteran called Bactiles, Melipas and myself.

'Bactiles, I'm sorry, but your finest days are behind you,' Polydeuces says dispassionately. 'This quest requires our most able.' Then he looks at me coldly. 'And you, Ithacan, have been disowned by your own father. If he doesn't value you, neither do I.'

'We're taking him,' Bria says flatly.

'I don't see why,' Polydeuces says, turning to her guardedly. I remember the way she humiliated him back in Sparta, and I can see that he's seeking any excuse to get even.

Bria pauses. 'Because Odysseus is a *theios*,' she says at last.

Fourteen faces swivel towards me, including the boatman's, whose cavernous eyes burn deepest.

'Who is your patron?' Polydeuces demands of me.

'Hermes,' I lie.

'How did I not know this?' Alycus asks.

Bria shrugs. 'Have you asked him? No? Didn't you notice how fast his wounds healed? And how easily he manages to string that massive bow of his? His mother is Hermes's grand-daughter.'

Laas frowns. 'So he's only a great-grandchild – he shouldn't have enough divine blood.'

'The blood can run thick or thin,' Bria replies. 'Some strains last many generations. Either way, he has the blood, and we need him.' With that, she puts her mouth to Polydeuces's ear and whispers something.

Polydeuces looks far from pleased, but he gives a curt nod. 'Odysseus comes.' He turns and faces the other men still waiting to board. 'I'm sorry, Melipas, but you will stay.'

The young warrior's eyes had widened in shock. Now they narrow. 'Wait! What did Bria say to you?'

'I asked that you be spared this,' Bria replies, before Polydeuces can speak. 'Out of friendship.'

'Then unsay it! I wish to accompany my princes! You can't leave me here!'

This time Polydeuces speaks. 'It's my decision. I charge you to return home with our tale, should we not come again to Sparta.'

'No! I will *not* stay!' Melipas shouts. 'I know the tales. I'll walk this bank one hundred years before I can leave. You can't do this. I'm one of you!'

'My decision is final.'

The chosen men clambering onto the barge look uncomfortably from Charon to the two men left on the shore. Bactiles seems accepting, but Melipas is still furious, his eyes flying from the prince to Bria to me, as his fingers clench and unclench.

Then, once we're all on board, and as Charon's great frame bends to his pole, Melipas gives a strangled cry. In a blur of motion he hurls his spear at me, at almost point-blank range. But I've been half expecting some such move and arch away, my *theios* reflexes engaging without conscious thought, and the bronze spear point flashes past to strike Samo in the belly. The Spartan falls to his knees, groaning, his face filled with disbelief.

As the barge pulls away Melipas leaps across the gap, *xiphos* flashing out and levelled at Bria's chest.

She braces her feet and slams her shield up in one fluid motion. The sword punches into the thick oxhide, Melipas's free hand scrabbling at the shield rim while his feet slither on the gunwale as the barge tilts wildly.

Then Bria shoves, and Melipas topples backwards, screaming as he hits the water. Somehow, thrashing madly about, he manages to struggle back to the bank. Something large surges up from the depths but with Bactiles's help he scrabbles out of its reach, soaked and howling.

'You said you wanted me!' he roars at Bria. 'You said I made you feel whole!'

Already the mist is closing about the two men left on the bank. Bria stands woodenly, staring back. The silence around her is like a wall of knives.

'Bria! You said we had something. Bria!' Melipas's voice is already distant. *Too distant to be natural.* In a few moments, the only sound we can hear is the splash of the pole, the ripple of the hull sliding through the water and the wheezing breath of the old boatman.

I am shivering, and not from the loss of my cloak. Again I've come within a finger's breadth of death. And Melipas had been a friend, a decent man, destroyed by Bria's cold-hearted games. At least she has the decency to look sick about it all. The Spartans are eyeing her with expressions ranging from disgust to fear. Laas kneels beside Samo, speaking quietly and urgently – a spear through the belly is a wound no man can recover from.

The princes both give Samo a blessing, then Laas draws his dagger, and with the stricken warrior's own whispered consent, slices open Samo's jugular while Samo's eyes lock on Laas's face... until they empty.

I draw Bria aside and mutter in her ear, 'Which is it? One hundred years or an open cave?'

'There is *no* way back from there,' she whispers. 'If you come through that gate, you must cross the Styx and find the Dusk or Dawn Gates, or you die.'

So she lied. Bactiles will wait until he starves or chances the river... And she's prepared to leave Melipas stuck in eternity as well... Right at this moment, I am utterly disgusted by her. 'You slept with

Melipas – you used him for your own pleasure then got rid of him afterwards. Is that how you end every relationship?'

'Oh, bugger off, Ithaca! It wasn't a "relationship", it was a fuck. And yes, I was heartily sick of him. Now stop moralizing and start dealing with the problems ahead. We have to find a way past the Hound of Hades, and you hold the key.'

Part Three: In Hades's Realm

14 – Cerberus

'At Cerberus's rear, beneath his shaggy belly, lurked the snakes that formed his tail, darting their tongues about his ribs. Dark rays of light flashed, deep within his eyes. Truly in the Furnaces or in Meligounis such light blazes into the air, when iron is worked with hammers, and the anvil booms beneath mighty blows...'
—Euphorion, *Fragments, 121*

Erebus

With little warning, our ferry-boat journey comes to an end. Charon heaves back on his pole to slew the barge athwart a gloomy riverbank, overshadowed by massive cliffs of razor-edged black granite, slick with vapours. The skies above are lit in bronze, smeared with black clouds that shift in strange patterns. One could never mistake it for the world above.

All the way across the river Styx, we've been haunted by whispering sounds and, far off, the bleating of a goat. The river has swirled with the passage of unseen creatures beneath the surface; once I glimpse what looks like Aendros's face, staring up at me. Led by Alycus, most of the Spartans leap ashore the moment the barge touches, eager to be on dry land. I follow, clutching my bow tighter than ever. *What did Bria mean, that I hold the key? Or is it another of her manipulative games?* I glare at her as she pauses to exchange murmured words with Charon before joining us, her face unreadable. Laas, last to disembark, carries Samo's limp body in his arms.

I drop back and join Laas. 'If a man dies when he's already in Erebus, what happens to his spirit?' I ask.

Laas grunts, shifting the weight on his shoulders. 'Best I know is that it'll still be inside his body, but it'll pull free at some point.' He shudders a little. 'Damned if I want to be holding him at the time.'

Charon's visage gives nothing away as he poles his barge off into the murk.

A dog howls somewhere ahead, the cry echoing about the cliffs. Even Laas and Alycus look ill at ease as the Spartans huddle around the two princes. Polydeuces turns to Bria for guidance. 'You've been here before,' he says. 'What comes next?'

Bria beckons me to join her at the centre of the group. The revelation that I am a *theios* has surprised the Spartans, but it hasn't enhanced their trust in me, judging by how they draw away.

'So,' Bria says, addressing Polydeuces but speaking so all can hear. 'From here, we must pass into a cave which will emerge near the grove of Persephone, the beginning of Erebus itself. But to traverse that cave means passing Cerberus, the Hound of Hades.'

I can sense them hanging on her every word, their nerves tightening as it sinks in that this is a place we might never leave. A fairy story about a dog that guards the Gates of Erebus, a folk tale to chuckle or shiver at, is about to become a real menace we must face.

'Tell us of Cerberus,' I invite her, trying to project a calm I don't feel.

'Sometimes the stories say Cerberus has many heads, or that he's huge; in other accounts he's no more than an ordinary hound. That's because Cerberus becomes what he needs to be. Three travellers will be met by three heads, five by five, and so on. He is a daemon in canine form, fearsome but not unconquerable.' Bria thumps her spear on the ground. 'Heracles wrestled Cerberus and choked him with his own chain.

However, none of us, by themselves, is a Heracles. But together we can be as strong as the great hero.'

We'll need to be more than that. I clear my throat. 'I have an idea.'

–

The cliffs are split by a narrow canyon, hemming our party in as we leave the riverbank, and forcing us onwards towards a dark cleft in the bare rock. Though both sun and moon are absent, there is plenty of light – despite the brazen colour of the sky, it is the air itself which seems to illuminate all it touches, giving our faces a grey-green, ghoulish sheen.

The stink of dog increases, of rotting meat and unwashed fur, a gut-churning odour so concentrated I have to force myself to breathe. *I'll never eat meat again, as long as I live. However long that is…*

Some hundred and fifty yards short of the cave, we pause, as the canyon narrows even further.

'That cleft looks like my wife's cunny,' Laas growls, his attempt to lighten the tension greeted by nervous grins.

'Hey, you're right, it does,' I reply, provoking snorts of laughter.

Alycus holds up a hand. 'Well, men, you know the plan. It'll be rough, and some of us mightn't make it. Play your part, don't move until the moment comes, then go like the Hound of Hades is after you… because he will be.' He turns to me. 'All yours, Ithacan.'

It isn't a sophisticated plan; we have too few options, too few tools, and only one way to go: straight ahead – and a guard dog almost impossible to overcome or avoid, if the stories are to be believed – which in this place they should be.

Slinging the Bow of Eurytus over my shoulder, I heft Samo's body, my *theios* strength making light of the burden, while Bria and the others retreat behind an outcrop on the left-hand side. I hug the right-hand wall as I advance, my heart thudding so hard it almost chokes me. But it's my plan, and I'm obliged to take the most dangerous role.

A hundred yards before the cave, the silence is split by an ear-shattering howl as the hound erupts from the darkness within, doubling in size as it hurtles towards me in leaps and bounds. It's black, the size of a pony and of no distinguishable breed. Its eyes are blazing coals, its serpent tails hiss and swish, and its bronze claws screech and clatter on the bare rock. When it sees that I'm carrying another man, its single head morphs into two.

I stop, stock-still, as the creature jerks to a halt at the limit of its chain, a point marked by claw marks, piles of dog excreta, bone fragments and old bloodstains that cover the ground up to this point.

Theseus's party will have come this way. Is any of this blood theirs? Did any of them survive? How can we imagine we'll do better?

With hot, sulphurous breath Cerberus's bronze teeth snap a few feet from my face. I can see now that the creature's fur isn't fur at all, but tiny writhing snakes with hound heads, its whole body made up of many thousands of creatures mimicking the shape of one.

Very carefully, I lower Samo to the ground and edge the body just inside the hound's reach. The monster is enraged and excited to be so close to a live, edible human – me. But Samo's corpse puzzles Cerberus, as I had guessed it might.

In legend, the dead come as daemons – souls – not as dead flesh. Cerberus is here to keep the living out while welcoming the dead. My reasoning is that a dead *body* might confuse the beast, especially as the soul is still trapped within, because Samo died here in the Underworld. It's taken some persuasion for the Spartans to permit their comrade's body to be used this way, but they've not been able to come up with a better alternative.

I step back and watch as the beast sniffs cautiously at Samo with one head, while its second head snarls at me, warning me to stay away yet clearly desirous that I come within reach. Then a third head forms from one of the tiny, hound-headed snakes, its neck coiling about, and with the additional head, the hound grows in size – it's now larger than a horse. I take that as a sign that the beast is wary, on edge, but it remains focused on Samo and me.

Two of Cerberus's heads now sniff at Samo's body, increasingly agitated as it catches the scent of the soul within, which is what I've been hoping for. But even I'm not prepared for what happens next. The dead man's body begins to writhe, bulging around the midriff as if some immense parasite is trapped inside.

A spectral human face forces itself out through Samo's belly wound, accompanied by a gush of foul-smelling blood. Cerberus yelps excitedly, its serpent tails lashing about, its heads gaping and barking in fascination as the spectre tries to pull clear of Samo's belly, like a hideous birthing.

This lurid sight is why Cerberus doesn't react as it should do when Alycus emerges from behind the outcrop, moving down the left-hand cliff face slowly towards the cave. As he appears I deliberately step back and nock an arrow, to draw the attention of the heads that aren't focused on poor Samo's body.

Even if they don't look away and see Alycus, I'm hoping Cerberus might not realize that behind Alycus, standing pressed to his left shoulder and directly in line, so his body is hidden from view by Alycus's, is Laas. And behind Laas is Pandos, and behind him Myrcos, Eunomos and Thaumas, then Philoton, Bria, Polydeuces and Castor, each standing in the other's shadow so that from the perspective of the hound, there's only one person…

…and the daemon emerging from Samo's corpse is *so distracting*…

It can't last, of course.

As Alycus comes closer, the head that is watching me catches the movement and barks wildly, swiftly joined by a new, fourth head. When Alycus doesn't stop, the hound bucks and slathers, torn between the fascination of seeing a blood-soaked spectral figure pull itself from Samo's belly and this *diversion* on the edge of its vision.

Then someone stumbles, the line behind Alycus becomes ragged, and Cerberus finally realizes that there are many more intruders, and they are all *living meat*. Within a heartbeat, ten more heads erupt from his neck to deal with this new prey.

'*Run!*' I shout, firing at the base of Cerberus's central neck, as Alycus's men break ranks and sprint for the cave mouth. The arrow plunges in, black blood fountains out and the creature howls from fourteen gaping throats...

But then the hound comes apart in a flesh-tearing, ripping movement – and thirteen hounds, each separate now, tear free from the main body and race towards the Spartans, leaving just one before me, still held by his chain.

Cerberus roars, more hydra than hound now, as more bodies break from his main body. I fire arrow after arrow, faster than I've ever managed in training, both at these new creatures and at the ones pursuing the Spartans, sending shafts lancing into their flanks and necks and watching them shriek in agony and fall limp. Even as Cerberus spawns new beasts, I realize that he's growing smaller, not larger – there are limits to his power, even here. And the Great Bow seems to impart some potency to the arrows, for every shaft is deadly. Perhaps there are beliefs about this bow that hold true, in places like this.

My fear evaporates, wiped out by sheer exhilaration born of danger and the unleashing of skill and superhuman strength, sufficient to execute the near-impossible. These moments feel like reward and justification for all those brutal months training with Bria, and for the years of taunts over being unable to string this bow.

I feel like a... a *hero*!

'Come on, you runt of a hound,' I shout at the monstrous shape before me. 'Is this all you can do?'

I'd almost forgotten, in the rush of excitement, that quivers can empty, that Cerberus is far from down, and I still have to get past him myself. But then I grope and find only one arrow in my quiver, and reality smites me. The Spartans seem to be escaping, but I'm still here... and then Cerberus's main body leaps at me. Although my arrows really have done some damage to him, he's so immense that nothing has penetrated his body deep enough to actually kill – if he's not immortal anyway.

As I sprint for the cleft in the rock, a massive set of jaws lunges, seeking to clamp on to me. I roll out of reach, come up and *run*. I feint left, go right and burst past him as Cerberus spins and is briefly wrapped in his own chain. Perhaps he's slowed by his wounds, because my burst of pace opens a gap. Ahead I can see the Spartans are almost through to the cavern entrance. Many of the lesser hounds are down, transfixed by my arrows, but the remainder are hurtling after my comrades, though Thaumas has fallen and is already being ripped apart, his screams cut off short. At the cave mouth, Alycus and Laas have taken a stand, covering the flight of the rest. I dash towards them.

But Cerberus is snapping at my heels, gaining even though I'm running as fast as I did that day I pursued the Trojans on foot, chasing down their horsemen all the way to Kirrha.

Theios energy pounds through my blood and flesh, my heart thunders and my whole body moves in a fluid unison, but some of the hounds have seen me and come bounding to intercept me. I meet one head-on, duck under its leap and slash open its belly with my *xiphos*, sidestep another and almost charge right into a third, managing to plunge my sword into its throat and wrench it slantways as black blood sprays. I hack another down, and then I'm almost blown over by the trumpeting howl behind me.

I glance back, and find Cerberus looming over me, even his lesser selves scattering to avoid being trampled. In the dozen heartbeats since I've fled before him, he's grown. He's the size of that great tusked creature from the remote kingdom of Punt, the *elephas*, and causing the earth to tremble at every bounding step.

I'm not going to make it, I realize. *Then he'll go over the top of the Spartans like an avalanche.*

I have that one last arrow in my hand… and without real thought I spin, kneel and draw the bow string back even as I nock the arrow. A wall of monstrous flesh pounds towards me, massive jaws open in the largest of his heads, a gaping maw big enough to swallow me whole…

And I fire the arrow straight up into the roof of its mouth, and into its brain pan.

Cerberus lurches, shudders… and collapses at my feet.

I back up, shaking like a leaf – just as the other heads begin to lift again, and the body rises once more, the dead head sloughing away, taking its bronze chain with it. It, and all the other lesser hounds, bark and snarl, bounding straight at me.

I turn and run like a crazy man down the barely lit tunnel that bores into the stone, with the remaining Spartans fleeing ahead of me. We are howling in a wild mix of triumph and terror, straining every muscle as bronze-toothed jaws clash and snap behind us. Myrcos, just in front of me, accidentally clips the heel of Pandos and both go down. There's no time to save them – I leap over their sprawling bodies, knowing they will be engulfed. And I'm next…

It's at that moment that my right thigh muscle, never properly healed from the boar's tusk at Pytho, chooses to tear. I shriek in agony and despair as my leg gives way, falling face first, slithering and rolling. Sharp teeth snap shut on my right calf and I expect death a heartbeat later. But Bria appears, plunging her spear into the hound's skull. Its jaws go slack and I pull my leg free as fire gouts from Bria's left hand, torching some hounds and driving the rest back momentarily. She heaves me to my feet and hurls me onwards. Yet more fire streams from her; the hounds recoil, shrieking and snapping as fur singes and ignites, then they surge forward again.

We're both going to die…

Bria shouts something in a high, shrill voice. It sounds like an incantation, a spell. I hear the word '*chain*' and a deafening clang of metal, then countless howls of frustrated fury. Suddenly Cerberus is only one beast again, albeit gigantic – but the chain is back around his neck, bronze links taut and straining.

I lurch to my feet and limp away, gasping for breath and shaking with pain and relief. Bria joins me, panting hard but with a huge smile on her dark face. 'Don't you love this,' she purrs, throwing my arm around her shoulders and helping me move.

We make it through the final few paces, stumbling around a bend and into a cavern, as Cerberus falls silent. Alycus, Laas and the two princes are waiting, Castor winded and shaking while Polydeuces is pale but bright-eyed. But only two of the soldiers have made it: Philoton and Eunomos.

The rest of us have survived... but no one is looking at me with any particular gratitude.

'I suggest we move on, in case the chain snaps,' Bria pants. It seems like *excellent* advice.

With her help, I hobble after the others as we penetrate deeper into the cave, leaving the yowling hounds behind. 'Why did you fall?' Bria asks.

'The boar wound,' I reply, through gritted teeth. 'It's never come right... Starting to think it never will.'

She gives me a rare, sympathetic look. 'I've brought healing herbs with me, and some water from the world above. Wait till we find a place to stop and I'll have a look.'

I have more questions for her. Where did she get that fire from, and why hasn't she used it before? How did she conjure up that new chain and stop Cerberus eating us all? But I can barely speak through the pain.

Finally we reach the end of the cave, emerging onto a slope beneath overhanging cliffs, with a path winding down through scattered trees into a forest, mist-filled and ominous. I look up at the blank, bronze-coloured sky. 'How big is this place?' I ask Bria.

'As big as our imaginations,' she replies, helping me to a boulder so I can sit. Alycus, Laas and the two princes join us, the two captains clearly distressed at the loss of Myrcos, Pandos and Thaumas. The two remaining soldiers, Philoton and Eunomos, look shattered, physically and spiritually.

'What's wrong with the Ithacan?' Castor asks as he heaves down gulps of air. There's no concern in his voice, only curiosity.

'He's been bitten,' Bria snaps. 'Can't you see?'

The teeth marks on my calf are grey-rimmed and the wound feels oddly numb, a sharp contrast to the fiery pain of my thigh. 'I can make a poultice for this wound, but we need to move on,' Bria adds.

'Is he going to slow us down?' Polydeuces asks.

'No, I'm damned well not,' I retort. 'Are you?'

'I've not been bitten by the Hound of Hades.'

'Enough!' Bria cries, turning on the princes. 'Odysseus's plan got you through. You owe it to him to help.' She jabs a finger at Laas. 'Give him your shoulder while I find what I need for my poultice – we need to reach the shelter of the forest before something really nasty arrives to find out what upset the dog.'

Laas takes my weight. 'Don't worry about the princes,' he has the good grace to mutter. 'I doubt any of us would have survived without your little ruse.' He looks sidelong at me: 'How would Theseus and his party have got through?'

'Pirithous is one of Hades's champions,' I say, sharing a thought that has only just occurred to me as though I've known it forever. 'He probably gave Cerberus a haunch of meat and patted its head, then they all strolled past, whistling.'

'Probably. So, you're one of us, eh? The half-secret brotherhood of the *theioi* – famous for backstabbing each other, then pointing at an icon and saying "my god made me do it". When were you awakened?'

'Recently.'

'And King Laertes wasn't best pleased, I'm guessing, considering that you're disowned and wandering the Peloponnese like a mercenary for hire?'

Laas is perceptive – and uncomfortably close to the truth. 'It isn't something he feels comfortable about,' I lie, cautiously. In fact, Laertes has no idea.

'Old Laertes?' Laas cocked an eyebrow. 'An Argonaut who hunted the Calydonian Boar? He's been around *theioi*.' He gives me a shrewd look. 'I heard he was in despair of ever having a child until you happened along.'

Not just perceptive, uncannily accurate. 'I'd remind you that my father's honour is my own,' I warn.

'Don't get touchy, Odysseus,' Laas drawls. 'I just need to know that you want our princess returned home as much as I do. Because I'm wondering what her nibs there,' he indicates

Bria, 'is really up to. Does Athena want Helen back in Sparta? Has Theseus really gone rogue, or is he doing exactly as his mistress wishes?' He fixes me with a cold stare. 'What really happened in that culvert?'

I know better than to look away, even for an instant. 'I told you all exactly what happened.'

'You're either a brilliant liar, or telling the truth. And for once, I can't say which. You're too smooth and worldly for a bumpkin island prince.'

'Hardly a bumpkin – I spent four years in Lacedaemon, remember? And before that, I had well-travelled tutors. And I'm not stupid. I think you're looking too hard for things that aren't there.' I wince as my injured leg jars. 'While not watching the bloody path close enough,' I add.

He grunts unapologetically, but he shuts up.

We hobble on together until we reach the forest verge, where I find a fallen tree trunk to plant my arse upon. Laas takes a quick look at my bite wounds, shakes his head and ambles away.

The pines have a ghostly aspect, their needles greenish-grey and sickly. There's little sign of life here – no paths or trails, no birdsong, no animal scent or spore, not so much as a spider or an ant. The Spartans huddle together, subdued by the desolate place.

Alycus checks each man's well-being, but leaves me to Bria, who bustles up with a clutch of starry white flowers. 'Asphodels,' she tells me, handing me most, then pulling out a small mortar and pestle from her pack and grinding up some dried herbs of her own with a splash of water from her flask, along with a few of the petals.

'What are the rest of these flowers for?' I ask, peering doubtfully at the asphodel posy I'm holding.

'To cheer you up. And there, they have,' she winks. 'There are whole fields of them on the far side of this forest. We'll see them tomorrow.'

I lay the flowers beside me. 'Today? Tomorrow? How can you tell time here? Does it ever get dark?'

'No, it's unchanging. But we aren't: for us it's night, and we need to rest.' She finishes crushing her paste and smears it onto my bitten calf muscle, then binds a strip of cloth cut from her cloak about it. 'Let's have a look at your thigh,' she says, pushing up my tunic and digging with thick strong fingers around my knotted scars. Each probing stroke is painful, but there is something in her touch that soothes. 'I'll make another poultice for the inflammation,' she tells me, 'but beyond that, the only remedy for this is time, rest and a gentle easing back into full movement. Of course, we're in Erebus, so that's not going to happen. But try at least to protect it, Ithaca, or you'll be limping for the rest of your life.'

However short that is.

She makes another batch of paste, rubs it roughly into my thigh, then bandages me tightly. 'If you meet another monster,' she advises, 'try reasoning with it.'

'Talking of reason,' I ask, 'what did you do back in the tunnel? You threw fire at Cerberus then chained it – how?'

'Things work differently here, Ithaca. This isn't our world, this is Erebus. For want of a better explanation, we're walking around inside a place that has been invented by human imagination. That gives beings like me a certain discretion. The stories say that Cerberus is chained – I "reminded" the chain to be there.'

'Why couldn't you do it earlier?' That Thaumas, Myrcos and Pando might still be alive is something I don't need to point out.

'Before we entered the cave, we hadn't truly entered Erebus,' Bria explains. 'Passing Cerberus marked a transition and opened up my options. It enabled me to use fire in a way I couldn't before. There are certain energies sloshing around here, and I used them. I've been drawing on the same energies to try and speed your healing. Test the limits, when you're able.' She pats my shoulder and gets to her feet, her black skin glistening with sweat from the strain of whatever magus arts she's been performing.

There hadn't been African slaves in Ithaca, but I've seen them in the slave quarries near Mycenae, and spoken with freed slaves and Libyan traders in the ports too. The cast of her face is rounder and softer than an Achaean face, and her skin so much darker. It's not unattractive – but of course it's just another mask Bria wears. I remember that I am still angry with her, nod a grudging thanks and look away.

She takes my change in mood in her stride and goes to join the Spartans, who are discussing how to make camp here. 'We can build a fire, but don't touch anything but fallen wood,' she instructs Alycus. 'This forest is sacred to Persephone, and she annoys easily.'

She follows that up with a diatribe about not eating the berries, drinking the water or hunting, but her voice fades to a murmur as I drift towards sleep. I roll onto my side, close my eyes and everything falls away.

–

I dream that I'm floating through the air as if swimming through water, riding unseen currents. There is neither sun nor moon, but the sky is a brazen colour and that tells me my dream is set in Erebus. To my left are giant cliffs, rising sheer, a mile high and topped with jagged ridges. Below me is a ribbon of silver fluid, a river: the Styx, I guess. To the right is darkness, shot through with stars, and a chill that frightens me. *Don't go that way*, every instinct clamours. *Follow the river.*

I see other people float by, drifting across the skies, their bodies like glass, or an empty chrysalis or a cicada husk. They are all focused on their own journey. Other dreamers, perhaps. Or dead souls.

The river below is sluggish, and I glide lower. The waters are foul with rotting vegetation and the submerged roots and branches of fallen trees. Then I see a ship, no wind in its sails but drifting with the current, making a slow and tortuous journey on Death's river, rowing through the debris.

With the logic that dreams have, I know that it's Kyshanda's ship.

I swoop in closer, hearing the muffled drum keeping time for the rowers, and noting that all else is silent. Fear rises from the ship like a smell, unsurprising when they're navigating the waters of another culture's concept of death and the afterlife. And from my high vantage, I can see things they perhaps can't – dozens of dark shapes are trailing the ship, beneath the surface. Some are almost as large as the galley, stalking it menacingly.

The moment I think of Kyshanda, my focus zooms in, as if I'm being propelled by thought alone – perhaps I am. I find myself hovering near the starboard beam, where the strained faces of the Trojan soldiers watch the deathly shore float by. Then I spy Kyshanda, huddled with Skaya-Mandu and a man who is perhaps captain of the galley. The two men are fully armed and armoured, but she is clad in her formal eastern robes, her head veiled and only her eyes showing amidst the silks. They are speaking their own tongue, but if I concentrate the sound carries to me, and I know enough Luwian to follow the conversation.

'We need to find somewhere to beach,' the captain is saying. 'The men are shattered. They haven't rested properly for two days and a night.'

'There'll be no rest here,' Skaya-Mandu replies sullenly. 'We cannot afford to pause. Our enemy is far ahead of us, and if they reach the Achaean Death God before we find them, we've lost.'

'The men worry that we might never escape this place,' the captain says.

'We'll find a way out, Gan,' Kyshanda puts in, and my senses quicken to her lyrical voice. 'Theseus is travelling on foot, and he won't know that we've breached this place by way of another entrance. Every hour we're gaining on them, even by this circuitous route. Our paths will soon intersect.'

'How do you know that?' Skaya-Mandu demands.

'Because I've studied maps of this place, given me by our mother,' Kyshanda answers. 'Like our own realm of death, this place has a geography. This river, the Styx, joins the Lethe soon and spirals into the heartland, to a place called the Pantheon, which Theseus will certainly aim for – it's where visitors must go to seek audience with Hades. To reach it on foot, Theseus must pass Cerberus, traverse Persephone's Grove and the Asphodel Fields. All of these are perilous obstacles.'

'Whereas this river journey is safe?' Skaya-Mandu asks, in sarcastic tones.

'I didn't say that,' Kyshanda replies. 'I only said it was swifter, and given that we had no other way to pass the hound, infinitely more likely to give us success.'

Suddenly they all three fall silent, and I realize that Kyshanda has turned towards me, with piercing, glistening eyes. There's no recognition in her gaze, only concern at some perceived threat. She says something, words that crackle and roar in my mind; I feel my whole form fray and come apart, an agonising sensation that makes me shriek...

...and then I'm gasping and thrashing in my cloak, back at the campsite. My eyes fly open, and for a moment I fear I've shouted aloud and woken everyone, but apart from the sentries, everyone's sleeping.

It takes time for my heart to stop hammering, and even more for my brain to stop churning over that vision. I'm nervous about sleeping again, but when exhaustion finally claims me, I tumble into a dreamless pit.

15 – *The Grove of Persephone*

'Therefore we must not be persuaded or permit it
to be said, that Theseus, the son of Poseidon, and
Pirithous, the son of Zeus, launched themselves
into such appalling rapine, nor that any other hero,
a child of a god, would have been reckless enough
to perform the dreadful and impious deeds they
now falsely accuse them of.'
—Plato, *Republic*

Erebus

I am half-awake when Bria touches my shoulder. 'Rise and
shine, Ithaca. It's about as morning-like as its going to get, and
we've got a lot of ground to make up.'

I look up – the sky is unchanged, a sheet of bronze fire
and black smoke, slowly swirling. But perhaps it's lighter? The
Spartans are all rousing, stretching their cramped limbs. I accept
Bria's offer of a hand, gritting my teeth as I put weight on
my right leg. 'I'll need a spear to walk with,' I admit, cursing
inwardly.

Castor and Polydeuces saunter over, arm in arm. 'We'll
not let you slow us down, Ithacan,' the younger brother
pronounces. 'Our sister's life is at stake, and she's worth a
hundred of you. We'll travel as fast as possible – it's over to
you to keep up.'

They swagger away without a backward glance.

'I wish one of those damned gods at Olympus might have
blessed Polydeuces with a shred of humanity,' I mutter to Bria.

'A simple "thou shalt not be a total heap of *kopros*" would have sufficed.'

'None of the gods except our mistress would have understood the concept,' Bria replies, drily. 'Sadly, you'll find that most *theioi* are like them. But seriously, can you manage?'

'Certainly,' I lie. 'I just need to loosen my muscles up. They're a bit stiff.'

We breakfast from the meagre remains of our food before warming up for the day's march. The next ten minutes are about the most painful I've ever endured. Exercising with a ruptured muscle is far from ideal, but Bria guides me, and by the time Alycus calls a halt to the session, I can limp along at a reasonable pace.

Thankfully, Bria's tracking – she's seeking signs of Theseus and his party – means we travel at a pace I can manage. The path she takes leads through a tangled pine forest, where she finds a path, a muddy swath of ground about two feet wide where nothing grows, meandering through the undulating forest. When Laas asks her who made the trail she replies, 'Persephone comes here – everything dies that touches the hem of her dress.'

It's not a comforting thought, but she does find fresh footprints in the mud, made by Achaean boots with nails hammered into the sole – Theseus and Pirithous, almost certainly.

'Is my sister still with them?' Castor demands.

'This set,' Bria replies, pointing out a smaller print with a pointed toe, 'either belongs to Theseus's mother or to Helen. They're not far ahead of us.'

'So we can run!' exclaims Polydeuces, giving me a malevolent glance.

'With all respect, my prince,' Alycus replies, 'if we lose their tracks, our mission will fail. We cannot say if they have stayed on this path or have taken another route further on. Care and accuracy must outweigh haste.'

Good man, I think, fervently. Even walking is anguish for me, and I'm drenched in sweat.

The morning passes in surges and pauses. When the way seems obvious we jog, with Bria in the lead. I inevitably fall behind, catching up only when they stop to examine more tracks. We see the first animals since Cerberus's cave – a flock of dead-looking crows feasting on an even more dead-looking trio of wolves. Nearby, a fresh, hastily abandoned campsite at the side of the track is marked by prints of nailed soles and, this time, two sets of women's slippers. We conclude that one of the women must have been carried, up to this point. So – at least when they reached this campsite – both Helen and Aethra were still alive.

'Theseus's party was attacked by wolves, but the pack drew off,' Bria declares, just as I limp in.

We move again before I can catch my breath. To my surprise, Laas drops back. 'How do you fare, Ithacan?'

'I'm… just about… done, until… I can rest,' I pant, hating to admit it.

'Do you need help?'

'No! I… can manage… better on… my own. Just need… a break.'

'Hang in there. Even Prince Poly will have to accept that Castor is as exhausted as you. We'll all rest soon.' Laas gives a wry smile. 'It'll be good for our blessed prince, having an elder brother who's mortal.'

'I understand he's going to fix that,' I grunt.

Laas chuckles. 'He speaks big, does our Poly. But he'll find out things don't just happen because he wants them to. We all have to learn that lesson.' He pats my shoulder. 'You've got grit, Ithacan. I just wish I knew whether we're on the same side.'

I'm not even sure which side I'm on, after what I've seen of Athena. All these gods seem cold-hearted and self-serving. *But no young girl deserves to be kidnapped by brutes like Theseus.* 'Trust me, on this matter, we're very much aligned. I'm just worried the damage is already done.'

'Aye. I think even the princes realize that, though they won't voice it. Helen is late to begin her cycles, so no man of honour ought to touch her. But Theseus bedded every girl he fancied, so even her youth mightn't stop him. And there were already signs of—' He stops himself in mid-sentence.

'Signs of what?' I say, feigning innocence. *Does Laas know what happened at the Olympian Court?*

'Why do you want to know?' Laas gives me a probing look.

Because gaining her powers requires losing her maidenhead. And – cycles or no cycles – she might well want those gifts unlocked now *and at her fingertips.*

'I just want to know all the angles we're dealing with,' I tell him.

'Fair enough,' Laas grunts. 'There was a slave boy – Leda found him and Helen half-undressed and kissing.'

So that was what Tyndareus started to refer to, that night I overheard him talking with Menelaus in the palace courtyard, back at Sparta. 'What became of the boy?'

'He died under the lash.'

'Harsh,' I comment. *Especially since the poor young fool would have had little choice but to obey her.* I wonder how that incident affected Helen.

'Harsh? See how *you* like it, when you find your sister bedding a slave,' Laas retorts. 'Ah, here we are!'

We've arrived at the latest resting place, to find Castor kneeling, red-faced and dry-retching. I grip Laas's shoulder in thanks, then hobble over to slump down beside Bria and recuperate as best I can.

Alycus and Laas sit with the two remaining soldiers. One of them, Philoton, recently lost his wife in childbirth, and claims to have dreamt vividly of her last night. This sounds ominous, but there's no turning back.

'How's Castor?' I ask Bria, as we share water.

'Done in. He's only sixteen. Polydeuces isn't much better off, for all that he's a *theios* – he's still growing into his potential.' She jerks her thumb forward, 'We're almost through these woods – next is Persephone's Grove.'

'What's that?'

'Don't you know the tale? Persephone, daughter of the Harvest goddess, is whisked off by Hades to the Underworld and ravished. A crisis develops, with crop failures and famine, until it's agreed she can spend the winter here, and the rest of the year in the natural world.'

'A made-up tale to explain the seasons.'

Bria gives me a withering look. 'You really do need to stop thinking like that.'

'Are you going to enlighten me?'

Bria harrumphs, but then concedes, 'Of course it's a tale to explain the seasons. But remember, this Underworld we're visiting is made of such tales. Here, they become real. Once the story of Persephone became widely known, and *believed*, who should pop up in the Underworld but a new queen called Persephone. As for her grove… well, let's just say it's her special place.'

'Is it safe?' I remember the sinister, half-faced goddess at the Olympian Court.

Bria snorts. 'What do *you* think? Let me tell you of Persephone – she's part-winter, part-summer; part-living, part-dead; part-goddess, part-victim. A lot of contradictory parts can drive someone part-mad.'

'Shouldn't we stay away?'

'If it's where Theseus went, we have no choice.'

'Laas is worried Theseus might already have raped Helen,' I say, dropping my voice. 'Or seduced her – Laas told me she was becoming precocious.' *Though there's a world of difference between kissing a slave boy and embracing a murderous thug like Theseus.*

Bria pulls a face. 'Maybe. But his original plan, to take her to Troy – and now this flight to Erebus – requires exchanging Helen for gain. Gold or, perhaps, immortality. Either way, her value is lessened if she loses her virginity, even if that does result in her gaining her *theia* powers. Helen unsullied is worth far more to Hades than Helen already debauched by Theseus. Our favourite Athenian would be stupidly reckless to do such a thing.'

'But "stupidly reckless" pretty much sums him up,' I point out.

'I know. That's the worry. But they've got Theseus's mother with them. Theseus would do anything for Aethra. She's not what you'd expect: ruthless in defence of her son, yes, but otherwise she's dignified old gentry, and quite maternal. She's my hope that Helen is being treated well.'

Bria's logic allays some of my fears, leaving me free to concentrate on sipping water and getting my breath back, while massaging my leg muscles. Our water skins are almost empty, but Bria reassures us that we are approaching a spring where it's safe to drink. 'Persephone has made a place here which contains a small part of the world above,' she tells us. 'The water flowing directly from the spring is safe. But don't drink from the pool below – not that you'll want to, when you see it.'

Castor perks up at the mention of water. He's just drained his own water skin and then his brother's.

'Come,' Bria says, getting to her feet. 'The grove is this way.'

–

As we descend towards Persephone's Grove, the deathly pines give way to lowland forest, cypresses and oaks, and even figs and wild olives. The spaces between the tree trunks are filled with undergrowth, most of the bushes heavy with berries. There are birds here that seem no different from those in the world above, and we glimpse squirrels flitting through the branches. As we pass the berries it is almost a reflex to reach out and pluck—

'Don't,' Bria raps. 'You've much to live for, Ithaca. It'd be a shame to throw it away for a morsel of fruit.'

I snatch my hand away from a luscious red berry, and refocus on picking my way along the now overgrown and root-bound path, my right leg muscles burning from the exertion. A livid bruise now covers the entire inside of my thigh, purple and yellow and swollen, under the scarred welts left by the boar tusk.

I have to care for it better, as Bria warned. I don't want to be a cripple all my life…

To distract myself, I think of all the things I want to live for… to see Ithaca again and my family – together, happy, smiling. Laertes proud of me; Mother safe and restored to his affection; my sister Ctimene in love and wed to a good man. To see Kyshanda of Troy, as a friend, not an enemy.

I grit my teeth, struggling to keep up as the Spartans increase their pace again, eager to reach the spring Bria has described. Castor, not far in front of me, seems almost as distressed as I am. Polydeuces has come back to assist his brother; it's nice to see, once more, that concern for his brother can temper his ego – perhaps that augurs well for him. *He might become less of a* priapos *as he matures.*

By now my leg is cramping badly, reducing me to a slow shuffle. Even the brothers have vanished up ahead. Suddenly I hear a cry of horror. Alone in the tangled woodland, I'm immediately fearful for our party, burning through much of my reserves to catch them up.

As I lurch into a clearing, I see Bria and the Spartans, and feel a surge of relief that they're safe – a relief that doesn't last. The Spartans are huddled beside a spring which feeds into a large pool surrounded by ancient willow trees. Their eyes are all drawn upwards and I follow their gaze – and choke on my breath.

In the nearest tree, three young women are dangling from twisted rope vines, choking and kicking as they strangle, drool running from their mouths and blood from their chafed necks. Their dresses are torn, and their inside legs are coated with excrement. The stench is vile and both the air and the bodies are thick with large, squat flies.

Appalled, I drag my eyes away from the ghastly sight, only to find dozens more twitching bodies dotted about the glade. Even Laas's hard-bitten face has turned a sickly grey-green colour.

Bria's voice is matter-of-fact, as if she were a guide in a historic temple or shrine. '…And this tongueless nymph's name is Lara – she tried to seduce Zeus. Hera was furious, so Persephone helped her out by seizing Lara and bringing her here, to her Sacred Grove. Persephone likes to hang them, despite – or because – they're immortal and can't die. Every so often she "harvests" a few to be harpies or *Erinyes*, but they could as easily just choke here for the rest of eternity.'

It's too much for most of the party. Alycus and Laas have probably seen enough atrocities to be hardened to suffering, but Philoton and Eunomos turn aside and lose the meagre contents of their stomachs, as do both the princes, and I take that as licence to do the same. When I've finished retching and stand wiping my mouth with the back of my hand, I find Polydeuces looking at me with what seems to be a shred of empathy.

We've finally shared an emotion, this bold young prig and I. Revulsion – basic enough, to be sure, but it's a start.

'The spring water is safe,' Bria reminds us. 'Use it to rinse and drink. This is the only drinkable water in Erebus, so fill your water skins.' She fills her helm and tips it over her head, the water briefly flattening her tightly curled Nubian hair, which then crinkles again. 'The tracks indicate that Theseus came here, but moved on quickly – we need to do the same. They're still a long way ahead of us.'

'But shouldn't we do something for these women?' I ask, trying my best not to look about me at the kicking, convulsing nymphs. 'This is monstrous!'

'Are you mad?' Bria responds. 'They're here because Persephone wants them to be! You help even one of them, and you'll be sharing their fate! Come on, let's move!'

'I never thought Persephone could be so cruel,' I mutter to her, as we prepare to move again.

'What did you think "suffering in Hades's realm" entails, Ithaca? Bad wine and boredom?' She stamps away.

'If that's what all Athena's ladies are like, I'm glad I serve Ares,' Laas notes drily.

'What do you gain from serving your patron?' I ask, remembering what I'd been told: the *theioi* of different gods have slightly different gifts.

Laas shrugs. 'The usual *theios* gifts for a champion: speed, strength, stamina, durability; but with Ares, you also gain another thing: a double-edged weapon called *bloodlust*. When the blades are drawn, and the wave of madness hits you, the world turns to red, and you're invincible, inexhaustible, until that wave sweeps on by. You barely recall it afterwards, bar the trail of bodies and carnage you can follow back to the starting point of your rage. War is savagery, Odysseus. It's not about strategy or skill, it's about who wants it more, you or them. That's why Ares will always be greater than Athena.'

I weigh my words, keeping in mind that to these men, I represent Hermes, not Athena. 'With the greatest respect,' I reply, 'I think you're wrong. In the end, I believe, the skill of Athena will be held higher than the bloodlust of Ares. But I'm just a man of Hermes, so what do I know?'

'Think what you like, Ithacan. Blades speak louder than thoughts, and mine has had plenty to say over the years.'

'Is Ares aware you're here?' I ask.

Laas gives me a shrewd look. 'Wondering if he knows about this matter, are you? I've not told him so – I'm only a champion, not an avatar. He can't enter me, nor anyone I know. Avatars are the rarest of the *theioi*.'

Then the loss of Iodama is a more grievous blow to Athena than I realized.

'If gods can take animal form, why don't they do it more often?' I wonder.

'Because it weakens them,' Laas replies. 'At least, that's what an avatar of Ares once told me. But it's not for me to educate you, Ithacan.' He slaps me on the shoulder and trudges away.

A few minutes of walking takes us out of the ghastly grove, past more dangling bodies and other victims also, male and female, some being crushed by grappling vines studded with thorns, some tied to stakes and being pecked by crows or stung by clouds of wasps. Then, mercifully, the land opens out, the trees giving way to a shimmer of asphodel flowers, a sea of white that stretches out before us, a strange contrast to the gloomy backdrop. Again, I fall behind.

When I catch the Spartans up, they have been resting and are readying to move on again. To my surprise it is Polydeuces who speaks for me. 'Another few minutes, to allow the Ithacan to recover,' he says. Another glimmer of hope he mightn't turn out a complete arsehole.

From the small rise where we sit, eating the last of our food, Erebus spreads before us, circled by mountains. A clinging mist has crept in as we watch, smearing the asphodel-covered plains, obscuring much but leaving enough gaps to reveal a distant, forested hill crowned by a white-pillared building, near the edge of a marshland forest through which we glimpse many trailing lines of silvery water. The asphodel fields reach to the near side of the hill, and are bordered to their left by a jagged line of low hills. Several paths wind through the flowers – more lifeless soil touched by Persephone's hem, Bria confirms.

'What's the building atop that distant hill?' Alycus asks her.

'A holy site that Hades calls his "Pantheon" – "pan" meaning all, and "theon" meaning what you'd expect it to mean. It's a place where all the gods can sit enthroned when they visit Erebus.'

I'm still in a state of horror over Persephone's Grove. 'This is a dreadful place,' I remark.

'Sure, but if you want to see real cruelty, go to Tartarus. I've not had the pleasure myself, and I hope I never shall. I trust in Athena that when I finally die, I shall be conveyed to the Elysian Fields, and dwell with the Blessed.'

'May we all be similarly rewarded', I mutter fervently.

'What about those hills?' Laas asks, indicating the foothills that border the left flank of the asphodel fields.

Bria snorts. 'Do you think I'm a local? I've only been here once before, with my mistress, and we went directly to the Pantheon to discuss some theological matters with Hades and Hera.'

No wonder she was sketchy about dealing with Charon and Cerberus. I forgive her a little.

'And this "Pantheon" is where Theseus is going?' Poly-deuces asks.

'That's my belief,' Bria replies. 'The protocol for any visitor is to burn an offering on the altar inside the Pantheon, which summons a representative of Hades. After that, you just wait for the Death God to show up. Beyond Pantheon Hill – and after many more miles of Persephone's damned asphodels – you reach the Hall of Judgement, where the spirits of three wise kings of old – Minos, Aeacus and Rhadamanthys – sit in judgement over the dead. Beyond that you've got the Elysian Fields, for the Blessed; the Vale of Lethe for most of us, where we can reflect on life until we drink from the river of forgetfulness and cease to be; and Tartarus for those with whom the gods are truly annoyed.'

'Where's Hades's palace?' Laas asks.

'Overlooking the Hall of Judgement, so I'm told.'

I remember my dream – in it Kyshanda had spoken of a 'Pantheon' that Theseus had to reach, to summon Hades. If I can trust the dream, she's going to the same place as us. I wish I had an eagle's eyes, to see what might be transpiring on that green, far-off hill. Theseus must have reached it by now. How long would the Athenian have to wait before Hades arrived to hear his petition? And where are the Trojans? Has their ship successfully traversed the rivers? Could they even now be climbing the hill?

All too soon, Bria stands up. 'When I was here last,' she says, 'Hades arrived on a flying chariot amidst storm clouds. I'm not seeing any yet, but we have to reach that hill and reclaim your princess before he turns up.' She raises her voice. 'There's only one rule when crossing the Asphodel Fields: you must remain silent.'

'Why?' Castor asks.

'Because the dead will hear you, and you don't want that.'

We clamber to our feet, Alycus taking the lead. 'We're running again,' he tells us, before turning to me. 'Sorry, Ithacan, but we've lost too much time already. And a one-legged man's no use in a fight, especially if his bow hasn't any arrows left.'

I can't dispute his logic, and looking around me, I see a little sympathy but no disagreement. I nod acceptance, knowing that being left alone in Erebus is akin to a death sentence, but I can offer no counter-argument. I've got them alive past Cerberus but I'm no longer of any use. Laas, bless him, gives me his cloak. In one sense, I'm doing him a favour – it will only get in his way while he's running. Even Bria can do no more than spare me a pair of her own arrows. I wonder how many of Athena's champions she's seen die. A fair number, I judge, from her barely sympathetic face. I guess serving a cold-hearted queen like Athena rubs off.

Then off they all jog through the asphodels, following Persephone's deathly path, and though in my heart I know they have little choice, it's difficult not to feel bitterness. *They haven't even thanked me. No 'You saved our lives; we'll remember you in our prayers.' Bastards.*

In moments I am alone, limping along, waist-deep in white flowers, and before long it becomes apparent that the Pantheon Hill is also fading from view. A ground mist is rising, blotting out the middle distance and beyond. Soon I can't tell where the asphodels end and the mist begins. The Underworld has shrunk to a flowery field surrounded in mist. I hobble on for what seems an age, consumed by bitter recriminations, muttering to myself at the injustice of fate.

Basically, I'm done for. Bullied by Athena and betrayed by her turncoat champion. So much for her omniscience. And so much for my grand plans to help my mother, and prove myself to Laertes…

Round and round my thoughts circle, until I fear they'll strangle my brain. The pain of moving dulls my awareness of what is before me, and my inner war against despair. But then the whispers start.

It's not just mist that surrounds me, I realize – but also the pale wispy forms of men and women, wraiths of the dead. They're drifting in clumps, pale as clouds and radiating cold. I see old faces and young, even children lost and afraid. I'm staring, but none look back – they don't even seem to see me.

You have to stay silent, Bria warned. I follow her advice.

I don't know how much time has passed, but it feels like aeons. I realize that I've lost the path, and am limping directionless through the asphodels… Then I hear a distant voice, a man howling in despair, and I recognize Philoton, calling his wife's name… then he suddenly falls silent and that silence chills me. Fear closes in, borne on those vacant, deathly faces.

Then I make a mistake: unthinkingly, I speak aloud: 'No, Philoton,' I whisper, wishing him silent when I should have remained so myself.

The mist churns, as if stirred by a gust of wind – then, chillingly, I realize that the wraiths in the mist have spun my way – and they *can* now see me.

The nearest, a dead warrior with a wound in his chest, bares his teeth and snarls. His arms rise, reaching out, and they hem me in.

I turn and run – well, stagger – frightened now, more than frightened, scared nigh witless. Cold, barely substantial hands pull at me, like frost on my skin. I thrash about, tripping and falling, hauling myself along as the wraiths gibber and plead.

'Stay, stay,' they call. 'Stay with us, Living Man. Stay… feed us…'

My panic rises, and I know I have to fight it or I'll be destroyed. I spin about, lurching through the asphodels with no goal in sight, but then the merest tear in the mist shows me a bare, stony slope. *The Pantheon Hill?* I make for it, stumbling onwards, slapping aside the spectral hands that reach for me.

Behind me, the dead are massing, their ranks closed tight, led by that dead warrior whose eyes are now alight with a feral kind of hatred. I hobble on, the long grass and the flowers seeking to entangle me, and then I burst from the foliage and onto a barren slope. I look upwards, but can't see the crest.

And now I'm remembering that the Pantheon Hill appeared green and lush from a distance…

I turn, see the massed dead gathered on the verge of the hill. They come no further, just standing there silently, watching, reaching out, their faces hungry. I back away, and then low cloud sweeps in and I'm alone again on this lifeless hillside.

Then I hear another wail of despair, from somewhere above me, followed by a huge resounding roar like an avalanche, filling me with dread. I'd once seen a cliff give way during an earthquake on Ithaca, carrying four houses with it, and I've never forgotten the sound.

Again, I hear that wailing, anguished cry, and stare blindly up into the mist, aware that I'd been unable to aid those poor nymphs being strangled in Persephone's Grove. Perhaps this is someone I can help? And perhaps they might aid me in return? It seems far-fetched, but I'm alone, and one truth we humans cling to is that most of us need other people to endure. I'm no different in that respect.

And perhaps, if I can climb above this wretched mist, I can get my bearings again. So I head up the slope towards the fading cry.

–

The last clattering echo of the rockfall has died away. I pull a fold of Laas's cloak over my head so my hair won't be soaked by the moist, heavy air. The deathly cold makes my bones ache, but curiosity draws me onwards, clambering over loose rocks and shifting shale, the stone hard-edged, awkward to walk on and treacherous.

After a time, with the mist already lifting a little, I hobble through a gap between steep slopes, into a faceless gully, the ground choked with fallen stones. One giant boulder, many times the size of a man, lies atop the pile, but as I approach, it crumbles and falls apart, becoming a gritty sludge that runs away, leaving only a round core, as small as a man's fist.

Puzzled, I slog up the pile of sludge to look at that core stone more closely. I've already reached down to pick it up when I hear a footfall above me and look up, braced to fight.

Only some ten yards away, a man is standing, perhaps the most magnificently piteous figure I've ever seen. He's tall, and once he was strong, with wide-shoulders and a deep chest. But now he's so emaciated that every bone can be seen, every muscle a thin cord straining at the pale skin that clings tight to his wasted frame. His back is hunched, his legs locked half-bent, and his skin bruised and bleeding and covered in stone dust, as is his ragged loin cloth – all he has to wear.

But it's his face that draws the eye: crudely moulded features affixed to a large skull, striking rather than handsome. His age is impossible to tell, for his expression is locked in a rictus of pain, but his beard and the thin hair that clings to his scalp are white, filthy and hang to his waist. A wild light burns in his eyes: not the insanity of the confused, but the madness of the fixated, who exist for only one thing...

I leave the stone where it lies, and draw my *xiphos*.

The old man snorts. 'If I thought that thing could kill me, I'd help you push it in.' His voice is rasping, as if his throat is coated in rock dust. Grasping his knees to support his upper body, he coughs up blood-flecked grey phlegm and spits, then clambers down towards me. 'Don't worry, boy,' he says. 'I'm not going to hurt you.'

I clutch my sword tighter, seeing no reason to believe anything he says. 'Where am I?'

He chuckles grimly. 'If you don't know that, you're in more trouble than I thought.' He gestures expansively at the mist, mimicking a king overlooking his realm. 'This is Erebus.'

'I know I'm in *fucking* Erebus,' I growl. 'But which part of it?'

The old man blows his nose onto the ground, one nostril at a time. His snot is grey with rock dust, like the phlegm he's just coughed up. 'I don't think it has a name. You could call it "Soulcrusher Peaks", maybe. Or the "Hills of Hubris", for all the proud men brought low here. Or just "Losers' End", because in the end, that's what we all are... Those who fought the gods and lost.'

Something in the burning intensity of that last line, the bitterness, the fury in the old man's eyes as he utters them, lights a spark in my heart, because that stubborn, fiery, focused will feels strangely familiar. 'Who are you?' I ask, sheathing my sword.

The old man straightens painfully, lifting his head as if the memory of who he is has freed him, for a brief moment, from the bent, crippled creature he's become. You might call it towering pride, arrogance even, but I see indomitable self-belief. Hubris, we call it – the arrogance to challenge the gods. It's the sin the gods hate more viciously than any other.

'My name,' he says slowly, 'is Sisyphus.'

16 – Son of Sisyphus

'CHORUS: Is it possible you transgressed even further?
PROMETHEUS: Indeed, I prevented mortals foreknowing their death.
CHORUS: What kind of physic did you find for this sickness?
PROMETHEUS: I caused them to be possessed by blind hopes.'
—Aeschylus, *Prometheus Bound*

Erebus

For six long heartbeats, I can't breathe.

I just stare, stomach churning, heart stuttering, at the ragged old man. *My father.* A wave of dizziness sweeps over me, so strong I have to lean on the bow to stay upright. Everything I'd imagined I might say to him – given such an impossibility as this – every question, every accusation, every curse evaporates from my brain. All I can do is gape, like a stranded fish.

'And you?' Sisyphus says, frowning. Getting no response, he clambers down to tug the cloak free of my head, catching his breath at the sight of my thick red hair. 'By Atlas, are you Anticleia's boy?' the old king chokes out. Without waiting for a response, he clasps me to him, shaking uncontrollably, his eyes welling tears. His arms are thin, but his strength is immense – I can scarcely breathe in my father's iron grip.

Slowly, tentatively, I return the embrace.

Finally, he holds me at arm's length and stares. 'What did they name you?' he asks.

'Odysseus.'

'"Born of Grief",' he mutters. 'Apt, I suppose, in so many ways.' He waves at a pile of rubble. 'Sit, boy. Your body is warm, so you still live. How can you be here?'

I do as bidden, my legs too wobbly to stand. There are so many things I want to ask him – but I'm still burningly aware that Bria and the Spartans are pursuing Theseus, and that I need to be there.

But this is my father, and I will never have another opportunity…

The first question comes blurting out. 'Did you force my mother?'

Sisyphus flinches. 'Is that what she told you?'

I feel all my frustration well up. *I've lost my home, my family, my very identity because of you!* 'She tells Laertes one thing and me another! I don't know the truth! I don't even know who I am any more!'

'Slow down, son. Tell me what happened. How are you here? How did you learn of me?'

I breathe deeply, slowly, several times to calm myself, then begin. 'Close on six months ago, my family took me to Pytho, to learn the rites and be recognized by the Pythia – Anticleia's mother. In her prophetic trance, the Pythia denounced Mother as an adulteress. Father – *Laertes* – disowned me instantly. He also threatened to cast Mother aside – only the dishonour of exposing himself as a cuckold prevented him. They returned to Ithaca, but I was told to stay away.'

Sisyphus spits, a blob of grey mucus that sinks into the grit at our feet. 'The Pythia. Hera's tool, the vengeful bitch. And your mother told two tales?' He shakes his head. 'There was no rape. Seduction, aye, but no force.'

'What's the difference, when a powerful king traps an inno-cent young woman alone?'

'You're young, lad, with much to learn. Laertes wouldn't know the difference – he's a farmer at heart. He can get a bull to a cow, but he has no more idea of seduction than that. Don't get me wrong: I like Laertes well enough, a good and decent man, but he's no worthy husband for a woman like

Anticleia.' His eyes light up. 'Your mother shone. Not just her scarlet hair, wonder that it is, or her face or form, but her heart and mind! I'd met her several times at kingly gatherings, and she was the intellectual match of any man present. She was being groomed as a future Pythia, and her education made her blossom. As her understanding of the world grew, so did her passion for life. Then Laertes won her hand – and he *stifled* her. He felt threatened by her brilliance, so he punished her for "presumption" and dismissed her teachers on petty excuses. When the time came for her initiation as a future Pythia, her first steps on the Viper's Path, she failed – because he'd broken her confidence. She was so traumatized she could never open herself to those gifts again.'

I stare. This, I've never heard. 'So she could have awakened as a *theia*?'

'Yes, indeed. But for Laertes.'

I'm shocked – no, I'm *furious* that Laertes has so crippled her soul.

'I didn't just seduce her, Odysseus,' Sisyphus goes on. 'In so far as I'm capable – for I have my own failings – I *loved* her.' Sisyphus waves a hand, as if batting away a retort. 'I love all women – yes, I know, every man says that! But I love to see them bloom. They're half the world, and yet we belittle them. Why should a man feel so threatened when he sees a brilliant woman? They see things differently to us, and usually more sensibly. They should be our partners, not our slaves.' He looks at me gravely. 'Do you know of the *theoi*, the god-touched?' Then he answers his own question. 'Of course you do – how else are you here? Athena, yes? No other would appreciate you. Small blessing, to be in the hands of the Virgin, but at least your gifts are awakened. And I see,' he says, touching the bow on my shoulder, 'that my old friend Iphitus kept his promise.'

'Yes, indeed. I couldn't even string it until I was awakened.'

'Treasure it – it'll serve you well.' Sisyphus examines the bow, his voice softening in remembrance. 'Heracles slaughtered Iphitus's family, so he feigned death, stole the bow and escaped. He took refuge with me in Corinth. I hid him as long as I could, but my own life was under threat. So I told him of Anticleia and my hopes for you. I made him promise to give you the bow, if you both lived long enough to find such a chance.'

That's good to know, but it's trivia to me right now. 'What happened between you and my mother?' I demand.

He sighs heavily, then nods. 'You need to know. It was… well, how old are you? Twenty? Then it was twenty-one years ago. I was mourning the death of my favourite grandson. You must know his name: Bellerophon. The tales say he grew prideful, tried to assail Olympus and was destroyed by Zeus's thunderbolts. The truth was more tawdry: the gods lured him with empty promises and murdered him. Years earlier, my only *theios* son, Glaucus, Bellerophon's father, was slain by Hera. She possessed his horses with daemons and they *ate* him. Why such evil? Because we are the last of the blood of Prometheus.'

I know that, but it's been different hearing the tale from my own father's lips.

'With them dead, I almost despaired,' he went on, 'But I was still strong, still vigorous. Still potent. But because I am merely the great-grandchild of Prometheus, I cannot sire *theioi* on ordinary women. Those I fathered on my wife, a political match to secure Corinth, weren't god-touched. Merope, my lover, was a nymph who had taken a human body, but of our children only Glaucus was a *theios*. Now both he and his son Bellerophon were dead, I was the last of the blood of Prometheus. I knew I must sire another *theios*, so I cast about for someone of the divine blood.'

'My mother.'

'Yes – though fate played a part. I met Laertes at Dodona, while consulting the oracle to determine who I should approach. Not only did the prophecy point to her, it also spoke of a hero of the line of Prometheus as the future saviour of Achaea. This prophecy was swiftly suppressed and has not been heard since, but I still believe it. If I'm right, *you* are the hero. I confess I told Anticleia of this when I… ah, *persuaded* her to surrender to me.'

This is consistent with what Mother had told me at Pytho… but it still takes some believing.

Sisyphus sees my doubts, and grips my shoulder hard. 'Believe in that prophecy, Odysseus! Who but a follower of Prometheus will ask the right questions, follow the right path to free us of these accursed gods and their meddling? Our forebear was the only one of that Olympian brood who loved us more than himself. For that, they cast him down. But in you our bloodline endures, and the hope that he can be freed, that once again the gods will serve us, not we them.'

'What do you mean: "the gods will serve us"?'

'Exactly that. The tale – that Prometheus gave us "fire" – is a metaphor. The real fire he gave us was *knowledge*, son. Reason and logic, tools that lead you to more tools. Tools that raise us above the beasts. Prometheus was the spirit of knowledge, of understanding, of all that enlightens us. He served us, when the others just wanted our obedience. That's why he's imprisoned here in Erebus, and I also. And you'll end up here too, if you can't outwit our foes.'

'Are you saying Prometheus is *here*?'

'Aye, in the next valley. Come, you must meet him.' He clambers to his feet.

I hesitate. 'But my friends—'

'You're not alone?' His eyes narrow. 'How and why are you here, my son?'

I hurriedly explain my predicament – I can see no reason not to be frank, and despite having only just met him, I feel I can trust him, at least in this. He wants the best for me – needs me to carry on his struggle.

Once I've explained who I am with, and our purpose, Sisyphus half closes his eyes. 'I see them. They're heading for the Pantheon, but they still have some way to go.'

How he can do this, I have no idea – perhaps, like Bria, he has the magus gifts?

'That's where I must be,' I tell him. 'I must recover Helen and absolve myself of blame for her abduction.'

'Never fear, I can get you there, as quickly as you need, once you've met Prometheus.' He points at the ridge above us. 'We'll go that way, for the extra yards.'

What does he mean by that? I watch curiously as Sisyphus picks the small black stone that I'd been drawn to earlier from amidst the slush of the crumbled boulder. He lifts it in both hands, his face a paroxysm of hatred, despair, determination and reverence. 'Come,' he says. 'A good start is essential.' He begins to trudge up the slope, carrying the stone as if were many times heavier than it is.

'What are you doing?' I ask, as I hobble after him.

'This,' Sisyphus pants, 'is my punishment. Futile, of course. But I have to try.'

I have no idea what he means. I follow close behind, watching him with growing concern as with each step upwards, the stone grows perceptibly larger. Inside a few paces, the old man is shifting his grip, cradling it in his arms. 'Let me help you!' I offer.

'Too dangerous, Sisyphus grunts, as the stone grows even bigger. 'Must... do... this... on my... own.'

'But—'

'Shut up, boy! I have to concentrate!' Sisyphus's ravaged face sets into the rictus I'd witnessed before – fixed, anguished, the pain lines deepening as he staggers upwards, striving for footing. Now the stone is bigger still, a weight such as only an athlete in his prime might essay, but my father's muscles bulge, each one standing out like a giant blisters beneath his skin, as he heaves one step forward, and then another.

He's halfway up the slope... If this is a punishment, it's self-inflicted, as far as I can see...

The stone is now almost the size of Sisyphus's torso, and becoming nigh-impossible to hold. With a shout, the old man hurls it upwards, into a small basin of rock where it teeters until he throws his weight behind it and traps it. Then, with bleeding hands, he starts rolling it uphill, at first with some momentum, making a dozen yards or so, but the stone keeps growing. Soon

Sisyphus is bathed in sweat and shaking with exertion, his blood smearing the stone.

I realize that the slope is hard-packed by his footfalls, that he must have done this hundreds, or even thousands of times. It's appalling to watch. Wordlessly, I sling the bow over my shoulder and limp up the slope to put my shoulder to the boulder. He gives me a desperate, almost insane look of gratitude and burning hope. 'Perhaps this time!' he grunts. '*This* time!'

Together we heave it up another dozen yards, my torn thigh muscle screaming in protest. But with each upward roll, it becomes more massive still, man-height and almost impossible to shift. My legs can't take much more of this... and we are still only three-quarters of the way up the slope...

'We won't make it!' my father gasps. 'When it slips, get clear, or it'll kill you.'

We try for another push, three yards to the next lip where the boulder might catch, but the gravel beneath our feet gives way, the boulder rolls and we hurl ourselves out of the way, letting the giant stone crash between us and down, to shatter in the gully below.

We sit, Sisyphus glowering at the broken rock below. 'Shit of a way to spend eternity,' he remarks, eventually. 'Thanks for the help. You've got good shoulders, boy. Shame you aren't taller.'

Why is that the first thing anyone notices?

'Why do you have to do that?' I pant, massaging my burning right thigh. My body is definitely healing faster than normal – but I just can't get enough of a respite for the wound to heal properly.

'I told you. It's my punishment, for being a Promethean.'

'But why do you go along with it?' I ask. 'Stop doing it. Try something else.'

Sisyphus sighs. 'I tell myself that, every time I pick that bloody stone up at the bottom of the slope, and every time I end up hereabouts. But Hades promised me once that it's not forever. It's finite... there is a target, a vertical yardage. When I reach it, the stone will become light as a feather, and I'll walk out of here and be taken to the Elysian Fields! The Elysian Fields, son! Where all is bliss, where only the finest foods and wines are served, where the blessed while away their time in every pleasure. And I could reach that target with the very next step I take!'

'Hope and despair,' I mutter. 'The cruel bastards.'

'Aye, it's the hope that hooks us. That's what keeps us poor suckering humans going.'

'But Hades could be lying?'

'I've not discounted that, but he's not known for it.' Sisyphus exhales heavily. 'I can work at my own pace, I've got a goal, and it gives me time to think.' He clambers wearily to his feet, his skin still slick with perspiration, but he is shivering now with the cold. Wordlessly, I hand him Laas's cloak. 'I thank you,' he says, flinching as he pulls it round his skeletal shoulders. 'Damn but it hurts, though. Just to move. Anyway, you need to see our sire.'

We tramp up to the ridge and emerge from the mist, but there is little to see but these bleak and arid hills. Then we hear the thud of beating wings, too immense to be a natural bird. 'Hurry,' Sisyphus exclaims, breaking into a trot despite his obvious exhaustion. With me hobbling after, he tops another rise then plunges into a narrow cleft. I follow, to find myself in a stinking, three-sided canyon that encloses a pool of congealed, stagnant foulness. The unseen wings are still beating, and above our heads, someone groans.

I catch my breath in horror. About forty yards above, just below the rim of the cliff, someone is dangling, one hand nailed to the rock. His shoulder is dislocated, and he is clearly in agony. Rotting blood and excreta stain the rock wall, the source of the stench that fills this small enclosed place.

This is my nightmare come to life, unspeakably hideous to me, even though I am now only a witness, not the ghastly, corpse-like creature high above me.

'Great-grandfather!' Sisyphus calls, hoarsely.

Prometheus jerks in shock, then twists so that he can look down. '*No...*' he cries, '*No! You're still here?*' He wails in anguish at the grey skies above. 'I dreamt this morning that three centuries had passed. I dreamt you'd escaped.'

The sound of beating wings grows closer, and Sisyphus's expression becomes urgent. 'Sire, I bring you a kinsman, a *living* kinsman! My son, Odysseus!'

Prometheus twists again to stares down at us. He's handsome, beautiful even, and big enough to stand head and shoulders above Sisyphus. His eyes are aglow, their colour more red than brown. But his face is contorted in pain. 'Living? A living man, of my blood? Let me see you, boy!' His face goes from a rictus of despair to one, equally agonising, of hope. 'Why's he here?'

'For your blessing,' Sisyphus calls. 'Please, give him your blessing, sire!'

Just them a bird of prey shrieks, causing Prometheus's face to contort in dread. A giant eagle appears, so large its wingspan bridges the canyon. Somehow, despite its overwhelming presence, Prometheus keeps his fiery gaze on me. '*Odysseus, do you wish for my blessing?*'

'*Yes,*' I shout. '*Yes, I do!*'

The eagle lands on the cliff above Prometheus, peering with beady intensity, but Prometheus, though visibly petrified, ignores it. '*Then I do bless you!*' he shouts. '*Thou art my kin and heir, and I awaken you to every gift!*'

Awakened a second time – by my true patron, whose blood runs in my veins. It doesn't erase Athena's gift, but augments it. The effect, this second time, is less dramatic, more like a sense of doors opening and pathways shifting inside me, without the fierce burst of energy that had transfixed me with Athena. Perhaps that's because this isn't the first awakening; it's more akin to a realignment, a broadening of what is already in place.

…I awaken you to every gift…

My eyes lock with Prometheus's, wanting to tell him of this. But, as if it senses something untoward, the eagle shrills and with a brutal movement, seizes Prometheus's shoulder in one talon for purchase then lunges downwards, its foot-long beak ripping open the fallen god's abdomen. Prometheus screams in utter agony as it clamps on something, pulling and tearing and wrenching until a large blood-coloured lump of flesh – a liver – comes free. The bird gulps it down, before flapping away, leaving Prometheus howling in agony as blood gushes from the wound and runs cascading down the cliff.

'Catch it! Catch it in your hands!' Sisyphus commands.

I do as bidden, cupping my hands beneath the erratic flow. I only manage to collect about a spoonful, but Sisyphus seems satisfied. 'Drink it,' he commands.

I hesitate – civilized men do not drink blood.

'Do it!' Sisyphus shouts, in sudden fury.

His conviction and urgency convince me, and I force the bitter fluid down. This time, I experience something vastly different, a violent reaction as though someone has kicked me in the throat, or I've drunk lamp oil, then set fire to my tongue. I drop to my knees, frightened I might no longer be able to breathe, while Sisyphus holds my shoulder in his rock-like grip.

Above us, Prometheus lies against the wall, bleeding and sobbing.

'Every day is the same as the last for him, the pain just as fresh each time,' Sisyphus intones, looking up at his great-grandsire. 'He's healed by the touch of dawn's rays, only to be rent and torn again. Meanwhile, with no liver, he is in agony as his body poisons itself. This is Zeus's punishment for the sin the Skyfather hated more than any other: daring to elevate mankind.'

I can feel Prometheus's fiery blood beginning to radiate through my whole body. My thigh muscles are knitting, just as they did under Athena's hands, and my whole body is pulsing with energy and strength. I fumble for my flask and manage a mouthful of water from Persephone's spring, which gives enough relief for me to speak. 'Why would Zeus not wish the best for mankind? Doesn't he want his worshippers to prosper?'

Sisyphus snorts derisively. 'Oh yes, he wants them to prosper, if by prosper you mean breed like animals and cover the earth while never questioning who or what he really is.'

I stare. 'But we know what he is! King and Father of the Gods! The gods are rivals to each other – I understand that now – and they're not omnipotent, except in places like this. But they're still gods! They still made us!'

'You think so?'

I describe Athena's simile of the amphora and the holes through which their godly hands can reach to help mankind. 'It makes sense,' I try to say, but Sisyphus interrupts, barking with bitter laughter.

'Are they still peddling that shit? Well, fuck me! Look around you, boy! This place – did the gods invent it? No, we did – we men, with our piddling understanding of the world, and our burning need to invent greater beings to blame for our sorrows! *There are no gods!* Just monsters that we've imagined into reality! That is the knowledge that our sire – *one of them* – wished to give to us! And you've just seen the price he'll pay for eternity, unless you, his last worshipper and champion, can free him and all the rest of us!'

I stare again, aghast. *Ravings, the demented outpourings of a broken man, trapped forever in a recurring nightmare.* But… what was it Bria had said: *the bird or the egg*?

Something like understanding strikes me – too profound, too complex to take in completely, but Sisyphus recognizes it. 'Aye, it takes root. Ponder it, lad: take the time to understand and realize the implications. But you don't have that time right now!' He pulls me to my feet again, sniffing the air. 'Son, we're out of time,' he says hoarsely. 'Don't waste that taste of divine blood. Your friends are about to reach the Pantheon, but so is Hades. I wish we had more time together, but the eagle has seen you. It's only going to be hours at most until Zeus knows you're here, and that you, a son of mine, have been blessed by Prometheus. You have to go, now.'

'I'm sorry – I didn't know you were here—'

Sisyphus raises a hand: 'How could you? I'm just grateful that chance threw us together… or fate.'

I have many more questions for him, and wish fervently that I could in some way ease his suffering, or free him. But he's right. 'Do you have any message for my mother?' I ask.

His face softens. 'Tell her... tell her...' Tears stream down his cheeks again. 'Tell her she is the best of women, that our hours together were my finest. Tell her I think of her always. And tell her she should say whatever she damned well likes about me, if it wins back her husband and her happiness.' He pulls me to him, hugs me fiercely, then steps away. 'This place, as you've been told, is as it's believed to be. Strange thoughts can sometimes create strange results, for those with a touch of the divine. That mouthful of Prometheus's blood should be enough: think hard of a place in this realm where you need to be, or a person you need to find, and *will* yourself there!'

I wish I could freeze time. I wish I knew the right questions to ask to unlock my true father's mysteries and free him from this dreadful plight. But I have a task to perform, one of the utmost urgency. So I conjure the face of Helen of Sparta, as I remember her from that night we stole her from her bed in Sparta, and even as I breathe her name, the world spins away, then blurs in converging lines down a tunnel of swirling colour...

17 – Lost Hero

'By them stood Death-Blindness, gloomy and dire,
pale green, shrivelled, hunched over with hunger,
with swollen knees. Long claws tipped her hands,
her nose dribbled mucus, and blood dripped onto
the ground from her cheeks. She stood, her lips
parted in a hideous grin, and much dust lay upon
her shoulders, wetted with tears.'
—Hesiod, *Shield of Heracles*

Erebus

As I hurtle down that tunnel of light, I retain enough awareness
to not arrive *precisely* on Helen's shoulder: what is a white dot
in darkness ahead of me becomes a blockish building on a low
plinth, a strange edifice with open sides, pillars of pale stone
and a solid, low-peaked roof. A 'Pantheon', Bria had called it
– a place for all the gods. I glimpse people inside, and focus on
one spot, below the edge of the plinth...

...and an instant later that's where I am, without even the
impact of landing. That in itself is so disorienting that I almost
cry out and betray my presence.

'Did you hear something?' a male voice growls, and I press
myself low to the ground and against the wall of the plinth, as
heavy footsteps tread my way and I hear someone breathing.

'Hear what, Pirithous?' another man replies, and I know the
voice: Theseus.

I pray that Pirithous comes no closer – I've no idea exactly
to whom I pray, it's more like silent, desperate wish-babble –
but through luck or divine intervention, the former King of the

Lapiths stops, the sound of his boots on the stonework retreats, and I can breathe again.

'It was like the rush of wings,' Pirithous says, his voice already further away.

Once I am sure Pirithous has lost interest, I cautiously peer about. As we'd already seen from the edge of Persephone's Grove, the Pantheon stands on a hill, surrounded by flat land. If the direction from which the Spartans will be approaching, through the asphodels, can be called south, then the wall I'm hiding against is at the north end of the Pantheon, facing deeper into Erebus.

Now I know Theseus and his party are unaware of me, I crawl to the north-west corner, which gives me a view of the hills in which I met my father. The western flank falls away sharply, almost unclimbable. The landscape is still patched with mist, especially over what I can see of the ghostly asphodel fields. I can't see anyone out there.

I then creep to the north-east corner of the Pantheon, where the slope descends into a tangled forest, streaked with brazen smears of water reflecting the skies – the swamps that the river Lethe morphs into. If the Trojans come, it'll be from that direction, and I note that the slope is gentle on that side, an easy approach. The patchy mists cling to a reeking swamp, and the trees and mist are too thick for me to tell whether the Trojan galley is in there somewhere. If the Trojans are down there, they might be able to see me, so I draw back to the northern face of the hill, crawling beneath the lip of the Pantheon floor.

Now I steel myself for a risky task – finding a vantage point to observe Theseus and his party. There's a pillar at each corner, and three along this narrower, northern end; I use one of those to screen myself as I raise my head above the lip of the plinth – floor-level for those inside the Pantheon – and finally peer into the edifice.

The Pantheon stretches some sixty yards in length, half that in width, with a roof held purely by giant pillars. It all seems to be made of marble – an incredible structure unlike any I've ever seen, like something out of another time. Within, a giant table has been placed, with twelve thrones arrayed about it – two immense ones at either end, and five on either side. Each throne has a name blazoned on the headrest, front and back. The nearest belongs to Zeus, and the furthest to Hades. On the western side are arrayed the thrones of Hera, Aphrodite, Athena and Artemis, with Persephone nearest Hades. On the far side I see the thrones of Poseidon, Ares, Hephaestus, Hermes and – remarkably – Prometheus. It seems that things change slowly here. Or perhaps Hades and Zeus like to remind everyone of what happens when a god falls?

No Apollo, I note with some satisfaction. No Demeter either, or a host of 'gods' whose worship has been absorbed by others, or is on the wane. It all lends credence to much that I've been told.

Then my attention goes to the mortals present: Theseus of Athens is seated on Hades's throne – I catch a glimpse of the top of his boar's tooth helm. Further down the long ebony table is Pirithous of the Lapiths, the very same man I saw talking with Theseus on Mount Ida, with his shaved, tattooed head and his rough, bear-like demeanour. He's slumped in Prometheus's chair, gazing at Theseus with a watchful, brooding expression.

Aethra, Theseus's mother – a stately grey-haired woman with a gentle, tolerant face – has taken Persephone's chair, to Theseus's left. And leaning against a pillar at the far end, looking out over the asphodel fields, is Helen of Sparta. She seems moody, even sullen, occasionally glancing back over her shoulder, to cast long considering looks at the three adults holding her. There is a very adult coldness to her that's hard to read, surprising in one so young. How has Theseus treated her? I see no warmth in her when she looks at her kidnapper.

'When will Hades get here?' Theseus grumbles.

'We've performed the invocation,' Pirithous replies. 'All we can do now is wait.'

'I don't like waiting. I never have.'

'Stop worrying,' Pirithous drawls. 'We're in Hades's realm, my friend. Who's going to follow us here?'

'The sort of mad bastards we've been fighting all our lives,' Theseus replies. 'Those Trojans were led by *theioi*. The doors to Erebus aren't locked, or even hard to find.' Then he shrugs. 'Fuck it, let them come! One last glorious battle, before we're immortalized.'

I've been right all along.

I tuck my head back out of sight, my body pressed flat against the cold marble of the plinth. They're here seeking to trade Helen for true immortality. I take little satisfaction from guessing correctly; if they get their way, nowhere in the world above will be safe for me. I have to find a way to thwart them.

What worries me most is that glimpse of Helen. While she's clearly not happy, there's no visible trauma in her face. Despite her dalliance with a male slave, with its ghastly outcome, she'd almost certainly been a virgin still when Theseus snatched her away. She's only thirteen, but I don't see a child or a victim: I see self-possession and calculation.'

Theseus, what have you done?

'Those Trojans won't have given up,' Pirithous growls. 'They've invested too much in this matter to back out now. We should have stayed and killed that squinny little *kopros*, Skaya-Mandu – and taken his sister as an extra hostage.'

'Just as a hostage?' Theseus snorts.

'You've got a piece of ass out of this lark,' Pirithous says. 'Why shouldn't I?'

'And what a piece,' Theseus chuckles, leering down the Pantheon at Helen. 'Dreaming of tonight, darling?'

She flinches, shuddering then glaring back at him coldly. 'You don't know what I dream of,' she says darkly.

''Course I do,' Theseus says smugly. 'Same thing as every other woman: me.' He guffaws at his own hilarity. I'm watching Helen though, and I can see fear and anguish behind the brittle dispassionate mask she's erected.

She's been raped, whether violently or through coercion I can't say; certainly she's been awakened: I suspect it's only the *theia* gifts she's now gained that are allowing her to maintain this calm façade.

'Theseus, darling, don't talk like that in front of the girl,' Aethra says, in a prim but not especially outraged voice – like a queen complaining that her pet lion has made a mess while eating a slave.

'What girl? I only see a woman.' Theseus chuckles again. Then his voice drops. 'If those Trojans had played straight we wouldn't have had to come here. We'd have been in Troy by now, with all the rewards they promised. Blame them, not me!'

'Oh, I do, darling,' Aethra replies. 'I'm so pleased Pirithous suggested this contingency. I'd rather be a Lady of Erebus than live in some gilded cage in Troy.'

Right again, I congratulate myself, though not with any great satisfaction. *So it really was a private arrangement – Zeus might have been dangling Helen and all her gifts in front of the Trojans, but he hasn't committed to marrying her off to one them.* This implies that King Piri-Yamu of Troy decided to take matters into his own hands – but Skaya-Mandu overreached, thinking to snatch the prize while avoiding the payment. Perhaps he hopes to claim Helen for himself, when otherwise she might be given to another?

I drop my head and take stock, wondering how I, a largely unproven warrior, can take advantage of my hidden presence, and rescue this situation for Achaea, for Athena, for Helen and the Spartans… and for myself. If they were ordinary men, the two arrows Bria has given me might be enough… but Theseus and Pirithous are *theioi*, and living legends.

Then I see movement far below, in the trees bordering the Stygian marshland, and realize I'm out of time.

I'm not the only one paying attention; Pirithous snarls and I hear him stand. 'Theseus,' he warns, 'we've got company.'

The silhouettes of three-dozen men have appeared in the shadow of the trees below, their garb and gear marking them as Trojans. They are moving swiftly up the lower slopes, to the edge of arrow range.

If you can see someone, there's every chance they can see you; and I have no desire for the Trojans to spot me. So I duck down again, and wriggle over to the north-west corner, then peer over the lip from behind the corner pillar. I see Theseus, Pirithous and the two women, who all have their backs to me, facing towards the Trojans, who are now out of my sight.

It seems the easterners think they have no time to waste either, because I can hear no calls for a parley. Nor do I detect any attempt to outflank the two heroes by circling around the Pantheon, judging from Theseus's and Pirithous's actions as they nock arrows and take aim down the eastern slope.

Aethra and Helen merely watch, the Spartan princess making no effort to escape.

'There's as many of those phalloi as we have arrows,' Pirithous comments. He doesn't sound overly worried.

'Mother,' Theseus calls tersely, 'watch over the girl.' Then he raises his voice: 'Trojans!' he shouts. 'Go home! There's nothing but death for you here!' He's only going through the motions of negotiating, though; from his body language, he's eager for the fray.

Now what? I wonder. If I kill the two heroes while they have their backs to me, I'll be left facing the Trojans on my own. If I try to snatch Helen for myself, and somehow spirit her away while the two heroes are distracted, I'll need to deal with Aethra, and my morality doesn't permit me to murder helpless old women.

I could whack her over the head, though – my morals are fine with that.

But that still leaves my escape as a problem, relying on Helen's cooperation, not a given by any means. Theseus may well have told her of my involvement, so she may see me as no better than him. And I can't yet see a way of escaping with her, unnoticed. But I have to try – perhaps at the height of the fighting, and ideally with Bria and the Spartans close at hand. But where are they?

With that in mind, I creep back along the outside of the northern wall to the Trojans' flank, keeping very low. I need to be able to monitor the success or otherwise of the Trojan attack, so I can pick my moment. By the time I get there, staying low to remain unseen, the Trojans are halfway up the slope, darting from cover to cover, using the slight unevenness of the terrain. I'm on Theseus's left, and I glimpse him aiming carefully, picking his spot. Then I scan the advancing Trojans: is that Kyshanda, down in the trees behind her *phallos* of a brother?

Then a Trojan archer breaks cover, seeking shelter higher up. Theseus, with easy grace, aims where the Trojan is *going to be* and shoots him in the throat. The man drops and the rest dive behind any shelter they can find.

'Plenty more arrows up here, Trojans!' Theseus shouts. 'Plenty for all!' Then he lowers his voice. 'Where's your blasted god, Piri?'

'It might be hours before our invocation is responded to,' Pirithous admits. 'We might have to kill this bunch of phalloi first.'

Theseus hoicks and spits. 'So be it. I slew the Minotaur. I'm the true King of Athens. I will be immortal.' He lifts his voice. 'Come on, Trojans! Come and get us!'

It's enough to goad Skaya-Mandu and his men into action. With a ragged cry, the Trojans surge up the slope, shrieking their battle cries. Theseus just laughs: 'One last fight, Piri, before Olympus embraces us! One last, glorious fight!'

'For immortality!' Pirithous answers.

Together they raise their bows, and take aim.

And I creep back to the rear of the Pantheon, to await my chance to seize the princess, though I hold out little hope of getting far. I can't see an honourable way out of this, and right now I'd even take a dishonourable one. I'm beginning to appreciate Bria's flexible morality…

Speaking of whom…

Movement catches my eye below, and I look down the nearly unclimbable western slope, and my heart leaps. Bria is clambering hand over fist up the cliff, her black face glistening with sweat.

–

'Glad you could make it,' I whisper, as I help the Nubian woman housing my occasionally favourite daemon over the clifftop and onto the narrow ridge of ground below the western side of the plinth, both of us pressing low into the long grass.

'How did you get here first?' she hisses, glaring at my scarred thigh.

'I'd need to know you a whole lot better before I say another word on that subject,' I tell her – which is word for word what she said to me when I asked her about being 'compelled' to serve Athena. Yes, I can be that petty.

She grunts in an unladylike way and jerks her head to our right. 'Alycus and the Spartans are coming up the slope from the asphodels. There's good forest cover on that side and they're hoping the presence of the Trojans will distract Theseus and Pirithous enough for them to get close. I'm supposed to grab the girl.'

'Any losses?' I ask.

'Philoton,' she says, confirming my fears in that respect. 'He vanished into a cloud of wraiths, and we found only his bones.'

I bow my head, then indicate the Pantheon and those inside. 'Let's see what we can do.'

Keeping close to the ground, we slither to the plinth, the lip of the platform deep enough to keep us concealed, even though Aethra and Helen are only yards away. Pirithous and Theseus are on the far side, still with their backs to us. Suddenly everything is aligning: we can snatch the girl and manage the old lady at the same time, then pull out while Theseus, Pirithous and the Trojans hack lumps out of each other. After that, I know I have a choice to make: Sparta or Athena – but I'll deal with that later.

'Get ready to grab Helen,' I whisper in Bria's ear. 'Don't hurt Aethra. I'm going to find a vantage point overlooking the Trojan attack, to pick the best moment.'

Bria looks like she'd have preferred our roles to be reversed, but she nods agreement, pulling out a dagger and clamping it between her teeth. I creep along the outside of the wall again, to a point where I can watch the Trojan attack, so I can determine the best moment to strike...

…and, just quietly, to see if I can get Kyshanda out of this alive as well.

From my new lookout, I watch the Trojans attack. They're still on the lower slopes, three or four men dead and several more wounded already. I can see their hesitancy, and note that they've eschewed archery for fear of striking Helen. Skaya-Mandu is towards the rear, shouting orders, the smaller, shrouded figure of Kyshanda with him.

To my right, out of my sight but in clear hearing, I can hear Theseus and Pirithous breathing heavily from the latest volleys they've been firing. They've barely wasted an arrow.

'Did you get a shot at that skinny slip of a prince?' I hear Pirithous call.

'The little *kopros* is hiding still,' Theseus growls. 'Wait, here they come again.'

The Trojans are indeed advancing once more, this time in a line, with their shields locked against archery and spears out-thrust, massed together so they can overwhelm the two defenders by force. Theseus and Pirithous shoot again and again as the Trojans edge forward, concentrating on keeping themselves covered up rather than on speed. I see more men drop, but these seem only injured at most, apart from one man with an arrow through the eye. The two Achaean heroes begin to swear and curse as their arrows run low.

Then Pirithous calls out. 'Hey, princess,' he says. 'Are you serious about shooting?'

'And would you rather be married to a Trojan prince who hides behind his men, or given to an Achaean god?' Theseus calls to her.

'I've hunted with my brothers all my life,' Helen calls, her face grim. 'I already know how to shoot: give me a weapon!'

Is this loyalty, or survival? Does she actually want Theseus to be victorious, or is the alternative – capture and rape by the Trojans – even worse?

'Use mine,' Pirithous replies. 'I'm Hades's champion, and this is Erebus. I don't need anything so puny as a bow.'

That worries me enough to glance around the pillar, in time to see Pirithous toss Helen his bow and quiver, which she catches with a deft effortlessness that speaks louder than any words. Now I know for sure. *Her gifts are awoken. Theseus, you dirty* katapugon*!*

Then I catch my breath as Pirithous turns back to face the advancing Trojans, flexing his fingers and muttering an incantation. Purple light limns his eyes, and the air about him drops in temperature. 'Come on, little Trojans,' he rasps. 'Let's see what you can do.'

Her perfect face set and confident, Helen steps to the edge of the platform, between the two men. I curse under my breath: she's just made herself harder to reach, for Bria or myself – and where are Alycus and his men?

'On three,' Theseus tells Helen. 'Their shields are too small to cover all of their bodies, and they're holding them high. Aim low, where their groin and legs are uncovered… One, two, three…'

They fire together, taking down a man each, their victims screaming as their loins are punctured. *Belly shots: a slow death.* Theseus nocks another arrow. 'Beginner's luck, princess?'

'I have eternal beginner's luck,' she retorts, and proceeds to slam a shaft through the eye-socket of a man stupid enough to peer around his shield, while Theseus cripples another with an arrow through the left thigh. The odds are changing by the second.

Where in Erebus are you, Alycus?

Then Pirithous raises his hands to the skies. '*Klythi, anax nuktos*,' he shouts. '*Iketēs de toi euchomai einai.* Hear me, Lord of Darkness. I appeal to you for help.'

Thunder cracks overhead.

The Trojans finally realize that their phalanx isn't going to protect them; they have to get closer fast to neutralize the archery and whatever the Lapith champion is preparing to do. With a ragged shout they break formation and begin to run, shields still high, curved swords flashing.

'Three more shots, then it's blades, princess,' Theseus roars. His hands and arms work in a blur, bringing down one man then another as the Trojans pound uphill towards the temple, with Helen's arrows equally unerring. In the twelve heartbeats it takes the Trojans to cover the distance, six men are sent sprawling. And there's still no sign of Alycus and the Spartans. I'm beginning to wonder if I'm going to have to take sides in this fight. But which side?

'Get behind a pillar, girl!' Theseus shouts, and out comes his sword, a custom-made blade longer than the standard *xiphos*, to suit his strength and build. The platform is low on that side, only a foot above the ground, so he leaps to meet the first man, kicking his shield aside and thrusting with his blade as he staggers, in and out with brutal strength, then lopping the head from a thrusting spear, catching the spearhead in his left hand as he slashes open the next man's throat with a roundhouse cut, then thrusting the severed spearhead through the eye of the next man.

By all the gods, he's damned good!

'*Nux te kai moros kata panta dasontai,*' Pirithous bellows. '*Tethnathi.* May Darkness and Doom devour you utterly! Die!' The Lapith grips the air with both fists, and clouds of shadow spew forth, enveloping the two nearest men. A wrenching gesture follows, as if he were pulling the souls from their bodies, and both soldiers crash face down on the turf. I shudder with horror, especially when, a moment later, he uses whatever he's pulled from them – life, energy, substance – to blast a withering dark mist into the faces of the next two soldiers, their skin and bones withering and twisting as they die. The remaining Trojans falter, wailing to their gods as they realize they're next.

Theseus roars with the joy of battle-lust as he advances, cutting down another man. 'Skaya-Mandu,' he yells: 'Come to your doom!'

I see the Trojan prince clearly now, as the last remnants of the shield wall he's been cowering behind breaks. Kyshanda is with him, her veils loosening as she beseeches her Hittite gods for aid, here in Hades's realm. But unlike Pirithous, there is no glow of light or dark around her, nothing to suggest she's succeeding.

'Come and get it, you coward!' Theseus shouts as he advances, wading into the Trojans. Everything around him seems to be happening in slow motion. Next to him, Pirithous is ripping another Trojan's soul out, and both men are able to avoid the hurled spears of the Trojans with ease. Theseus catches one left-handed and throws it back, transfixing a man right through his shield.

'Is this all you've got?' he shouts, as the remaining dozen or so Trojans fall back. Skaya-Mandu begins to move forward, when an older Trojan grasps his shoulder and interposes himself.

'Try me, Athenian, man-to-man,' the Trojan says. 'I am a champion of Apaliunas.' The Trojan *theios* is well-built, stocky and strong, yet with a lithe grace to him. His face is handsome, in a horse-like, narrow way, and his beard is well braided – a court warrior, no doubt, but still formidable. He must know he's doomed, but he doesn't let it show. Or do all experienced *theioi* believe themselves invincible?

I see Theseus pause, assessing. A formal duel, even at the heart of a mass mêlée, isn't uncommon. It's been known for entire battles to be settled by two champions, and there are complicated traditions as to how such duels are conducted.

'You presume to challenge me, ahead of your prince?' Theseus sneers.

'A prince shouldn't lower himself to fight a common brigand, Athenian,' the man replies, haughtily. 'I am Ganatu-Missa, born to a daughter of your Aphrodite.'

'Well, the Clamshell does like to get around. I imagine she and I will be at it hammer and tongs once I'm a god. Welcome to Erebus, Gan – you're going to be here a long time.' Theseus wipes his blade on his thigh then sheathes it, walking forward with palms up. 'Right then, let's establish the rules for this duel.'

The Trojan returns his own blade to its scabbard and advances to meet him. 'In my land,' he begins, 'we—'

You really have to be watching carefully: the two men clasp right hands, the formal acknowledgement of a worthy foe, but as they do so, Theseus twitches his left wrist. A short spike juts from under his wrist guard, which he punches upwards under the Trojan's chin. The spike must have gone all the way into Ganatu-Missa's brain, for he collapses instantly, already dead.

'I acknowledge no rules!' Theseus roars, as Helen fires off another arrow and Pirithous conjures fresh darkness from his fists.

The Trojans recoil in shock. Theseus snatches up Gan's fallen shield and sends it spinning at Skaya-Mandu, who has turned to shout a warning at Kyshanda. The rim catches the prince on the side of the head – two fingers' breadth lower and it would have broken his neck. Instead it sends him sprawling down the grassy slope, with his sister shrieking in horror.

Bria and I have to act now, I realize – the two heroes are well down the slope, leaving Helen isolated. And that decision is confirmed when suddenly – *finally* – the Spartans appear, Alycus leading them around the side of the hill towards Pirithous and Theseus, storming forward with swords drawn and shields raised.

I signal to Bria, then step around the corner of the Pantheon wall, an arrow nocked but not aimed. As I break cover, Bria ghosts onto the platform behind Aethra and puts a dagger to Theseus's mother's throat, while placing a strong black hand over her mouth.

As I reach her, Helen is drawing her bow once more. 'That's enough, Princess,' I say. 'We're taking you home.'

Her eyes widen with surprise and then recognition. '*Odysseus?*'

I'd half hoped, given the years I spent at Sparta, that she might trust me, that she'd be pleased. Relieved. Grateful, even.

Instead she fires her arrow at my head.

–

'Half hoped' is another way of saying that when she does round on me, I'm not entirely unready.

Her damned shaft still grazes my temple though, as I jerk aside, opening a gash beside my right eye as I twist. Then I overbalance and fall off the side of the platform. Feeling more oaf than hero, I thump into the turf, losing my arrow, and lucky not to break the Great Bow beneath my body.

But I come up fast, even as Helen reaches for another arrow, while Bria snarls something behind her – probably some threat to Aethra. I doubt Helen gives a fresh turd about Theseus's mother, but she does glance around. The distraction allows me a moment to recover, just as the Spartans close in on Theseus and Pirithous, with Alycus and Laas in the lead. The remaining Trojans, already wavering, are on the verge of breaking but Skaya-Mandu, somehow on his feet again, screams an order and they turn to face the Spartans head-on. While Castor and Polydeuces, with Eunomos, attack the Trojans, Alycus goes for Theseus and Laas attacks Pirithous, bellowing their Lacedae-monian war cries.

I launch myself at Helen again, just as Bria shoves Aethra aside and does the same. Torn between two targets, the Spartan princess wavers for a fatal moment – gifts or not, huntress or not, she's not been in a fight before. Just as she decides that I'm the bigger threat, Bria punches her in the side of the head and Helen folds into my arms, dazed and staggering.

I thrust her at Bria. 'Watch her,' I shout, spinning to face the fray, drawing breath in readiness to shout something along the lines of 'Stop fighting, we have Helen.'

To be honest, I'm still thinking the whole thing through.

Theseus and Alycus slam into each other, their blades blurs of shining bronze, clanging like hammers on an anvil. Beyond them, Laas and Pirithous are locked in combat, two great bears of men, with Pirithous given no room to use his sorcerous tricks. Polydeuces, Castor and Eunomos are holding their own against the remaining Trojans, Castor fighting as well as any man despite his youth, while the younger Polydeuces has his *theios* gifts to aid him. All seems to be going our way.

Then suddenly it isn't. Theseus hammers aside Alycus's shield then rams his big sword right through the Spartan champion's chest. Laas manages to parry an overhead blow from Pirithous, but is smashed in the jaw by a punch that hurls him down the slope.

Castor and Polydeuces blanch, but prepare to sell their lives.

'We have the princess!' I scream, at the top of my voice. Everyone below turns and looks up at me, Theseus and Pirithous in fury, Skaya-Mandu and Kyshanda in shock.

A moment later I hear a choked cough behind me. I look over my shoulder in alarm.

Inexplicably, Bria has let Helen go. She staggers to the front of the dais... and falls off, face-down, her body twitching. There's a bloody wound in the middle of her back. Aethra is standing where the daemon had been, a dagger dripping blood in one hand, her other hand clamped on Helen's arm.

'Kill them, my son,' she calls to Theseus. 'Kill them all.'

Wasn't it Bria who said Aethra is a fine old lady? I race to Bria more than half expecting to find a corpse. I'm rolling her into a foetal position when she groans. *Still alive, thanks be to... to whom? Athena?*

I can't do more for her though, because Theseus, roaring like a bull in mating season, comes storming up the slope towards me. 'ITHACA, YOU RUNT!' he bellows. 'YOU'RE MINE!'

Fear keeps me there – fear for Bria and Kyshanda. Then it becomes fury; I whip out my blade and meet Theseus halfway, venting a defiant shout and unleashing as powerful a blow as any I've ever summoned, just as Polydeuces attacks Theseus's other flank, and Castor goes for Pirithous.

Then my thigh muscle tears again.

The leg gives way, my lunge falls short, and white agony shoots up through my gut. Theseus's foot slams into my face with such force it lifts me off the ground, even as he parries Polydeuces's thrust with ease.

'Ha!' Theseus shouts. 'I'll have you too, boy!' He crashes his sword hilt towards the young man's helm, and only lightning reflexes save Polydeuces from being stunned.

Still dizzy from Theseus's kick, I stagger to my feet, my bad leg buckling under me. Below us Laas, trying to protect Castor, takes a sword in the side and folds, then Pirithous twists round and drives his blade into Castor's thigh. The boy collapses, but Laas is up again, standing over the prince and defending him desperately.

A moment later Theseus has Polydeuces staggering from another glancing blow to the head. As the young prince loses his footing, I thrust myself between them, preparing to die in the boy's defence.

'This is a grown-up's fight, runt!' Theseus snarls, thrusting like a snake, a blow I barely turn. Instinctively I twist away as Theseus's off hand flashes by, that hidden spike he's had built into his wrist guard almost slashing my face open. I duck under a roundhouse swing that would have beheaded me, and take a boot in the middle of the chest which hurls me a dozen yards away, winded and barely able to breathe. Fighting Theseus is like facing a whirlwind.

The Athenian puts the tip of his blade under Polydeuces's chin, forcing him to lift his head. Then Castor whips off his helm, revealing his face, and his clear boyish voice rings out across the hilltop. 'Helen! It's us!'

Theseus turns his head, and so do I, looking up the slope to where Helen is standing, with an arrow to her bow.

This isn't just about power and politics, I realize. *It's also about family.*

Helen pivots, her aim shifting; her bow sings and an arrow strikes Pirithous in the left buttock. The Lapith staggers, howling in pain, then collapses as his leg gives way. Instantly Helen nocks and aims another arrow, while I inwardly cheer, because it's pointed at a speechless, white-faced Aethra. 'Don't move, Theseus, or your mother dies,' she calls, her voice as cold as winter.

'You little slut,' the Athenian rages, but he doesn't move. 'I should have—'

'Should've what? Fucked me harder?' Helen rasps. The faces of the two young Spartan princes have turned puce but she ignores their outrage. 'Keep your distance, and let my brothers come to me.'

Theseus looks like he would break Helen's neck with his bare hands if she were in reach. But with his precious mother's life at risk, he remains utterly still.

I'm wondering how this will play out, seeking some kind of opportunity for myself – but then the skies above us darken, changing from bronze to a deep, impenetrable black in moments. We all see it, and feel it, begin to react...

Then we all freeze – not through our own volition or lack of it – *we just can't move.*

From Theseus, standing over Polydeuces, to Laas protecting Castor, to Pirithous prostrated on the ground, and the remaining Trojans gathered around Skaya-Mandu and Kyshanda, none of us can budge an inch. Even the great host of black birds that have flooded the skies are held in suspended motion. I can still make tiny movements – my eyelids can open and close, my nose and mouth and lungs can breathe, my blood still pumps. But it's as if the air grips and holds us all immobile.

Then I realize that the 'birds' are not birds at all, but a huge flock of grotesque *things*. One of them is poised above me, a bare-breasted hag with a bird's hips and legs and wings, but with a wizened and contorted human, female head. Its charnel stench assails my nostrils, talons spread, ready to rake and claw. It too can move its eyes, and these are watching me with consuming hatred. It's a harpy, a creature I'd never truly believed in. I recall the Grove, where Bria said that Persephone harvests such beings from the suffering nymphs. There's no reason in the harpy's eyes, just shrieking madness, and there are thousands more in the air around her.

My eyes edge sideway as I focus on the only moving thing in sight. An ebony chariot the size of a small house swoops through the air, drawn by winged horses, and lands before the Pantheon. The winged horses seem forged from bronze, snorting and snarling, with sharp, predatory teeth and burning eyes, but still mere adornments to the dark majesty of their masters: Hades and his consort, Persephone.

When I'd seen them at the Olympian Court on Mount Ida, they'd kept their forms cloaked, giving only hints of their true nature. But this is their own realm, and they have no need to hide their splendour. The black cloaks are gone, and their rage, clearly directed at all the invaders who have dared to war inside their realm, shimmers about them like a black, incandescent force, shot through with lightning.

Hades is clad in kingly robes of gold-chaised black silk, disdaining armour as if it's beneath him. His normally pale face is livid with fury. Beside him, Persephone's two faces, Summer and Winter, are unshrouded, the bright side golden and glowing like an overblown peach in the last days of ripeness, gorged with juice, but the left side withered, a lifeless grey-green colour. She wears a flimsy dark dress beneath a gauzy veil of shadowy lace. Her whole body is a constantly shifting blend of crone and lush beauty, as if she can never be wholly one or the other. Her eyes are on Helen, with a virulent expression somewhere between jealousy and contempt. Helen is staring back at her with a mix of defiance and a haughty preening that I would warn her against if I could move my tongue.

'Trojans, Spartans and *theioi*,' Hades says, in a voice like hail on a tiled roof. 'Living men, in my realm without my leave.' He strides across the hilltop to bend over the fallen Pirithous. 'And here lies my beloved champion.' He makes a gesture over Pirithous, and the arrow in the *theios*'s buttock vanishes, the wound sealing instantly. 'Speak, my champion. What brings these men to my threshold?'

While the rest of us watch helplessly, Pirithous rises, still shaky but recovering, and clasps his patron's knees in a gesture of supplication. 'Great King, Lord of Erebus, Ruler of the Underworld, you know me. Thirty-five years I have fought for you in the world above. My son Polypoetes serves you also. I have endured the fear and slights of the ignorant, while bringing retribution to those that offend you. And now I bring you gifts.' He points to Polydeuces and Helen. 'Behold, these are the son and daughter of Zeus himself, by Leda, Queen of Sparta. I give them to you, for your glory.'

Hades draws himself up to his full height and chuckles – a profoundly unsettling sound. 'Your gifts seem to be somewhat ungrateful to their giver, dear Pirithous, judging by the arrow I removed from your arse.'

'We had unwelcome pursuers, Great King. The whole of Achaea is in chaos right now,' Pirithous boasts. 'Olympus itself will be in uproar! But we have the ascendancy.'

'We?'

'Theseus of Athens, my King,' Pirithous says, pointing out his comrade. 'This is his plan.'

Theseus doesn't look best pleased to be given so much credit.

'The same Theseus who is sworn to Athena – as is the youth near him?' Hades enquires coolly, looking from the Athenian to myself.

'My Lord, the Ithacan is no one! He—'

'I know who he is,' Hades interrupts, brusquely.

I feel a thrill of fear at that. If Hades knows *all* that I am, it cannot bode well – not when I've seen the fates of my father and of Prometheus.

Athena and Prometheus, I pray you, give me the chance to speak in my defence…

'I also know these other Spartans, and the wounded daemon over there,' Hades said, gesturing at Bria. 'But not these Trojans, bar two whom I have seen once before. I would hear all sides of this matter ere I judge it.'

Pirithous's eyes widened in worry. 'My King, I assure you—'

Hades looks down and his expression clamps the man's tongue to the top of his mouth. 'Did I command you to kidnap the Skyfather's children? Did I order you to bring them here? Did I say I wished for chaos throughout Achaea?' A rod of judgement appears in his hand and he thumps it on the ground. 'I desire an accounting!'

Suddenly the world goes blank. I lose all awareness for an unknowable amount of time, until I blink awake and find myself seated on an ebony throne. At first almost completely disoriented, I gradually become aware of others seated in the same way. We're around a table, flanked by nine more such thrones, with a giant seat at either end. We're seated in the Pantheon, I realize, in the thrones reserved for the greatest of the gods.

My skin crawls as I realize I'm in Prometheus's throne. Persephone is immediately to my left on one of the giant end-thrones, the lush right side of her face nearest to me. To my right, Bria, Laas, Castor and Polydeuces are arrayed, the young *theios* clearly overawed. At the far end is the dreadful presence of Hades, occupying the other end-throne. Opposite us are Helen, Pirithous, Theseus and Skaya-Mandu, with Kyshanda directly opposite me – all the *theioi* or ranking nobles from the conflict. I wonder where the mortals are – the remaining Trojans, and Eunomos and Aethra.

All those present bar Hades and Persephone look dazed, but recovered enough to sit upright at least. Bria is clearly struggling to breathe, and my own thigh is throbbing. Alycus isn't here, and I realize that he must be truly dead; I grieve for him, a true-hearted warrior. But my eyes return constantly to Kyshanda, sitting opposite me with her eyes on mine. I would give anything to take her away from here.

Persephone has been observing our shared glances; now she looks fully at me, her disconcertingly halved face freezing my thoughts. 'Do you know what my husband likes to do with trespassers?' she asks, casually. 'The men are fed to Cerberus – and I know the hound remembers you, Ithacan.' Then she glances at Kyshanda, who appears terrified beyond speech. 'The women are given to me, for my grove.'

Those slowly asphyxiating nymphs! I almost fall to my knees to beg for Kyshanda's life. But then Hades raps his rod of judgement on the table, and his dark voice rolls over us.

'None of you were invited here,' he says, coldly. 'Not even thou, Pirithous. But I am a just King, and I will hear from you all. You, Theseus of Athens, if it really was your strategy to come here, you had better explain yourself.'

Theseus rouses himself from a reverie and looks across the table, at Bria and then me, his intention clear in his sullen eyes.

He is going to reach for glory, and if we try to drag him down, he'll make sure we all join him in Tartarus.

18 – Hades's Justice

'O Gods, whom I see before me [O Hades, Persephone and the Erinyes], ye who rule over guilty
souls and over Tartarus where the damned are
punished, and Styx, livid in your shadowy depths,
and Tisiphone, to whom I so often pray, look on
me favourably, and further my depraved desire.'
—Statius, *Thebaid 1*

Erebus

'It's true,' Theseus begins, 'that I have been dissatisfied with
serving Athena for a long time. I ensured her position as *the*
goddess in Attica, but she helped my rival Menestheus – a man
I trained in combat – to take *my* throne. She left me with
nothing, but continued to demand my service. "I'll find you
a new kingdom," she kept promising, but she never did. I've
been played for a fool.' He glares across the table. 'As for this
plan, it was Athena's own, prompted by her fawning bootlicker,
that lying Ithacan, and the body-jumping *dromas* beside him.'

*Much the same tale he'll have fed to Helen… nor does she look in
any way surprised…*

Bria scowls, though being called a whore is probably not a
new experience for her. But the real revelation in that diatribe,
for the Spartans at least, is my true allegiance I see their eyes
narrowing. 'He told us he served Hermes,' Laas growls.

'He's a born liar,' Theseus comments, before turning back
to Hades. 'Dread King, I decided there were other gods than
Athena, less faithless, more rewarding. I hoped my friend Pirithous could gain me a hearing with you. But I did not wish to

come as an empty-handed supplicant, so I have brought you a mighty gift: this is Helen of Sparta, Zeus's daughter, blessed by all the gods. That her brother, equally gifted, followed us is a bonus – I'd not thought Sparta so negligent as to send a child into Erebus.'

Laas stifles Polydeuces's angry retort.

Theseus gestures at Helen. 'As for Zeus's virtuous virgin child, far from showing grief at her abduction, she crept willing to my bed that first night, and pleaded to be ridden. "Take me each and every way," she implored. And look at her! What red-blooded man could turn such a creature down?'

'You forced me, you animal,' Helen shouts.

Bria arches an eyebrow, but I shake my head at her, defying the cynicism in her eyes. To me, Helen's words ring true.

So why did she side with Theseus in the fight? Why did she shoot at me?

I decide it wasn't loyalty to Theseus, but cold-hearted, *theios* pragmatism: I'm guessing she thought the legendary Theseus was more likely to survive than some dupe from Ithaca, even if she did know me.

Put like that, I'd have shot me too...

Theseus is slapping his thighs in mirth. 'You begged me for it,' he crows. 'You revelled in the ride!'

'You'd have cut my throat if I didn't please you!'

'*Silence!*' Hades snaps. Both Theseus and Helen go rigid. For a moment, it seems neither can breathe, before they slump, gasping.

Pirithous leaps in, sensing his master's displeasure. 'I told Theseus all along that Erebus had to be our goal,' the once-King of the Lapiths says. 'These twins, Helen and Polydeuces, are the first *theioi* in a generation to be blessed by all of Olympus. Clearly Zeus has plans for them, for his own betterment and no other. It was our duty to bring them to you. Theseus is the greatest warrior of his generation, Dread King. He wishes to serve you.'

I glance at Kyshanda. *Theseus and Pirithous are pretending they've never tried to sell Helen to the Trojans.* It's tempting to throw that into the debate, but I bite my tongue. *Speak last*, Eurybates has always advised me. *Many men are swayed most by the final argument.*

I wonder if that applies to gods.

Skaya-Mandu can't help but burst in, though. 'He's lying, Lord Hades! They never intended to bring the prizes to you. They made contact with my father, King Piri-Yamu of Troy, who sent me and my twin to collect them. But they brought only one child and tried to claim the full reward. Faithlessness deserves to be treated in kind.'

Theseus snorts. 'There was no such arrangement.'

'Liar,' Skaya-Mandu snarls back.

'Prove it,' Theseus replies, with an almost admirable bravado. *There won't be any written proof – both parties will have negotiated by word of mouth.*

Skaya loses his temper. 'They're lying, Lord,' he exclaims furiously. 'What really happened is that they reneged on their word, so we tried to seize the girl. They fled, to the cave at the hot springs on the beach—'

'Thermopylae,' Bria clarifies.

'Aye, Thermopylae – the so-called Gates of Heat,' Skaya says, glaring at Bria for interrupting, but that small pause helps him regain some control, because his voices reverts to his usual teeth-grindingly irritating tones. 'We pursued, bringing our ship here thanks to the treaties in place between our own death god, Lelwani, and yourself, Lord Hades. We rode the Styx and the Lethe – our galley is in the marshes nearby. As to whether these men purposed to bring the girl to Troy or to yourself, Lord Hades, you must be the judge. But we brought two chests of gold – payment for the two children – all the way from Troy to Attica. They are there in the ship as witness to our honourable intentions. Why should we bring gold if there was no agreement – or good faith on our part to go through with the arrangement?' He stares straight at Theseus. 'If this *old man* had a shred of honour, the deal would have taken place.'

'It was you who betrayed me, you back-stabbing smear of dog turd!' Theseus bursts out. Then he clamps his jaw shut, his face going scarlet as he realizes he's been provoked into revealing the truth. He turns hastily to Hades. 'All right, I admit, we first sought to deal with Troy.'

'But I always advocated Erebus, Lord,' Pirithous puts in, in a wheedling voice.

'Enough,' Hades grates. 'Your falsehoods are revealed and noted.'

I suppress a smile: Pirithous and Theseus are both on something of a roasting spit now. But how can I turn that to my – and Athena's – advantage?

The Lord of Erebus turns now to Laas. 'What say you, man of Sparta?'

Laas has become increasingly angry, especially since my allegiance to Athena was revealed. But when he speaks, his words are carefully chosen. 'Great King, we of Sparta have been the victims from the very beginning. We are proud the Skyfather chose to lie with our Queen, and awed to be living alongside his blessed offspring. When Princess Helen was kidnapped, we acted swiftly to right this wrong.'

He then indicates Bria and me. 'We accepted the aid of this daemon, Bria, knowing she serves Athena, because she came to us, disavowing Theseus and pledging to aid us. As for the Ithacan, he lied to us, stating that he was trailing Theseus to thwart this plot – he even claimed to serve Hermes, not Athena. It's now clear to me that Bria and Odysseus were as guilty as Theseus in the kidnapping, but that, as I have long suspected, the thieves fell out. Lord Hades, I beg that you allow me to escort Castor, Polydeuces and Helen home, where they belong. As for these others, they are yours to *dispose* of.'

Castor gives Laas a grateful smile, but Polydeuces and Helen share a fearful look, as well they might. I have a sudden intuition that, while Hades is making a great show of conducting this court as an even-handed search for justice, the verdict reached will be the one that serves the Lord of Erebus best.

But the impassive gaze of Hades has turned my way. 'So, Odysseus of Ithaca, you seem to be a proven liar. Can we trust your account now? Or yours, *Bria*,' he adds, putting a strange emphasis on her name: I wonder if he's known her by another. 'What do you *creatures* of Athena have to say?'

I give Bria a warning nudge, fearing she will attempt to build some convoluted web of truth and falsehood. A single misstep will taint everything we utter, and I have a better plan. 'We are guilty, Great Hades,' I say, before Bria can speak. 'Guilty of all that we've been accused of, and more.'

That admission draws reactions on all sides, from Bria's horror to Kyshanda's sickened gasp, Theseus's satisfied grunt and the sibilant hiss of Persephone at my left shoulder. But before anyone can interject, I continue. 'Everything we did was for Achaea – and by extension, for you, Dread King.'

Hades raises an amused, ironic eyebrow. 'For me?'

'Indeed, Lord of Erebus. The oracles speak of inevitable war, and the destruction of Achaea by the armies of Troy. Kill the worshippers, kill the god. The eastern divinities know this; Zeus-Tarhum, who wishes to be King of the Gods in Troy as in Achaea, knows this, as do Ares, Aphrodite and Artemis, who are also seeking out their Trojan counterparts. Skaya-Mandu speaks of your own accommodation with Lelwani, their death goddess.'

Hades's smile becomes fixed – I'm pushing my luck in saying all this.

Persephone breathes, 'Have a care, Ithacan.'

I'm committed to the argument now though, and push on. 'Some gods and goddesses of Achaea have no Hittite counterparts, however, including Hera, and my mistress Athena. They fear this realignment, naturally.' I indicate Polydeuces and Helen. 'Athena sees these children as pawns, serving Zeus's ambitions at Troy – a demonstration of the worth he brings to an alliance with Tarhum. Naturally Athena wishes to disrupt the Skyfather's cosy little arrangement, when her very existence is at stake.'

I have Hades's attention now, which is encouraging, although I could be talking myself into an eternity in Tartarus. Beside me, Bria looks sick at the amount of truth I am revealing, but I'm less concerned at holding on to secrets than getting out of this fix – with logic and reason, the only weapons I have to hand.

'Say on,' the Death God invites me.

'The real point, Lord Hades, is how this affects you. Aligning with Lelwani is one thing, but do you wish to be Hades-Lelwani, or Lelwani-Hades? Or nothing at all? The dominant cult always subsumes the lesser in the end. And if Achaea falls to the Trojans, what will you be?'

'I take the point,' Hades concedes. 'But how does this mitigate your guilt, Ithacan?'

'It doesn't,' I reply, fighting to keep my nerve. 'Except that Athena is irrevocably for Achaea, where I believe your real interests lie. And therefore, how you judge *her* efforts to prevent Zeus from betraying his own people is relevant. I am only her tool.'

Hades's gaze shifts to his consort. 'What say you, my dear?'

Persephone is stroking her summer face thoughtfully. 'I am the peace offering between yourself and my mother, Hera-as-Demeter, Husband. You know where my loyalties lie.'

Here, in Achaea is how I read that. She studies me with a reptilian eye. 'But you also know this one's ancestry. Regardless of his present sagacity, or even *because* of it, I would counsel that he should share his father's fate.'

I try not to let this sentence of death and eternal punishment distract me. It isn't very easy to do, when images of Sisyphus and his terrible ordeal flood my mind, my ears ringing with Prometheus's screams as the eagle rips his kidneys out. But I now know I have a foothold in this debate. 'I'm sworn to Athena,' I remind Hades. 'My father's cause is dead. I look only to the future, as does Athena. Regrets and familial ties are wasted thoughts, to her and to me.'

Persephone's serpentine gaze flickers between me and Kyshanda – I worry that she perceives our emotional connection – but she doesn't allude to it when she speaks. 'If you were counselling my Lord Hades,' she asks me, slyly, 'would you advise him to keep these gifts Pirithous has brought, to safeguard Achaea?'

Pirithous and Theseus begin to protest, but Persephone silences them with a gesture.

'On the contrary,' I reply, 'I would argue for their return to Sparta, to King Tyndareus and Queen Leda. Yes, Polydeuces and Helen are precious. But if you seek to hold them here, you'll bring the wrath of Zeus and his allies down upon you, and perhaps precipitate a war no one can win. I know you are universally *believed* in. But belief is not *worship*. If I correctly understand matters, worship transcends belief, because worship is *active* belief. Therefore, even here in your realm, Zeus might be your equal – or even your better – in a direct conflict. So I would repudiate this gift, and...' I look across the table at Theseus '...I would repudiate the givers. Return them to Sparta as a peace offering, perhaps. And use the time this gives you to reach a fuller accommodation with Lelwani, or with Hera – however your interests can best be served.'

'You would have me deliver these "gifts" back to Zeus, who wishes to use them against Achaea?' Hades asks, his voice sceptical.

'That's the way it might seem, but it isn't how I believe things will play out,' I reply. 'After they were blessed, Zeus thought he had time, while they matured, to negotiate the strongest possible arrangement with the King of Troy. But now the twin's true identity is revealed; all Achaea will soon know who and what they are. And Tyndareus now knows what use Zeus intended for them, and Tyndareus is a proud Achaean. You gods might view your worshippers as compliant pawns, but men worship gods they believe will protect them. If Zeus no longer protects Sparta, Sparta will look elsewhere. I believe Zeus will be unable to marry Helen to a Trojan now: Tyndareus will refuse to let him.'

'We will never marry Trojans,' Polydeuces bursts out, supporting my case. He glares down the table at Skaya-Mandu. 'We loathe your kind.' Helen, beside him, nods emphatically.

'The feeling is entirely mutual,' Skaya-Mandu rasps. He reaches over to take his sister's wrist. 'No son or daughter of Troy feels anything but contempt for Achaea.'

I could tell him that isn't entirely true, but Kyshanda wouldn't thank me for it.

Then Helen speaks, in a high, clear voice. 'Do I not have the right also to speak?' she demands.

Heads turn. I'm watching Hades, wondering if she's wise to speak. But the Death God seems curious as to what might come out of the mouth of Zeus's daughter.

'The right?' he drawls. 'I determine who has "rights", whatever they are.' Then he waves a benevolent hand. 'Speak, girl.'

Far from cowed or overawed, Helen of Sparta, all of thirteen years old, lifts her chin defiantly. 'You call me "girl", even now, my Lord. But I have been dragged into womanhood. Against my will.'

'Lies!' Theseus snarls, but Hades silences him with a gesture. The Attican keeps trying to speak, struggling to move his tongue as it strangles him, his face turning red, then purple.

'Say on,' Hades invites Helen, while Theseus chokes.

'You've listened to this *beast* tell you I begged to be taken,' she says, her voice ringing through the hall. 'Yet never did you even look at me, to ask where the truth lies! Perhaps you feel some guilt for your own marriage, my Lord?'

I'm thinking, *DID SHE JUST SAY THAT? Cronos's cock, the girl has guts!*

Hades – he of the pale-as-a-wraith visage – colours. 'Speak not of that which you know nothing,' he grates. His eyes trail to Persephone beside me. 'What occurs between a man and a woman is more complex than you yet know.' His voice is like the sharpening of knives.

'Is it?' Helen fires back, and I reel again at her temerity. I've seen her brazen out the breaking of crockery in Sparta when she was a child; I recognize the tilt of the head and the dauntless glare, but this is madness. Unless...

My brain, as it is wont to do, shoots off on several tangents...

Helen throws out her arm, pointing at Theseus. 'This one held me down and violated me! Did you even wonder how I felt about that, Lord Hades? Did it even occur to you to question whether a thirteen-year-old girl might want a six-foot-tall fifty-year-old to take her virginity? Did it even occur to you to question his assertion that I "begged for it", O Just Lord? Or are you another of the vile "old enough to bleed, old enough to breed" fraternity?'

Hades – *the God of this place* – looks like he's just been slapped. But – at the very start of our trial – he asserted himself as a "just king". He's trapped, and forced to acknowledge her right to accuse.

I can't even look at Kyshanda, because suddenly every male is complicit in Theseus's crime. The silence is deafening, until Helen fills it. 'The first night, we simply fled,' she says. 'The second, he came to me when the others slept, pulled my blanket aside, clamped his hand over my mouth and... and...'

And then suddenly Helen's no longer a force of vengeance, an Erinys screaming against injustice: now she's the violated innocent, and that's even more powerful. I'm spellbound – we all are.

'He pushed his thing into me, and then suddenly *everything* happened to me at once. It was like claws of light that ripped open my brain, and worms of fire that invaded my flesh...'

She breaks off, sobbing, and I realize that I haven't breathed for too long. We all do; we gasp for air, shocked and shattered. My gaze trawls to Theseus – he's shaking his head but he can't speak, which at least saves us from more of his lies.

Helen's arm suddenly shoots out – at Pirithous. 'Then this one appeared,' she rasps, tears streaming down her white, trembling visage. '"Give me a turn," he says. "You've got a piece of tail out of this jaunt, Theseus – I want my share." That's what he said.'

'What a load of *kopros*,' Pirithous shouts. Then he collapses forward, his head pressed to the table, and I realize that's because Hades is doing something with the air in his throat. His face is going blue, and I can't say the sight displeases me.

Helen hammers home her words like nails. 'Theseus refuses, but he says "What about Hades's *kunopes*? That slut Persephone must be longing for warm, living meat inside her. Why don't we kidnap her too, Piri – all for you?"'

If I'd thought the universe had fallen silent before, when Helen began her accusations, it's utterly still now. We could have heard a bee fart in Luwia. I'm scarcely able to comprehend what she's just done…

She's destroyed them. She's condemned them for eternity.

My eyes lock on Helen's tragic, broken face. For a long few moments, we're all incapable of speech, but then Hades raps the table with his rod. When he speaks, his voice is – *almost* – emotional.

'I have decided upon my judgement.' He turns first to Pirithous and Theseus. 'I have no doubt you were seeking venal rewards in Troy, and that coming here was your second choice. I did not command this abduction, and nor do I wish it. Nor do I condone *rape*, for any cause. The lines of responsibility between the world above and below, between subjects living and dead, have been hammered out between Zeus and myself over many long centuries. Those who came intentionally to Erebus will be sentenced shortly, but Helen of Sparta was brought here unwilling. And so, I deem, was Aethra, mother of Theseus. They shall both go free.'

'But—' Pirithous begins to protest.

Hades makes another of his choking gestures, stopping the man's throat. Then he turns to Polydeuces, Castor and Laas. 'These three came willingly to this forbidden place, but it was duty that compelled them. They too shall be released, along with their one surviving soldier, to return to Sparta. As for the Trojans, both brother and sister, and their followers who still live, I find them guilty of trespass, and deserving of punishment. Have you aught to say?'

My heart jolts, but Kyshanda places her hand on her brother's arm to stifle an angry protest. 'I am daughter of Hekuba and sworn to Kamrusepa, akin to your Hecate, Achaean Goddess of Magic; and to Lelwani, our death goddess. In the name of my patron deities, I do have words to say.'

Hades studies her coolly. 'Go on.'

'The judgements you have announced show a willingness to undo the harm this abduction has caused, without burning bridges between yourself and the Skyfather. In that spirit, perhaps you might also use it to develop closer ties to Lelwani and Kamrusepa? I offer my services as mediator.'

I marvel at her composure and audacity; I know only a little of Hecate – she is very much a woman's goddess, associated with childbirth as well as magic, and like Hera she has a triple aspect. She'd not been present at the Olympian Court, and is said to have been the child of a Titan. That makes her loyalties suspect. Tellingly, she has no throne set aside for her here either.

Persephone places a hand over Kyshanda's. 'I favour this,' the goddess tells her consort. 'But if she is to mediate, she must learn our ways. I propose that she serve me for half a year.'

No, I protest silently, as Kyshanda looks across the table at me, her conflicting emotions – fear, regret and hope – reflected in her eyes. But she doesn't flinch. 'If that will secure the release of my brother and our warriors, I accept,' she tells Persephone.

My heart sinks, though I am mightily impressed with her courage, and her willingness to sacrifice herself for her brother. But I worry what six months here with Persephone will do to her.

'Then we accept,' Hades agrees. 'Which brings me to my *erstwhile* champion.' He turns to Pirithous. 'You brought me a gift unwanted, presuming upon my support while dragging me into a situation that, as the Ithacan has pointed out, could bring me into direct conflict with Olympus. What have you to say?'

Pirithous seems to be sensing that his many years of service mightn't get him out of this. 'I swear, it was always my intention to bring the girl here. I would have killed Theseus if I had to. I meant only to serve you.'

'Why, you piece of barbarian shit!' Theseus roars, twisting in his seat, fists bunching.

'Peace!' Hades shouts. Suddenly Pirithous is bound to his seat, serpents made of stone erupting from the ground to bind his arms and legs, pinning them in place, while his lips are sealed closed. The Lapith grunts furiously, his eyes imploring forgiveness. But Hades has none. 'I will find a place for you here… in Tartarus.'

Pirithous tries to protest – and another loop of the stone serpents gags him. He thrashes then goes still, eyes bulging as they dart frantically here and there.

The Death God turns away from his champion uncaringly, to look at Theseus, Bria and me.

'And so to our kidnappers. You admit conspiring to abduct the girl, but Odysseus of Ithaca says it was all to serve Athena and Achaea, and thwart these others. I do not wish to overly upset Athena, yet punishment is due. Lives are forfeit.' He narrows his eyes, enjoying his power. 'I see three *theioi* of Athena here. One of you shall be allowed to leave, to explain your failures to Athena. I am feeling generous, so I will let you decide which it will be.'

He clicks his fingers, and suddenly our surroundings shift again – to an arena of stone, a circular pit surrounded by tiered seating. The instant transition from sitting to standing throws my balance, and I sprawl on the ground, close to the perimeter wall. Across the arena, only thirty yards away in either direction, are Theseus and Bria, also prone, but now struggling to their feet.

Before each of us are our own weapons: Theseus and I have our swords and daggers, but Bria has a bow, half a dozen arrows in her quiver, and a long knife.

Why has Hades denied me my bow? To make more of a spectacle of this? A spectacle of my death…?

Above us, the seating fills: Hades and Persephone are on the presiding thrones, and arrayed on one side are the Trojans, Skaya-Mandu and Kyshanda, with the Spartans opposite them, their bewilderment at the sudden change transforming into a cold, intent curiosity. Then in a feathery rush, the harpies descend, filling the empty seats and screaming at us lustily.

None of them cares who will win – except Kyshanda. I meet her eyes, swallow, then look away, hoping against all hope she won't have to watch me die.

Hades gestures, and a small, slender candle appears. 'I will light this shortly, to mark the start of your contest. In the time it takes for this to burn out, I expect two of you to be disabled or dead. The victor will return to Athena to explain your follies. Any surviving losers will either hang in my consort's grove, or burn in Tartarus.'

Contemplating my chances against two experienced *theioi*, while recalling the fates of Sisyphus and Prometheus, is enough to freeze my blood.

Theseus shows no anxiety as he picks up his oversized *xiphos*, but Bria's hands shake as she takes up her bow and fits an arrow. *So even an age-old daemon can feel fear.* I remember her earlier admission that she might indeed die here, in the Land of the Dead. I watch that fear strangle her composure. But I don't wish her ill, not in the way I loathe Theseus.

My *xiphos* feels heavy, the grip already slippery in my perspiring hand as I grasp it. Gingerly, I try out my injured thigh. It takes my weight but I know this fight is going to have to be brief for me to have a chance.

'Bria,' Theseus calls. 'Remember all those nights, my honey? All the good times? For those, I'll make it swift.'

Bria bridles at his words. 'You stabbed me in that culvert, Theseus. There *were* no good times.' But when her eyes move to me, she looks no more welcoming. 'Why don't you boys slaughter each other? I'll take on the last man standing.'

With arrows from across the arena, no doubt. But I'm remembering the wound Aethra gave her, and note how sluggishly she's moving.

She has no more of a chance than I do...

Theseus snorts like a bull. 'I think you're the first to go down, sweet-cakes. That bow of yours might serve me well.' He twirls his blade, stretching and flexing, warming up his body for the exertions to come while seeking to intimidate us with a display of physical power and prowess. I recall how he battered me earlier, and downgrade my chances from low to none.

But there is one angle I can work... 'Bria,' I call. 'If I return above, I'll give Athena your bracelet.'

She glances down at the twist of copper on her black-skinned arm, the only visible sign that has linked the three bodies I've seen her wear. Then she looks back at me, perhaps with some sign of an understanding.

But then again, perhaps not…

Hades lights the candle, and Bria fires her arrow instantly – *at me* – the arrow streaking across the gap, perfectly aligned with my heart. *So much for our "understanding"; what is it about women shooting at me today?*

I dodge right, fast but not quick enough: the shaft gashes my dagger hand and sends the blade flying to the ground, while the shaft spins away. In the stands above, Kyshanda cries out aloud, while the Spartans and Skaya roar with excitement, and the harpies shriek like the carrion birds they are.

Theseus charges, roaring like a bull as he leaps across the arena, his blade hammering at me. All I can do is throw up my smaller, lighter blade to protect myself, staggering at the impact of each parry, my wrist jarred by each blow.

'Come on, runt!' he shouts, slamming me back into the wall, my legs buckling, while Bria circles. Theseus's face is lit with fierce joy as he goes through his repertoire of slashes and lunges, slicing open my side, then lashing out with his foot and crunching it into my damaged right thigh. I stagger, time slowing to a standstill as Theseus's giant sword swings back for the fatal blow, even as I fall to my knees.

Then Bria shouts; he hesitates, and I snatch up my dropped dagger with my injured left hand. Despite the appalling pain, I drive it upwards…

…and that damned *freak* of a warrior twists away from the surprise blow. 'Ha!' he shouts, as if the sneak attack has amused him. He kicks the dagger from my grasp…

Then Bria shoots him in the right calf. The Athenian almost falls, barely parries my reactive sword thrust and staggers out of reach as I try to rise.

'You faithless bitch!' he screams. His left hand sweeps back and he throws his dagger before Bria realizes her danger. The blade takes her in the throat and sticks there, quivering. She wavers, the bow falling to the ground as her hands paw ineffectually at her neck, trying to dislodge the weapon. Then she collapses onto her back, twitching into stillness.

I regain my feet, but only in time for Theseus to turn my way again. I'm fighting an irrational desire to try somehow to save Bria's life, and that wavering costs me the chance to get at Theseus while he's still reeling in pain. By the time I've regathered my wits, Theseus has already yanked the arrow from his leg and thrown it away.

'Now you,' the Athenian rasps, limping towards me. 'I've been wanting to do this from the moment I met you.'

The next few moments are a blur, as Theseus's sword slashes at me, each blow like an axeman levelling a tree. All I can do is parry once more, wielding my sword two-handed with my bloodied grip slithering on the hilt, my arms almost numb with exhaustion and my right leg threatening to collapse under me at any time. Theseus is relentless, a raging bull.

But in the months before the Spartan mission, Bria has drilled me to the point of exhaustion and beyond. Whereas Theseus, pudgy from drink and excess, is now slowing visibly, blood running down his leg from the arrow wound. The fight below the Pantheon must have taken its toll on his reserves. And he should have left the arrow in, or broken off the shaft – his mistake, my opportunity – because he's *bleeding*.

I reach deep within myself, finding resources I scarcely believed I had. Speed is the key: I have to move faster, darting the tip of my blade towards Theseus's face, forcing him to move. Every time I give ground I go sideways, left or right, forcing the larger man to turn. My damaged thigh muscle is screaming, but somehow I blank out the pain. It's attrition now, as I try to exhaust him while fighting my own collapse. Theseus is grunting now at every blow, sweat streaming down his face, as he tries to hack through my guard. *Keep moving... Just keep moving!* And there's my own discarded dagger again – I've come full circle. I thrust, forcing Theseus to back away, then in one fluid movement I stoop, pick up the hilt and throw, just as he did with Bria.

Theseus fails to evade it or sweep it aside, and the bronze blade punches into his left thigh, dropping him to one knee, roaring in fury and pain.

I limp as quickly as I can over to Bria's lost bow, while Theseus clambers painfully to his feet. 'One shot, Ithacan,' the older man bellows. 'Then I'm on you. Better make it count.'

I plunge my sword point in the ground, nock an arrow and take aim as Theseus charges, weaving left and right. Then, defying wounds and gravity and pain, the Athenian leaps, covering the intervening distance so fast I only have time to loosen my shaft before Theseus's blade hammers down on me. I throw up the discharged bow in desperation, and the outsized sword smashes through it, gouging my left shoulder.

But the arrow has slammed into Theseus's right thigh and punched clean through flesh and muscle, and he falls past me, slamming face first into the dirt, hard. I stagger out of reach, snatching up my sword as Theseus tries and fails to rise, his nose pulped and pumping blood.

I circle behind him, forcing Theseus to roll to face me, the arrow shaft that impales his leg grating on the ground, causing him to howl in anguish. 'Coward!' he shouts, spraying spittle. 'Let me up!'

He tries once more to rise, and I slash through his left hamstring. Theseus collapses, shrieking, to lie writhing in the dust. 'Coward!' he roars again. 'Runt! Dwarf! Poisonous little half-man!'

'Yield!' I call. 'Don't make me kill you.'

'I am Theseus!' the Athenian screams back, his eyes mad with fear and pain and delusion. 'I am the hero of the age! I am the King of Athens! I do not yield!'

Once more he tries to rise, but now both legs have failed him, leaving him dragging himself towards me, brandishing his blade weakly. The harpies jeer, flapping their wings, their grotesque faces contorted with bloodlust. 'Kill him!' they yowl.

Instead, I hobble to the space beneath Hades's throne. 'Blow out your candle, my Lord King,' I call.

What the Trojans and Spartans are shouting, I neither know nor care. I have eyes only for Kyshanda, who is sitting hunched over, crying and shaking with relief.

But there is one more, crucial thing to do. I limp back to Bria's corpse and take the bracelet from her arm. Then I cross her black-skinned arms over her chest and close her eyes. 'Ikumbi, this woman was called,' I tell Hades. 'Have mercy on her soul.'

When I look back, Theseus is lying face down, weeping in the dust.

19 – Homecoming

'But you must be gentle with your father.'
—Hesiod, *Fragments of Unknown Position 21*

Erebus

'I wish you didn't have to stay here,' I say, softly.

'It's only six months,' Kyshanda replies.

I ache to kiss her, as I had that one glorious time in Krisa, but there are too many eyes on us, too many people who could use affection between an Achaean and a Trojan to ruin us both. But damn, I hate partings! Especially this one. I am desperate to touch and hold her, my longing stronger than any I've experienced. Is this love? Or just infatuation? Right now, I only know that it hurts beyond belief to be so close and so unable to reach out.

We're below Pantheon Hill, under the gaze of Hades and Persephone. Kyshanda has already farewelled her brother, and Skaya-Mandu has taken his surviving men into the trees, heading down to the swamp and the river Lethe. Hades has said he will give the Trojan ship passage out of his realm.

'Do you know what you've agreed to?' I ask Kyshanda.

'No,' she admits. 'But I think I'll learn much. Kamrusepa and Hecate, Lelwani and Persephone... there are links there to explore. And you? Will you be safe?'

'Safe? I don't know. The Spartans could turn on me the moment we're back in the world above. But Hades has charged me with reporting to Athena, so perhaps they'll let me be. For now.'

'Come to Troy, once you know I've returned,' she urges. 'You will be welcome – with me, anyway. And I think Mother would like you.'

Could I do that? Live in Troy, with the enemies of my people?

'One day, perhaps,' I reply. As I speak I have a vision of myself, standing on the walls with her – we are older, much older, but she is still heartbreakingly beautiful. *Is it prophecy?* Right now, I'm certain it is – has Prometheus not said he was giving me all the gifts?

'Yes,' I say, meaning it with all my heart. 'One day I will come.'

'I won't feel fully alive until you do,' she replies. Then she blushes shyly and adds, 'Of course I won't feel fully alive for the next six months anyway – I'll be in the Land of the Dead.'

'Are you coming, Ithacan?' Laas of Sparta calls, his harsh tones breaking the moment.

'I won't forget you,' I promise, my voice thick with emotion.

Then Persephone joins us, simply appearing and startling us both. She lays one of her pale hands on Kyshanda's shoulder, looking from her to me. 'How interesting,' she says. 'Two who should be enemies, smitten by the arrows of Eros.'

'We're just friends,' we chorus, but Persephone cackles harshly.

'Do you think I'm a fool?' she asks. 'I know more of partings than any.' She strokes Kyshanda's cheeks. 'Look at your eyes, brimming with tears. And his clever tongue, tied up in knots. I know what I see.'

'What are you going to do with her?' I ask, foolishly daring.

'I'm going to open up her mind, and let the light and darkness in.' She meets my gaze. 'You should leave now.'

I should, but I don't. 'Lady Persephone, was your union with the Lord of the Underworld... er...'

'That's none of your business, mortal,' she rasps. Then she softens. 'I have no axes to grind, Prince Odysseus. I am content with who I am.' She meets my eye. 'The pomegranates people say I ate, that condemned me to my months below ground... I ate them willingly.' She puts a hand on Kyshanda's shoulder.

'This young woman and I are going to have the most extraordinary time together.'

I'm not going to get more than that from her, or escape so easily. I bow in the eastern manner to Kyshanda, raise my hands in salutation to Persephone and turn away, feeling my heart bleed with loss as I limp down the other slope to join the Spartans, refusing to look back.

Hades flashes into existence beside me. 'Convey my greetings to Athena,' he tells me. 'And suggest that she doesn't meddle in the affairs of my realm again.'

I bow my head. 'I will tell her.'

He half turns away, then pauses and asks, 'By the way, Ithacan, did you by chance happen upon any of your ancestors in your travels in my realm?'

'No,' I tell him, taking care to keep my face blank. *Does he believe me? Or not?*

'You might have heard tales of the fates of Sisyphus and Prometheus, told in the world above?' Hades continues, his expression giving no hint as to what he knows or guesses. 'Those are true tales. The punishments visited upon your father and your divine ancestor were decreed by Zeus, not by me. I do not condone their sins or their hubris, but I do not condemn you simply for having their blood... unlike others.'

'Thank you,' I say, cautiously.

'You interest me,' he says. 'You speak well, fight resourcefully and possess a cunning intellect. If Athena ever lets you down, I may be able to offer you shelter.' Then he turns to Laas. 'The Ithacan is bearing messages for me. You will not harm or spread malicious tidings of him. Tell your king he's innocent of any crime.'

The Spartans don't look happy, but they touch their clenched fists to their hearts to signify obedience. Then Hades lifts his right hand and makes a gesture. 'Be gone, and do not return to my realm without my summons.'

It's a command I will be very pleased to comply with.

–

The hillside in Erebus disappears, to be replaced by a rocky limestone beach bathed in sunlight.

Predictably, Polydeuces flies at me, fists flailing. But before I'm required to defend myself, he's caught by Laas, the veteran warrior having to use his utmost strength to contain the boy's rage. 'No, my prince! No!'

'Why not? The lying bastard admitted he came to kidnap Helen.'

Castor, his wounded leg heavily bandaged, growls in agreement. 'We should drag him back to my father to stand trial.' He turns, seeking agreement from Helen, standing radiant beside him. But she only smiles, cat-like. For a moment our eyes lock.

I was able to destroy Theseus and Pirithous for what they did, her eyes say. *I could find ways to do the same to you.* 'Castor,' she replies instead. 'Hades has commanded us to spare him. Besides, Odysseus is our guest-friend. We grew up with him. We owe him the benefit of any doubt.'

I'm not fooled; she knows I conspired to abduct her. She *must* blame me – in some part at least – for Theseus's rape. I'm torn between pity for her and awe at this iron-willed control of her emotions.

Her gaze says, *You owe me… and I own you.* But there's another undercurrent as well: recognition.

This new Helen is cunning, dangerous and devious – and she sees the same in me.

'Aye, we must comply with Hades's wishes, Lady,' Laas agrees, his voice grudging, but tempered by shrewdness. 'And in truth, Odysseus saw what none of us did. Whether this alleged plot he speaks of is true or false, it forces us to ask what Zeus wants from you, his son and daughter. Indeed, what does Zeus intend for Sparta, or for Achaea?'

I wait, hand on sword hilt, for the danger to pass. Hades has returned the Great Bow to me and it's over my shoulder, though the quiver is empty.

After a pregnant pause, Castor and Polydeuces turn away, shepherding Helen from me. I would have loved to speak to her more, to understand her better, and somehow convey my regret for all that's happened to her. But she just throws me one of those over-the-shoulder looks that some girls can deploy like weapons, as she leaves with her brothers.

'Her new status as *theia* is one she wears well,' I comment eventually.

'Aye,' is all Laas says in reply.

'You must care for her as a victim,' I say to Laas. 'She's been abducted, and used unwillingly. She needs to be healed, body and soul.' I pause, then ask. 'I imagine the tales about this rescue won't mention me?'

'You were never involved,' the Spartan confirms. Then he becomes thoughtful. 'You've learnt fast, I'll give you that. The gods and their games are complex – you need a labyrinthine mind to see all the angles. Most *theioi* are mere pieces, tokens to be moved on the board. But you're a player, and that's a dangerous thing.' He shifts uneasily. 'I've had to kiss and make up to many a sworn enemy in my time. Religion is all about ideals, but it's pragmatists that last longest. So I expect I'll be seeing you around.'

'We're both Achaean,' I remind him.

'That means little, in this game.' He points northwards. 'Walk far enough, and you'll reach the fortress town of Messe. Take ship, and don't come back until you're welcome, if that time ever comes round.' He swings on his heel and stalks away.

I watch him go, then I pull Bria's copper bracelet out, studying it. In moments it has turned green with verdigris, and inside sixty heart beats, it has turned to dust.

See you soon, Bria. But not too soon, I hope.

Three miles up the coast I meet someone coming the other way, a tousle-haired man with an Egyptian complexion and a lopsided smile. Only when I hug him, beating my fists against his back, do I truly believe that I've survived.

'Eurybates,' I manage to choke out. 'Let's go home.'

–

As the trading ship slogs into Ithaca's port, my eyes are drawn to my father's squat, mud-brick fortress-palace on the hill above. Compared to the giant stone citadel of Mycenae, or the gleaming, brightly painted walls of Sparta, it's a primitive construction, unlikely to strike fear into the hearts of any serious war band. The strength of Ithaca is the people, who will snatch up weapons without hesitation to defend her.

There isn't a trade in the town of Ithaca that I haven't tried, nor an alley I haven't roved. This is home, and I'm incomplete when I'm not here. But in the past months I've seen marvels – Erebus and the Olympian Court, gods and heroes – and I belong to that world too now. Little Ithaca is going to feel very, very small…

The ship docks, and Eurybates and I climb the long hill to the gates of my family's fortress, silent and contemplative after all we've gone through. And we both know we'll face more. The oracles say war is coming, a war for survival.

The guards at the palace gate have no idea how to react when a long-absent prince returns unexpectedly. I suspect they've had their private doubts about Laertes's official story, and they're happy to let us sit inside the gatehouse while a runner searches for Ctimene, at our request.

I know them both well, ask after their families, and receive a quiet, 'It's good to see you, Prince,' from them in return, while they eye me up surreptitiously – I daresay I've changed since last they saw me. I still have a limp, but I've not had anyone try to kill me for days now, so perhaps this time my leg will get a chance to heal. I have the Bow of Eurytus over my shoulder – strung – and a well-used *xiphos* in my shoulder scabbard. The eager young man who left half a year ago for Pytho is now a man.

Eurybates exchanges gossip rapid-fire with the guard captain, but I remain silent, composing myself. Then Ctimene appears, shrieking with joy as she flies into my arms. We squeeze each other so tight we can barely breathe, sobbing into each other's shoulders.

'Thank all the gods you're back,' she gasps. 'I've so missed you.'

'How have you been, since Eury was here last?'

'It's still awful,' she tells me. 'Mother and Father pretend happiness in public, but they never share a bed. They don't even look at each other, unless they have to.' She seizes my hand, her face coming alive with hope. 'But you're back! Now things will be all right! But what about you? What've you been doing?'

'Oh, nothing much,' I reply, keeping my expression bland. 'Sleeping, mostly. You know me.'

She does – well enough to know I'm lying through my teeth. But bless her, she doesn't ask, just takes my arm and pulls me along with her into the house.

But we still have a huge obstacle to overcome – my father's anger and rejection. 'Father might send me away again,' I try to tell her, but she's not listening.

'We're not a family without you, brother,' she says, her voice breaking. 'I can't believe you're here.' Then we're walking into the megaron, the central hall. Mother must have been alerted by Ctimene, for she's walking towards me with a semblance of restraint, only to stumble as she reaches me, as if she's about to faint. I catch her and she clings to me, Ctimene joining in a three-way embrace that is both painful and wonderful.

Finally Laertes stamps in, eying the embraces of his women-folk sourly. 'Crown Prince Menelaus has written, asking that I hear you out,' he says. 'That doesn't make you welcome.'

I gently disengage from my mother and sister, and limp over to face my not-father. 'I know that. But I have learnt something that should make you relent, at least towards my mother.'

'What have you to say that could possibly make any differ-ence?'

Up close, Laertes looks dishevelled, neglected, his hair dusty and matted, his tunic stained. And he stinks of manure. *He's retreated to his farm – just as he always does when he can't deal with the world.* 'I descended into Erebus, and met my true father. And he told me something you need to hear.'

Laertes's eyes bulge, while behind me I hear Mother give a strangled cry. Then the King shakes his head. 'Your father is dead. And men don't wander into Erebus to natter with ghosts.'

'*Men* don't – but I'm a *theios*, god-touched. Don't pretend you don't know what that means. You were an Argonaut, and hunted the Calydonian Boar. You've seen the *theioi* up close. You know what they are and what they can do. And you know from my blood that I've inherited that blessed curse, on both sides. So don't you pretend disbelief when I say that, through the aid of Athena, I've crossed the Styx in Charon's boat, and faced many-headed Cerberus. That I've walked Persephone's Grove and seen the fruit hanging there, and traversed the Asphodel Fields. In the hills beyond, I met the man who fathered me, and heard his tale.'

Laertes's face takes on a sick expression. 'What makes you think I'd want to listen to anything *he* said?'

'You'll want to. And Mother too. The tavern tales are true: Zeus has determined to break Sisyphus by setting him an impossible task. My father must roll a boulder up a hill, but the boulder grows larger with every step, until it slips from his grasp and hurtles to the bottom again. He is barely more than a skeleton, bloodied and torn, but his spirit remains defiant.'

'He was always a stubborn *phallos*,' Laertes growls. 'Good – he deserves such a fate.'

Anticleia turns her head away, biting her lip.

'He told me how I came into existence,' I continue. 'And why. After his grandson Bellerophon died, Sisyphus was desperate to breed another *theios* but, because of his age and his debauched habits, he was *impotent*. So he came here, to Ithaca, intent on evil. Somehow he'd obtained a goblet from Aphrodite that, with the help of powerful spells, would cause a woman to conceive from his saliva, which he secretly placed in the wine.'

'A fairy tale,' Laertes snaps. 'Like your wild tale about descending into Erebus.' But he's looking doubtful.

'Hear me out, I beg. Sisyphus said that Mother became dazed and then unconscious after she drank the wine, but no sexual union took place. He swore by all the gods that this is the truth. He's humiliated by what he did, and begs pardon of you both. When I told him you and Mother are estranged because of him, he wept, and prayed for your understanding.'

Laertes stares at me. 'I swear, if you're lying, boy—'

'*Lie?* I found out I was conceived through his *spit*, when I'd hoped he'd deny he was even my father! How do you think I feel?' I grab Laertes's arm. 'Your wife did nothing wrong! She has been faithful to you all her life! Yet you continue to blame her for something *utterly* beyond her control! What kind of *just king* are you?'

'But—' Anticleia begins.

'*You remember nothing*,' I rap out. 'Aphrodite's spell wiped your mind clean. You never fell from grace, Mother! You are a good and faithful wife. And Sisyphus is paying for his deceit.'

I step away, clearing the space between Laertes and Anticleia. Ctimene tiptoes over to take my hand, her face rigid with tension – I know she is just as desperate as I am that they reconcile.

And in truth, if this fabrication doesn't work – a lie that absolves Mother of any blame and lays all the fault on a dead man – I don't know what will. Can Mother stay silent, even though it adds to the vile stories that have poisoned Sisyphus's memory? She doesn't yet know that Sisyphus himself doesn't care if she maligns him, if it can save her marriage.

And will it appeal to Laertes's sense of honour? I know his nature: he has more than his share of pride, and sensitivity too, beneath that gruff exterior. He needs to believe that Anticleia has been his alone, that he's never been exceeded in his own bed.

Has he seen enough of the bizarre world of the *theioi* in his travels that he can accept the idea of a magical goblet of seed-bearing spittle? How many wonders and legends have already been brought to life before his eyes? Or has he wandered, blind and oblivious, along a path strewn with miracles?

The answer isn't long in coming. Laertes hesitates, glancing to right and left as though the walls might give him an answer. Then he clears his throat, straightens his shoulders and strides to Anticleia to hold her, tentatively at first, but then, as she returns his embrace, clutching her to him, shaking, eyes tight shut but cheeks wet with tears.

I lead Ctimene over, and we twine our arms around our parents' shoulders, until they envelop us also in this tentative rekindling of family love.

Now, truly, I have come home.

Epilogue – Crowned Once More

'Justice beats Hubris when she arrives at the close.
But only after suffering does the callow fool know
this.'
—Hesiod, *Works and Days*

Erebus

The next time I see Athena is about a week later. She wakes me with the sense of her presence, while I lie buried in a dream. There is no time to react: no sooner am I aware of her ghostly daemon figure sitting beside my bed than she's taken my hand and she's pulling my spirit from my body. We spin away, two blurs in a swirling tunnel of light, until I find myself beside her towering presence in a darkened place, where I sense marble pillars, and can feel the night air.

'I thought potions were needed,' I gasp.

'I'm a goddess,' Athena says drily. 'I can do things you wouldn't dream of.'

I'm still digesting that when a new voice – chilling yet familiar – says, 'Greetings, Odysseus of Ithaca. We thought you might wish to be here.'

Torches flare, and I can see where I am: in Hades's Pantheon again, and we're not alone.

Hades is sitting on the main throne, with Persephone standing beside him, her two-sided face eerie as ever. I look swiftly about, but to my disappointment, Kyshanda isn't here.

But across the table from us sits Theseus of Athens. He's bound to a throne by stone serpents, gagged and motionless, but his eyes bulge as he glares at Athena and me, sweat beading on his brow. He's looking at us with the deepest hatred I've ever seen on a man's face in my short life.

'Well, well, well,' Athena says theatrically. 'My faithless champion, the legendary Theseus. How delightful to see you thus.' She turns to Hades. 'You sent a message telling me you wished me to have no more to do with your infernal realm. Have you changed your mind, dear Hades, or is this a peace offering?'

The Lord of Erebus gives his melodious, dark laugh. 'Neither, Athena. By now Olympus knows you attempted to abduct Zeus's children. That Theseus turned renegade is irrelevant. You moved against Zeus and failed. The lines the Skyfather is drawing are a little firmer now. You're not welcome on Olympus. His brave new court of Achaean and Hittite gods, scrambling to align their dual identities, are gathering together to rule a greater empire. But not with you. You are now *irrevocably* beyond the pale.'

I feel my own heart sink. This is about as bad an outcome as possible – for her and therefore for me. But Athena lifts her chin defiantly. 'Then what are you doing? Taunting me?'

'No. I'm merely wondering what this man is worth to you.'

She indicates me. 'I've already replaced him. So if you wanted me to plead for his return, I tell you here and now that I don't need him.'

'I understand your bitterness,' Hades replies. 'But I am giving you a chance to re-establish your prestige in Attica after this recent debacle. Otherwise, future bards will make little sense of that strange, brief period when a virgin was patron goddess of Attica, just before she disappeared without trace.'

I watch Athena nibble her lower lip, uncertainty crawling across her face.

I decide that if I'm here, I can speak. 'What is it you want in return, Dread Lord?' I ask.

Athena frowns at my temerity, but Hades only looks amused. 'Well, when all seems hopeless, and every rat is leaping from a wallowing ship, I begin to wonder whether the odds have been misread. I am accounted a lord of wealth, enriched with all the gold buried with the dead. So the movement of riches – and its investment – interests me, as does the lure of a good wager. There is little gain in backing a certainty, but much to be made from the rank outsider who might win through.'

Athena makes a small dismissive gesture – which tells me she's hanging on every word.

'My wife and I are *believed* in,' Hades goes on, stroking Persephone's hair. 'But we're not *worshipped* – we're *placated*. That's a subtle difference but I think you understand it, Athena. Here's my offer: you have shrines all over Attica, and a few in other places too – Crete, for example. Command your priestesses to place altars to Persephone in them, and I'll give you back Theseus, your champion.'

Athena raises an eyebrow. 'Is this an alliance, Hades?'

'No, it's you accepting a crumb from my plate, in return for some favour in the future. It's me placing an *obol* on a long shot. It's you punishing yourself to feel better. It's my dear consort planting a seed in arid ground for you to water.' He waves a hand playfully, enjoying his own eloquence. 'Do you want my tacit, hidden aid in the years to come, Athena, or do you wish to go quietly into oblivion?'

She accepts, of course. I look at Theseus again – he'd barely seemed to be listening, but now he's glaring at me again, triumphantly this time. He can see himself reinstated, his crimes forgotten – and I know that I'll be watching my back until the moment one of us dies.

I suppose Athena can ill afford to lose any champion, especially one so experienced as Theseus. 'What is the fate of Pirithous?' Athena asks Hades.

'Oh, he's still bound to a throne... in Tartarus,' Persephone smirks. 'The Furies are rather enjoying their new plaything.' She runs an eye over Theseus. 'They'll be sad not to have his friend for company also.'

'I understand you have a new toy yourself?' Athena enquires.

I stiffen, but try to feign an uncaring stance, especially when Persephone's gaze meets mine.

'The Trojan princess?' the Queen of Erebus titters. 'Yes, she's rather amusing. I'm giving her new perspectives on *many* things.' In her enigmatic voice, her words take on a multitude of meanings.

I manage to suppress the urge to plead mercy for Kyshanda. Athena *must not* know of my dreams of her.

'I think I approve, Persephone,' Athena says, breezily. 'I hope that when you send back Hekuba's daughter, her own mother barely knows her. I don't like Trojans.'

'I'll do as I please, of course,' Persephone replies. 'Remember, Athena: I want altars in all your shrines. Renege, and we'll help tear you down.'

Theseus is jerked from his bindings, laughing, freed against all hope. In a moment he has vanished, transported bodily by Hades back to the world above, leaving me glowering, and preparing for the worst.

Athena lays a hand on my shoulder and once more we're wrenched into a whirlpool of light. We shoot upwards and flash across the Underworld's sullen, coppery skies, and then out into the stars, leaving Erebus behind.

But it isn't to Ithaca that we go.

–

Suddenly it's just Athena and me again, on a stone floor in a darkened building. I almost stumble and fall, but she catches my shoulder, and hushes me with a finger to her lips. 'Watch, and remain silent,' she commands, drawing me into the shadow of a pillar, in a torchlit throne hall I've never seen before.

I look about, taking in the rich decorations and the promi-nence, on the painted walls, of images of owls and olives – Athena's own symbols. The two giant doors to the hall lie open to the night. Moonlight coats a sprawling city, with a gleaming harbour in the distance. Stars glitter above, the haze of cooking smoke has been blown away by the night air, and all is quiet.

It has to be Athens – we're in the palace atop the massive outcrop of rock the Atticans call the Acropolis. This is Theseus's home… And there the man himself is seated, as solid-fleshed as I am ephemeral, on the King's throne, staring about him in joyous disbelief.

No… no, no, no! She's going to restore him, after all he's done.

I look about me, my mind racing. In this form, can I fly under my own volition? A silver cord, Iodama showed me last time. Can I make it appear?

Theseus flexes his arms, then he laughs. 'Where are you, Athena?' he calls. 'I know you're here!'

She emerges from beside me, drifting like a ghost across the painted floor, into the light. It passes through her, but *theios* that he is, he can see and hear her daemon.

'Theseus,' she says, softly. 'Welcome back to Athens.'

'Ha! I knew it!' the Attican hero crows. 'I knew you couldn't do without me! Who else is good enough for you, eh? That stupid cow, Bria? That fucking Ithacan runt? I'm the best you've got!'

He starts to rise, but Athena gestures, and the throne seems to fold around him, lashing him in place. 'You forget, my dear champion, that I own your soul.'

Theseus snarls, though more in annoyance than fear. 'Let me go, Athena! Stop playing games!'

'You stabbed me in the back, as surely as you plunged that dagger into poor Bria's chest, back in Sparta,' Athena replies icily.

'Bria's a body-jumper. What's a little discomfort to her? Perhaps the whole thing was fated? You can't blame me for destiny, eh?'

'Can't I?'

'You can't do without me!'

She walks in front of him, her expression disdainful. '*Can't I?*'

In the shadows, I just stare, wondering what the point of this actually is. Am I here to witness the fall of a rival – or am I to be dangled in front of Theseus as a reward for his renewed fidelity? The longer it plays out, the more my anxiety mounts, but I fear to speak in case Athena reacts angrily against me.

'Oh, stop pissing about,' Theseus chides her. 'You *love* me, Athena, that's the truth of it. You live vicariously through me. Every little maid I ride is a proxy for you. I know you *long* to slip inside them. So stop messing around. I've been your champion for over thirty years; I won you Attica! You'd be nothing without me. I don't blame you for being angry over the Helen affair – I admit, I was wrong. But nothing is irrevocable. I did nothing you can't forgive.'

At that precise moment, I decide I'm doomed.

But then Athena laughs. 'Theseus! Oh my...' She puts her hand to her mouth. Then she bends over him, and her face turns to frost. 'You're obsolete, my darling – an antediluvian relic. An ageing, bloated shadow of a once mighty *athlete*, who I taught how to *think*. A wall of muscle I once placed at the forefront of a deadly world for a short window of time. You think you can betray me, and laugh about it? I'm not here to forgive you! I'm not here to reward you! I'm here to watch you get torn apart!'

Even then, he doesn't believe it. Perhaps he's incapable of hearing such words. 'Come on, I've had enough of this scene,' he says, as if she hadn't spoken. 'Let me loose, and I'll do whatever it is you want. Anything at all.' Then he turns his head, and I realize he knows I'm here. 'And then I'll break that runt with my bare hands,' he rasps. 'Come on, Athena, free me. Let me show you who's the better man.'

Her hand whips across his face, knocking out teeth and almost breaking his neck – a daemon striking a physical body. She really does have resources I don't.

'Don't speak again, Worm,' she rasps. 'You have no right to address me.'

Theseus is still reeling as she steps away. 'Menestheus!' she calls.

A male voice, cool and dispassionate, resonates through the throne hall, and many booted feet approach. 'I am here, Great Goddess. All my court are here, and Lycomedes of Scyros too.'

I turn to see a calm, even-featured man, someone who seems more bookkeeper than king, walking down the hall calmly, his fighting men behind him. I pick out Lycomedes, one of the men Theseus rode roughshod over in his reign as king, and see bitter antipathy on his face. These are the men who've supplanted Theseus's cronies: both *theioi* and ordinary men. The fathers and husbands of women he's had, willing or no. The brothers and fathers of men he's killed. There is no pity on their faces, only the desire for revenge.

It's mob justice, and it sends a shiver through me. But Athena is unmoved.

'You're nothing,' Theseus croaks at Menestheus and his followers, defiant to the end. 'You're all nothing. Athens is *nothing* without me.'

Athena's backhander smashes the other side of his face.

'Menestheus,' she says. 'He's all yours.'

I would as soon have not watched, but Athena makes me – I wonder initially if she thinks seeing a rival brought low might be something I would take pleasure in, but then I realize that this is an object lesson for me. I am being given Theseus's place at her right hand – and she wants me to know the consequences of betrayal.

So I watch these men close in; I see the fists, and the grasping hands that drag Theseus from the throne, the kicks that break his bones. I hear them crack, and I smell the blood and the shit.

Once they've vented their rage on him, they drag him to a clifftop just outside the palace, writhing in the slippery grip of reddened hands, a mob baying around him. He's dazed, his body a bloody pulp by then, but aware enough that, as they hold him over the edge, his last act is to turn his blurred gaze towards his patron, watching with me from beside a pillar, visible only to the *theioi* present.

Athena stares back, impassive.

Then he plummets towards the waiting stones, hundreds of feet below, screaming until the thud of his landing cuts his cries off short.

'There, it's done,' Athena says, as if this were just the spanking of a wayward child. 'I trust the lesson is learnt? Good. Then let's take you home. We have much to do, my dear champion.' She grips my shoulder and suddenly we're in Ithaca again.

This time she doesn't bother to catch me as the disorientation sends me sprawling. Instead she kneels over me, and presses a finger to the middle of my forehead.

'I know what's in your mind,' she says. 'I let him off too lightly.'

That is far from what I'm thinking, but I'm still too stunned, emotionally as well as physically, to react.

'But you know, I've not let him off lightly at all,' she continues. 'That was just his mortal death. His soul is in Erebus now... no, actually it's in Tartarus, at the mercy of the *Erinyes*. Persephone and Hades have promised he'll receive the royal treatment, for the rest of eternity. What do you think of that?'

That I hope I never find myself at the wrong end of your mercy...

'May he receive true justice,' I reply, fearful for my own life in that moment.

But she's already gone, and I'm alone in the dark of my room, rigid with fear.

The lesson is most assuredly learnt. If you go up against a god – or goddess – don't fail.

There's no way I'm sleeping after that, so I dress, then head for the battlements, finding a favourite spot to watch the stars wheel overhead, waiting for the slow approach of dawn. Waves kiss the beaches far below, the moonlight sketches the landscape in silver, and the cool salt-laden air slaps my skin. Ithaca is sleeping in peaceful isolation, a haven from the turmoil of the world. The sound of the sea reassures me that life goes on. But there's a call in it too, a reminder that our journey is never over.

It takes me a while to realize I'm not alone. Sometime during my reverie, a skinny maidservant has joined me on the walls, leaning over the parapet and gazing out to sea. I almost jump out of my skin when I see her, but she just laughs. 'Hello, Ithaca.'

'Bria!'

'Hebea,' Bria corrects me, pushing the copper bracelet up out of sight. 'I'm Hebea here. I've been taken on as a maid.

You'll be seeing me every day.' She wriggles in what I think she imagines is a flirtatious way. 'And every night too, if you want.'

'Don't even think I'm interested,' I advise her. Then I remember the last time we parted – in Hades's arena: 'Your arrow almost killed me,' I growl.

She makes a casual gesture. 'I knew you'd dodge it. But I had to make it look real. Damned Theseus still nailed me, though. That's two bodies that *phallos* cost me.' Then she meets my eyes and for a moment she seems sincere. 'Thank you for getting me out of Erebus. I owe you.'

'Noted. What are you doing here?'

'Oh, you know… I just wanted to make sure you got home safely.' Bria peers about, then sniffs. 'I don't know why you'd want to come back to this dump. And don't say "family". Athena and I are your family now.'

'You've forgotten what family is – if you ever knew.'

Bria spits sourly over the side of the battlements. 'Maybe so. It saves a lot of pain. Why am I here? Because you and I are partners now. Athena wants Hebea here with you, so we'll be ready to leap into action when she next calls. She approves of your actions in the Theseus and Helen affair. You kept your head and rescued a dangerous situation from disaster. You have her favour. That's no small thing.'

'I don't want her favour.' *Or to hear from her again*, I think, though I'm wise enough not to voice it.

Bria laughs, with more pity than mirth. 'Oh, you'll hear, Ithaca,' she says, somehow reading my thoughts. 'She *owns* you. When she has need of your services, you'll answer her call.'

We fall silent, until I remember something: 'I have an answer for your riddle. You asked which came first. It's the egg. The egg is the world and the human beings in it, and the bird is your mistress, and the other gods. We contain the potential that makes the gods real. We, the world, imagined our gods – we created them. This secret is their great strength, and their great weakness.'

She doesn't disagree. 'What led you to decide that?'

'Erebus convinced me, as well as the Olympian Court – they were created from *our* beliefs. So, however omnipotent the gods seem, they're just leeches, stuck to the skin of the world and sucking life from it. Athena's bullshit story about a clay vessel and the hands reaching in was just a clever lie. The world existed before the gods. They didn't create it or us: we created them, and when our imaginings change, the gods must also change or perish.'

Bria smiles slowly. 'You make the important mental leaps, Odysseus. But keep them to yourself – the gods don't like them expressed, for obvious reasons.'

'I take it not all champions and avatars have come to this conclusion?'

'No, nearly all are blinded by their own powers, and think only of how they can use them for personal gain. It's a rare being that looks deeper.'

One like you, I think. *Or me.* 'What do *you* want, Bria? You, not our mistress.'

I don't think she'll respond, but she does, and not with the evasive reply I'm expecting. 'Oh, I want to destroy Olympus, for all the suffering it creates. We don't need them. I want to squash those leeches sucking on the surface of our world. I want to lock the gods in Tartarus, their own place of suffering, and watch them burn. Then I want to be the last one to sip from the Lethe, before it evaporates and is gone. That's what I want.' Bria taps my forehead. 'I think you want the same, Ithaca. I think we're going to be very good friends.'

Then she makes a sprightly curtsy, like a singer after a song, and she's gone, leaving me alone on the walls. I don't try to follow her – my head's too full, and I suspect I'll be seeing far too much of her in the future anyway.

Right now, I've got rather a lot to think about.

Acknowledgements

David

Firstly, I have to acknowledge my *fantastic* co-writer, Cath Mayo. Neither of us has ever collaborated in our writing before, so it was very much a 'learning on the job' process. I'm still amazed she agreed to do it, and I'm delighted with the resulting work – I think working with a peer made us both bring out our A++ game – and the way we brainstormed ideas and worked through plot issues was fun and an education.

I'd also like to thank my agents Heather Adams and Mike Bryan, who worked so hard to find a home for these books, and to thank the good people at Canelo for their enthusiasm in adopting the series. Thanks also to our beta readers – Kerry, Heather, Paul and Lisa – for their input, without which this wouldn't be the *brilliant* read that it is!

And of course, hello to Jason Isaacs.

Cath

I can only echo what David has said about the co-writing experience, except with the names switched over! I was incredibly excited to be asked to share this project with such an inspirational and imaginative author as David. While my past work as a musician has often been collaborative, brainstorming ideas and words is a whole new buzz, and I'm amazed how creative and stimulating it is proving to be.

Again, many thanks indeed to my agents Heather Adams and Mike Bryan: for taking me on board, for their energy and dedication and for their belief in our books, a belief shared by the team at Canelo – we love their enthusiastic support for what we're doing. Many thanks also to our beta readers: I never cease to be surprised and delighted at what they spot, from tiny details to gaping holes you could haul a Trojan Horse through.

Thanks also to Dr Bill Barnes for his analysis of *polytropon* – literally translated as 'many-turning' – such a vital key to Odysseus's complex character and so often oversimplified. Thanks, too, to Sofie Wigram for checking my translations of Ancient Greek quotes. Any remaining errors are entirely mine.

Glossary

General terms, names and places

Achaea, Achaean
The whole of Greece. While 'Achaea' is also a minor kingdom on the north coast of the Peloponnese, 'Achaean' is a common term in Homer's *The Iliad* for all Greeks, who were united by a common culture and whose mostly-independent kingdoms owed allegiance to a High King. Hittite documents dating from around the time of the Trojan War refer to 'Ahhiyawa', as one of the great political powers they interacted with; 'Ahhiyawa' is now widely believed by scholars to be the whole of **Mycenaean** Greece, or a major kingdom within Mycenaean Greece.

Avatar
A **theios** or **theia** who has the ability to allow their god to enter them and take over their body, so that the god, who is otherwise invisible to all but the **theioi**, can be seen. The god may appear in the form of the avatar, or in their own mythic form.

Axeinos
The Ancient Greek name for the Black Sea; the literal translation of Axeinos is 'inhospitable'.

Cerberus
The monstrous hound that guards **Erebus**, allowing the dead souls in, while keeping the living out.

Charon

The ferryman of **Erebus**, who transports souls across the river Styx to Erebus itself. In later, Classical Greek times, he was paid with a coin, usually an **obol**, which was often placed in the mouth of the corpse. Before coins were introduced in the 7th century BC, *obols* were bronze skewers, which were used as a form of currency.

Daemon

A god or godlike creature. The term usually refers to a lesser deity or spirit, but can also describe the major gods, who are simply daemons who have succeeded in building up far more power, through a greater worship base.

Drachma

A unit of currency. Before coins were introduced in the 7th century BC, a drachma was a 'fistful' of six bronze spits called **obols**. Later, both 'drachma' and '*obol*' became names of coins.

Dromas

A whore, specifically a street prostitute, from the Greek word for "race-course".

Erinyes

Also known as the Furies, the *Erinyes* are vengeful deities of the Underworld, who are also able to pursue their victims up on earth. The singular form is *Erinys*.

Erebus

The Underworld, where the souls of the departed go after death.

Hamazan

Amazon, a member of a tribe of women warriors who live by or near the **Axeinos** or Black Sea, at the outer edges of the Greek known world.

Harpies
Part-bird, part-human female spirits associated with the storm winds. They are usually disgustingly ugly, with pale, hungry faces and long claws.

Keryx
A herald serving a royal master, discharging important public functions such as making proclamations, undergoing missions, summoning assemblies and conducting ceremonies.

Kopros
Dung, shit, dunghill.

Kunopes
Bitch, shameless one, slut (from Greek 'kuon': a dog).

Laertiades, Sisyphiades, Atreiades etc.
These are patronyms, the equivalent of our modern surnames, except that they always refer back to the father's given name. They translate as 'son of Laertes', 'Son of Sisyphus', son of 'Atreus' and so on. This form parallels Scandinavian and Scottish names like 'Anderson', which initially meant 'Son of Anders'.

Magus
A sorcerer; a **theios** or **theia** with magical powers, who can bend reality.

Mycenaean, Mycenae
On a specific level, it refers to the kingdom, city and people of Mycenae, seat of the Achaean High King, in the north-eastern corner of the Peloponnese. The term is also used nowadays by archaeologists to describe the whole of Late Bronze Age Greece and its culture.

Nymph, naiad, dryad
A female **daemon** associated with nature, presiding over various natural phenomena such as springs, clouds, trees, caves and fields.

Obol

A unit of everyday currency. Before coinage was introduced in the 7th century BC, an *obol* was a bronze skewer which was used as a form of exchange. A 'fist' of six *obols* was as many as a grown man could be expected to hold in one hand, and was called a **drachma**, after the Ancient Greek word 'to grasp'. Later, *obols* and drachmas became coins.

Olympians

The select group of powerful Greek gods who dwell on the mythic Mt Olympus. The physical Mt Olympus is in northern Greece.

Pantheon

This word translates literally as 'all the gods'. It can also be a building. The most famous Pantheon was a religious building created for the worship of Rome's pagan deities. We have anticipated its basic form and function by many hundreds of years, creating an open-sided building in **Erebus** with a roof supported only by pillars, intended as a meeting place for the **Olympians**.

Phallos, Priapos

Penis, prick.

Satyr

A male **daemon**, a nature spirit associated with fertility who consorts with nymphs, *naiads* and the like.

Styx

A river that guards the boundary between the upper, living world and the true Underworld of **Erebus**.

Suagros

A person with a romantic attachment to wild pigs; a pig-fucker.

Theios, theia, theioi

A human who has some measure of divine blood; the Greek word translates literally as 'god-touched'. They are born of a union between a god and a human, or of a union between their god-touched descendants. A man or boy is a '*theios*', a woman or girl is a '*theia*', and the plural form (which we have applied to both male and female, for simplicity's sake) is '*theioi*'.

A person's *theios* nature is latent until it is awakened; this awakening can be carried out either by their ancestral god or by another god whose nature is in tune with that of the latent *theios* or *theia*, allowing gods to claim the descendants of other gods. In rare instances, a *theios* or *theia* can have affiliations with more than one god. *Theioi*, once awakened, can switch their allegiance to another god, but this is perilous, for it invokes the extreme anger of their original god and usually leads to their death.

There are four types of *theioi*: seer, champion, avatar and magus. The seer has prophetic powers; the champion has superior physical strength and talent; the **avatar** can become the physical vessel of their god, who is otherwise invisible; and the **magus** is a sorcerer, with magical powers. Sometimes a *theios* or *theia* can be more than one type, though usually one aspect is dominant, and generally each aspect is weaker than it would be in a *theios* or *theia* who has only one attribute.

In later generations, *theios* blood can become too diluted to give *theios* powers to new offspring. How long this takes depends on the power of the ancestral god, and on the mutual *theios* strength of the *theios* couple who produce the child.

Xiphos

A sword. Achaean swords of the Late Bronze Age, around the time of the Trojan War, were broad, straight and relatively short. They were made of bronze, as were all weapons of the time.

The Gods

Around 1300 BC, religious worship in the western Aegean region is dominated by the gods of the **Achaean** peoples. They are worshipped throughout Achaea (geographically equivalent to modern Greece); and their influence has recently begun to extend as far as the kingdom of Troy, on the Anatolian coast (modern western Turkey).

These Achaean deities are divided into the **Olympian** gods (those aligned to Zeus, the Skyfather and head of a **pantheon** of allied sects); and the unaligned gods whose worship is independent of the Olympic pantheon.

However, in Troy, a client-kingdom of the Hittite Empire (modern central and eastern Turkey), worship is dominated by the Hittite gods, with some Achaean influences through settlement and trade. As Troy's influence grows, so too does the influence of their gods; especially Apaliunas (known in Achaea as Apollo).

The Olympian Gods

Zeus is the senior god of the Achaean peoples, but his worship has spread well beyond the **Achaean** kingdoms. As a sky god, he is actively aligning himself with other such deities as his priests seek to make his worship universal. The Zeus cult is now questioning their alliance with the primary Achaean goddess, **Hera**, whose worship is limited to Achaean lands.

Hera is **Achaea**'s strongest goddess, aggressively absorbing other fertility goddesses (such as **Leto**, Gaia, Themis, Hestia and others) into her cult to increase her worship. Most of her followers are women, though she is still the dominant deity at the Achaean High King's capital of Mycenae, and her priestesses control the main oracular site of Pytho. As a purely Achaean deity, her cult faces challenges in a changing world.

Athena is a lesser goddess whose cult promotes wisdom and skill in war and peace, and whose primary power base is Athens, capital city of Attica. Outside that kingdom, her cult is in conflict with **Ares** the traditional war god. Like **Hera**, she is worshipped only in **Achaea**, and is even more vulnerable than Hera, if Achaean culture were to fail.

Ares, an Achaean god of war, personifies the belligerent warrior culture of **Achaea**. Recently, his sect has joined forces with that of **Aphrodite**, the goddess of love; a deliberate alignment to match the cult of **Ishtar**, the Trojan/Hittite goddess of love and war. Ares is the particular rival of **Athena**, who inhibits his worship in Attica.

Aphrodite, the **Achaean** goddess of love, promotes an alternative view of femininity to the **Hera** cult, idealising beauty, love and marriage in an outwardly submissive context, compared to Hera's traditions of strong womanhood. The cult of Aphrodite is in the process of breaking from the failing cult of the smith, **Hephaestus**, and partnering with that of **Ares**, leading to a spate of new "legends" that depict Hephaestus as being a crippled lecher. Aphrodite's cult follows that of her new ally Ares in seeking alignment with **Ishtar** (in the hope that they will usurp the eastern deity in due course).

Hephaestus is the smith-god, harking back to an earlier time when smiths were community leaders venerated for their 'magical' skill in metal-work. But society has changed, the smith is now just an artisan, and their cult is in decline. Tales now portray this failing deity as crippled and cuckolded; the first step in a process designed to erase him from human worship.

Apollo is revered already by the Trojans as their patron god **Apaliunas**, and his cult is aggressively expanding into **Achaea**, aligning him with the Achaean hunter goddess **Artemis** to capture the next generation. He is worshipped by the Trojans as a source of light, which brings him in conflict with **Helios**, the Achaean god of the sun, whose cult is collapsing in the face of his more sophisticated rival.

Artemis, the Huntress, is the traditional goddess of young **Achaean** maidens, and for centuries has dovetailed with **Hera's** cult, though in a subservient role. However, threatened by Hera's dominance, the cult has aligned with that of the new shooting star, **Apollo/Apaliunas**. The next generation, they believe, belongs to them.

Hermes is a nature deity from the **Achaean** mountain region, Arcadia, whose cult has been subordinated by that of **Zeus**, and is tolerated by the Skyfather's priests as it gives them access to the Achaean heartland. With Hermes personified as Zeus's herald, his cult exemplifies masculine cunning, in the grey area where skill morphs into trickery, and functions as a 'political' wing of the Zeus cult.

Demeter is an **Achaean** goddess of fertility and harvests, the latest to find her cult overwhelmed by that of **Hera**. To survive, the cult of Demeter has built an alliance with **Hades**, god of the Underworld, personified by the figure of her 'daughter' **Persephone**, a subordinate deity "married" during winter to Hades. As an Achaean alliance, it is threatened by eastern expansion, but believes the universality of death will enable it to survive any circumstance.

Dionysus is god of wine and the intoxicating power of nature. His cult has – like that of **Apollo** – pushed westwards into **Achaea** from the east. While appearing to align with Apollo and **Zeus**, the core rites are highly secretive, and the cult's true allegiances remain unknown.

Poseidon claims mastery of the sea and as a result gains worshippers throughout **Achaea**, primarily those involved in sea-born trade and travel, a vital part of life in such a mountainous, sea-girt country. His equivalent god in the mostly-landlocked East (Aruna) is a minor deity, so any foreign invasion of Achaea will diminish Poseidon's cult. As a result, he is in potential conflict with **Zeus**, but his cult believes his worship is universal and unassailable.

The Unaligned Achaean Gods

Hades is the Achaean god of death and the afterlife, conceived by **Achaeans** either as an eternal limbo or as a reward or

353

punishment, as appropriate. This universal concept affords the cult great durability, but *dread* of death is not *worship* of death: the cult has therefore limited influence in daily life. As a consequence, it has sought alliance with **Demeter**, goddess of fertile life (as personified by a 'marriage' to Demeter's 'daughter' **Persephone**), as a direct challenge to the **Zeus/Hera** hegemony.

Persephone, a seasonal harvest deity, has become 'daughter' of **Demeter** and 'wife' of **Hades**, enabling followers of both sects to bridge the divide between life and death, fecundity and sterile extinction, and make their worship more universal. Persephone's worship is growing as this duality of life and death in harmony gains appeal in **Achaea**.

Helios, the ancient god of the sun, has suffered from the growing worship of **Zeus**, who claims dominance over all the heavens; and more recently by the emergence of **Apollo/Apaliunas**, the Trojan god of light. As a consequence, the cult of Helios is collapsing almost unnoticed.

Eileithya is the **Achaean** goddess of childbirth, appealed to by pregnant women, and by men who fail to get their wives with child. Once a much-worshipped fertility goddess, she and other primal goddesses have seen their worship eaten up by **Hera**, whose worshippers now claim she governs every aspect of an adult woman's life, from unmarried virgin through to wife/mother and aged crone.

Eros is a primal god of procreation. Recently his worshippers have been increasingly lured away by **Aphrodite**, forcing the cult of Eros to subordinate itself to the rival cult to survive.

Leto, like Gaia, Themis, **Eileithya** and Hestia, is now a minor goddess. Her cult is seeking to regain their earlier influence by putting her forward as 'mother' to **Apollo** and **Artemis**, hoping to be instated as **Zeus**'s consort if or when the Skyfather's cult renounces that of **Hera**.

Heracles was originally a powerful '*theios*' – a god-touched human gifted with extraordinary powers. Such was his strength and ruthlessness that he has become a subject of worship among **Achaean** warriors after his death; which has seen his spirit ('**daemon**') elevated to godhead by the **Zeus** cult. He is now seen as a powerful figure in Achaean religion, closely aligned to Zeus – and a potential rival to both **Athena** and **Ares**.

Hecate is a goddess of magic, a personification of the mysteries of womanhood and born of a time when women's cults excluded men and handed down secrets and traditions only to their own gender. It has not survived the increasingly urbanised and domesticated lot of women and is increasingly marginalised, but still maintains a following.

Notable Trojan and Hittite Gods

There are many Hittite and Trojan deities – these are the ones who impact on this tale (so far).

Tarhun is the Trojan sky god, the most important deity in the Hittite pantheon, who is placated to gain favourable weather and therefore crops. The priests of Tarhun foresee the dominance of the Hittite Empire over the entire Aegean region through their client kingdom of Troy, and are more than willing to merge their cult with that of their **Achaean** equivalent **Zeus**, to undermine the Achaean people and extend their own dominance.

Ishtar is a goddess of love and war, who personifies a union of warrior-man and fecund-woman that has captured the imagination of the Trojan and Hittite peoples. This powerful notion has forced the Achaean cults of **Ares** and **Aphrodite** to seek alignment: the priests of Ishtar are happy to swallow up both, and foresee a time when they, not **Zeus-Tarhun**, dominate the Aegean.

Apaliunas is the patron god of the Trojans, who worship him as a source of light. In **Achaea**, he is now called **Apollo** and

355

revered as the son of **Zeus** and **Leto**, and the brother of **Artemis**.

Kamrusepa is goddess of magic, the equivalent of the **Achaean** cult of **Hecate**: her cult however enjoys the powerful patronage of many influential women in the eastern kingdoms, especially Queen Hekuba of Troy, and is therefore a powerful cult among women.

Lelwani is the Hittite and Trojan goddess of death, believed by her followers to preside over the Underworld in much the same way that **Hades** rules over **Erebus**. Her priests also attribute her with the power not only to induce sickness but the ability to heal it.